JULY COMES
ONCE A YEAR

William Schwartz, M.D.

Llumina
Press

Requests for permission to make copies of any part of this work should be mailed to Permissions Department, Llumina Press, PO Box 772246, Coral Springs, FL 33077-2246

ISBN: 978-1-60594-283-4

Printed in the United States of America by Llumina Press

Library of Congress Control Number: 2009902964

For Susan

Acknowledgements

I appreciate the interest and support of many people who shaped my interest in reading and then writing. Harry and Sylvia Schwartz were role models for the love of reading and education plus the value of hard work and strong family relationships. Our home was always filled with books, interesting discussions and methods to build strong self esteem. Dick, a loyal supporter reviewed and commented on many drafts, making good suggestions, most of which I followed. Lis spared me the wrath of her red marking pen for this work. Her previous markups rekindled the fear of Miss Bowman, Miss Seltzer, Mrs. Klett and, most of all, Battle Ax Smith. I value the comments of Charlie, Bob, Ann and Gail whose early encouragement spurred me on. Gracie Mille. Likewise to those who remained silent and did not return their critiques, my thanks for staying positive, following the axiom, if you can't say positive things, say nothing.

I treasure the comments of Shelby Foot, the Civil War Historian whose interview on the book channel indirectly stimulated me to start. He told of his method of writing with the old fashioned pens, well outlined, small output each day that was edited and recopied by hand before adding the new text to the manuscript. I could never do that but when he described his friend Walter who did not outline, had the story evolve as he wrote and kept writing so he could find out what happened. Following Walter's lead, I began the story.

Prologue

"To understand better what is really happening, I want to know the players, what game they are playing and what else is the going on in the club house."

Caroline Mitchell

THE PLAYERS

There are about 3500 people involved with the Children's Hospital of Union County, a major pediatric center serving both the citizens of South Creek, NJ, Union County and patients referred from the United States, especially people requiring medical consultations for yet to be diagnosed problems and for cardiac surgery. The highly qualified doctors chose to practice in this clinical hospital and to teach the next generation of pediatricians and pediatric surgeons. The nursing staff consists of veteran nurses who provide the best care to the sick children and new graduates who most likely will work for a few years and then move on. There are other people who support the mission of the hospital:the social workers, laboratory technicians, environmental services and dietary workers. Stars in the lineup are: John Esposito MD, Chief of Radiology, David Grunberg MD, Chief of Pediatrics, Carter Randolf MD, Chief of Surgery, Robert Farmer MD, senior Physician and Kirby Jackson MD, cardiac and transplant surgeon. Three hundred physicians cover all the surgical and medical subspecialties. The Vice President of nursing, Jackie Lawrence BS, MS PhD FAAN leads the staff of nurses, nurse managers and nurse specialists. Richardson Beardsley BA, the CEO, heads the administration.

THE GAME

Caring for children is the main reason that brings all these people to the hospital. The activity centers include the Emergency Department that serves as the entry place for the active trauma service as well as the primary care office for many people in South Creek who do not have a primary care doctor or whose doctor is not available, the intensive care units for newborns, major medical and surgical cases, the operating suites and the consultation offices. Like any busy place, there is much activity in other sites, some well known and others not fully appreciated by the public.

WHAT ELSE THEY ARE DOING IN THE CLUB HOUSE?

That you will find out in the following pages.

SUMMER

"You're so vain; I bet you think this song is about you."
Carly Simon

Chapter 1

"Hello, Dr. Randolf. This is Dr. Victor Didichenko. Right. Didi. You haven't forgotten me. I moved from South Creek to Winchester in the Pine Barrens. Say, Dr. Randolf, I hope you can help with this sick newborn I just saw in my office. Seems she was born at home with a midwife in attendance. Yes, one of those Pineys who do not like hospitals and all institutions. You know the story- no prenatal care, called the midwife when she was almost ready to deliver and the baby surprisingly looked good for about an hour, now she is having trouble breathing. She is not cyanotic but working fairly hard to breath. I listened to her chest and she does not have much air moving in her left chest. I bet there is a collapsed lung or some kind of mass. I wish we had an x-ray machine here but you know these rural clinics, understaffed and under supplied. ...... No, she did not have labs so I don't know if she has HIV or syphilis. No prenatal care, no labs, no in..... no insight into modern medicine, typical Piney."

"Say Dr. Randolf – will you take a look at her and see what is going on. I have great trust in you and your Children's Hospital of Union County- CHUC is that what you call your hospital? Great place- great care. Great doctors. I know I could send her to a closer hospital but I want her to have the best. I called the ambulance from the firehouse and they will take her to you if that is OK. Thanks a lot Dr. Randolf, You are the best!"

• • •

At about the same time, Anthony, age 12, is looking for new excitement in his neighborhood near his house. Always a daredevil, he will ride his skate board over curbs, down stair railings and hop on benches fearlessly and often, skillfully. As his medical record attests, he does fall, but nothing serious, one broken wrist, one greenstick fracture of his leg and some oral surgery to stabilize some teeth that were loosened when he fell from a trapeze. Today he and his buddy Bob have found some scaffolding put up by painters who were sprucing up a neighbor's house.

"This is more fun than the free fall at Dorney Park," screamed Anthony as he grabbed the scaffold top bar and dangled his feet. Then he moved, hand over hand, across the scaffold to get to the corner. He glanced down at the traffic along Sheppard Street. "This is like Leonardo DiCaprio in the Titanic— I am king of the world!" As he got to the corner and tried to make the turn he felt the top bar of the scaffold give a little. He was strong enough to hold on with his right hand and quickly move his left hand back to the spot where it was before he tried the turn. He hopped on the plank and looked at the loose bar. Someone had placed the bar in the right slot but did not tighten the clamp that should have held the bar in place.

"Wow! That was close!" Even for a daredevil, first class, his pounding pulse in his chest betrayed his outward bravado. "I think I won't do that again." He walked across the plank and looked for the ladder so he could make his way down from the 30 foot perch. At the second rung, his foot slipped; his hands slipped from the side of the ladder. His foot touched the lower platform of the scaffolding but this did not stop him from a free fall flip.

Bob screamed for help just as Anthony hit the ground head first.

The 911 operator took the call from a man who saw the fall and dispatched the fire rescue squad to the accident. After reaching Anthony in about 3 minutes, Ralph Scott, the EMT surveyed Anthony's limp body as he talked into his phone headset to the command post in the Emergency Department.

"He is still breathing- about 16 per minute; Blood was coming out of his nose and skull wound. Looks like an open skull fracture on the left, dried blood in the hair. His pupils are dilated but not fixed. He cannot move his extremities. Oh, no! Some of his brain tissue is on the ground! He looks like he is going to have a seizure. There is twitching of his hand now moving up his right arm. I am fixing a neck brace to stabilize his head. Joe is putting in a venous catheter and we are hanging saline. Then we will slip in an oral airway. We have a portable heart monitor on him- the heart is beating in a regular rhythm- amazing he is still alive. No other obvious broken bones. We are now getting the BP, just a second... A little low, 70/50 but better than nothing. Traffic is not so bad so we can bring him in on the ground. No need for a helicopter. This will be faster. Yeah. The EKG looks good. What do you think? We have the pressers in the IV, starting amp and sulbactam as this is a dirty wound and one sick kid. I hope he makes it."

It took about 5 minutes for the team to stabilize Anthony enough to get him in the ambulance, turn on the siren and head back to the trauma unit. Looking at the limp Anthony on the stretcher, it is wonder they are called the MASH unit. They were the slickest and the best in the city. Anthony was ashen, his skin damp. He moaned a few times and had some more of the mild shaking spells. The beep-beep of the cardiac monitor began to slow.

"The BP was now 60/35. Not good."

The transport doctor at CHUC, now connected to the ambulance speaker system, shouted, "Increase the pressers and get the defibrillator ready."

"Can't you go any faster, Pete?" Ralph asked nervously.

"I'm doing the best I can through this traffic hold up. Once we get past the boulevard we can roll," Pete responded.

"This is CHUC trauma command. What is the oxygen running at?"

"7 liters per."

"That should be good. Is there any chance you can get a blood gas?"

"Not with this bumpy ride. I have a pulse ox and it is 88, not so bad."

"Good luck, we will be waiting for you."

Ralph Scott turned off the phone and added "you might be waiting for me but I hope you keep those new interns and residents away from this kid. We don't need any amateurs getting in the way. I know this is the time of year that you should not get hospitalized. Summer is scary with those new smart asses messing up my trauma cases. But let's get on the way, the traffic is building up. Turn on the siren, there is a lot of traffic. Away we go to CHUC! I am not sure if this poor kid will be alive when we get there."

Two blocks later, at the intersection of Pine and 5th, the ambulance was almost hit by an old Honda. The driver, looking through the view-finder of his video camera, ran a stop sign. Pete swerved just in time and they made it safely to the hospital.

Up on the third floor, Carter Randolf, chief of surgery, was not worried about new residents; he was happy that a baby was going to be transferred to his service and would need emergency surgery.

"This is going to be a good day, a really great day. Time to play surgeon." After Dr. Randolf ended his conversation with the referring doctor from Winchester, he called the chief resident to tell him about the newborn being transferred to the surgery service for a chest mass. He was so excited about the referral that he ignored the obvious, the patient most likely did not have insurance and care was refused at the local hospital that was already overburdened with caring for non-paying patients. Even though the State of New Jersey had a fund to compensate hospitals for care of non-insured patients, it would not cover a third of the cost of the operation. That was someone else's problem; Randolf was here to save lives, not worrying about economics.

Although he comes to the hospital at 6AM each day, his practice has not been very active recently. He spends a lot of time in his office, looking at his many certificates, photos and diplomas from his past accomplishments. "Yes, things are looking up, finally something to do. I'll show those young ones some of my special tricks. A newborn with a chest mass that is one that they can't get with those new laparoscopes. You have to get in there a cut that thing out. I am glad that I did not have more than one cup of coffee this morning. I still have steady hands." He paused to look at his well manicured fingernails. "Wow! What a great way to start the month. Maybe my luck will change. My old referring doctors have not forgotten me." His resident, Peter Bird, had hung up, went to the ED to check the baby and the chest x-ray and then headed to the OR to get the team assembled for this operation. Carter was animated, even excited, at the opportunity to get back into doing more than fixing hernias and removing moles. He walked out to tell his secretary that he had a case scheduled for emergency surgery.

"What are YOU doing here?" he shouted at his wife Carrie, who had dropped by his office unexpectantly. "I came here prior to one of the many hospital committee meetings I attend; I was planning to kill some time by chatting with Ann , if she is not too busy being your secretary. I also would like to send an email to my sister in California, if that is OK with you."

Carter did not like her in the hospital, particularly in his office. "I don't need any spies in my office." Carter stormed out of the chief surgeon's suite, headed for the OR complex.

"What was that all about? Carrie asked Ann, maintaining her calm countenance. I just dropped by to say hello and write a note to my sister. I owe her an email." Her intestines were burning while she tried to cover up the embarrassment from her paranoid husband.

"Please don't be upset, Mrs. Randolf. He always gets snippy before he goes to the OR to do a big case. This one was a newborn who is having breathing trouble. Between you and me, he is getting a little old to do such complicated cases. But I would never tell him that. We just let him flare up and expect a latte or espresso when he gets back from the OR to make up for his antics."

"I guess I am getting older, I am more sensitive, but I am not that old. I will be OK but thanks for the insights." Carrie went into Carter's office before the tears appeared. Carrie retreated to the large leather chair in the inner office to write the email.

"Hi Liz, I understand you are having a hot spell out there. Hope you can cope with the 90 degree weather. It is even hotter here. As I told you before, things are not good with old Carter. He continues to expect me to act as if I was a parent of one of his adoring patients, thankful for his saving a sick child's life. I am not going to be like one of his dedicated nurses who put up with his tirades as he works through a difficult surgical problem. He can't seem to leave the aura of the operating room when he comes home, but I am not either an obedient nurse or thankful parent. He is so needy for praise and so fearful of moving out of the spotlight. Things have not been good for the last few years but now as he ages and finds himself falling behind the younger surgeons who have more technical skills and innovative ways to fix things, he is becoming unbearable. I am about to make my move to leave him, although it would be difficult to give up the life style that he has provided. If things do not change I will be pushed to act. Thank goodness, we don't have children to suffer through this mess! Maybe I will come out to see you. Right now the only trip west of Pittsburgh I have planned is a trip to Denver in the spring. I have to introduce our CEO who is getting an award from one of my national groups. He is a creep but a trip is a trip so I am going to take it. I love Denver. So maybe we can get together before that. I have a lot of miles on my frequent flier program, so I may surprise you.

Thanks sister for listening to me, I am so upset, I needed to let some of it out to someone and you won the lottery this time

Love
C."

She thought for a minute about canceling the email but then she clicked Send. Next, she erased the letter from the Sent file so the old bastard would not see what she had written. But that is past history now. She went into Carter's private bathroom to check her makeup in the mirror. She wiped her eyes with a tissue as the mascara had slightly smudged at the corners. Dropping the tissue in the waste basket, she noted a lipstick tinged tissue.

Strange, she thought, I know Ann does not wear lipstick and does not use these facilities. Maybe this was from one of Carter's friends in the hospital. She knew that Carter had several liaisons during their marriage; she had a 3 carat ring that came with the apology for one major infidelity. Good for him, she told herself, maybe these girls will keep him satisfied and away from me. She took a deep breath and left with a cheery, "Ciao, Ann. Off to another glorious meeting of the library committee."

Carter Randolf entered the locker room to change into clean scrub suit. It was easy to find his locker as it was at the end of the row, #1, of course. Before he became chief, he did not have the #1 spot, but as soon as he got the promotion, he needed every one to know he was the top man so he rearranged the locker assignments so he would be #1. No detail of authority escaped him, including the pressed scrub suits with sharp creases. After changing into the greens, he scrubbed up and entered the surgical theater, #1 room, of course. The scrub nurse put on a high intensity lamp over his surgical cap and adjusted the magnifying lenses over his glasses. He was ready for the case.

"Let us pray. Lord, please give us strength to help this young child do well in this operation we are about to perform. Help me make the right decisions and sustain life. Amen." Carter Randolf always began each operation with a prayer. He found religion about 10 years ago, now he was not afraid to let others know of his convictions. He wore his religion on his sleeve, whether it is on his custom made suit or scrub shirt. As part of this new spirituality, he developed his own surgical rites. When he got through the tense part of an operation, he would start with humming a hymn and then break out in his strong baritone voice singing his favorite "I walk in the garden alone." By the time he got to "and he walks with me and he talks to me" he had the whole OR team joining in.

Carter held the most powerful position in the medical staff. His position as chief of surgery gave him great clout in the hospital as all the surgical operations made a major impact on the hospital finances, so the administration tended to go along with his conservative principles. No abortions were performed at CHUC, no birth control advice or contra-ceptives were dispensed in the hospital pharmacy. All life must be saved no matter how ominous the prognosis. No case was inoperable, no breathing machine turned off, even when the parents were against further intervention. He countermanded Do not Resuscitate orders, threatening to get legal affairs to take the child away from its parents and become a ward of the court. When challenged, he repeated his mantra, "Life is a gift and we are here to help children live. Death is the enemy. To do nothing is to work for the devil." The surgical suite was the red state in an otherwise mostly blue state hospital. He also lived by the credo that "when in doubt, cut it out" which increased the number of procedures each year. If an journal article appeared that suggested a non-surgical approach, Carter would review it to find the flaw in the design or logic. He was not one to worry about statistics as he felt experience trumped any scientific method. Because of this non- academic approach to deci-sion making, his department has not maintained its stature as it had in the last decades as other hospitals had younger surgeons, who were trained in evidence based medicine used results from clinical research rather than opinions gained from experience from a few cases. Clues to this waning reputation were the topics of his lectures, mostly review of past times when pediatric surgery was evolving where he quoted his experi-ences since there were no formal studies to test the value of the intervention. "We did this and it worked so that is the way to do it" was good enough for him. Today, that would not be acceptable as medical journals would require a study that compared two techniques and meas-ure outcomes of survival but length of stay, cost, maintenance or loss of function and patient satisfaction to prove its value.

Carter went to the conference room outside the OR so he could re-view the baby's x-rays on the computer screen there; he knew that the Emergency Staff would see the baby first and get the necessary studies. Although he would listen to the chest, there was no need to as the x-ray was classic for one of his favorite diseases. He scrubbed up and went to OR #1. "Look here, this is classic C-CAM." He pointed to the mass in the left chest on the monitor in the OR. He reviewed the case with the OR team. He loved to teach, feeling that if the nurses and technicians knew about the disease, they would be more involved and feel part of the team. Carter loved teamwork, as long he was in charge.

"This baby has Congenital Cystic Adenomatoid Malformation or C-CAM, a mass in the lungs that replaces normal lung tissue. You can see

7

on the x-ray that the whitish area on the lung fields is quite large, pushing away normal lung tissue. That cuts down the amount of oxygen that can get into the lungs and eventually into the blood and body tissues. What is his blood gas?"

"82" called out the anesthesiologist, pointing to the monitor screen. "Stable. But I don't see any labs on this young lady. Shouldn't we wait to make sure she is not full of germs?"

"I will be careful and not stick my self with any sutures or needles. We can do better than that by getting that devil out of the lungs before she stops breathing and dies. So let's continue. The baby had no prenatal care so there was no way we could have diagnosed this condition prior to delivery. Usually the OB diagnoses this condition from the prenatal ultrasound. After birth, the baby seemed to be doing well for an hour but then there was trouble breathing and the oxygen levels dropped. We could have watched her a little but I know from other cases, we would eventually take out the mass, I decided not to wait. Enough talk, let's go and save a life."

The operation started with the usual rituals of scrubbing the chest with yellow antibacterial soap followed by covering the chest with clear plastic drapes and finally, layers of green drapes that covered the baby except for the small window that allowed the surgeon access to the rib cage. The anesthesiologist took over by giving a sedative and a muscle relaxant, then slipped a tube into the trachea, the size of a straw, and connected the endotracheal tube to the respirator. Kitty Brown, instrument nurse had the scalpel ready for Dr. Randolf to make the first incision. His adult sized hands contrasted with the tiny chest of the baby. Thanks to small instruments and magnifying lenses, pediatric surgeons are not fazed by the small organs and vessels.

"Thanks, Kitty, let's go."

The opening of the chest went well exposing the lungs, about the size of half an orange. He pushed aside the lung tissue to better expose the C-CAM tumor.

"How is the BP?"

"80/60- perfect. Keeping the BP stable is like trying to land a plane through turbulence, but we are doing it, Carter."

"Just keep your seat belt on; we don't want to lose you. There is the bad guy, give me some clamps so I can get those arteries and veins tied off. Everybody OK so far?"

This tense part of the operation required teamwork between the surgeon, the assistant surgeon and the instrument nurse. The only talk was the request for sutures, cautery to burn small vessels and gauze sponges to clear the blood from the operative site so the surgeon maintained a clear view of the operative site. Carter was unusually quiet until he took the tumor out of the chest and placed it in a sterile pan for the pathologist to examine later. Carter stepped back from the operating table.

"Let's pause to see if the lungs expand into the newly emptied space. Anyone see any bleeding? Things better look good before we close the chest."

"The oxygen is not normalizing yet. Let me push some air into his lungs."

"Thanks, Cal. You are ahead of me, as usual.

Cal Norse, chief of anesthesia, manipulated the black bag connected to the respiration tubing. "Done."

Although the lung was not as fully inflated as the other segments, the pink color indicated that air was getting into the lungs and the arteries were open so that blood flowed into the region. When he saw there was no bleeding and the lung almost fully expanded, finally, Carter began to hum "I walk in the garden alone" signaling to the team that they could relax since he was over the critical part of the operation. He was not ready to sing, not until he was confident that there was no further bleeding and that his sutures were holding. "How about the vitals?" Carter continued to hum.

"PO2 is 95, BP 90 over 60, Lytes are normal"

"Couldn't be better. I think we did this little fella some good today, as long as he does not bleed. Call the NICU and tell them we will be coming there in about half an hour."

The rest of the case reversed the steps that started the case, closing the lining of the lung, bringing the ribs together, closing the chest wall muscles and then the layers of the skin. This was routine to a skilled team of surgeons and anesthesiologists who specialized in children's procedures. Carter began to sing his hymns and let the assistants join in the chorus and make the final skin closures.

"Off to see the parents and I will be back to take this little man to the ICU." Carter repeated his post op mantra. "Most errors happened during the transfer of care from the surgical team to the intensive care doctors. I don't want to drop the ball and damage my statistics." After a brief stop in the locker room to change his scrub suit, he was off to the parent lounge.

"Good news, Mr. Monroe, we got the mass out completely and the oxygen levels are much better. I can't tell you about the breathing as the machine is still doing all of the work. That will last a day or so, and then we see how well your son can breathe on her own. He is going to the intensive care unit where we can keep monitoring his vital signs and breathing. I am pleased with the results and know you are relieved that the worst part is over. Your baby did well, very well. We have a great team here and they did their best for your little one. The next few days will tell us a lot, we are going to watch him carefully for infection and check his oxygen levels quite frequently, first with the tubes in his arteries and then with the light we place on his fingers." Carter extended his left index finger and pinched it with his right thumb and index finger to show how the oxygen sensor would look. As Carter was continuing his monologue, he did not recognize the father's blank stare as Mr. Monroe stopped listening when he heard the mass was out.

"This is a lot of information but please, please ask me questions. There are no bad questions so don't hold back."

"Thank you so much for helping him. I will never forget you. When can we see him? Is he in pain?"

Carter continued his soliloquy. "You will be able to go into the ICU when they get him settled. Of course, since he cannot tell us about pain, we look for changes in blood pressure and body activity for signs of pain after the anesthesia wears off. Since we have a tube in his airway, he cannot cry but our nurses can see crying efforts. But we will watch him carefully for signs of pain. Any other questions? I am sure you will have many in the days to come. When your wife gets back on her feet after the delivery, I will be happy to review the case with her. Now, how about a short prayer of thanks?" He put his arm around the father's shoulders and closed his eyes.

"Thank you, Lord for giving us the power and skills to help this young lady. It is our faith in you that allowed us to complete this operation, safely and with great skill. Amen. Now I have to get your little girl to the ICU. I always stay involved with the care until I see that the baby's airway connections were switched to the ICU machines and monitors and feel that the staff had all the information about the surgery. Then I have to go to the coffee shop to get the lattes and espressos for my office staff. I was a little rough on them this morning."

He looked at his watch; he had time to stop by Jackie Lawrence, chief of nursing to chat for a few minutes to see if she had time for some TLC for a tired surgeon. "Nothing like revving up the libido than a few hours of delicate surgery, saving the life of an infant, I always say." Carter could not decide which better, surgery or sex but the scientist as he was, he wanted to find out. But in the back of his mind was the worry that others would find out what he was doing with the chief of nursing.

• • •

Adrienne Cunningham MD, new resident in pediatrics, closed the door of the stall behind her and took out some Listerine mouthwash sheets to help clear away the bad taste in her mouth from the acid reflux; her hands were still shaking. She looked into the bathroom mirror to make sure the sweat did not ruin her make up, ran a brush through her newly straightened hair and then looked for her roll of Tums. Nothing seemed to help the queasiness in her abdomen. She fixed a smile on her face, looked into the mirror and softly said to herself. "This is not as scary as you think it will be; everyone is a little nervous when they start their residency." She thought of her mother's words to her when she left home to begin training at the Children's Hospital of Union County- "Remember sweetie, we are all cheering for you, you are the answer to our dreams- a college education, a scholarship to medical school and now training at a hospital where I used to work in the housekeeping department. You are the one and we love you. You go girl."

Up to now, Adrienne excelled in academics, taking tests,   rarely making mistakes but now this was the real game, taking care of patients who depended on your brains and decision making as well as your medical knowledge.

"I don't want to screw up, if I do, the kids could be harmed or die," she told the face in the mirror.

She took a deep breath, walked out of the ladies room and bumped into a fellow resident; she could tell he was a resident as he was wearing the ID badge with an orange border. The blue tooth headset attached to his ear was not part of the standard uniform.

"Hi, I am a little bit lost, where is the newborn nursery? I am supposed to meet my group there."

He turned to her, looking like he was woken up from a deep sleep. "Oh, the nursery! That is on the fourth floor, Go up these steps and when you get to four and turn left after you pass through the door way. You can't miss it. Or no, you best take the elevator that is down this hall, about 49 steps on the right. Then get off on 4 and turn right. You can't miss it." Adrienne could see that his first name was Lester but the last name on the ID badge was hidden behind papers that were jammed in his shirt pocket. He turned away and walked in the opposite direction. His gait was almost as strange as his affect. He kept his head erect but his trunk was tilted forward from his ample waist. His shirt tail was hanging loosely over his unpressed khaki pants. He appeared to drop back into his sleepy zone and shuffled down the hall. Adrienne opted for the elevator rather than walking up 4 flights.

When she got out of the elevator, her beeper sounded, causing more burning in her stomach.

"Oh, shit, that is the well baby nursery calling. I hoped I could get to the unit before being paged." Adrienne looked at the text message. "Come ASAP to nursery ---major problem with a parent."

"How major could a problem with normal newborns be? I hope no one is dying." she said to herself as she crossed the passage way that connected the children's hospital with the general hospital. She arrived panting. "What's up?"

"The man in room 45 wants a blood type on the baby to see if he is the father. He is roaring around the hallways and creating quite a mess. He wants to speak to a doctor."

"OK, I'll take him on. I wonder what is bugging him."

"Hi. I am Dr. Cunningham, the resident in the nursery. Do you have a question?"

"Yes, I want a blood test to prove that I am the father."

"Is there any question?"

"I don't think so; my wife says I am the father. She has not been fooling around if that is what you are thinking."

"So why the blood test?"

"Well. My buddy, he had a baby."

"Well, we are pleased that he is a father. But what has that got to do with you?"

"Well my buddy, you know, he was told that they were having a boy after they did the x-ray thing when she was pregnant. Then at the time of delivery, the doctor said it was a girl. Then they had to do a blood test to prove that he was the father of that baby. Seems that the belly button cord was between the baby's legs so on the x-ray test, it looked like – excuse my words- it was his water works on the x-ray so they said it was a boy. So I want to have a test. I took one look at my baby and fell in love with her. I don't want to get too involved until I make sure that they did not make a mistake with this beautiful baby and after I fall in love with her; they might take her away and give me some other baby. I might not fall in love with the second one. This one is a honey. I love her to death."

"Were you in the delivery room when the baby was born?"

"You betcha, I was there, I had the whole thing in video."

"Well did you see them put the little bracelet on the baby?"

"You betcha. I got that scene on my video."

"So the baby was born, the bracelet with the mother's name was put on the baby. There is no way that they could mix it up in the delivery room. You have it on video, you say."

"But they took the baby to the nursery to clean her up and keep her warm."

"Did the bracelet fall off?"

"I don't think so"

"So we have a smooth move from the delivery to the nursery to your room."

"You mean that cutie is mine? Is that what you are trying to say?"

"I guarantee it. Then we have a match. You have a baby and that one is yours."

"Mine? Really? I can't believe it. That baby is mine. That baby is mine. Thanks doc. Thank you Jesus. You are the greatest. Wait till I tell my cousin. That baby is mine and I love her to pieces."

Adrienne felt relieved that it was just an excited first time father and not some real question of paternity. Now that she was back to work, she started for the chart room to check the computer for lab results.

"Hey doc. Wait a minute. Can I get you on my video? I am going to make a whole program about my new little girl. I started when we went to the OB for the first visit and have all the big moments. I even took pictures when we were driving to the hospital. Tricky stuff to drive the car and take videos but I did it. I think I almost hit an ambulance that crossed in front of me. Near miss, thank goodness."

"You will be a great dad, but next time don't drive and shoot video. It could be dangerous."

"Good advice, thanks for everything, doc."

"Now that was easy, just use common sense. That is the trick. I know this year will not be easy and I will mess up. I just don't want to harm anyone."

Beth Hano, the unit clerk, looked up from her computer screen. "Did you say something, honey?"

"No just talking to myself, sorry." Adrienne smiled warmly, but felt the burning again and put her hands in her pocket so no one could notice the trembling as she left the room.

• • •

In the general medical unit, a medical student, Mia Nuygen, looked eager in her new white jacket, shiny stethoscope in her pocket and blue name badge that identified her as a first year medical trainee. She was also scared beyond any fear she had ever experienced. This session with a real doctor, observing how clinical medicine was conducted, an unscripted interaction, in contrast to lectures or conferences, unnerved her. She felt more secure sitting in a seat in a darkened room taking notes and trying to figure out what point she would see again in a test. Although she had read about a physical examination and had done several on classmates, she was anxious because this was live patient. For someone who is usually in control, she was nervous in this new role as a clinician, causing her to speak rapidly.

"Come in, I am Robert Farmer and you are?

"Mia Nuygen, first year medical student."

"Hi Mia. Sit down and tell me about yourself."

"Where should I begin?"

"Well you can skip the delivery room and the milestones of walking and talking. How about home town, college and interests?"

"I am from Hackettstown NJ, I went to Swarthmore. I am a field hockey player, play the cello but not on a concert level and like to sail in the summer and cross country ski in the winter. How is that for starters? Is that enough? Do you want to hear more? Did I do OK?"

"Fine. Today we have a full list of patients to see. The usual, too short, too fat, too many infections, not enough friends and a variety of stomach aches, headaches and joint pains. Most of the problems will turn out to be normal children with issues stemming from the parents' expectations for them to perform better in school or sports or adjustment problems as they grow and socialize with friends. Practice of pediatrics challenges the doctors to sort out these kinds of cases from the rare problem that are mainly diseases such as cancer, rheumatoid arthritis of inflammatory bowel disease for example."

"Why don't you watch me see a few patients and then I will put you to work. I want you to see how I approach the child and the family. You will see how I don't go through the exam from head to toe and at the end of the session. Then I want you to tell me what you saw that you liked and what I did that bothered you or was not what you expected."

"Sounds good to me. How do you know what to do? Aren't you afraid of making a mistake?"

"Me? I have made my share of mistakes. Hopefully I've done more good than harm. But now I have you to check on me, I doubt if I will make more than a few mistakes.

After a few patients, Farmer stopped. "How am I doing? What do you think, Mia?"

"All the cases were exciting but how do you make a judgment with such limited information and so few laboratory tests?" I thought everyone got an MRI so you could see what was inside, the anatomy."

"If I did that, we would not get much done in an afternoon. I rely on experience, recognizing patterns of diseases and some luck. Let's see the next patient. I peaked at the next chart; this girl's parents are worried about her lack of growth. That is a little unusual as most parents bring their sons, not their daughters in because of short size. I will have to find out more about the details. This should be fun."

Mia looked quite relieved that she was not going to be put in the spotlight and would not be able to harm anyone because of her inexperience and nervousness. But she could not keep from asking more questions. "What do you think is wrong? Is it anything serious? Do you think she will get to grow eventually? Should I look up anything in the book? Do you have Google in your office?"

"Let's wait until we see the patient."

"Sorry, I tend to ask a lot of questions when I get nervous."

"I noticed. Just take a few breaths and follow me."

They entered the examination room where a small girl, about 5 or 6, was sitting on the exam table, playing with her doll, not looking up at Dr. Farmer.

"Hi Jackie, I am Dr. Farmer and this is Mia Nuygen, a medical student. What is the name of your doll?"

"Sweetie."

After a little more tries to chat with Jackie, he turned to the parents, "how are you? Did you have any trouble finding a parking place?

"Not really."

"Good. Will you tell me your concerns about Jackie?"

"We are worried about her size. She is 8 years old and has not grown much in the past few years. She is now the shortest in her class and some kids are teasing her. We wanted to check her out to make sure she does not have some serious disease. We are not a tall family but she is much smaller than her brother was at this age. What do you think?"

"Let's back up and get some more information and then we can discuss what I think. She has been small for several years. What was the reason you came in now, now rather than next year or last year?"

"I think we came here now since the teasing began and her stomach aches that seem to be increasing so much that she does not want to go to school. I don't like that she is not happy. She was never the life of the party but now she avoids social contact. A lot of people in our family were late bloomers, not growing until high school, so the size was not the main issue; it is how being small affected her."

"What do you wish to accomplish with this visit today?"

"I want to know if she can be treated with growth hormone."

"Good question but let's not get ahead of the evaluation. First we need to find out what is wrong with her and then we can talk about growth hormone. OK?"

Dr. Farmer continued the history that revealed average sized parents and late growth spurts of the males on the father's side. She seemed to grow like other kids for the first few years and then she dropped to the bottom of the growth curve that our doctor had plotted. The rest of the history did not provide any clues to the small size. She was a good eater and had no diarrhea. Nothing so far.

"I think it is time to take a look at Jackie. Will you help her take off her shirt?"

While Jackie's clothes were coming off, Farmer took out a growth chart where the average height and weight measurements for each age were displayed in a graph. "Today, Jackie at age 8, measured at the bottom 3%. If 100 girls her age were lined up from tallest to shortest she would be one of the three at the end of the line." He then took the medical records that Jackie's mother bought with her and plotted out the heights for her yearly measurements that were made at her checkups.

"See, she dropped to the 5% at age 4 and slowed down even more for the past 4 years. He took another look at Jackie, noting she did not seem to mind standing there in her pink panties.

"Put your arms down to your side, please."

When Jackie dropped her arms at her side, Farmer leaned forward and then sat back in his chair. "Hmmm."

"Mia, what did you see and what is the diagnosis?" He did not expect her to answer correctly but trying to get her involved in the evaluation.

Mia was perplexed. Medical students have a hard time transitioning from college where they usually got all or most of the answers correct to clinical medicine where they rarely knew the answers at first and could not spit back facts from lecture notes.

"Here was a small girl with her arms to her side. Period. What do you want me to do? Should I get the diagnosis? Is this something I should know? What did I miss?"

"Wait a minute with those questions. Now it's my turn. Do you have a boyfriend?"

Thinking that was a strange question and wondering if she was getting into a sexual harassment situation, Mia blushed and said "no, sir."

"Do you write letters home?"

"Yes, sir"

"Well then write a letter home and describe what you see. The diagnosis might be in your words. Sometimes it helps to talk out loud." Mia felt the urge to blast out with a series of more nervous questions, but she held back, trying to see exactly what Dr. Farmer was seeing. She still looked like a short girl in pink panties. Silence seemed to be the best way not to look stupid.

"First. Don't worry about the diagnosis. Just look. Begin with the wide angle lens taking in the whole picture and then zoom in at areas of interest. OK. When in doubt, start at the top and work down. Anything in the head, eyes, ears, neck?"

Not wanting to embarrass her, Farmer pointed out the low hair line in the neck region. "See the neck; it looks wide even a suggestion of extra skin folds. The ears look small and seem to be rotated a little. Now Jackie, turn around, please. You are doing fine."

"Ok Mia, your turn. Put your arms to your side. Notice where your hand is in relation to your hip. There is a little space, right?"

"Right"

"Now look at Jackie. See that the space is greater. In medical school, we were taught that girls have a wider space than boys since they milked cows and the wider space allowed them to carry the milk pail without it hitting their body. Like Jack and Jill. I am not sure that is the real fact but girls have a wider carrying angle than boys. But in Jackie this angle is greater than other girls. We call this cubitus valgus. Cubitus refers to the elbow and valgus means away from the body. Think of the L in valgus. L stands for lateral. The opposite is varus. Not sure how to remember that. So we have a young lady with an extra neck fold, wide carrying angle and short stature. Anything else?"

Mia could not hold back. "What else should I see? Am I missing something? Is it in the front or back?"

"Mia, just tell me if you see anything."

I am afraid I don't see anything. I'm sorry."

"This is harder, but if you look at Jackie's chest you will see that the nipples are wide apart, more so than other girls. It does not mean anything but it is something that I see. You are doing fine Jackie. Can I listen to your heart and feel your tummy." He listened to the chest in front and back, poked around her belly and felt for pulses in her hip area.

After he finished the exam, Dr. Farmer smiles at Jackie, "you did a great job and now you can put on your clothes. Jackie, now I have an important job for you to do. I want you to go to see my secretary and draw picture of your house for her. Here is some paper. Oh, and you can use my pen. Mia will take you out to the other office and then she will come back into the exam room?"

When Jackie leaves the room, he then turns to Jackie's parents. "Let me review what is in my computer. Jackie comes here because of how her size is affecting her school and outlook and the question of growth hormone therapy. She has been at the low end of the growth curve for the past 4 years. There is nothing of note in the history to explain this. Her physical shows the features of her arm angle and chest. I heard a murmur in her heart- I'll come back to this in a few minutes- and felt no masses in her abdomen. I see her nails are not all full size. Of course there are some tests to do but I think I have an answer to your questions about Jackie. She looks as if she has Turner Syndrome. Are you familiar with chromosomes, men have XY and women have XX?"

"Yes, I remember an article in Newsweek about genetics and read a few novels where they discussed the difference between male and female patterns."

Farmer smiled and continued. "Good for you. That makes my job easier. Of course, I will order the tests to confirm the diagnosis, but I want you to know my thinking. I feel she has a problem with one of her chromosomes so that instead of having the female pattern – XX - like you do Mrs. Allen, Jackie is missing one of the X chromosomes or XO. The test I am ordering will most likely confirm my suspicion. Many of the features that I saw today are the result of not having both XX's. I know this can be confusing but I will go over this with you when we get the results of the tests. I have a sheet of information that I will print out for you so you will be an expert in this disease in short time." Farmer writes down Turner syndrome and XO, not XX on a sheet of paper and hands it to Mrs. Allen. "OK, with all the attention to her chromosomes, I don't want to forget about this murmur. I heard a sound that is common in girls with Turner Syndrome so I will arrange for you to get that evaluation by a cardiologist who can make a definite diagnosis about her heart. Right now, she does not need any more activity restrictions than she had yesterday. My secretary will schedule this at your convenience and also the endocrine appointment, as they are the experts for this problem."

"She will also print out the information on Turner syndrome for you. I will order a blood test to check her chromosomes that is called a karyotype. That is a lot of information for one day so now is your time for questions. In fact, I will answer the question that most people think of but do not ask. No, it is not your fault or something you did. This is a problem that just appears for some reason, not caused by anything the parents did. Now for your questions."

Mia watched in awe. The power of observation, amazing.

The Allen's went through a list of questions about what other tests, what are the treatments and what does this do to fertility, if she does not have functioning ovaries.

"You ask good questions, very good. Let me outline the tests that the endocrinologist would order. When they are done, they will talk about hormone therapy that will help her grow, develop into an adult female but if she wants children, she will need in vitro fertilization and care by obstetricians specializing in high risk pregnancy. At least we know what Jackie has and that there is a treatment to help her grow. We do not have to worry about the pregnancy issue right now."

"Thank you Dr. Farmer. We enjoyed the free physical diagnosis course, too. Good luck Mia. You had a good teacher today. Do mind if we call you when we have time to digest this visit and the diagnosis."

"Absolutely, call me anytime."

When the family left the room, Dr. Farmer sat back in his chair and looked at Mia. "That is why I love this job. Although there are more lucrative jobs in medicine and more with chance to have public acclaim, this is where I belong, seeing patients with all kinds of problems and working through the facts of the history and physical so that I can order the right tests to make a diagnosis and arrange for proper treatment. The actual therapies are not as exciting to me, find out what is wrong and help the child and family get the best care. I stick with them and make sure that all is going in the right direction. My motto is "If they are getting better, keep going with the plan; if they are not better, arrange for a new plan. You always should have a plan B."

"Does it bother you that you don't know all the answers?"

"No, if I only took care of patients for whom I know all the answers, I would not be very busy. I am here to help them or find the best person who can manage the problem. Then my role is to get in the boat with them and help them through the rough waters which in many cases is a difference of opinion between the specialists or in other cases, how far to push the treatments or balance the treatments with the side effects. In most cases, I am just the ears to listen to the machinations of the parents. Should we or shouldn't we; what ifs and whys. I am here to help them. This is my kind of fun. I don't even call it work. When it becomes work, I will think about doing something else."

"That is easy for you to say, Dr. Farmer. I know I can't learn everything and I don't want to be in a position where I am not in command of all the facts. I am scared I will harm someone because of my ignorance. I am already thinking of dropping out of medicine."

"Don't get ahead of yourself, Mia. You are here to learn what you can, that is to learn what you can do and recognize the situation when you need help. We are here to help you. You will do fine."

"See you are saying things with confidence but you really don't know how I will do."

"I am reacting what I see; a nice person, highly motivated and just beginning to learn how to be a doctor. I see no problems. I spend a lot of time seeing patients whose diagnosis is not clear, the treatment is not certain. But I am there to help them through the problem until we learn more. That is why they call it practice of medicine."

● ● ●

Upstairs in the administration suite, Richardson Beardsley, the CEO of the hospital was also experiencing signs and symptoms of sweating and a burning in his stomach when he heard his private phone ringing. Having arrived at his desk at 5:00 am, the same time he has arrived for the past 5 weeks, he has not moved from his desk, exhausted after a sleepless night of worry and concern for his organization and his financial problems, brought on by his newly acquired expensive tastes. The empty coffee cups and overflowing ashtrays that have accumulated during these solitary early hours testify to his anxiety.

"Who the hell is calling me so early in the morning? Not many people have my private number." His mind raced through the possible reasons someone was contacting him. His public face was that of a confident executive; only a few people knew about his private deals that he engineered for his personal profit, hidden from his board and administrative team. If these financial manipulations became public, he was finished. His queasiness was not belly butterflies but more like his high powered Harley revving up its engine exhaust, against the stomach lining, the fumes leaving a horrible taste in his mouth. He had no choice than to pick up the phone after the caller ID listed Wally Finley, the CEO of the UPS Children's Hospital in Cincinnati.

"Bad news, Richardson. I just got called by the District Attorney about a whistle blower's claim that my hospital using an illegal software package. That was the one we sold you that altered the computerized medical records to upgrade the acuity level of the outpatient visits. Too bad, since the billing here rose about 12% and you know what that means to the year end bonus."

"How far has it progressed?"

"Just a phone call, no real charges or publicity....yet."

"Any chance your phone is tapped?" Beardsley never left a paper trail or sent emails but did use the phone after weekly checks by his security service for bugs or phone taps.

"Not in Ohio, we don't have to do that." Walt's chuckling annoyed Beardsley even more.

"So what did you do, Wally?"

"Well for starts, I had the program removed from our system."

"But they can still trace it. Didn't you destroy it?"

"Oops, never thought about that."

"Let me get back to you after I get our IT man on this right away. Thanks for the heads up, Walt. I appreciate your fast action."

"No problemo, buddy. I still owe you a few things from some of our other deals."

Now Beardsley was sweating. Once the news came out in the Medical Insurance Association's newsletter, investigators would be looking at other hospitals to see if they were using similar programs. Up to now, the people who reviewed charts focused was on how many MRI's were ordered or how many open heart procedures were performed. Monitoring groups compared mortality rates of more serious diseases such as staph infections and surgical complications, not common colds. Usually the inspectors had not bothered with mundane conditions such as flu and colds to check to see if hospitals exceeded the national averages for diagnosing common illnesses. Nor they would also check to see how many sutures were being placed in lacerations. Then who knows what else would turn up in the billing of common problems. Fortunately for CHUC, the auditors spent more time looking at adult patient records, ignoring the children's hospitals, up to now.

Beardsley liked this insurance scam. It seemed hard to detect a system that increased the billing for routine outpatient visits. Insurance companies reimbursed hospitals according to the amount of service preformed. A longer history or more complete physical exam would be classified as higher severity; thus higher pay per visit. First the computer looked for how many items in the history were recorded. Adding more items translated into extra time spent with the patient and more allowable fees. If the doctor had entered only 2 or 3 pieces of the history, the program would add information about social situations and allergy history thus justifying the higher payment. In the physical exam, the program would change normal breath sounds to a few wheezes and alter the temperature by adding a few tenths of a degree. By these changes, a level 2 visit for a cold, low severity became a more serious level 3- URI syndrome, a difference of $20 dollars for the visit. Twenty dollars was not much to worry about but since there were about 30,000 visits a year in the general pediatric offices in the hospital system, this amounted to over a half a million dollars return for a $2500 computer program; a clever way to add big bucks to the hospital income without attracting much attention. There was another program that added an additional suture to the bill for repairing lacerations. Chalk up an additional $50,000 for the ER charges each year. For some reason the insurance companies paid for each stitch that was used to sew up cuts. Since Beardsley had engineered a performance clause in his contract, these extra charges created over an extra $50,000 plus in year end bonuses. Although he did not know the source of the aphorism, he always attributed it to Benjamin Franklin- "it is easier to take a few pennies from a large group of people than try to steal a large sum from a few." For those who knew his patterns, when he did not know the source of a statement, he attributed it to Franklin. So far either one cared about his quote or they did not challenge his attributions.

Beardsley lost his brio; he was scared, his power and income were in jeopardy. He had to come up with a way to defend against a possible audit and the negative publicity. At this point he did not think about possible jail time. He phoned Tom Stevens, his VP of Information technology.

"Hey Tom, we better stop using the billing program and destroy the records. I think that this system has run its usefulness. Since I know little about computers, I don't know how to handle removal, but that is what I pay you for. Right? I saw on TV that even though you erase a file, the computer nerds, eh- people can still retrieve information. So I suggest that you get to the server, whatever that is and destroy it. That should erase all the programs and prevent others from finding what we did......... Yes, if you send me a P.O. for a new server, I will approve it and you can get a new one today...... Good."

Then he then called the Maserati dealer. "Justin, I have to cancel the order for the convertible I was going to buy when I received the bonus check. There was some delay in accounting and the checks are delayed." He then turned to the file on helical scanners as he had a meeting shortly with the salesman. "Hopefully this scam will not be caught before my contract is renewed and then I can retire in a few years."

• • •

"Thank goodness, July comes once a year." Dr John Spirito could not stop his worrying and moaning to the people who joined him at the doctor's table in the cafeteria. At 10 AM, many people headed there for the morning coffee break. Since most doctors arrive about 6:30 AM, they have already made rounds on their patients, answered phone calls, checked emails, seen a number of patients and fielded a few problems that aides bring up. 10 AM is time for a break before returning to the clinical duties. Coffee time also has the advantage of making contacts with colleagues, setting up consultations about problem patients and maybe catching a few choice bits of gossip about the administration's latest power grab or to discuss national politics. The doctors sat at their corner tables, not that it was prized real estate but rather an area that they knew their colleagues would be meeting.

John continued. "The chaos in the hospital in July with changes in the house staff and turnover of medical staff is a necessary evil of a teaching hospital. In order to train the next generation, we have to accept their rookie ways. Chaos and disequilibrium."

"Oh John, new residents are not that bad," replied Isa Stella, a senior cardiologist. "Along with their insecurities, they bring new juices to this place that keeps us old farts on our toes and prevents us from depending too much on our clinical impressions that cannot stand up to these young people's questions and challenges to our traditional way of doing things. I am here because of these young ones, but I do agree that July is a scary time in the hospital. I always advise my friends not to get sick in July. After all that good advice, guess who got chest pain in July and had to be admitted to cardiology. To make things worse, the new intern was a former student who had the unfortunate but unique status of being a student that I actually gave a failing grade to when he was on cardiology. Fortunately it was a false alarm for me and I got discharged before he had a chance to harm me. I was more worried about him than my chest pain."

"You are right about the new juices, Isa," replied John, "But this place is out of control"

John is the heart of the hospital, loyal, a dedicated and 100% institutional player for his 35 years as chief of radiology at the hospital. He is the lowest paid chief, even though radiologists have typically one of the highest incomes in the medical hierarchy. Until the union got after him, he used to sweep the floors in the x-ray department to save money for the hospital. Sleeves rolled up, the ever decreasing tuft of hair on his head askew, he is ready for diagnostic challenges and opportunities to pass along his vast knowledge.

"John, you are still in control of your radiology kingdom, nothing goes on there without your approval."

"I like to see the patients sent for x-rays, talk to them and decide if the test that was ordered was the correct one. If not, I will do the test that I think is appropriate. That worked well when life was less technical. You either got a plain x-ray, a barium study or an injection of dye to outline the kidneys. Today it is different, ultrasound, too many choices: ultrasound, Doppler, MRI, PET scan CT, with and without contrast and nuclear medicine. This makes my personal touch outdated and unproductive. Plus, now all tests are ordered via computer entry, so I cannot change the tests without the obtaining the patient's doctor's approval. We process over 500 studies a day so I am no longer the hands on radiologist. This place is just too big!"

The staff and patients appreciated his loyalty to the hospital, but some of his dedication is avoidance home life where his wife, Emily, likes to get an early start on the afternoon cocktail hour. Her favorite tune is "its 5 o'clock somewhere."

"So what is the big deal? We are on alert and we can watch these young ones until they get dried off. September is not far away," continued Isaac.

"Summer scares me; new residents who are afraid of everything but won't ask for help, old doctors who are past their prime, offering to teach the new people what they think is current practice, administrators who sense an opening to occupy the void of change of staff and those pesky lawyers who know that July is the time when there will be problems in patient care that just might be grounds for a big malpractice case. I always fear the chaos of July." As he added more milk to his coffee, he rubbed his balding head, the usual mannerism when he was upset.

"Oh, John, you sound like Jeremiah, wailing about the upcoming doom." Bob Farmer said as he stirred his coffee watching the cream blend into the drink.

"Just look around this cafeteria. Those young kids with new ID badges and fixed smiles. I tell you, Bob, this is a scary time."

"So what are you going to do about it, John? The senior residents leave at the end of the June and the recent medical school graduates take their place. At least we get the cream of the crop of these birds so think what it would be like at some other places. You know New Jersey is not the medical center of the universe so we are one of fortunate places that get great applicants. Their enthusiasm and idealism overcomes their lack of skills."

"Great applicants make mistakes, especially in July." I remember.."

"Stop with the history lessons, John. We all were new residents at one time and did not doubt our competence, especially those of us who went to good schools."

"Good schools have nothing to do with it. The kids from New York are not safer than those from Nebraska. They are young, inexperienced and make mistakes. You need to get on the playing field with them. I see what studies they order, wasting money with those new toys, MRI with contrast, PET scans, Doppler's, you name it. All those CT scans can cause cancer. They order them when they don't even take a good history. Test first and ask questions later. That is what they do."

"Don't shout John, you are in the cafeteria and people will hear you. Besides, all that anger is not good for your pressure. Are you taking your medicine?"

"Those doctors are trying to kill me with all those pills, diuretics, inhibitors, blockers. Why don't they just get one pill that does everything and stop giving me all those side effects. But I guess without them I would not be here."

"And don't forget John, without the new residents, you would have no one to teach and no one to listen to your stories."

"You mean, Bob, you think you have nothing to learn?"

"I didn't say that, I just heard your lectures on the chest x-ray so often I could give it and repeat your stories."

"But they laugh at some of them."

"Right. But you have to admit some of them are boring too. Just think what it would be without these young ones."

"Maybe you have a point about that. I am still worried, something bad is going to happen and some child will be hurt because of these new people."

"We will watch them for you. John. Now sit back, have your coffee and let's talk about the Yankees."

"I don't like the Yankees and you know it. Bob. I can't wait until football season starts."

"By then the kids will be smarter, they will know where the toilets are and what time to get to work to find a good parking spot."

"You laugh but I am still worried."

Robert Farmer, chimed in. "The problems that impact patient care and hospital functioning are not limited to the trainees. It's the same all year long; the three issues, power, people and money lurk in the offices, board rooms and conference spaces of the medical staff and administration. People on the power trip find certain human barriers that need to be moved aside while those in authority want to maintain their control of committees, decision making and financial opportunities. I bet someone up there has his eye on my office space and position."

John continued his lamentations. "Not you Bob, you will be here forever. But there are staff problems too. Since the academic year ends, kids go on to college so the parents decide that a divorce is the best way to celebrate. That means staff openings as some docs leave here. Others are distracted by their new social problems. We doctors and nurses, like everyone, have issues outside of work or for a few, in the hospital. Affairs among the staff are not limited to TV shows and hospital novels. They happen, causing more challenges to the stability of hospital operations."

"I guess you are right, John"

Farmer chimes in. "Is that why you don't leave this place in July, John?"

"You know, Bob, I am the self appointed guardian of sick children at CHUC; I don't take time off in July as I know about problems with inexperienced staff. My place is in the radiology suite. These new trainees love to order tests. I like to read the studies and meet the new people but I would like to do it with less radiation and expense."

"Worst of all," interjected Robert, "this is the time the administration, identifies these vacuums in the medical staff and move in, taking space from medical services and reassigning it to the vice presidents. We will soon have more vice presidents than surgeons."

"That might be a good idea," quipped John.

"What would you do without us?"

"Oh Kirby, I did not see you here. Excuse my bad suggestion but maybe we should do a trial run with less surgeons at CHUC."

"Good idea," replied Kirby Jackson the star of the surgical staff. "I know you love CHUC..."Don't trust your luck, Go CHUC, cha cha cha." John smiles at this mild tease. The staff lets him wail because he is the best pediatric radiologist in the world- at least in this part of the world.

"I am tired of the administration cutting back on our budget while hiring more vice-presidents and redecorating the executive offices. Now they want to get a new MRI when the one we have is only a year or so old."

"I don't care what they do, as long as they build another OR for my heart surgery patients."

"Kirby, my boy, we will get a new OR after they open up a new clinic on the west side. There is more need for services to our kids than a fancy OR."

Kirby Jackson loved to goad John, knowing full well that all the hot air they could produce at the coffee table would not affect the CEO who made all the decisions because he controlled the budget.

"Let's go on and get to some real issues like should we allow the radiologists to use those horrible catheters to open narrow arteries and put us surgeons out of business; that is a real problem."

"A real problem for your knife happy wild men who get real pleasure out of cutting into young kids- shame on you."

"You are jealous, John. Look how much good we do and how much publicity we get- who ever read an article in the paper about great things going on in radiology. We do the drama and we get extra columns in the press" chided Kirby.

"But we are winning the battle; I see the number of interventional studies have increased while the number of cardio-vascular procedures has actually dropped in the past year or two."

"Sadly, you are right, John, and Beardsley has notice this too. He is against opening new clinics because they lose money and reduce the profit in this not for profit hospital. He has also noted that with more interventional procedures, there is less total income as there is no long OR times, not as much supplies used and fewer days in the hospital. You guys are going to break the hospital if you continue to invade our surgical territory."

"I don't see you selling your scalpels outside the hospital door."

"You know John, I am not in this for the money, I love to operate and fix kids that need my talents. My joy is to stand for hours in the OR fixing holes in the heart or making blue babies turn pink. Sadly for me, I work every other night, missing half of the fun that goes on in the hospital."

"Do you mean in the OR or behind closed doors?" interjected Sam Salivari, neurosurgeon.

"I am talking about the OR, big mouth. What goes on behind closed doors is what I do on my night off, or on my night on while waiting for the OR to get set up. And enough of you or I will tell stories about you know who."

John Spirito slid his chair back and stood up. "I think it is time to get back to work before the TV stations come in to tell the world that all we do is to drink coffee and complain."

• • •

Anthony Herman, chief of environmental services was making his rounds of the hospital. He was heading for the basement where there were always debris from the trash collector pick ups and empty boxes from the central supply. "What have we here? This looks like a good computer that someone is throwing out. I could use that in my office." He was looking at a Dell that IT must have replaced with a new one. "They are always getting new equipment, while our requests are always being turned down by the administration." His suspicions were confirmed when he saw the ID tag on the box that indicated it was from CHUC IT dept. "I will take this baby to my office and see if Cliff can tell me if it still works."

• • •

The Emergency Room director, Donna Barstow missed the coffee hour today as she was meeting with a new group of medical students, teaching them how to think and get organized. She constantly challenges them with "what would you do now? Why? What else? She never tires of teaching. She realized that being a doctor would fulfill her hope both to help people and to teach the next generation of doctors, not a choice to become rich but comfortable, a job that she would not trade with anyone. Looking at her ill fitting, mussed up attire, you can see she does not spend her money on clothes. Donna, a CHUC institution and lifer, first entered the doors of the emergency room as a pediatric resident, stayed there for emergency training and now directs this division. Coming from Loyola Medical School, she always felt inferior to the group of Easterners, making her try harder to succeed now that she joined the big team. Every institution has a few doctors like Donna that students, residents and young staff members seek out for medical or personal advice, wisdom, or chance to discuss the latest happenings of the Philadelphia Eagles, her team. She thrives on the excitement of the emergency department, yes, not the emergency room as most people call it. It is a department, with its 24 hour staffing by board certified emergencicologists, cool under fire nurses, radiologists with their MRI and x-ray machines at their side and a slew of respiratory therapists, pharmacists, LPNs, and college students, volunteering in the emergency department as a prelude to their medical school applications.

"Aren't you afraid of getting sued for the mistakes?"

"That is always an issue in the back of my mind but I can't be paralyzed by that fear. I like to treat all patients as my family so most like most families, they may yell at each other but they rarely sue their relatives. Only the rich children sue their families."

The discussion is interrupted by the overhead pager "Dr. Barstow, please come to the triage booth." "Excuse me, folks, duty calls. I have to be in the pit to see some patients. It is not like last month when everyone knew what to do and no body needed me to solve problems. Now we have a new bunch of players and Lordy, Lordy, they need me whether they know it or not. But I love teaching and not afraid of making small mistakes as I have had my share of diagnostic and treatment mishaps. I learn from them and hopefully do not repeat the errors."

"But why the page?"

"I hope one of the new doctors did not mess up already but just someone who wants to have me check a patient."

Chapter 2

Anthony was still alive when the ambulance arrived. The ED team wheeled him into the head trauma bay, outfitted with monitors, an x-ray machine and a cabinet full of emergency medications.

"Vitals were slightly better. BP 80/65 pulse 120, respirations 20 pulse ox 88."

Anthony continued to moan softly, fortunately, there were no more seizures.

The trauma team went into action, cleaning up his wound, cutting away his clothes and putting in another venous IV line and an arterial line.

"Let's get him to MRI."

"Since this was an emergency, we will bump the patient with chronic headache who is next on the schedule. "That headache can wait for another hour for this emergency" commented Raoul Hernandez, the head of neuro-radiology. He rushed into the MRI center and watched as the frame slices that sequentially appeared on the reading room screen. "I see a skull fracture opening up a 2-3 centimeter space in the skull. Fragments of bone were cutting into the brain white matter. There was another closed fracture at the base of the skull. Look here, the cribiform plate was also broken but the sinuses were intact, fortunately for him. Over here, an epidural hematoma formed where the middle cerebral artery was severed. Brain swelling was already apparent. See the area of decreased blood flow that had injured brain cells, now we have brain swelling."

Raoul pushed back from the flat panel monitor. "This was not the time to do fancy studies; this muchacha needs to get to the OR. The bone fragments are doing no good. The wound needs to be cleaned out and the bleeding needs to be stopped. Thanks for the fast MRI, in the old days; we would still be waiting for the slices to come out of the machine. Not bad for a three minute study."

We are on our way. Who is the neurosurgeon on call today?" In a place like CHUC, there are 4 pediatric neurosurgeons, more than are in some entire states or even some countries."

Barbara White, head nurse of the trauma unit answered that question. "Sam in on for today" referring to Sam Salivari, chief of neurosurgery and the ultimate WASP, even though he was Catholic and Italian. WIC White Italian Catholic does not have the same caché. Besides WIC is the nutrition program to provide formula for low income families- that is not a group that includes neurosurgeons. " "He will meet us in the OR. I am glad it is Sam; he is so cool in his Ralph Lauren costumes. But you can tell he is not a real WASP since he polishes his docksiders. He is the only doctor that has custom made scrub suits that are pressed by his housekeeper each day. Salivari is the best, even if a he's a little eccentric."

Sam, alerted by trauma central when the first call came into trauma center, went to his office to get his personal collection of surgical tools and tissue sponges that he requires for the operation. Not trusting anyone, he cleaned and wrapped his own instruments and prepared the gauze sponges, referred to as 'spongee-wongees,' (SW) that were used to mop up the blood from the operative site so he could see what he had to fix. The spongee-wongees were arranged in 5 rows containing 12 individual gauzes and held down to his sponge board by rubber bands. These all had to be accounted for by the circulating nurse in the OR, before and after the operation. He took them to the OR to have them sterilized in the autoclave.

Today the team included Ray Bartlett, resident in neurosurgery, graduate of Temple University Medical School and resident in surgery and neurosurgery at Temple University Hospital, spending an additional year of training in pediatric neurosurgery and Larry Mitchell, 4th year student from NYU Medical School. Sam always needed a resident to teach and a student to observe his surgical genius.

"Andiamo," Sam called to the team. "This should be an exciting case. Maybe we can do some good for this lad. Let's wash up and get started." The team headed for the sinks next to the OR and began the ritual of scrubbing up to the elbows. Sam shows Larry how to put on the cap and mask before the scrubbing begins.

"What is your name, doctor?"

"Larry Mitchell, sir"

"Where did you go to school?"

"University of Alabama, Sir."

"Oh! I went to Princeton, Ever hear of it."

"Yes sir, we always referred to UA as the Princeton of the South."

"Strange, at Princeton, we never thought of ourselves as the UA of the North." So be it." Sam never tired of setting up that old joke, dear to the Ivy Leaguers when talking to Southerners who were trying to put their university into the Ivy League. One never heard of schools claiming to be the Harvard of the Northwest or the University of Alabama of the North.

"Ever hear of George Patton, Larry?

Ray's head bowed as he has been through this drill on Patton so many times.

"Yes sir! He played for the Crimson Tide in 1964."

"Not that one. George A. Patton, the general in World War Two. He was played by George C. Scott in the movie Patton."

"Sorry Sir, I forgot about that movie."

"Well, Patton is my man. He has a lot to teach us about life and neurosurgery. Did you know his nickname?"

"No sir."

"Well what do you think it might be?"

"Tough as nails, sir"

"That is pretty good but wrong."

"I don't know, sir"

"Well, it was Old Blood and Guts."

"I was pretty close."

"Close does not do it."

"But what does Guts have to do with neurosurgery?"

"Guts and neurosurgery, good question. But let's get this straight- I ask the questions. Just pay attention to his biography and you will come up with the answer. Ok, what was his problem at the end of his career?"

"He slapped a soldier."

"How did you know that?"

"I saw George C Scott do it in the movie."

"What happened to him?"

"He died."

"OK how did he die?"

"Fell on his head?"

"Close."

"He was in a car accident and died from an embolism."

"Did he have any medical problems?"

"Not sure, sir."

"Well he had multiple head injuries from horse back riding and car accidents; some kind of traumatic brain damage. That may explain his outbursts and inappropriate behavior. Kind of fits, Patton and neurosurgery." Sam then flashed the most insincere toothy grin.

"Do you know where his museum is?"

"No sir. But I bet it is somewhere in the South."

"Fort Knox, Kentucky. Visit it and see the car that was involved in the fatal accident. I have been there at least 10 times. Amazing man!"

"I see that already, sir."

"I expect you to be an expert on Patton when you finish this rotation, even if you don't learn any neurosurgery. I may even let you read the draft of the biography that I am writing about Patton. Let's go to the big show and see what we can do for this lad." Salivari puts down the scrub brush, backs into the door to the OR with his arms bent at the elbow, palms facing him. Diane Murray, one of the circulating nurses empties the towels on the sterile setup table and then holds up the paper sterile gown. Sam dried his hands, drops the towel in a bucket and puts his arms into the sleeves of the paper gown. Moving tango fashion to Sam's back, Diane ties the gown at his neck and back.

Larry Mitchell, knowing the student's place, put on the sterile gown and moved to the left of the surgeon at the operating table. The resident, Ray Bartlett was across the table, ready to help but wishing he could do this case. After all, he was well trained, 6 years of neurosurgery residency after a year of general surgery. But Sam was not a sharer as he does not get many cases referred to him. "Not many Princeton graduates are in the area doing primary care that can refer patients to me. They send the patients to me and then expect me to do the case." Ray had no choice but to accept this rationalization. He did not want to argue with his chief that this was not a referral case, but an admission from the ED.

So Sam had the case and Ray was the assistant. Larry had been warned by the trauma nurse in the ED that his role was to be there to praise Sam for his skills and to stay out of the way. For Larry, this was a thrill and a scare because he has heard so many stories about the unusual way Sam operates, especially the spongee-wongees.

"The goal of this operation is to stop the bleeding, clean out the wound and try to fix the edges of the broken skull bones to allow healing without infection and hopefully restoration of brain function. Scalpel and hemostats, please."

First Sam placed about 15 hemostat clamps on the scalp wound edges. "OK, Larry, we need to keep these stats away from the operative field. Take this sterile tape and put one edge in the blood. That is the red end. Now take the red end of the tape and pass it through the finger loops of the hemostats."

Larry passed the red edge through the loops as he was directed.

"Now take the white end and clamp the tape so that all the hemostats will be away from where I am going to operate."

"Wow, that is a clever way to keep things neat, I'll have to remember that trick."

The next part went smoothly. First a section of bone from the skull was removed. A hand drill was used to make a small hole in the bone. Then a wire was passed from one hole to the adjacent hole. This wire had serrations so that the wire was pulled up on one side and then the other, acting like a saw. When the cut was complete, the wire was passed through the next hole and the sawing repeated.

"I know there must be more modern ways to open the skull, but I like the old ways better. Let's get that bone lifted." The bone flap was removed and placed in a covered sterile bowl on the instrument table. "Here is the middle cerebral artery there is the trouble maker! I need some crazy glue to seal the artery. I need more of my spongee-wongees." The nurse took a card board filled with these small white sponges and moved them closer to Dr. Salivari. "We need to ligate or burn these small bleeders with the cautery."

Ray Bartlett manned the spongee- wongees mopping up the blood on the surface of the brain while Sam squirted some saline to clean up the operative site and gently pushed on the brain to see if there were any bleeders under the skull. Identifying and closing off the bleeders continued for about 30 minutes. Larry Mitchell was thinking to himself that it is not clear why neurosurgery was a benchmark for medical skills. So many people rank people by comparing them to neurosurgery. He remembered his relative's comments. "He is so smart, he could be a neurosurgeon! He has good hands; he probably will be a neurosurgeon!" In reality there is not much skill needed to do this clamp the bleeder, tie it off and mop up the blood routine.

"Maybe Patten could have been a neurosurgeon; one needed a strong dose of aggressiveness to open people's heads" commented Larry.

Sam smiled at the comment. "The wound site was finally clean and blood free. Let's flush out the wound with saline. Have we started antibiotics yet?"

"They were started in the ED."

"Good! How is his BP, Skipper?"

"100/78"

"Blood loss estimate?"

"We are down about 500 cc's- I have some blood hanging."

"Thank you for watching that." Sam was definitely not the old time neurosurgeon who would have yelled at the anesthesiologist for not asking permission to give blood. "We are a team. Skipper watches the anesthetics and vital signs and I will do the surgery. It is now about 2 hours into the operation. The exterior of the brain is bloodless. The color is good. Do you see the swelling over in this section, Frank?

Larry smiled, ignoring the misnomer. "Boy I sure do not- this is some expert surgery today sir."

"Every day, not just today, young man. After we trim up the bone fragments, we can close up," Sam announced.

Larry tried to make a comeback. "This would have been a great case for the Discovery Channel's surgery shows. See how nice the rows of hemostats lined up and held together with the tape, one end red and the other white make the field so visible."

"We are a team and smooth operators. Most important it looks like we will have a good result. That is if this little lad cooperates and regains some motor and cognitive function. Did you label the skull piece so we can return it to Anthony when the brain swelling is over? We don't want to put the wrong lid on this pot. Ray, I will let you do the dressing but please protect the open wound, but you know that, sorry."

"Dr. Salivari, how many residents have you trained?" Ray asked.

"About 100 or so."

"Did you ever think you may have done more harm than good?" There was a pause where no one in the OR took a breath, not sure where this was going.

Sam leered at him over his magnifying glasses. The steely blue eyes served as potential lasers that were ready to fire across the operating table and kill Ray with his double beamed weapons. The nurses froze, wondering why Ray would say such a thing.

Just when an explosion was imminent, Ray continued. "You make this seem so easy, that residents and students will get a false sense of confidence that they can do the same operation since it went so smoothly. Then when they get on their own, they could try to fix a case like this and find themselves in deep doo-doo. You are really slick."

Sam quickly changed his look from rage and attack to a smile. He loves compliments, even sidewinders like this one.

"Thanks for the compliment, good for the ego, you know."

Larry reversed his red end and white end of the tape routine, released the clamps and removed the hemostats. Diane Murray called "sponge count, please."

"12 on the rack, 40 in the bucket, 144 personal sponges on Dr. Salvari's board. Sponge count correct."

The anesthesia was lightening up. Anthony moaned a little. Most likely from the irritation of the endotracheal tube that remained in place so his breathing can be controlled in the intensive care unit.

As they were finishing the case and getting ready for the transfer to the ICU, Larry whispered to Ray, "Sam is not as crazy as I was led to believe with his own surgical tools and spongee-wongees." Then as he stepped back from the OR table and gasped. There was Sam on his hands and knees scrubbing the floor under the OR table where some blood had dripped down from the wound. Fortunately Sam did not hear this as his scrubbing noise was louder than Larry's whisper. Sam stood up, looked at the closure of the wound and placement of the drains. "I am off to the locker room to polish my shoes so I can speak to the parents, gotta be clean, you know."

Ray and Larry helped the OR techs lift Anthony from the OR table to a hospital bed and then they pushed the bed down the hall to the neurosurgical intensive care unit. "We need to take time and go over the details of the case, what we did and what are our concerns. Skip LaFayette, anesthesiologist is there to report to the team about the anesthesia. We will stay here until he seems stable and then make rounds at 6 PM to check him and sign out to the neurosurgery resident on call tonight. There are 10 beds in the ICU; we take post-op patients to room 4, next to the nurse's station. You will meet his nurse who will watch the vital signs, look for bleeding and make assessments almost constantly until the condition stabilizes."

When they arrived at the ICU, Ray smiles as he sees Katie Burg.

"She is a top notch nurse who adds an extra dose of compassion and care to her patients. You find a lot of nurses like her who work in the intensive care, a special breed. But Katie is the best."

Katie sat in at the transfer meeting to hear about the surgery and the special concerns voiced about Anthony. After the conference, she put her notes on the chart and did her own examination so that she can see the baseline condition and then will be aware if anything changes. The i.v. lines, blood pressure lines, antibiotic lines, oxygen monitors, respiration detectors, EKG lines, pulmonary pressure lines coming out from arms and legs made it difficult for Katie to determine if the arms and legs could move. The endotracheal tube rested at the side of his mouth. A urinary catheter from his bladder emptied urine into the measuring plastic receptacle hanging from the side of the bed. He had the classic post-neurosurgery white gauze turban covering most of his head. The skin around his eyes was puffy and pale; tomorrow there would be black and swollen eyes from bleeding from the injury and the operation. His pink lips and toes were the only positive signs of good circulation.

"Ray, will you hold his head still while I check his lungs. This is the best I can do as I do not want to move him too much."

Katie then checked the i.v. rate on the electronic monitor, the label on the IV bags and flushed out the second i.v. line reserved for antibiotics.

"Things seemed to be in good shape, at least for now since the troubles usually come the next day or two."

"See, Larry, that is what I like about Kate, she does not miss a step."

Kate did not seem surprised at Ray's kind words as everyone knows he is a true gentleman; being a bachelor made him even more attractive.

"Are the parents around?" Katie asked the unit secretary Margaret, the real boss of the unit. She knows everything that is going on in the hospital and knows who can fix things, speed up getting replacement parts, and get extra pizzas from Cicero's pizza. Margaret called on the intercom, "Will the parents of Anthony Packson come into the ICU when you are ready."

After they were finished speaking to Dr. Salivari, Fred and Sandy Packson came into the ICU, holding each other, overwhelmed by the accident, the hyperactivity of the ICU and the beeping of the monitors. Fred, looking somewhat gray when he saw his son, squeezed Sandy "I am glad the ICU was a series of private rooms so I can not see the other children. I have heard the saying that when you come to CHUC and see the sick children, you feel lucky that your child is not as sick as the others. If that is true, I am glad I don't see the rest of the kids here. This is as bad as it could be. Poor Anthony."

"Welcome to the ICU," Katie greeted the parents. "I know this all looks quite scary but you will soon get accustomed to it. First, let me show you around the room and explain the equipment." All the time keeping her eye on the monitors and Anthony, she moved next to Anthony's bed. "His color is good, his BP is 90/60; pulse is 88; respirations 16; pulse-ox 94- these are good readings."

Fred, a chemical engineer, was entranced with all the monitors, tubes and i.v. lines. "This was comparable to flying a jumbo jet," he told Sandy. A philosophy major at the University of Chicago, she was eager to get to the library to read about the physiology of head trauma and the long term issues. "When in unfamiliar waters, go intellectual" was her motto. Katie realized that Sandy felt helpless to aid her son so she wanted her do feel part of the recovery. "Will you bring in some familiar things from home? You can play his favorite music, posters, pictures anything that he likes so when he wakes up he will see some old friends." Katie made sure that she said when and not if he wakes up.

Sandy, heard that nuance, tried to smile. "Thanks for your optimism; we have had enough bad news for one lifetime, today."

• • •

6 o'clock rounds were uneventful as predicted. Ray first checked the orders. "Larry, we need to make sure that all the things we talked about were on record and more importantly, were administered. Computerized records made rounds much easier. But one still had to check to see that the patient's appearance matched the numbers. Sometimes there is a discrepancy between the chart and the visual check, I favor what I see in the patient as the lines may be clogged or the monitors may have lost their calibration giving us false information, electronics do not equal perfection. Don't be like these young doctors who worship the numbers; they are happy sitting in a conference room making sure the numbers line up neatly, even if, much to us older doctor's dismay, they do not come to the bedside to look at the patient."

• • •

"What I am proposing to you is a good basic price for the helical scanner then, as you can see, I added the 5% for the administrative approval."

"Well, here we call it icing." Beardsley corrected the salesmen.

"Ok, let's write up a pro forma." Tom Nelson, the Commonwealth sales rep wanted to get the order started before the end of the month sales reports went out.

"No, I do not want to put anything in writing, no paper trail, if you know what I mean? OK, the call for bids will go out in a week or so. I

39

will let you know what the competition is bidding and you will go under that plus the 5% icing. After the contract is signed, then we will talk about the options and revisions to the contract. You will do well. I estimate your commission is about 70G's On the other hand, if this does not work out for any reason, the next batch of purchases will go the company that plays our game. Selling this beauty to our hospital will send a message to the other children's hospitals then you, …. and I will profit from the sale. Right?"

"Yes sir."

"I am sure you could use the cash to pay for that new house you just purchased with a double mortgage. Right….I am here to help you. We will talk later. I have to get to executive committee meeting." Richardson Beardsley collected his file for the executive committee meeting.

Walking past the executive offices, he looks at the framed document on the wall outside the administration office suite. He smiles as he reads it for the 500th time.

Mission Statement of the Children's Hospital of Union Country

- *Provide the best care possible to all children of Union County and all who come through our doors. We serve all children of all races, religions and ethnic groups without regard to ability to pay.*
- *Support the community by providing up to date services to our citizens*
- *Support education and research to advance the science of pediatrics*
- *Provide leadership in developing new techniques and treatments for improving health of our children.*

From the bylaws of CHUC updated June 21, 2007

He joins the executive committee in the pathology department conference room; a group of doctors assemble for the weekly meeting to fix hospital problems and make policy decisions. That location is the closest thing to neutral territory for the members who represent the major departments in the hospital, pediatrics, surgery, anesthesia, laboratory medicine, technical services, information technology and the administration, the CEO, the COO, the CFO and the president of the medical staff. In a hospital this large and centralized, the executive committee is the one place that the power brokers can have a voice in the operation and direction of the institution. Each person has chance to make an announcement. In true democratic style, no one is supposed to lead the meeting. The town meeting effect makes sense on paper, but in reality, the staff talks and the administration does what it wants to do. The dialogue is used to establish the fact that the ideas were discussed; references to the discussion are quoted when there are disputes about the administrations actions. "But we discussed it at the executive committee meeting last fall," is the salve that the CEO uses to soften some of the pain of their self serving decisions which are made outside of the committee between the CEO and the particular division head who is often bought off by the approval of a pet project or purchase, just like the relationship between many in the U.S. Congress and the lobbies. Richardson Beardsley follows his management policy called the BLAAC system - buy loyalty at any cost. Pay the leaders enough so they follow his instructions. Several of the recent appointees in nuclear medicine, ENT, orthopedics and laboratory were paid premium salaries and given a large endowment for their department to improve the quality of care to the sick and injured children to assure their loyalty to the administration.

Greer Messic, chief of laboratory medicine, sat at one end of the table, his usual spot. This position allows him to block any sudden lunges at the throat of disagreeing debaters. Carter Randolf, chief of surgery sits at the other end of the table unless he arrives after the meeting starts, then Richardson Beardsley will take that spot, much to Randolf's displeasure. David Grunberg, chief of pediatrics sits facing the window, any seat. John Spirito sits opposite David Grunberg because the bright light from the windows bothers his eyes. When she attends, Gail Grange, president of the medical staff takes any empty seat.

"Well, what is on the table today?' asks John. He is always one to poke fun at the heavy bureaucracy of the administration. "I see that there is now a vice-president of information added to the staff. So I called her and asked her what the capitol of Mali is. She got angry and hung up. Don't you think that is important information that this info guru should know?"

David Grunberg started the next topic. "I would like to discuss the possible expansion of the addition of another health center in West Cedar. I know we have gone over this before and it was deferred while we look at costs and return on investments etc. But this seems a good time to re-air the issue. Dick, what is going on with the study group?"

Richardson, or Dick, to his colleagues replied. "The study is still going on. There are some abandoned buildings in West Cedar that can be had for a reasonable price. There is no problem getting an architect to duplicate the center we have down in Alpha. We certainly need to get these people out of the main hospital building; I mean to provide services to them in their own neighborhood. But…. But the return on investment is a problem. The Medicaid just does not pay enough to make this a profitable venture."

"I thought this was a non-profit organization" chided David, opening up the old argument of non-profit or not for profit. The administration's stock answer is that they can make a profit and have to make a profit; the profit, called the margin, is plowed back into the institution to create new programs or replace old equipment etc. Unlike profit organizations, the non-profits pay no dividends. Beardsley is defensive when this topic comes up as the so called profit determines the CEO's bonus so the more profit, the larger the bonus paid to him on top of his 1.5 million dollar salary.

Beardsley interrupts the discussion. "It is a not for profit institution but we cannot build up losses or our main mission of caring for sick children will be threatened and we will be forced to cut back on services. Believe me; I am not doing this for the money. I could be in hedge funds or M and A's, if I wanted to make big money. The other option is to add on three new operating rooms. These will cost about the same but will produce about 7.5 million a year in income from procedures, charges for renting the room and markup from supplies and drugs. Many times we get a minimum one hour charge for the operating room when the procedure takes 15 minutes, 10 to clean up and set up the next procedure and away we go! Two hourly rentals in 60 minutes. Bam! Money in the bank."

"And in your bonus," mused John.

Ignoring Spirito's jab, Beardsley continued." Unless we can see some way to erase the losses from the community program, I can't approve the project until the numbers look better."

"How about the annual fund raising program?"

That is designated for the new helical scanner we promised the new radiologist that we hired from Johns Hopkins. He is a hot ticket and should bring in a lot of new cases and profit to the institution."

"And to your bonus" John repeated to himself. John did not want the new helical scanner as the present one is only one year old. He did not want the new radiologist hired. He can do the work without the added expense but he was overridden by Beardsley who was hell bent on getting this newest helical scanner.

John whispers to Gail, "Beardsley suffers from the Got to Keep Up With the Big Boys Syndrome. I hear he has 1400 bottles of wine in his cellar, another symptom of the big dick competitive complex that he learned from his buddies on the hospital board ."

Gail smiles and blushes after hearing about the big dick. "He gets that part right but still gets his suits off the rack at Sears, on sale, and doesn't shine his shoes."

John is feeling a little paranoid as he seems to be in the line of administrative fire. He knows the drill. His requests for equipment are denied. He is excluded from decisions and special meetings. He fears that soon he will be reading x-rays at another hospital. Even after 35 years of loyal service, the present is past; the future is how much profit you can make and forget the past. The helical scanner is another example of the soft push out.

"The fetal medicine center is ready to roll," J. Rendell Pickering, chief medical officer, announced. "We have the tie in with maternal fetal medicine at the OB department. The fetal surgeons are on board; the fetal ultrasound equipment has been replaced with color Doppler and rapid scanner. Nursing has hired a manager. The only issue left is control of the nurse manager. Should the hiring be done by the fetal center or the Nursing department? If we turn it over to them, there will be all sorts of delays, trying to figure out where the manager sits on the TO and how many degrees she should have. I think we should keep the manager in the center where there will be less meetings and more work."

"Does public relations know about this?"

"We have Channel 24 ready to do a special. The PR department has the paper writing a story. The Health Channel is working up a proposal for a program. The women's committee is planning a special booth at the flower show with the idea of making the center the recipient of their profits."

"Have you passed this by legal and the Diocese?" asked Randolf. "It seems to be pressing the envelope a little. Operating on a fetus. Maybe some will be aborted because of the procedure. This is new territory for the hospital. You know we don't provide abortions here to the teens. I fear a major reaction from the anti-abortion groups and the Evangelicals."

"Maybe we should get modern and change the policy" chimed in David. David Grunberg, an example of what happened to the protesters of the 60's who did not drop out, but entered the mainstream andnever gave up his liberal credentials. He enjoyed his prodding the conservatives from the inside rather than on the street.

"The backlash would be horrific. Our donor base would not stand for it."

"But does this follow our mission of providing first rate care to all children?"

"That is a tricky one. I rather not mention it because it is hard to defend. Fortunately, not many people know about this contradiction and I would like it to stay that way." Beardsley replied. "Anything else?"

"Yes, two things. The hall ways are still dirty. I collected a bag full of cups and dirty diapers in the hall way on Seven and a number of soda cans in the stairwell. There is even one over the air conditioning duct, but I could not reach it" John spurted out.

"If the growth hormone shots don't work and you don't grow 8 inches, I will look into it. What else?"

"What do you expect? Parking. The lot is full early in the morning, making it hard for the patients to find a spot. Then they are late for their appointments and the day gets crazy" continued John. Seems administrative parking has taken 15 more spaces that were for patients. Can you find them other spots?"

"What would a meeting be without reference to the dirty halls and the full parking lot? I thought when we added 300 spaces across the street that this would be taken care of but it did not make a dent. I will contact housekeeping, eh environmental services, to send someone up there to patrol hallway on Seven. Otherwise, I will see you all next week."

Beardsley pulled out his Palm Treo and saw that he was due in the front lobby for a picture session with South Creek Community Committee, the area near the hospital, who has awarded him their Man of the Year Medal for all the support and service given to their citizens by the hospital.

Chapter 3

Tonight both Anthony's condition and the laboratory results were in agreement, predicting smooth sailing for the resident covering for the night, at least for now.

About 4 AM, things changed. His blood pressure started to rise; Anthony was moving in the bed as if he were in pain. The intensivist on the night shift was called to check things over. After the usual monitor check, tube check and lab check, he examined Anthony's eyes, reflexes and his reaction to a painful pinch.

"This is a sign of either brain swelling at the base of the brain where the blood pressure was controlled or too much fluids or a reaction to the drugs." Almost reflexly, the intensivist went through his check list. "The heart rate was unchanged. There was no rash to suggest a drug reaction. The urine output was good, his veins were not full, the liver was not enlarged from excess fluids, it was hard to tell if it were tender. The venous pressure was not elevated as it would be in heart failure. Looks like we have some edema in the brain." Randy Pellote, the intensivist concluded. "Increase the rate on the respirator and increase the steroids. It is early so we may beat this problem before it gets out of hand. It takes a few hours for the drug to work, so let's get cooking. How are the I and O's?" referring to the fluid in and the urine out. "We don't want to get him overloaded. Check the electrolytes to see if the sodium changes. Tomorrow is the day we expect all hell to break loose so let's give him time to rest up for the turmoil. It seems that there is one bad day when things seemed to be unglued as the body recovers from the trauma and surgery."

On rounds the next day, Ray Bartlett took over. After going through the same examination, he wrote his progress note. "6:30 AM. Still no major complications. The BP elevation early this AM is under control. 126/82 now. A minor spike in temperature to 100.5. Checked the lungs, clear, good exchange of air in all lobes. Will increase chest percussion and suctioning."

Katie did her best to clear the mucus out of the airway. Fortunately, the fever disappeared in a few hours. She was glad to see the monitor readings were normal indicating that the pressures in the lungs, brain and aorta were in acceptable ranges. She wrote her note in the chart- "vitals normal, the cultures of blood, urine, IV sites were sterile so far; the lab sheets were all in order with no unusual values. Still no signs of improved brain function."

Ray came back at noon and added to his note. "12N-The chart is in good order but poor Anthony did not wake up," Ray summarized his condition. "We have to be patient."

Fred and Sandy were not patient; their worries began to show the strain of the ordeal. Fred became obsessed with watching the monitors. He was good at sequencing the worries. If the blood pressure dropped, he would look at the urine catheter to see if urine was flowing indicating that good blood flow through the kidneys. If Anthony looked pale, he checked the latest hemoglobin. This was like monitoring a complicated machine at his job. Sandy became more intellectual, sitting at the bedside, reading the books from the library and printouts of material from WebMD about head trauma, outcome studies of brain injury especially the cognitive abilities of survivors. Although she was silent, her brain was racing with many questions. What would happen to Anthony? Would he graduate college, become a lawyer or investment banker? Would she have grandchildren?

The next day about 6 am, Dr. Salivari was the first one on the team to make rounds. He was accompanied by the nurse manager of the unit, Libby Nichols. Anthony's parents were still asleep in the parent's overnight room down the hall. Sam moved quickly, always in a rush to get to the next patient. In his wrinkleless, fully starched white coat, he looked as if he spent a few hours in the makeup room, getting groomed for a TV interview. Libby, likewise looked very professional in her long sleeved white uniform; her French cuffs closed by beautiful jade cuff links. She had pulled the charts of his patients and was following around behind him, a throwback to the 50's when that was the expected nurse's role. Her only nod to the present was her not wearing a starched white nurse's cap. Libby liked tradition and formality. Everything looked so sterile and professional, except for the mild flush in Libby's cheeks and erect nipples pushing on her starched uniform. The clerk at the nurses station noticed the two protrusions and commented "Rounds cannot be that exciting at 6 AM."

Sam looked over the chart and pinched; rather he grabbed the skin on Anthony's chest and gave a twisting squeeze. Anthony groaned and moved his arms and legs. "Great" Sam concluded his exam. When the parents were not at the bed side, that twist was Sam's complete physical. Pinch and see of the arms and legs withdraw. For many days, this reflex reaction to pain was all the patient could muster. At least it was better than no response. When the parents were present, He took out his stethoscope to make an effort to listen to the lungs. "Remind me which end of this thing goes into my mouth" Sam asked the resident. So much for comedy routines in a very tense and sad room.

Later in the day, Dr Salivari came back to speak to Fred and Sandy. "It takes time and although it is hard on you, you have to keep up good spirits in front of Anthony because he probably could hear what we are saying." He stepped back and whispered to them, "It was too early to have doubts about recovery since patients with head injuries have recovery times measured in months rather than days."

Katie joined in. "It is good to read stories to Anthony, tell him what you are doing and play his favorite music."

Fred apologized "I would be glad to get his music but unfortunately I do not have any idea what Anthony's favorite groups are but I will bring in whatever CD's are found in his room at home. Sounds like strange noise to me."

Katie smiled and began then checked over his skin. "We don't need any bed sores on good old Anthony. You can see I put half splints on his ankles and wrists; he is getting daily physical therapy to keep his arms and legs supple. Lying in bed without much movement is an invitation for bedsores so we turn Anthony frequently and keep him on the air mattress. We check the area where the IV fluids and medicines passes through the skin for redness. Nutrition was here to advise on feeding. They suggest switching from IV feedings of amino acids, sugars and emulsified fats to tube feedings through a tube passing through his abdomen into his small intestine."

She checked the faces on Sandy and Fred who seemed to be listening so she continued. "Our nursing care goal is to remove as much technology from him as quickly as the condition allows. So far, the breathing was good enough to turn down the settings of the respirators and soon we can remove the tube that was in his airway. So things are on track right now, let's keep our fingers crossed."

Ray Bartlett frequently stopped by to check Anthony and then asked Katie to about her assessment of Anthony's condition. Since both were unmarried, the gossips on the floor, were trying to make something out of this couple's conversations. There was no place for traditional social graces in the intensive care; one was either arrogant and unfeeling or trying to take someone to bed. So when Ray stopped to talk to Katie, the ladies at the nurses' station were watching and over-interpreting all moves and gestures. The consensus from the nursing station: Katie had the look of 'it's ok to continue this over a few beers at Oakstones on 35th street.' Ray remained all business, at least for now. He knew that something was about to happen; the crash that occurs a few days after major surgery.

Chapter 4

Sergeant Cranford is manning the triage booth today. Sarah Cranford RN, 30 years experience in the emergency department, teacher of hundreds of interns and nursing students about emergency medicine is another CHUC legend. Built like a Hummer, she runs the unit with confidence and authority using her experience and common sense. She can pick out the sick kids in 2-3 seconds, not needing any labs or x-rays to make her decisions. She also can pick out the child abuse cases, and differentiate a child with pain from appendicitis from the bellyacher trying to get out of school. The new residents were told "When the Sarge says jump on this one; you jump because she knows and she is right." But things were not that straight forward for Cranford. The new wave of PhD Nurses has determined that the triage duty should go to a master degree prepared graduate. Experience not necessary is the unstated corollary. This causes a great deal of tension in the ED as no one could match the Sarge but she has only a RN degree, not even a Bachelor degree. But even the tough old Sarge is worried that after the next nursing accreditation board inspects the hospital staffing pattern, she will no doubt be replaced.

In the triage booth, she took a brief history, eyeballing the breathing, posture, facial movements and evidence of blue or ashen skin color. She quickly decides that this patient goes to the emergency unit, the urgent care, to see the doc in the box or given an appointment to come back to dermatology or dentistry in the morning. The computer monitor in front of her updates the status of each patient she has processed in the triage booth and moved them to the next section. She can tell how many open rooms there are in the urgent care, how many are waiting for lab tests or x-rays or who is being admitted to the hospital. This patient flow system is the only token of modern technology she allows in her kingdom. Next patient.

Linda Forrest, 33, well dressed and composed, brings in her third son, Peter, age 18 months.

"He woke up from nap and refused to walk. He had not fallen, had no bruises was irritable and definitely would not walk. I left the other two children with the maid and headed off to the CHUC Emergency Department."

"Rays and sugar" calls out the Sarge, which translates into "get an X-ray of the leg and here is a piece of candy to make Peter a little less crabby." This way when the ED doctor comes to see Peter, the x-ray will be available, speeding up the visit and treatment time. Not all the cases are seen this quickly but Peter's father, Robert Forrest is the vice-president of community services at the hospital, explaining the expeditious triage and treatment. It is also the reason the Sarge called for Dr. Barstow to meet the parents and check Peter.

• • •

While Peter heads to radiology with his mother, Samir Abazz age 19 months, sits in his crib at his home on Peach Street, constantly crying, with his face buried in the dirty crib sheets. His mother, Shana, 23, does not attend to him as she is trying to keep Aziza, her 30 month old from trying to feed some miniature cars to her 6 months old brother Tamir. She extracts the cars from Tamir's mouth and puts Aziza in from of the TV to watch Arthur the Mouse for the 150th time. Now, Shana looks at Samir to figure out why he is crying. "This cry sounds different," she noted because it was more intense and slightly higher pitched. "Hey, his leg is swollen, much larger than the right one. He don't move his leg. This does not look good. I better get to the hospital. Where is that damn Allen?" referring to Allen, her boyfriend and father of the baby Tamir. "He was here a few minutes ago," she continues. "There was no way I can take all three to the hospital and wait the usual 5-6 hours. Dammit, where is Allen? Since he does not have a job, the jerk usually sits on the couch watching the cartoons with the kids. At least then he spends time with the older two children who are not his. I wish I could get him out of my life!"

Allen finally arrives home about an hour later, obviously after a hit of crack. He calms down enough to get the assignment of baby sitting so Shana heads out to Locust Street to catch the 33 bus that will take her within a few blocks of CHUC. It took about 45 minutes to get to the Emergency where the Sarge greets her.

"Not walking? Come in and tell me more. Who else lives at home?"

"Me, my friend and two other kids besides Samir."

"Who is your welfare worker?"

"Miss Edith, but I don't see her very often."

"How about your family? Who's on the team?"

"My mom and sister Debby, but they don't come around much. I see them on Christmas when I can make it."

"How far did you go in school?"

"I dropped out in 10th grade, when I got pregnant. Most of my friends had babies before I did," Shana tried to rationalize her lack of education.

"You sure have a full plate. How old are you?"

"Twenty three. People say I look a lot older. What do you say?"

Sarge tried to be diplomatic. "I guess you are as old as you feel."

"Rays and sugar" spouts the Sarge, "what is going on with all these broken babies? Here Shana, take this form for an x-ray and go through that silver door next to the red sign. Here is some candy for Samir."

Sarge got on the phone to call the Child Abuse team. "She did not miss many of the check points for possible child abuse. A loner, isolated life, no family support, overwhelmed by three young kids. This is not good, this smells like business for you guys who will take a better history and begin to work with the mother if needed."

• • •

In the laceration room, Bob Gardner, on his first day in the emergency was assigned to seeing walk-ins with colds or sewing up minor lacerations. Today he has sutured a few cuts on the legs and forearms. He, in his naive way, felt quite competent and for a few seconds, was considering switching to surgery as a career. So when he looked at the next chart, saw it listed a 4 year old child with a small cut on her palm. His face glowed, "I am glad that it was nothing more complicated than a small cut. I can do that one. Send her into my treatment room."

When Mrs. Dilson sat down with Irina, he confidently tells her, "I will put you back together again, even though she does not look like Humpty Dumpty. Does it hurt?"

"A little."

"Is she allergic to any medicine?"

Mrs. Dilson nodded.

"Did she have her shots?"

"She is up to date."

"Good. Let's get started to fix up your cut."

After washing off the wound, he injected a small amount of anesthetic. "Obviously this requires 3-0 suture material. Hold on honey, you should not feel anything now that the numbing medicine is in."

The wound extended from the mid palm to the thumb. "Thenar eminence, I think this is called. Let me at 'em."

In about 10 minutes, Bob was able to put in a row of sutures to bring the cut ends together. "Just one more minute, honey, I have to have this checked by my boss."

Bob, obviously proud of his clinical acumen and sartorial skills, left the room to find Dr. Barstow. "Hey Dr. Barber," Bob was not very good on names. "I have a suture job for you to check out. Pulled the whole thing together with 3-0 suture. Looks good to me, what do you think?" Dr Barstow, looked at the wound, used a sterile needle point to touch the tip of the thumb. "Can you feel this? How about this? And here?" "Ok Bob, did you check for nerve damage? Rule 1- always test for nerve damage in lacerations, especially cuts on the hands. See here, no feeling on the thumb." She turned to Mrs. Dilson and explained. "I am worried about the lack of feeling in the thumb; the nerve may be cut so I am sending you to see the hand surgeons. They will give you their opinion about whether or not she needs further treatment. Is that OK?"

Mrs. Dilson nods.

"Good. Fortunately, the hand surgery section is on the next floor. I will call them and tell them you are on your way."

When they left the room, Dr. Barstow turned to Bob. "So off they go to the hand surgeons so they can reconnect the nerves before they sew up the hand. No harm done, since you checked with me, but a lesson you will never forget. Right?" Bob nodded in agreement and kissed good bye his surgical career.

Upstairs in the outpatient department Sarah Wright picked up the next chart on her door. This was a 4 month old coming to see her for a so called well baby check. "Hi, my name is Dr. Wright; I am new here, taking over for Dr. Shannon who left the hospital since your last visit. I am happy to meet you. You are here for a check up? How are things going? Any questions for me today? Is she eating OK?" With each question, Shelia Vinson, the mother was trying to answer the question as the next one was fired off. Sarah was astute enough to realize that her anxiety was getting in way of any meaningful communication. She took a deep breath and started again. "Tell me, how are things going?"

"Do you think there is something wrong with her head? I had a hat for her Easter outfit and it no longer fits.

"Let's take a look. Her head does look large. Let me check the chart and see the previous head measurements. We are in luck; the head circumference measurements for the last 2 visits were charted on the head size graph. Oops, the head is large. It was always average, running below the 95th percent range and now it is slightly over the 95th percentile. No question she has a large head but we only have a few measurements so I can't say if it got larger or the measurements were not accurate. Since as you can see, they wrap the tape around the head. Usually, the person who does the measurement may place the tape in different positions. But with this change, we have to make sure that there is nothing going on in the head, like hydrocephalus, water on the brain, you know."

"Where did she get water on her brain? She drinks formula, not water."

"Pardon me. I got ahead of myself, thinking out loud. We need an MRI to look inside the head and seeing what is going on." Totally forgetting the well baby visit agenda, Sarah raced out of the room to find the preceptor. "Hey Dr. Casey, I am about to order my first MRI. I have a case of hydrocephalus. Can you imagine, she was coming in for her shots but I saw her head was large and I want to get an MRI to prove that she has hydrocephalus? OK?"

"Hold up a minute doctor! She was here for a well check. How is her development? Is she eating OK? What tricks is she doing? Sleeping? Eating? Pooping? What about these things? Is there any thing on the physical to suggest hydrocephalus?"

"Yes, she has a large head."

"OK let's start with that. What else can cause a large head?"

"You mean what is the differential diagnosis of large head."

"Right."

"Oh, could be craniostenosis, Could be macrocephaly. Oh, that is the same as large head. I take that one back."

"OK but lets think of a history question that may help us. Maybe we can go talk to the mother and ask her a few questions."

"Be my guest."

"If I could ask only one question, I would ask the mother the size of the father's head. I say father since you already know the mother has a normal sized head.

"OK, Shelia, I am Dr. Casey, Dr. Wright asked me to come in and take a look at your daughter. Tell me, the baby's father, do you have a picture of him with you."

"No, why do you want to see his picture."

"I wanted to see the size of his head."

"I don't have a picture of him but they call him balloon head since he has a very big head."

"Aha! You were right, Dr. Wright. The baby has familial macrocephaly. Big heads run in the family. Like father like daughter. Now you can get back to the purpose of the visit. Checking her out and getting her shots. You can cancel the MRI. See how one question can save about 1000 dollars.

"No problem. Thanks Dr. Casey."

Down the hall in the acute care section, three new interns were trying to use their collective skills to find out what was wrong with Carlos, who was brought here because of a fever. As this was their first day, they could not call upon their vast experience so they decided to triple team the next patient.

'I know how to treat otitis, but I don't know what an infected ear looks like."

"I saw a red ear once so I will look in his ear and then you can write the prescription."

"What if the ear is normal? I think we should get a CBC since it could be leukemia. I am worried about missing a case of leukemia. That would be truly sad if Carlos had leukemia. I read that many cases present with a fever."

"Maybe we should start with the history and then see what we come up with. I don't think we can get checked out when we are totally disorganized. He could have bird flu but I doubt it."

The circus, starring new residents, continued in the acute care section of the emergency room. Beth had a case that she thought was cystic fibrosis but was finally diagnosed as pneumonia. A suspected brain tumor turned out to be a normal child, a case of possible appendicitis turned out to be severe constipation. Fortunately, the faculty was present to check each diagnosis, proving again that most people have what most people have or commonly, people have common problems. This was not the first time nor would it be the last group that a new resident thinks of leukemia before URI and cystic fibrosis rather than a cold. Unfortunately, making mistakes is part of the learning process.

Chapter 5

John Spirito flashed the next image on the console. "Look, there is the demon, a break in the femur. Bones look good otherwise." He called the ER and spoke to the Sarge

"Peter Forrest's x-ray showed a fracture of the thigh bone, no displacement, rather straight forward for this little guy. He was a good trooper through the exam, must have been that sugar you dosed him with. Are you sure there is no rum in it?"

"Thanks Dr. Spirito." I'll get the pods here to cast him.

In a few minutes, the cast was on. "Mrs. Forrest, here are some instructions about how to care for the cast and treat his pain." The Sarge handed her the papers just as Peter's father, Robert, arrived just when Peter was discharged.

"Isn't this strange? This is the second fracture for Pete."

"Dr. Sprito says the bones look good, aside from the fracture- good calcium and density." Robert did not like the news that there was another fracture. He also thought to himself that if this was some other child, child abuse would be suspected. "What is going on in my home?"

Samir also had a fracture. In contrast to Pete's case, the SCAN team arrived with all their forms and empathy to deal with Samir and his mother. Vivian Nussbaum led the group of nurses, social workers and their students. "Classic" was the first impression of all the members of the team except Vivian. She had been well trained. "Look for reasons why such a classic case is not child abuse. You know that this may go to court, what will the public defender argue? What else could this be? At one end of the list is a fracture, plain and simple, at the other end of possible causes, there could be a bone cyst, a genetic disease such as osteogenesis imperfecta, or even cancer in the bone or metastasized from a organ or bone marrow. Let's ask Dr. Donna what she thinks."

"This is what makes the job so much fun- being asked for a consult, especially by someone with a lot of students with them. Some to tease, some to stimulate and all to teach. "This is a tough one," warned Donna Barstow. "It looks like child abuse, smells like child abuse, but Vivian was either suspicious or just making a point to her flock just as her mentor had done for her, many years ago. Let's make this a teaching case, they will never forget."

"Hi, I am Dr. Barstow, the head of the emergency room. How are you today? Good. Can you tell me what happened to Samir?"

Shana, looked a little peeved after having gone through the story twice before in the past two hours. "I already went over this with the other group. Well, you see, I was home, watching the kids. I had been out getting groceries while my friend Allen, was watching the kids. When I got home, they were all asleep. So I did some wash and slowly one by one, the kids woke up from their naps. Samir was the last one to get up, like he must have been tired. But he was cranky, not like him. So the other kids watched the cartoons, and I let Samir stay in his crib. About a half an hour later, he had not settled down. I went to pick him up when he cried even more, I figured something was wrong. I figured that his leg was the problem since he would not stand on it. His cousin has the sickle cell anemia and I know he gets pain in his leg but I don't think he has sickle cell, do you? Then when Allen, my friend came home, I had him watch the other two kids and I got the 33 bus to come here. Is it a bad break?"

"We have to check the x-rays to see about the break. Thanks for that good history; I see you must have told it to others before since you gave me important information."

Turning to the students, Donna began. "OK, let's get started. Suppose you are a movie camera man. Pull back the camera and get a wide angle look. What does the baby look like? What I mean, is he well nourished, active, moving around? How is his color, not black or white but is he pale, blue, yellow. Does he relate to his mom? Donna has been doing that routine for many years to sharpen the student's observation skills. Once in awhile, she gets burnt by an over serious, sensitive student that does not want to be questioned in public, afraid that a less than A performance in the eyes of the others in the group would permanently mark her as unskilled. Many students are part of this generation who wants praise, not questions. Continuing on with a smile, Donna continues with this exercise asking them to write this imaginary article and describe in detail, how the child looks. "So?" she nods to the student to begin.

"He looks like he has a broken leg."

"No," interrupts Dr. Donna, "wide angle, fill in the blanks of the items that I just mentioned. Is he well nourished?"

"Yes"

"How is his activity?"

"He is active."

"Color?"

"Not pale, blue or yellow, I guess the color is OK."

"Does he relate to his mom?"

"He is looking at her, seems to be happy with her holding him."

"Good, now let's start to zoom in. look at his face. Does he look worried or happy, how about his breathing, his hands, does he have any scars on his skin, any cigarette burns, any bruises, any marks that might indicate that he was hit with an electric cord?

"No to everything, he appears normal," chimed in the little one in the front row. Donna marked her as an eager learner and someone that has already got caught up in fun of this detective work.

"Now," Donna continues, "zoom in some more with your camera. I will feel his head to see if there are unusual lumps from healing fractures, look at his wrists to see if they are swollen from rickets that would indicate that he either did not get vitamin D in his milk or he has not been in the sun to make his own vitamin D. No, the wrists are fine. The skin has a few marks on the shin but that is par for a recently skilled walker and runner. How old was he when he began to walk?

"Eleven months"

"Good that was early. Now let's move on the more subtle findings" Donna continues. "I want to look into his eyes with my ophthalmoscope. This is hard to do since cooperation from a little one is impossible so a fleeting glance is all we can hope for. Many times we can't see inside the eye because of the baby does not stay still."

Donna picks up the ophthalmoscope while Jeff Marian, the intern holds Samir's head. A few flicks of the dial and Donna says "Success, the retina is red, the optic nerve is sharp and the vessels are clean. No hemorrhages. Thanks. We will be back after we go to the conference room to check the x-rays." she nods to the mother and leads the group to the conference room.

"The way I look at problems is to look at a classic case" and holds up her left hand with the fingers extended. "Then I look at this patient." She holds up her right hand and extends the fingers. "Then see how similar the classic and the actual cases are" as she moves her thumbs and fingers so that the tips touch. "Is it a good match or" moving her hands apart "not such a good fit? In a classic case of child abuse, there is an injury, the history has some hard to believe stories about how the accident happened. The person who injured the child is not so attentive to the child. In severe cases, the child is almost motionless, may have a fearful look on his face. Some even have what we call 'radar gaze' – eyes moving back and forth looking to make contact with someone. This occurs when there is little stimulation at home. Remember, when I said to look at the body movements? In severely abused cases, the child will not move, for fear that any movement will provoke more injuries. There will often be bruises or linear marks from being hit with an electric cord. If there were severe shaking of the baby- the shaken baby syndrome, there might be small hemorrhages in the retina of the eye or if there were hemorrhages around the brain, the optic disc will be blurred from increased pressure in the head. So that is the left hand. Now to the patient. Not much of a fit except for the injury. Samir's mother went to a lot of trouble to get here, she gave a reasonable story, the baby's movements were normal, and he related well to his mother, he was interested in what was going on here, no radar gaze. There were no other marks on the skin, no other broken bones that I could feel, normal eye exam. Only the broken bone."

Donna looks up at the group and asks. "Now comes the hard part. Do we file a report of suspected child abuse to Child Protection Agency with such little evidence on the initial exam? How many would file a report?" One of the six raises her hand. "How many would not file a report?" 4 signals no. "Come on you all have to vote. So let's do it again. For? One. Against? Five. Well 5-1 for not filing a report of suspected child abuse."

Turning to the solo voter, "why did you vote to send in a report?"

Sarah Wright, the intern in the emergency room, turned red when signaled out. I think this is a clear case of child abuse, despite the lack of evidence so far."

"I like your method of ignoring facts and going with your gut. Once in awhile you will be right."

"How about you?" pointing to the tall resident, Keith Aaron, who was leaning on the EKG machine, obviously more interested in where he was going to eat tonight than this discussion about subtle signs of child abuse cases.

"I don't think this is child abuse, it's just a broken bone."

"And what are you going to have for dinner?" The tall one almost fell over the electric cord to the EKG machine. His jaw dropped as he had a look on his face, "how did you know what was on my mind?"

"In this democratic society, the 5-1 vote should hold but I did not vote. I have 6 votes so now it is 6-5 for filing a report. Remember that filing a report is for suspicion; we were all suspicious that this might be child abuse. Right? Look at it this way, If there were no child abuse, the SCAN team will pick this up immediately and it will go no further, but if you return the child to an abusive situation, then we have done major harm. I bet the mother is innocent but maybe someone else is the culprit. She will most likely not be very upset when we tell her, as she seems like a good mother, overwhelmed as she is. Think too, about the possibility that this is an abusive situation and the newspaper will report that he was seen in the ED but sent home."

"Do you mean we have to report this family and save our behind?" asked Beth.

"Not at all. What do we know about the current boy friend? Nothing except, he is the father of the baby, not Samir. Often, the adult male in the house will abuse children in the house that are not his. Samir is not his child, so we need to look at this man. Any one else?"

Blank faces...

"Remember there was an older sibling. Sometimes they will see a leg sticking out of the crib and give it a yank, getting back for all the attention loss. So we need more information about what is going on at home and filing a report is the mechanism that will allow us to proceed. Let's talk to the team and get their advice."

Chapter 6

Karl Strem, the chief resident sent out a reminder via the beeper system that the first house staff meeting would be held at noon in the resident lounge on the 9th floor. A graduate of Yale and Harvard Medical School, he gave up a career in baseball for medicine when it was clear that he could not hit a curve ball. If he stuck with baseball, he could have been a manager for he could detect subtle patterns in the opposition and knew all the strategies about when to take a pitch, steal a base or change pitchers. Pediatrics was a natural for him as he liked kids, did well in his pediatric rotations and most important, he liked to associate with pediatricians, probably the main reason that people pick specialties whether or not they recognize that determinant. Raised in Michigan, he was a Big Blue loyalist but favored the East for professional baseball and football teams. Red Sox and the Giants were his favorites. Looking like a cross between Brad Pitt and Robert Redford, he had a trail of swooning women waiting for any sign of attention. Unfortunately for them, he was so kind and interactive with all women, they could not tell if he was showing interest or just being a nice a good guy. He had been at CHUC for three years and had been a groupie in social settings, always with a gang of residents and nurses, not paring up with any one person. For some that was enough attention but for others it was not close to being acceptable, they wanted more interaction. He was obviously quite bright and had good people skills, a major reason he was picked to be the chief resident. This job combines administrative oversight of schedules, vacations and assignments to various inpatients and outpatient units to guarantee a good experience and training for the residents plus being in loco parentis for a lot of bright, but at times, immature residents. Karl had the fastest and funniest comebacks to any situation. Unlike other chief residents who use this year to buff up their resume as a prelude to a career in academic medicine, he had no plans other to do a good job this year and see what will happen come next June.

"What kind of bullshit is this?" Bob Gardner, first year resident. "Another meeting after a week of orientation. I wonder if they know how much it costs to have a meeting. Even at our inmate-like, below poverty level wages, it is still expensive to gather 50 some house officers in a room to tell them what they could be told via the hospital intranet. So many meetings and rounds, it is impossible to take care of the patients and read something so I can get smart. I thought that is why I came here, not for meetings."

"Take it easy," Kathy Conley advised him. "There may be something important that has come up, like a new brand of toilet paper or a new form to select our menu from the cafeteria. It is amazing how sarcastic one can become when you mix anxiety of a new job and responsibility with fatigue and inexperience. At least sarcasm is better than depression like some of the birds here."

Felix Cinemo, a second year resident who has made his life's quest to seduce at least 100 different people in the hospital before he finishes his residency, looks over the first year group to see if there are any worthwhile challenges. "Not bad" he notes as he wets his lower lip as a sign of impending action. "She is not bad." He has taken his glasses off so he cannot clearly see the reaction of the tall blonde as he stares at her. She obviously has seen his ogle as she is smoothing her skirt and then running her fingers through her hair. The lion king has marked his target and so far, he is pleased with her response. "This is going to be an interesting year," as he replaces his glasses and continues to review the other new faces in the group.

Like any collection of people that always seems to have one of each personality type, one who takes over the leadership, another who is an enthusiastic cheer leader type, and one piano player and one who likes to perform, there are the usual types of characters in this group of new doctors. Adrienne Cunningham, a bubbly chatterbox was discussing her new apartment with Beth Conover, a good listener. Keith Aaron, obviously not doing well in new situations, had a scowl on his face, stared at the clock as if it would speed up if he concentrated enough. Jeff Marian was talking with Sarah Wright about their first rotation in the emergency room. Bob Gardner was the confident one or at least that was his presentation of the group. He had been at CHUC as a medical student so he knew where the bathrooms were and how to get extra portions at the cafeteria after he took care of the child of the lady who made the sandwiches at the Deli counter. His good looks and 6 feet, 2 inches stature seemed to add some validity to his confident demeanor. Unlike the medical staff discussions about power, sex and money, the residents were too caught up in their own insecurities and worries to think of any thing except themselves. Those thoughts would come later. Right now they were learning the rhythm of the hospital- what time to arrive, what to do before they started patient rounds, how to prepare for teaching rounds, the idiosyncrasies of the medical staff, who liked brief histories who liked detailed presentations, whose bark was loudest; realizing no one would actually bite. They learned that the cafeteria was the all purpose meeting room, communication center and news central for hospital activities. Although fear was the main emotion for the new trainees, they knew the value of training at CHUC so the anticipated excitement that would come in time propelled them through these early July days

"I guess we better get started," shouts out Karl Strem, trying to get the group's attention as the room is full of loud and nervous chatter. "There are a few things on the agenda for today. First announcement from Edgar Grimely, assistant vice president for transportation. Just one of many vice presidents at CHUC. Grimely is important since he takes care of parking and elevators as well as other transportation issues. Here it is."

To: House staff of CHUC
From: E. Grimely AB, FAHTS (Fellow in Academy Hospital Transportation Services
July 8, 2006
Re: Misuse of the elevator call buttons

Problem: Excessive double punches of the elevator call buttons
It has come to my attention that many people are pushing both up and down buttons when they are using the elevator services at CHUC main building. This causes the elevator to stop unnecessarily at floors when the originating button pusher has already accessed services on the elevator, slowing down the elevator as it tries to perform its function of transporting patients and staff to their desired destination.
As you are aware, the up button indicates your need to go up and the down button indicates that you need to go down. We have observed on numerous occasions that both buttons are lit, even though one individual is near the button panel. It is obvious that that <u>one</u> person can only go in <u>one</u> direction, up or down, not <u>both</u>. It is not clear to our department how

widespread this practice is but we are forming a task force, headed by my assistant Chloe Brittan, to survey elevators in the main building as well as in the ambulatory services building. At present we do not have enough staff to do an extensive survey of some patient unit elevators as well as supply services but intend to do that in the near future, unless other issues take precedence over this important transportation research issue.

As we are collecting the data in order to make final policy changes, please cooperate with this department in the following way.

1. When approaching the elevator button panel, please pause for a moment of your precious time to decide the direction you would like to go.

2. Next make your choice, UP or DOWN

3. If you decide UP is the desired destination, then push the UP button. You will notice that some elevators will have an arrow pointing UP or be labeled with the letter U. That is the button to use when desiring to go UP.

4. Conversely, if you go want to go in the down direction, then push the DOWN button. You will notice that some elevators will have an arrow pointing DOWN or be labeled with the letter D. That is the button to use when desiring to go DOWN.

Thank you for your cooperation in this important transportation issue. I expect the task force will be formed in the next few weeks and will report back to you no later than 50 working days.

As always, getting you there is our business, our only business. Keep moving.

EG/cb

"Be nice to this man, he has real power---- he controls the parking lot assignments." Warned Karl. "I think the first week went well. Sorry about the prolonged orientation. Everyone thinks that if he or she speaks to the group that there will be no further problems. It is more like covering their asses as they can fall back on "we covered that in orientation."

"Next is moonlighting. As you know moonlighting is not permissible for first year residents, unless there is an emergency problem. But if you are interested in putting your name on the list, contact Eva Masters, assistant to Dr Saltzman in Medical Education."

"There will be a picnic this Saturday at Dr. Saltzman's house along the river. For directions, check the hospital intranet."

"Hospital records. House staff is responsible for dictation of all patients hospitalized for more than 36 hours. Dictation time is not charged to the 80 hour limit on weekly working hours. Remember, someone potentially will read the discharge summary so keep it brief as possible."

"Volunteers needed for doing school physicals at the Washington Elementary School. Sign up with Eva Masters. This is part of our community action program. I am looking at the third year residents to take this on."

"This just in…. Pharmacy reports a shortage of ethyl alcohol. Seems that a cartoon of bottles is missing from the supply area just outside the pharmacy."

"Next week we will discuss whether or not we will accept pens from the Drug companies. Until then, return all trays to the cafeteria and recharge your beeper batteries."

"Heavy stuff" quipped Felix as he found another new resident to give the stare test to. This time it was not a blonde but still a tall slim one. Seems Felix, all 5 foot 9 of him, liked the tall ones. This time the stare did not work, seems that she had taken off her glasses too and had not put in the contacts so she was unaware of Felix's gaze. He then went to plan B. He walked right up to her and asked her, "Are you the one who took the alcohol from the pharmacy and why did you not share it with the group?" Beth Conover laughed at his question and replied, "I am an only child and I never learned to share."

"Pretty good" replied Felix as he moved on to the spook test by patting her on the shoulder." He noted she did not recoil at the touch test. A positive test.

"Where are you working this month?"

"On the 5th floor, young kid's things."

"How is it going there?"

"Little scary at times, I am so new at this."

"Don't worry, they don't break and we will be around to help you, especially at night."

"That was what I was afraid of. Especially at night."

"No cause for fear, Felix is here. And what would be your name?"

"Beth Conover would be my name; I think I know your name is Felix."

"So some one warned you?"

"I heard about you when I was interviewing for a residency. You are known at many places on the East Coast as well as California, listed both as an asset and a liability depending on how you view oversexed junior residents."

"How do you view being oversexed?"

"I have never been accused of that so it is hard for me to make a judgment. Have to go."

Felix never took no for an answer so he accepted this brush off as a challenge for this year's activity. In the meantime he moved on to his assignment as resident in the consultation service. This was a good post as he had chance to move around the hospital, mostly without supervision. He headed to the endocrine unit.

• • •

After Samir was OK'd for discharge by orthopedics, the SCAN committee met to finalize the follow up. Vivian Nusbaum summarized the case so far. "Of course the mother, Shana, must be supported through this investigation. Although she is not the prime suspect, one can never be 100% sure. Maybe Allen, the boyfriend is attracting our attention because of the similarity to many other cases. So we have to support Shana because she is the one that cares for Samir. So far, she has done what seems like a very good job. I wish we could get her to the family planning docs. Maybe three kids is the magic that will get her there. The next step prior to discharge is to complete the home assessment, including a talk with Allen, the current adult male in the house. Who is up for that visit?"

"I have been doing the background checks so I will go visit Allen at the house." replied Rosemary French, the assistant social worker on the team.

The next day, Rosemary took the 33 bus to visit Shana's home, a typical row house in the northern part of town. The area formerly was the place where the owners of the mills and breweries once lived but now the area long past the good days, now is run down and neglected. Most of the people are on welfare or working for minimum wages at unskilled jobs. This did not seem to bother Rosemary as she routinely makes visits in this neighborhood. She goes past an old Ford Taurus, once dark blue but now rust and reddish blue thanks to the sun and rain. There is no front yard; the screen door has a few traces of paint while the screen is separated from the frame at the bottom, evidence of many young hands pushing through the screen door on the way to a fast exit. Not expecting the door bell to work, she knocks on the door. She hears a baby crying; soon Allen appears and asks her what she wants.

"I am here to make a home visit as part of Samir's discharge planning from the Children's Hospital. May I come in?"

"Sure."

"How are you today, I am Rosemary French from the social service department."

"Fine and you? How ya doin? I'm Allen. My, what a pretty shirt! I always liked daisies. My favorite flowers."

"Thanks for noticing it. How is Samir?"

"His brother misses him. Come sit down. Let me push aside the pillows and toys to make room for you. I would offer you tea but we used the last tea bag this morning."

Rosemary looked around the room that serves as the eating-living-family room. A picture of Jesus on one wall, the American Flag on the other wall; many hand prints were scattered along the bottom part of the walls and peeling paint at the top. One light fixture in the center of the room and a few lamps with what used to be lampshades on end tables added shadows to this scene, making even more desolate. Not quite the Ritz Hotel but livable, Rosemary writes in her note book. Also that there are no dangerous objects or bottles of liquids that could be harmful if swallowed. "Let's get started. I know you are busy. Tell me what you know about Samir's broken leg."

"Well, I saw him in the crib when I went out in the morning. I had a good lead on a job possibility and I wanted to get there early. The baby was in the crib and the older one was watching a Shrek video. I had to get across town to the new hotel that was opening up. My friend, you know, knew someone there that was doing hiring so I had my hopes up. I need a job real bad. So I went to the hotel and tried to find my friend, but didn't see him. So I waited in line with the hundreds of others who were looking for work, too. I stayed there all day and finally got an application and tried to fill it out the best I could. Then I caught a ride home with a buddy and got back just before she took poor Samir to the hospital. I don't know how in the world he could have broken his leg, being in the crib all day. His brother misses him so much. I bet you must get tired of listening to all these stories. How long have you worked at the hospital?"

"Too long. How do you think Samir broke his leg?"

"Not from playing football, that's for sure" Allen chuckled.

"Do you think he fell?"

"I don't see how he could fall from the crib. We always keep the sides up; I must admit that I haven't figured how to get them down. Something is wrong with the latches on the side. Do you have kids? I bet they are cute."

"Do you think he got his foot stuck between the rails of the crib?"

"That may have happened. That is a good idea. Yeah, I bet he got his legs caught between the crib rails. Yeah, the crib railing."

"What else could it be? "

"Donno."

"So what do you do with yourself all day?"

"I watch sports and the weather channel. You know I have a nutty friend that tapes the weather channel. What do you think of that? I check around with my guys about jobs. Sometimes I get some day work but most of the time I am checking with the guys."

"When was the last time you worked at a regular job?"

"A few years ago I had a job at Home Depot, cleaning up. But they hired some other people to do the work. Outsourcing, I think they call it. I didn't like the job because the boss was always after me. I don't think he liked me. After that I was sour about jobs so I got my welfare check. They are always after me about getting work, but I have to like the boss to be good at showing up. It is hard to find a good boss, you know whad I mean?"

"What do you think happened to Samir?"

"I dunno, like I was away all the time. My lady is here all the time; I dunno how she does it, three kids and all. She hardly has time for me. I know she gets upset with me when the kids get on her nerves. She looks calm but I know three kids can get to you. I have another boy that lives with his mother. She only has 2 and that is a lot. That is why I moved out of her place since she was always on edge. She kind of had the PMS's all month. You know whad I mean? Now this place has three kids, only one is mine, Tamir. He is the baby, my boy. I think he is the cutest but everyone says Samir is cuter, whaddo you think?"

"I am still puzzled about how a little one can break his leg. He was in the crib. Do you have any idea?"

"No, I was away all aftanoon. He was OK when I left in the morning."

Rosemary, sensing that this was not going to produce any more useful information, closed the session, "Thanks Allen. Here is my card. You can call anytime.

Outside she called the office dictation machine and began her notes of the visit as she walked to the bus stop.

• • •

Day 21, Anthony was moved to a new room in the transition unit. This was still intensive care but for patients who were stable and hopefully on the recovery phase. Katie stayed with him for these first days to provide continuity; the intensivists were still in charge but a different doctor headed the transition care team. If you had a good imagination, you would think Anthony's coma was lighter, that is, he seemed to respond to sounds with movement of his arms and legs. But another setback! He had a seizure; his right leg began to shake. This was noted by the night nurse and reported to the neurosurgery resident who immediately came to see Anthony, checked him over and reviewed his medication. Since he was already on phenobarbital, the resident added atavan. The seizure stopped before the medication was given but it returned about 3 hours later, this time involving the leg and arm.

This news upset the parents when the parents arrived in the morning. They had adjusted to the routine so they knew that if they got there at 6 am they would meet Dr. Salivari. They also learned that they could lay a Sam trap, i.e. jelly filled doughnut at the bedside, would keep Sam there for a few more precious minutes so they could chat with him. Actually, Sam was not that busy but he came from a surgical tradition where one always made rounds at 6 AM if they had one or ten patients to see. Part of the busy surgeon façade. Of course Libby, the nurse manager accompanied him on the rounds, carrying his charts.

"We are so upset by the news about the seizure" Fred began.

"These things happen, especially in patients with head trauma." Sam was always careful to talk about patients with ...... rather than saying "these things happen to head traumas." He remembered his first day in medical school when the chief of medicine, Frank Lombard, greeted the class and made that point that they are seeing people with diseases not diseases. If a student wanted to get in trouble he would present a patient on teaching rounds by starting with "this is a 49 year old diabetic." Dr. Lombard would jump in and repeat his introduction to humanism-day 1.

Sam continued, "seizures come from electrical activity in the brain, the same activity that you would have if you wanted to shake your arm or leg. This time, however, Anthony did not want to do this. The activity came from an irritation in the brain causing electrical activity. We could see it on the EEG if he had the wires connected to his head."

"But what does it mean?" Sandy asked. "Will he always have them?"

"My best thought, (Sam never guessed) is that the swelling is starting to decrease and the scars from the injury are now irritating the normal brain causing the electrical stimulus to the part of the brain that controls motion of the arms and legs. Just about here, pointing to the area near the ear and moving up to the top of the head, the motor strip. With the decrease of swelling we should start to see more progress toward recovery and possibly more seizures." Good old Sam, pump them up and then stick a few downers. No one would say he was overly optimistic.

On the 28th day, Anthony opened his eyes and appeared to look around. Only Katie saw this. When the parents came to the bedside, Katie tried to lift their spirits with this good news.

"Come on Anthony, open your eyes for your mom and dad. You can do it."

No response.

"OK, Anthony, wake up and see what I have for you."

No response

"Sorry for this false alarm. But I really did see this. He will do it. I promise."

"Anthony never liked to perform for small audiences. I know he will do it Katie. But look. I think he can hear as he tries to move his head towards us when we speak."

Fred and Sandy welcomed the news as the stress from Anthony's lack of progress made them irritable and impatient. One day Fred was discouraged while Sandy tried to support him. Sandy then lost her optimism but fortunately, Fred now was back on the positive side and helped her. This was fine except some days they both lost hope and started to snap at each other. Katie knew this pattern so she tried to intervene. "Why don't you both take a break get some fresh air, maybe go across the street to the book store and do some browsing. Maybe even go out for dinner?"

Sometimes that advice worked but she could tell they were not ready for the dinner diversion. Her optimistic slant helped them in the dark times to be refreshed and regain their strength. Fred was back on the monitors and Sandy resumed her reading.

Fred looked up from the EKG patterns on the screen and told Katie, "this place is getting noisy. The beep, beep, beep are getting to me... Too many lights on in the room. And the noise from the elevator doors closing and the chatter of the nursing staff at the nurses' station near Anthony's room are worse than before, aren't they?"

Katie smiled. "You are now veterans of the unit. When you start complaining about noise that has always been here and lights that were always on, you are adjusting to this place. The noise is the same, it has now become amplified. It was obvious, that it is time to go home and get some rest and quiet. Every body was ready except Anthony. But he will surprise us very soon, I am sure. Sorry to tell you, I am moving back to the ICU as another major trauma patient was being admitted."

Day 40

As predicted there was some progress. It was as if Anthony's brain was a rack of circuit boards, all but a few unplugged from the main computer. But in an almost random way, one circuit would reconnect. The seizures were less frequent now; he opened his eyes and began to look around. He had begun to swallow better but still could not be fed. He pulled out his feeding tube several times but it was quickly replaced as it was his only source of nutrition. No bed sores, thanks to the program Katie started with careful positioning and physical therapy. Progress was slow and mostly steady.

Sam told them "We are applying Kaye's rules- referring to his old mentor, Nigel Kaye who said. If they are moving in the right direction, don't change anything, if they are not moving ahead, better do something else. Good advice when dealing with patients with chronic problems since changes is not sudden and improvement is measured in weeks and months rather than hours or days."

But even optimistic Sam was getting worried but tried not to show his feelings as he had to support the family as well as oversee Anthony's care. He did not know what was going to happen, but acted as if things would get better. Part of being a compassionate doctor was being an actor. He tried to give a perspective to Fred and Sandy by mentioning that "many of children with similar injuries walked out of the hospital. Most continued to have seizures but some went to college, others could not do that level of mental work." A few months ago

Sandy was thinking of Princeton or Haverford for Anthony, now she was ready to accept walking out of the hospital as a big success.

Sam tried not to show his fears, but in the quiet of his office he prayed, not in a recitation of a religious script he learned in catechism class, but his own words spoken to himself. Surgical spirituality was how Sam classified this quiet reflection. He had left the official church when he got to college but retained some of the practices. Respecting those who practiced formal religions, he always suggested that, if they like, they could have their priest, minister, rabbi or iman come to the hospital, in addition to the hospital chaplain. But today, he was now losing hope for some meaningful recovery. Things were not moving fast, in fact they were not moving at all, Most of the patients with severe head injury had made more progress after 6 weeks. At least Anthony was not regressing, but Sam wanted to see slightly more improvement. Since he thrived on success, it was hard to accept that someone under his care was not going to get better. Sam was good at propping up others when they were down and discouraged, but no one was around to give him a boost. Because he did not discuss patients at home, he could not look for support from his wife who was so caught up in her own world and activities that she could not see that Sam's demeanor had changed. Being down is one of the hazards that one takes on when working with very sick children, but dealing with Anthony got to him in a different way. Maybe it was that he had a son about Anthony's age or just that he was breaking one of the rules of success, not getting too close to the patient or maybe it was just that he was tired and his defenses were being challenged, probably a combination of all these. Sam really needed someone to talk to about his feelings.

Libby seemed more tuned into the change in Sam's mood. Despite her icy demeanor with families, she did have feelings that she could not always hide. Although she rarely spoke on rounds other than saying "next patient, here is the chart on ...." this time she whispered in Sam's direction, "think pink." Sam turned his head to her, initially giving the look that "I am the surgeon and I do all the thinking here," but quickly he picked up on the hint. He nodded "good idea" to Libby. Sam turned to Fred and Sandy and began the probe of their spirituality. He did not try the usual ploy that his friends would use when meeting a new person and not sure of their religion. These people led with the line "did I see you in church last Sunday?" He did ask if their minister had come in to visit. Fred laughed a little and replied that he is afraid that the minister would not recognize him as he has not been a regular attendee on Sundays; in fact, he has not been there since his marriage but returned the question with "why do you ask?"

"Nothing, just trying to be a holistic surgeon, if that is not a contradiction for the find it, fix it creed of our specialty. Some people get comfort in visiting the Pink Sisters and asking them to pray for them. Their real name is the Holy Spirit Adoration Sisters, a cloistered-contemplated missionary order who live in a convent of perpetual prayer, never speaking to outsiders. But they will accept requests on paper passed through the gate at the convent. They stay at Sheppard Street near the art museum."

"What is the address?" Sandy jumped in. "I do a little better at church than Fred but whatever might help, I am all for it. Pink Sisters, I don't care what color they wear, if they might help, let's give them a try!"

"Come on," Fred said. "You know you don't like pink. This is the silliest thing that we have heard about since the accident. But if you want to go, I will take you. So let's put something on paper to give the Pink Sisters and get over to Sheppard Street. Might as well cover all the bases, that's why I light candles when we visit the old churches in Europe."

The area near the convent has seen better days, beautiful old houses, now mostly apartment buildings for students and artists, surrounded by row houses in various states of disrepair. One of the old mansions, probably owned by some wealthy merchant in the 1880's and given to the Pink Sisters when the heirs of the original owners would not live in the neighborhood, stood behind a 10 foot stone wall with a small gate. The door was bas relief iron made by Samuel Yellin, a famous Philadelphia decorative iron worker. There was a slot for passing the prayer requests. Sandy, oblivious to the surroundings, jumped out of the car and stuffed the paper outlining Anthony's condition and requesting the sisters to pray for him. Since the order was one of perpetual prayer, this was not a burden for the sisters. Fred, keeping some distance from this activity, sat in the car while Sandy lingered for a few minutes, offering her own prayer. She returned to the car with some of the worry and stress removed from her face. So far this trip was good for Sandy. Fred did not share the same peaceful look but knew enough to keep quiet and not disrupt the serenity.

Day 45

The 6 AM rounds were the same. Sam Salivari arrived, 10 minutes earlier than usual, with the perpetual smile on his face and the same starched and pressed white coat. The grin, hopefully showing some forced optimism, sometimes helped encourage some of the parents. Libby, the nurse manager, was with him as usual to carry the charts and report on any changes in the patients' condition. Sam kept up the cheerleader's role to boost the parents' morale and to let the patient know that someone was optimistic about the recovery. "I got a good feeling about Anthony, today. I feel it in my bones." It may seem strange that he would do this for the patient but he has learned from many patients who recovered from head injury that although they were in a coma, they could hear what was being said around the bedside, even though they could not see or speak.

Libby, Larry Mitchell, the medical student, and Ray Bartlett made up the rest of the rounding team. Libby still had a flushed look on her cheeks but no longer were her nipples erect. The gossips at the nurses' station noticed this, of course, causing them to wonder what happened to Libby Nichols. Seeing the smoothness of Libby's blouse today, Margaret asked "What happened to the Nurse Nipples? Is she getting tired of 6AM rounds?" Since Anthony's condition had not changed, social interactions of the staff were the only news.

"And how are we today? Asked Sam, as he did his morning pinch of Anthony chest skin. As usual, Anthony responded with a groan and withdrawal of his arms and legs.

"No" said Anthony.

"My, my. What have we here? Sam's eyes bulged and he looked shocked to hear words from Anthony. "Let's try this again" another pinch and another groaning "No."

"This is getting interesting." Sam took out his reflex hammer, the one he got at Queen's Square in London, the Mecca of neurology training for the British and for many visitors from the U.S. Instead of the usual metal and triangular rubber reflex hammer, the English use what looks like a drummer's stick stuck into a skinny flat doughnut rubber disk. He tested the reflexes at the elbows and knees. "Still 4 plus" noted Sam. Ray looked into Anthony's eyes with his ophthalmoscope to see if there were any changes in the back of the eye, the only area where one can see the optic nerve, an extension of the brain. "Disc is flat, no change. No hemorrhages." These findings were expected and indicated there were no changes in the neurological examination except for the wonderful "No."

"The first step in a long march upward. This is great!" Sam seemed a little upbeat but cautious as these things may happen with no further progress.

Katie had heard about Anthony from the night nurse report so she quietly joined the team to see Sam's reaction to her boy. She wanted to over interpret this encouraging finding but knew that so many things were not working that she was afraid to be too optimistic. Yet she could not hold back "a No is a No and there were no No's yesterday so maybe this was something. I can't wait until the parents arrived."

She combed Anthony's hair and looked for a new pajama top for him so he would look his best for his parents.

"I'll be back later," Katie said to no one in particular but Ray looked up as if she were talking to him.

"Why don't you take her out?" asked Larry, a bold question for a medical student, but he could not miss the electricity that seemed to be in the air when the team came to Anthony's bed. "If you don't, I will ask her for myself, I am no John Alden, Miles." Larry had been watching the two people smile and whisper to each other. But it was the body language that made him suspect that something more was going on. Larry, unattached at the present time, had a lot of experience with hospital dating, unlike his mentor, Ray.

Ray returned to the NS ICU about 10AM which was also time for Katie's coffee break. The timing, noted by the gossips on the floor was perfect.

"Back again, how is your new patient doing? Not as dear as Anthony, I see. Speaking of Anthony, has he done any more Anthony tricks?"

"No, nothing."

Ray picked up the chart of the patient that Katie was now caring for and took on the professional manner. Let's go over her medications, is she still on seizure meds"

"Yes she is, No changes."

"That is good. No seizures in how many days?

Three weeks.

"Skin is clear, vitals are good. Seems to be ok

"Right."

So let's take a coffee break"

"I thought you would never ask" blurted Katie before she realized what she had said. Along with this retort, her face turned red.

"I was saving up my pennies so I could treat you to a latte at the coffee bar. No home brew from the staff room for me. I go first class."

As the blushing faded and she regained her composure she was glad that a monitor was not connected to her for it would have shown that her heart was racing and occasionally skipping a beat.

She seemed to float down to the coffee shop. "This is my day and some good things were going to happen, I am sure."

Ray made small talk about the neurosurgery service and the different personalities of the staff doctors, especially Sam, who was the character of the team.

Katie ordered a latte with skim milk and Ray asked for a black coffee medium sized. He could not accept the skinny or grande Starbucks lingo. They had a lively conversation, Katie did most of the talking and Ray seemed happy to listen. When the break was over, Ray took over.

"How about going to dinner on Friday, I have the night off." Katie was tempted to delay and check her social calendar but she grabbed the opportunity to accept and not play games with this long awaited invitation.

"That would be fine."

"I look forward to seeing you for dinner. That should be fun."

The next day things changed dramatically. Anthony seemed to say "water."

"What did you say?" Diane, Anthony's new nurse asked, happy to hear him say a word but bothered by the lack of witnesses. She hoped he would say some more words. That did not happen.

Ray came by, after going through the physical, he noted that Anthony was beginning to use his arms and seemed to move his feet when he tried to raise his arms.

"Pulling away from my touching the bottom of his feet does not count because that is a reflex, just as he grabs my finger when I squeeze his palms. But things are happening. Some of the swelling is leaving the motor strip of his brain," pointing to the area over his ear as he always did when he mentioned the motor strip.

When Fred and Sandy appeared, Diane did not tell them about the word or the movements but asked Anthony if he wanted some water.

"Water" said Anthony more clearly than before.

"The Pink Sisters strike again," shouted Fred, now a believer in the power of prayer, at least as if the Pink Sisters were involved." What other words can he say? Does he know his name? Does he recognize me and his mom? This is great. Maybe we are ready to toss around a football."

The speaking did not return after that for a few days causing some of the optimism to fade again. This time it was Fred who seemed to be the support while Sandy seemed to be losing hope. She went back to reading about speech after head injury from the internet on any topic that remotely applied to speech mechanisms. She seemed to be more interested in the bad news today as Anthony lay quietly in his bed.

A few days later

Now Larry the medical student was feeling cocky about his romance advice to his resident. "Here's how you do it. You bring flowers, you knock on the door, and you extend the flowers. As she reaches for the bouquet, you bend a little, pick her up and take her right to the bedroom. Lay her gently on the bed and give her a big kiss on her lips- no cheek to cheek stuff. Then you get a feeling of how the date will go. This is what I call the 'take 'em by surprise test.' How did this bold move affect her? I mean did she get defensive and push you away, or did she welcome cutting through all the date dancing of chatting, searching for clues of future success. You will know immediately what her thoughts are about you. This is not rape; it is just a mega-spook test. Believe me it always works, in my experience."

It was that last statement that seemed to wet down the advice. For Ray, in all his aura of man about town, good looks, pleasant smile and easy chatter with the nurses identified him as a real lady's man but medicine was his love life, giving him little time to function outside the emergency room, OR, or ICU. The 80 hour limit on house staff working hours did not seem to apply to Ray and his fellow neurosurgery residents. Ray did not consider it work but his life and it was fun, even though exhausting. 'In my experience' dampened the validity of the medical student's battle plan. Ray thought, just how much experience does a medical student have? 4 years of college grinding away to get high grades and extra credit plus medical school when pressure continued to get high grades to get a prized residency. That allows for some social life but nothing compared to those who went into investment banking or consulting. Medical training is more like delayed adolescence with prolonged dependency.

Ray responded to Larry, "good advice, I will consider the battle plan.

"Just think ---what would Patton do?"

Anthony remained the same for rest of the day; Fred and Sandy did not leave the bedside. About 3 PM, Katie visited them often and tried to cheer them up pointing out the little positives and put the few bursts of activity that were improvements from the first week. "If he did it once he could do it again. So keep talking to Anthony and help with his PT exercises. I hope he continues because if Anthony reaches a plateau in his recovery, the utilization review people will start to push for a transfer to the rehab unit, less expensive care and opening up the bed for new patients with acute injuries or serious operations."

This worried Fred. "I do not like to hear that he may be moved; I am accustomed to being in the security blanket of the intensive care monitors. Instant read out of vital signs, pressure and EKG. It would be hard to leave this unit, I even blocked out the constant beeping of the monitors and the noisy hall way. One thing I will not miss- the hospital food. The sight of the dried fish or the watery vegetables has ruined my appetite. I have lost 5 pounds since Anthony's fall." Sandy remained quiet as she has gained that much and a few pounds more as she used food to calm her down when her intellectual approach to the problem failed.

"See you later, gang. My break is over so I have to get back to my unit and check on my patient."

Laura, her pal in the ICU checked in with Katie to find out how she was dealing with Anthony's stalled recovery. "It must be hard to come here each day and see how little progress Anthony is making." That is advanced communication skills 200, a course she took in her Masters program. Instead of saying "I know how hard it is," which is not really true; since one never knows exactly what the other person is thinking or feeling.

"Not so bad" is the usual response. But it is the facial expression and look of the eyes that say more. Katie seemed to appreciate the few words, 'it must be hard.' "I know you understand how much energy I expend trying to be cheerful when many nights I have cried myself to sleep worrying about a patient."

Laura picked up on this glimpse of emotion and asked Katie about her boyfriend, Cal. "Oh, Cal is old news; we haven't seen each other for several months."

"Time has sped by so quickly. We have not had a chance for a personal talk in a few months. I moved in with my boy friend in June that is working out well, so far." Too bad about you and Cal, he was a nice guy, I remember him at the Memorial Day picnic."

"As my father said. They are like trolley cars, they come and they go. There will always be a next one." That was the days when they had trolley cars, probably before his time but he liked the expression.

"So is there a new trolley car?"

"As a matter of fact, yes. I have a date tomorrow."

"Someone I know?"

"As a matter of fact, yes. Ray Bartlett."

"No! Ray, the Neurosurg resident? Now that is a real first class trolley! What are you wearing?" Laura was instantly interested, almost as if she, rather than Katie, were going on a date with Ray. "Something sexy, I hope" Katie was surprised by this question as she had one uniform, Laura Ashley. Baggy top, long skirt look in small flowers or faded plaids.

"What do you think I should wear?"

"Not too low cut but show your boobs a little. I think a mini skirt would scare him so make the skirt longer than a mini or maybe pleated pants. Four inch heels and you are a sight he can't resist.

"Sounds like you are dressing me up for a whore house parade. I am not sure I can be that revealing."

"Of course you can."

"And get your hair cut, I know a great place; go to Sally at the Royal Crown on 22nd street. She is the best. Do it!"

• • •

"How is my honey today," Adrienne gave a hug to Edith, the chief clerk on the 4th floor newborn nursery. Edith ruled the floor, checking on all visitors, making sure the medical students do not leave the crib sides down after they examined the children, arranging transportation for patients going to x-ray, keeping the supplies at appropriate levels and most important, looking after the young ladies of the nursing staff.

"Fine Sugar, what brings you back to our den of ill repute? You are my girls and I'm your momma away from home. Have you found the man of your dreams yet?"

"Not yet but I am still looking. Any prospects?"

"Get in line; I have a long list of honeys that are waiting for the bees to buzz."

"Thanks for thinking of me but I am looking for Dr. Farmer, I am supposed to be with him this afternoon."

"He is seeing the new baby that was just born and transferred to the nursery for well baby care. Room 4572, around the corner."

Adrienne left Edith and turned the corner. Before she walked through the door of 72, she peeked in the window and saw Dr. Farmer with a couple hovering over their newborn. The Alexanders appeared to be in their late 30's, looking both tense and happy as they marveled in the miracle that they produced. Such a different sight than most other situations in the hospital where the child was usually quite ill, connected to a number of IV lines and multiple monitors beeping and blinking their measurements. This was more like a Mary Cassatt painting with soft lighting, pink baby and glowing parents.

"Hi, I am Dr. Farmer, just saying hello and welcoming your baby to Children's Hospital. Congratulations. I see this is your first so you must be doubly excited."

"More than double, this has been a long trip to get here," sighed Rose Ann.

"Long trip?"

"Yes, this is our first after a long time of trying. We had a few miscarriages but this time you are seeing the result of a pregnancy from a frozen embryo. Thanks to Dr. Guido, the miracle maker fertility doctor. We had a few unsuccessful runs but this time we were fortunate and happy to get to term and be here, especially in the well child nursery."

"Wow, you have been through a lot. I can see why you are so happy, what is the little fella's name?"

"George, for Dr. Guido, and Harrison for my father. We are going to call him Rusty as it looks like we have a red head."

"Is there anything else I should know about you or the pregnancy?"

"We are both working for Lockheed in the information technology section, working with cable companies' data exchange systems. Our families are in good health, one grandparent has hypertension, and the others are well all in their late 50's and early 60's. No other illness in the family."

"You sure know how to give a concise history. I guess you had a lot of practice. Well let's take a look. He is pink and kicking. That is a good sign. Let me flash my light on him and listen to his heart and lungs. I do that first so he may be quiet then. If I push on his belly, it may start a long aria that will interfere with my listening."

Adrienne watched Dr. Farmer as he listened to the chest. "Lungs sound normal." As he moves to the heart exam, Dr. Farmer paused a little. He listened again to the back of the chest.

Oh my, thought Adrienne, "he must have heard a murmur. I hope it is an innocent murmur that will go away and not a sign of a serious heart problem."

As he listened to the heart again, Dr. Farmer was also thinking – "it is too loud and too harsh. It sounds like a VSD. But this is something more complex. Why me? I only agreed to check the baby as a favor to one of Dr. Simpson. Why do I have to ruin this family's day? I only agreed to come to do the check up because it was a supposedly a well baby. OK, I will finish the examination and come up with some plan."

"How is your tummy, Rusty?" Let me poke around and see if all is well. Yes it feels good. "And the hips, they are fine. 5 fingers and toes on each extremity."

The parents were too busy watching Dr. Farmer that they did not process the omission of any comment on the heart exam.

"This is a keeper, besides we don't take returns at CHUC." The parents smiled at this attempt of humor. "Here is the plan. You work on getting some rest and the breast feeding and I will be back in the morning to give him another check up. If you have any questions, the nurses or I will be here to answer them. I am on call tonight so don't be shy. We are here. Any questions?"

Silence.

"I guess that means I did a good job or you are too excited to ask any questions. OK, I will be around today and will see you in the morning. Call me if you think of something" He walked out of the room, motioned to Adrienne to move away from the door.

"What's up?"

"This kid has a strange murmur; I don't like the sound of it."

"So call Cards and get an echo. I was listening and noticed you did not say anything about the murmur."

"Good ears. I am worried about the murmur but I made a decision to let them have one more day of enjoying their offspring. He is in the hospital and not going any where so if there is a problem, we are here to take care of it. It is not like he is home and has to come back to the hospital. I am going to delay the bad news. They have been through so much. Maybe this was a false alarm and the murmur will disappear in the next day. I think one more day will not cause Rusty any harm. So let them enjoy him."

Adrienne, because of her low confidence, was in a mild sweat, not sure about this decision. "I know that about half of the babies will have an innocent murmur sometime in their early life as the heart adjusts to changes in circulation present in the fetus to the extra uterine life, especially in the changes in lung pressures. The way you listened to the back and paused, I have a feeling that the murmur was serious. But what if there is a problem and the cardiologists ask why they were not called before. How would you answer this?"

"The doctor in the delivery room did not hear the murmur; neither did the nurse who saw him when he came to this unit. This is why they like to keep babies for two days since things change from day one to day two, especially heart examination. He is pink and breathing well. So I made a choice. Treat the whole family; give them a breather from all the worry for at least a day. Some people call this patient centered medicine. If something goes wrong we will be around. Let's go see some more patients and then you keep an eye on Rusty for any changes."

Adrienne was concerned that this was right. Later when she sat in the resident's office and mulled this over again, "why not call cardiology right away and get the diagnosis today? I know that he is going to die and they will blame me. I know I should report this to the chief resident, so I won't get blamed. I knew I was going to make a horrible mistake but I did not think it would occur so soon and it is not even my fault. I am scared but I will follow Dr. Farmer's recommendation. I hope Rusty makes it through the night."

The next day, Dr. Farmer came to see the Alexanders still hovering over their baby but still glowing with happiness. "How was your day? From the look of the room with the McDonald wrappings, cups and pizza box, it seemed that you did not leave the room for a second."

"We had the best day. It is hard to believe that Rusty is here and looking so good. He did cry a lot last night, is that OK?

"Just exercising his lungs. I call it music. How was the breast feeding?"

"I think I need a little practice."

"Of course you do. It is like playing tennis, no one is skilled after one or two tries at hitting the ball. Takes a lot of practice but you will get better each day. Now let me check him."

Unfortunately, it was not better. The murmur was there and more distinct. The baby was pink and active, eating and breathing normally Time to act: call the cards, order the studies and get this baby treated. Dr. Farmer was now holding Rusty in his arms as he sat on the edge of the bed.

"We have a problem." he announced to the family. "When I listened to the heart, I heard a sound that I did not like, a heart murmur. There are good murmurs and serious murmurs. I feel this one is serious and needs evaluation. I think the best thing to do is to run some studies including an EKG and chest x-ray, an echocardiogram and contact the cardiologists to listen to Rusty and evaluate the studies. Since it is early in the morning, I can pull some strings to get the tests run immediately; I will call Dr. Stella of cardiology to come to see Rusty. I do not know what his schedule is today, but if he has something already scheduled, he will send someone from his team to come but he will get here as soon as he can. I expect that we will have some early answers in an hour; should be more definitive in 2-3 hours. I like to get all the information together before discussing the next move. That will obviously range from watching him over the next few months to scheduling OR time today. So with that wide spectrum of possibilities, it is best to get the full picture before we talk about the path we are taking and decrease your anxiety of not knowing what is going on. Let me pause and answer your questions. I know this is a lot to put on you so early in Rusty's life."

"I knew something was wrong. I just knew it." cried Roseanne. "Is he going to die? I just can't think of losing him."

Seeing the tears running down her cheeks, Farmer paused. "Here's a tissue. We all worry about our children. You have reason to be concerned, but first let's find out what is wrong. I will push the heart team to get an answer as soon as possible and then we can outline the treatment. This will be helpful in focusing on a problem rather than where we are now, just floating in fear."

As she was dabbing her eyes, she got back on track, "Thank you Dr. Farmer, I am sure you are helping, we had such a good day yesterday that this is such a shock. We spent the day looking at him, holding him and trying to feed him. What a great day! I am superstitious so I knew something was going to happen because we are not used to being so happy. I was waiting for bad news, I am such a worrier. I worry about the weather, if it is going to rain or if it is sunny. If it is sunny, I worry about melanomas."

"Worry is natural but let's keep our focus. We are all here to help Rusty. If worry will help him, then keep worrying, but I think Rusty needs us to be strong. But lets not allow our anxieties paralyze us so Rusty will suffer. Again discuss your worries but keep our goal in focus. Being upset can paralyze your breast milk production. So we need to let the worries out. Can you tell me more about your worries?"

"That makes sense, thank you for your advice. OK, my worry is, will he need a transplant?"

"Whoa! That is getting ahead of the specialists. Let them come and see Rusty and review his studies. I found that many parents have a great sense of guilt when they are faced with the news about a child with a medical problem. What sorts of guilt do you harbor down deep?"

"Guilt? What do you mean?"

"Oh something you ate or took during pregnancy, a fall, a fight, something counter to what your doctor advised. Many people tell of all sorts of thoughts or fears that occurred during pregnancy."

"Do you mean like skipping my prenatals vitamins on occasion."

"Something like that. How many times did you skip your vitamins?

"2 or 3, I guess. But I took a double dose. Was that wrong?"

"Not one bit. I don't want to talk you into guilt. I just wanted to open the discussion. You think about what I said and let me know if you want to discuss the topic again."

"My father has heart problems and I guess I did worry a lot about my baby having a heart problem."

"What kind of problem?"

"Angina for the past three years. He takes pills and seems to be under good control. They are not ready to do any work on his arteries yet. But they are watching him. Do you think worrying about my father could have caused this?"

"Not really, but I am glad that you mentioned this. Oh here comes the EKG technician. The radiology tech will be here in a second to take a chest x-ray. Things are rolling."

The lady taking the EKG placed the wire leads on Rusty. In a matter of seconds, the machine uttered a mild sigh and produced a pink page with a lot of lines running across the page. The report on the top of the sheet said bilateral ventricular hypertrophy with Right axis deviation (+120° to +150°) and left ventricular hypertrophy.

"This is a computerized evaluation, not quite as good as an experienced cardiologist who can put together the sound of the heart and the condition of the baby with the EKG readings. The EKG is a record of electrical impulses generated by the nerves and muscles in the heart. Right now I can say this is not a normal tracing for a newborn. It will take a little longer to get the official reports, but they are not as important as the echocardiogram, the ultrasound study of the heart's anatomy."

Dr. Farmer returned in about 15 minutes. "I see that the chest x-ray shows a normal heart size and clear lungs. So far we have a baby with a loud murmur on the left central part of the chest, a normal looking chest x-ray and an EKG that shows more work on the left sided pumping chamber than usual. Hopefully the cardiologists will show up shortly. So now go back to hugging Rusty and read him a book or sing a song."

In about an hour the cardiologists came to see Rusty. Isa Stella, the cardiologist on consultations that day, was a tall, gray haired man about 60, with slightly pink cheeks and rimless glasses. Right out of central casting for a wise and experienced doctor. His demeanor suggested a great deal of kindness as well as competence. It is hard to tell how competence looks but once he approaches the bedside, you immediately get that impression. After greeting the parents, recognizing their fear and worry, he gently listened to Rusty. "I am old school; I listen to the heart before looking at the studies. The new doctors go right to technology then listened to the heart more as a token to the old days since they could see the lesion on the echo. In addition, Dr. Stella had an old fashioned stethoscope instead of the titanium headed, space age inputs that the techies would have. The 300 dollar price for the fancy scopes added to the allure of the specialist but Isa Stella did not need that extra equipment, he had experienced ears. The Alexanders were searching for a clue from his facial expression. There was none. He raised Rusty to a sitting position and listened to the heart again. He listened to the back of the chest, felt for pulses in the groin.

"There is a loud murmur in the chest in this area pointing to the left side of the small chest. This is not normal so we have a problem that I am sure we can fix but I need to look at the other studies. Come on." He pointed to Adrienne and took her into the conference room to view the chest x-ray. "What do you see?"

"Looks OK to me." Adrienne responded, actually believing that the chest was normal, but could not see how this could be with the murmur being so loud.

"Talk to me like a doctor, how do you look at chest x-rays?"

"OK the drill - big heart no, little heart no, normal heart size, yes. Dirty lungs, no clear lungs yes, referring to the fullness of the blood vessels in the lungs."

"Actually the lungs are a tad fuller than they should be. The EKG?

"There is more left sided activity than normal for a newborn. That means the left heart is working against an obstruction or a fistula.

"You are on a roll. Would you like to try the echo?"

"After you, señor," smiled Adrienne, trying to get off the hook. "I am here to learn at the foot of the master. It was easier to read the EKG since the printout came with an interpretation but they have not yet written the program to electronically read the Echo."

"Well the master could not make it today but asked me to come instead so we have to go back to the heart station echo lab. So let's talk about the possibilities.

"What are the best bets?"

"VSD works for me"

"That is a common problem. Not cyanotic, systolic murmur fits but the murmur is not very loud which would mean a large defect between the ventricles. EKG kind of fits so maybe you are right. The chest x-ray shows full vessels so there is extra blood going into the lungs."

When they got to the echo lab, they signed on the computer and called up the study from the list of patients on the monitor. Fortunately, a cardiologist was in the room and she showed the lesions.

"This is a VSD. Look at the blood flow- out the aorta and through a humongous hole in the wall that separates the left ventricle from the right sending blood into the lungs. But look at the mitral valve. There is some regurgitation back into the atrium too."

"I thought this was more complicated."

"Right you are, Bob. I'll get Kirby Jackson on the phone to tell him what we found He will need an operation but the timing will depend on how he can handle this extra work of pumping blood into two places, the normal pathway to the aorta and through the abnormal hole in the heart wall."

Dr. Stella went back to the floor to tell the Alexanders what they found and what they planned to do to fix the lesion. That is the excitement for the cardiologist, sorting out the clues and interpreting the data then turning the case over to the surgeons to reroute the plumbing to as normal a circulation as they could.

The Alexanders were almost relieved, "At least, that the unknown is now known. We knew that they we're in an excellent hospital with a top staff. We picked the medical center for the delivery and the remote possibility that specialized pediatric care was right there, in the remote possibility that it would be needed. Well, the remote was not so remote now for here we have our son with a serious defect. At least we are not in nowheresville and had to be flown into CHUC."

"Wow, you sure have thought a lot about this. Right now we will take Rusty to the Cardiac Intensive Care Unit to watch him."

"Doctor, we have a question."

"Yes, I am here to answer you. Anything."

"Does this happen often in babies born from frozen embryos?"

"We used to think that the rate of heart problems is the same in babies who come from frozen embryos as they are in the general population but recently, some studies show that there is an increase in certain types of heart problems in kids like Rusty."

Over the next three days, Rusty was showing signs of heart failure. His heart rate increased, the liver was enlarging and he was having trouble taking his formula despite being treated for heart failure. It was time to make an important treatment decision.

It is hard to imagine the skill required for congenital heart surgery. The heart is the size of a lemon, small to medium sized. To operate on a heart the size of a lemon, the instruments have to be tiny. First the heart opened up so that the defect can be seen and the hole in the heart wall closed, using very small sutures. This is all done without damaging the heart muscles or cutting important nerves that control the heart beat. Speed is critical since the longer the baby stays under anesthesia and connected to heart lung machines, the more complications such as bleeding or infection arise and the greater chance for dying during or after the procedure. It takes a special type of personality to do pediatric cardiac surgery.

Kirby Jackson, the heart surgeon, was the perfect man to do such a procedure. He was made of steel, loved, even salivated at the thought of spending hours in the OR opening up chests to expose a beating heart and then fixing the problem. The more complicated the case, the better. His steel blue eyes sparkled with the challenge. His stern voice commanded the respect of the team. His demanding perfection among his assistants assured him that they would do what he wanted and nothing more. He was not a screamer but his voice had a steely edge that communicated "no bullshitters allowed. I am the star so don't upstage me. Does what I say and watch me for you will rarely see someone sew neat stitches, make decisions on the fly when unexpected problems arise and get the results I do."

One of his favorite expressions to the resident who shot off a wrong answer was "did you make that up or did someone else misinform you?" For the students, he was kinder when he listened to a wrong answer. "I love that answer; it makes me feel like I learned something since I got out of medical school." To students who were not interested in surgery, this ego trip convinced them that they made a good choice about a non-surgical career while the future surgeons stood in awe but cowered at the thought of a wrong answer, fearing that their career would be over before it started. They did not realize that he did not know their name, did not care about their name and had no interest in what they were fantasizing about their career. He was there to fix hearts and set some incredibly high standards for the next generations of doctors. The nurses just ignored his sarcasm and quiet outbursts. They loved the teamwork, the anticipation of what instrument that he would need in the next stage of the operation. They picked OR nursing, knowing that there would be tension in the room and high levels of adrenaline that would cause words to be spoken that would vaporize as soon as they were said. No hurt feelings, no internalization of emotions. They put up with Dr. Jackson because they knew that the children were getting the best care and they were part of the team. The rest of the team, the anesthesiologists, the heart lung machine team and nurses manning the control room elected to be on the heart surgery team so they could not complain too much. To the outsider, some of the dialogue between the surgeon and the staff seemed to be a small war not appreciating the underlying pressure, life/death events and instant problem solving that resulted in many tense moments during the operation. When things were less tense, Kirby would talk about hunting in South Carolina or racing cars. Shooting ducks or racing his Porsche were ways he relaxed from the tension of the OR. His wife was busy organizing fund raising projects for the hospital and serving on various local boards. She attended bible class on Tuesdays and choir practice on Thursdays and shopped most every day she could; things to keep her occupied while Kirby was busy at the hospital.

Kirby came to see Rusty about 4 in the afternoon, after a long day in surgery. He always traveled with his team of residents and students and at times visitors from other countries. His nurse, Mary Ann served as the team manager, making sure he got to see all his patients as he raced through rounds. After he examined Rusty, he told the parents. "I hear the same murmur that Dr. Stella and the others heard. Fortunately, there is a cardiac surgery/cardiology conference scheduled for 5 today so we will go over his records and lab tests and talk about options for Rusty's care. I am certain with the increasing heart failure despite the excellent treatments to strengthen his heart muscle with medications, we will have him in the OR soon. Mary Ann will get back to see you after our conference."

"Thanks, Dr. Jackson. Your plan sounds good to us. We would like to take him home fixed up."

At the cardiology/ cardiac surgery conference, the interesting dialogue allows all participants to opine about the appropriate diagnosis or treatment. Although both the cardiologist and the cardiac surgeon want the same outcome, they try to emphasize their specialty when there are several ways to treat a heart defect. In babies, sometimes a balloon can open up a blockage in the heart chambers or create a connection between the chambers to establish blood flow, saving an operation; most of the time surgery is needed. But for Rusty, there was no real debate about which approach was correct; Rusty needed an operation but not this minute.

Stella started off the discussion. "That VSD is huge. Until today, he was handling it as his lungs are relatively clear; his liver is not down so he is not in failure. But now he is losing his ability to handle both the VSD and mitral regurg- a double stress on his heart. And his drop in formula intake shows his heart is failing."

"As always, I agree with your wisdom, Isa. He is on thin ice so we should plan to fix him before all hell breaks out. I can patch up the hole and tighten up the mitral ring and he will be ready for the Olympics."

"Which event?"

"Spitting up and pooping out."

The time has come for the cardiac OR.

• • •

The show was about to begin. Initially the activity followed the script, somewhat like a traditional religious service. Before the surgeon, the high priest, entered the temple, the underlings, residents and junior staff people would scurry around the altar preparing the patient, putting in tubes, scrubbing skin and checking the equipment while the heart lung team set up the equipment that would provide oxygen to blood and circulate it thourgh the body when the heart stopped beating during the surgery. Often the junior levels would start the case by opening up the chest to expose the heart. Then the surgeon would back into the OR from the outside room where he had scrubbed up just as the tenor arrives on stage after the chorus and minor singers started the opera. A nurse would dress him in the sterile gown, adjust his head light so he could better see the operating field. When he approached the operating table, the lower priests would step back to allow the surgeon to assume the place of honor. Then the ritual was over. Depending on the surgeon's mood, the music would be selected, ranging from Gregorian chants to baroque to Salsa. "Today let's hear some Hank Williams." This portended a fast and non-combative session but Sue Gratzinger, one of the circulating nurses and self appointed analyst, mumbled "he must have had a country girl last night." Some surgeons will go to bed early and not drink coffee before a big case as the caffeine may cause their hands to have a minuscule shake; Kirby roams the hospital after rounds to see who is available for a quick fling.

The music started as soon as the CD was located and put into the player. Kirby Jackson looked around to make sure the underlings prepared the patient correctly. "OK, let's do some home repairs and fix up this babe to he can become a national league star for the Mets. Then the chanting started as Kirby tried to emulate Hank wailing about his lost love, his lost house, his lost dog and broken car. The OR theater would continue moving away from the formality of the church service analogy towards a ballet. The surgeon, the assistants and the nurses would develop a rhythmic dance, cutting, mopping blood, handing off instruments as they worked through the body layers to get to the heart. The experienced nurse would anticipate the surgeon's next move so there would be an instrument ready for the next request. He took it into his hand in a graceful sweeping motion. The people in the control room sounded like an off stage chorus as they announced the numbers of the blood pressure, the amount of blood lost, the oxygen levels of the blood, electrolyte levels and hemoglobin status as they appeared on their monitors. Circulating nurses would move equipment from sterile shelves to the equipment tables next to the operating table. The more the team worked together, the less commands were needed. During the critical time of the surgery, in this case, sewing a patch over the hole in the heart, the chatter ceased while the surgeon manipulated the instruments so that the sutures would hold up when the heart began to beat and the heart chamber filled with blood. This extra time taken with the suturing would hopefully prevent the patch from breaking away from the heart muscle. Usually the cases that Dr. Jackson did went well without any unusual problems. His stitches were placed better than a machine could do, even spaces between sutures and the tissue edges intact, not torn by the sewing. But when a suture slipped off, a needle broke or a blood vessel leaked, the mood changed, the rhythm interrupted. Some days, Kirby spewed out expletives, learned from his days working in a factory during college while other times he would wail "Why O Lord, why me?" Or he may try to be a comedian blurting out puerile jokes. Because the hearts he was operating on were not anatomically normal, there was always some variation in the position of the various landmarks in the heart chambers. When he had a medical student with him, he would pull out his brand of self deprecating jokes, or at least, he thought they were jokes. No one would be brave enough to tell him that he was not funny. Only Fran Wright, the scrub nurse would be able to get away comments like "Now Dr. Kirby that joke was one my grandfather told me and he told me his grandfather told it to him." Since Kirby was focused on the surgery, he could not see the rolled eyes from the rest of the team. Today things went well, the patch was placed, the EKG showed good electrical conduction, pressures were normal. Tightening up the mitral valve went smoothly. "Let's get this baby off the by-pass and back to his mama." Coming off by-pass was like piloting a space probe returning into the atmosphere, always some tension as the transition was made from full support of the circulation by a machine to full independence from technology. Here again, the experience of the team allowed an almost automatic success. But today something was not right. As the tubing was being removed, a suture tore the edge of the heart muscle. The blood flowed freely until Sam Mathews put a clamp on the tear and Kirby put his hand out for sutures to close the tear. No panic, the team was well prepared for this as if they expected this emergency so what could have been a disaster turned into a routine event. Kirby stood there to make sure there were no surprises. "We don't charge extra for the additional sutures. Time to go huntin." He left the assistants to sew up the chest as he went to speak to the parents.

Outside the OR, Dr. Jackson always dressed in the green scrub suit with sport coat rather than white coat, something that marked him as training at the Mayo clinic where the chief always wore tweed sport coats over his scrubs. He always polished white OR shoes after the surgery. He learned about neat shoes in Ann Arbor when he was doing a fellowship in pediatric cardiovascular surgery. He could not stand blood stained shoes that many of the less fastidious surgeons would wear in the hospital. His trainees were known by the sport coat, white shoe attire. Now to see the parents. Not that he spoke to them too often; he had an assistant Mary Ann Hamilton that did most of the talking. He did not like to repeat himself which conflicted with the needs of anxious parents liked to ask the same question each day. He recognized that he had no bedside manner so he made social rounds each morning and let MaryAnn take care of real communications. The parents did not seem to mind, they had fear of him just as the medical students did. After they thanked him for his help, they were happy to deal with MaryAnn. She was an excellent communicator and empathizer.

Dr. Jackson met the Alexander's in the parent's lounge and discussed the operation with them. He drew a picture of the heart with both hands, saving precious seconds from the discussion. Recently he added color pens to his pocket so he could show red blood with oxygen and blue blood with carbon dioxide. He showed them the diagram of Rusty's heart and with a green pen sketched in how he fixed the heart so that the flow of the blood would closely resemble the normal traffic flow. The fix seemed easy when it was on the paper but the drawing did no justice to the skill needed to put the tiny stitches into the heart muscle and the Dacron grafts that were sewn in to close abnormal openings.

"Will you autograph this drawing; I would like to put it in Rusty's baby book?"

"Sure, but when you auction it at Sotheby's, I want a cut of the sales."

"That is a deal!"

Kirby Jackson felt he had overstayed his visit and nodded to Mary Ann to take care of explaining the rest of the usual recovery process.

"When can we see him?"

"Soon, just give the nurses in the CICU time to get all the tubes arranged, get the correct settings for the respirator and oxygen flow, adjust the iv rate, add the antibiotics, send off the zero hour blood studies, oxygen levels, connect the lines that measured the pressure in his aorta and pulmonary circulation and the EKG leads, thermometer and respiration transducers to the monitor at the head of the bed. No wonder they call this Intensive care.

Carla Allen, a veteran of 5 years in the ICU, was the nurse assigned to Rusty. She had been at CHUC for about 5 years. She came there because she wanted to be taking care of the sickest children at the best cardiac center in the East. She needed to be in the East because her family was in the East, the New York Giants were in the East and the New Jersey shore was in the East. She was married to an engineer who worked for Lincoln Technology. Although they wanted children, they were having trouble conceiving so they had a dog, Eloise, instead. When she finished her jobs of connecting tubes and lines and sending off the tests, she called to the waiting room for the parents to come in.

"Welcome to the cardiac intensive care unit. I am Carla Allen and I will be taking care of Rusty. Come in and let me show you around. This has been quite a day for you. Hopefully we will have only good news for you from now on."

The Alexanders gasped when they looked at Rusty. He was covered in tape and tubes, the little skin they could see was ashen. A tube coming out of his mouth was connected to flexible tubing that led into the respirator that grunted every few seconds causing Rusty's chest to rise and then fall.

"He is so pale!"

"That is the because the skin is not getting good blood flow, that will change in a few minutes, now that we have him hooked up to the monitors and he is getting warmed up on the blanket. Let me show you all the measurements we have here. Don't mind the beeping, when something goes wrong, you will hear the alarm. Since he is still under the effects of the anesthesia, he will not be very responsive. But look at the good things. He made it through the surgery, he is moving his arms and legs and all the readings are normal. He cannot cry because of the tube in his throat but just remember this day, the day you wished you could hear him cry. We are going to do just fine!" She put her arm around Sally and gave her a little hug but Sally was not convinced that Rusty was doing as well as they told her.

The next day it was hard to believe it was the same little Rusty who was now moving around, looking pink. The IV fluids were all the nutrition he was getting but hopefully he would be strong enough to eat.

"You were right, Carla, Things are looking up. I hope this continues."

• • •

Peter Murphy, a member of the SCAN team, conducted the follow up meeting of the case of Samir "What do we have? Anything new? How is Samir?"

"His fracture is healed and he is back at home, walking and playing with his sibs," chimed in Sarah Wright, the intern from emergency.

Vivian, the social worker, did not look happy. Not that she would look happy for worry was the badge of honor for social workers. They could imagine so many horrible events that might happen. If there were no problems, they would just announce, "I am concerned," as if that announcement took them off the hook if something bad happened. Of course, she has seen many horrible events working in the hospital, but happiness was saved for being with her nieces and nephews. She was a charter member of CWA, Certified Worriers Always.

"This case is frustrating because we cannot get enough information. The mother is helpful but she does not have any new insights about how the fracture occurred. The boy friend, Allen, is too glib and seems to be hiding something. At this point, he is number one in our suspect list. He has a story and he is sticking to the original version. He was out of the house, playing dominoes at the corner with his buddies. He left before the child went to sleep and came home as Samir was being taken to the hospital. So he was not involved. He says since he was abused as a child, he never hit any of the kids,. He is a church goer and the pastor has warned the congregation that under no circumstances should an adult hit a child. That is his story and he has not changed one word. Sounds fishy to me but we have to deal with what we have, not what we suspect. It is usually the guilty person that stays with the original script. But you know, the judge will throw us out of his court room if we came in with feelings about a case without evidence to support the feeling."

Donna Barstow, the emergency room doctor who saw Samir on the first day, chimed in. "Battered children batter their children. I am not sure about Allen. His story is too fixed. He sounds like the White House staff that memorizes the talking points of the day and like robots, they go out and spin the same story. Maybe Allen has a career in politics."

Murphy, getting frustrated at the lack of progress and the worry that there was child abuse, scratched his ear, a good sign that something was brewing. When he had gas pains, he rubbed his head but when he had an idea, he scratched his ear. "Maybe it is time to call the electric company for a service call. This may be my desperation shot. I mean going to the house posing as an electric company employee, mess around with a few meters, begin to chat with the people in the house, get invited for coffee or iced tea and then shift the conversation to raising kids, dealing with crying and punishments. I have done this before with more than occasional success. You can't take this information to court but it's an opportunity for someone to unburden their secrets."

The team gave its OK and then discussed a few other cases and adjourned until next month.

Chapter 7

Ray's date with Katie went well. He came to the house with the flowers he bought at the cart outside the hospital. Katie was in full bloom, new hair style, a pale turquoise blouse that seemed too low cut for her but she had to wear a cardigan over the blouse to hide some of the newly exposed skin. Her trousers were Adobe brown, earth tone combination was her advisor's suggestion. Ray handed her the flowers but did not throw her into the bedroom as his medical student had proposed. They walked a few blocks to the new Italian restaurant, Finalmente, where they did the initial steps of the dating dance, talking about the hospital, tough patients, and the screw ups of the administration and the Eagles and Giants. Ray came from Giant territory while Katie was following her father's loyalties to the Eagles. Italian food could have too much garlic so Katie looked for ones that had olive oil; one had to prepare for eventual close contact, thought Katie. Ray did not care, Katie ordered Mozzarella and tomatoes. Ray ordered grilled mushrooms. Ray picked out nice Chianti. He had heard about the best Chianti has a purple rooster on the band around the bottle's neck. He hoped that the one he selected had a rooster. It did! After a glass of wine and some food, things seemed to take on a glow. Katie told about her wish to become a nurse, just like her mother. Her father was involved in public health, working for the state department of health. She picked neurosurgical nursing because there was an opening in that department and she liked what she saw there when she was a student. Ray finally opened up about his personal life. "I came from a Northeastern Pennsylvania, small factory town that was all football. I was the first one to go to college in his family, getting a scholarship to play football at Moravian College in Bethlehem. I did well in school and OK in football. The athletic director had dreams of greatness so he scheduled games with teams from larger schools which led to a losing season so no professional scouts came to see the team play. I did get a scholarship to Temple University Medical School where I did well so getting a residency was straight forward and uncomplicated, not like some of my classmates who spent the fourth year of school perseverating about specialties and residencies, while losing an inordinate amount of sleep. I was a little naïve about all the potential difficulties that my friends could conger up to make their life miserable. I just worked hard and stayed pleasant. Doing research on head trauma at the Center for Head Injury at the school helped my chances for a residency." The bio was interrupted by the waiter who brought Sole with sautéed tomatoes and linguini with pieces of fresh tomatoes in olive oil and basil.

The body language changed too, Katie leaning forward towards Ray and he likewise moved his chair closer to the table. At times, for emphasis, she would tap him on the arm. He did not flinch, a negative spook test by Larry's standard. He touched her hand to show where he had a football injury. Katie held her ground, another negative spook test. After some more wine, the gossip started.

"How is it to work with Dr. Salivari?" Katie opened the cat session.

"He is great, a great surgeon with a lot of good ideas and he is fun to be with in his custom made scrub suits and starched white coat." I am learning so much from him. Speaking of starched white uniforms. What is with Libby Nichols? Does she ever smile, so serious and old fashioned."

"Oh Libby Nipples, she is our mystery girl" Katie blushed a little when she thought that she revealed an ICU's secret name. Businesslike Ray, not realizing that the nickname was used and never noticing Libby or her chest when he was in the ICU, let this one pass.

"Mystery girl?"

"You mean you don't know she is Salivari's downtown girl? She lives in the Bainbridge Towers in the penthouse condo. Each morning she leaves the garage in her BMW yellow convertible, dressed in either her cashmere jacket or mink lined raincoat covering her Armani suit or Calvin two piece gray silk dress, hair flowing in the breeze. When she arrives at the hospital, she turns into Clark Kent. Off with the designer things and into the white starched suit of armor. From amour to armor. Her hair pulled tightly back as a tango dancer, her cuff links placed into the cuffs of her uniform, she is off to the ICU to cure disease and stamp out illness. She gets there early so no one can see the transformation but most of us have been there once or twice to witness the butterfly transform back to the cocoon. Some days when I can't sleep late, I come in early so I have seen her make the transition."

Not being used to gossip and in shock about his boss and the nurse manager, Ray did not know what to say at first but then he asked about Mrs. Salivari.

"From what I know, she is happy being the committee member of the century. You see her name in the paper as the head of many organizations or causes. Save the trees, save the red turtles and anything that is connected to England. It is as if she is waiting for the next tragedy in Europe so she can head up a committee to save something there. I saw her on TV once and heard that fake English accent. Gar'-auge for garage and shed- ule. Not a wrinkle on her face since she does not smile enough to get laugh lines. As she is aging, I think she dips into the Botox but that is being catty."

"Good old Sam," Ray smiled.

"Speaking of Sam, I think I better get going since 5 AM is coming too soon. I had such a good time; I wish I could stay longer."

"Well there will be other times, soon I hope. I had a good time too."

When they got to Katie's apartment, she was beaming, thinking about whether or not she should invite him in. She decided to hold that off, partly for the need to get some sleep and partly afraid of what may happen. Her old fashioned ways appealed to Ray so he did not seem bothered by this plan of action. He did manage to move in to give her a kiss good night- a real kiss albeit an unromantic cheek to cheek one. Ray, a regular church attendee had taken a vow of abstinence so he was not eager to be sexually aggressive. So far, he was able to keep this pledge. This might be a test of wills. Katie was wondering where he came from. She was not oversexed or frustrated, but she would have welcomed a hug.

The next morning the ladies at the desk in the ICU, who already knew about the date, had their dissecting microscopes out looking for clues of what happened with Katie and Ray. Katie was beaming as she entered the transition unit to check on Anthony before she went to work in the ICU. Good sign, thought the ladies. Katie's glow turned to amazement. There was Anthony looking at her and trying to raise his arm to say hello. Anthony was waking up. It's been about 8 weeks, about time, but hopefully this would be a real advancement and not a false hope of recovery. Katie gave him a kiss on his cheek.

"Hi." Anthony responded as he lifted up his arm towards her.

"I knew this was going to be a good day, a double good day." Peggy, the night nurse, filled her in with more details. After Katie saw it for herself, she wanted to know more. There had been a change in his vital signs, pulse had slowed down to normal range, breathing increased slightly, Oxygen levels were perfect, urine output increased. It seemed that brain swelling had lessened, at least in some critical parts of the brain. Peggy knew something was up. When she turned Anthony and tried to clear his airway, he said "don't" and moved his arms. He continued to look around the room, as if he were trying to determine where he was. He then fell asleep for the rest of the shift.

Ray came by for rounds, business like as usual, as he examined Anthony. No signs of any emotion. Night is night, work is work was his motto.

"These movements are real, not reflexes. Let's get another MRI and see what the brain swelling is doing. His arm and leg on the left side do not move, but some movement was better than no movement."

Katie saw Ray come into Anthony's room so she came to the bedside. "Reflexes were still increased on both sides but somewhat less so on the right. The pupil on left was reacting to light."

"How do you explain that?" Ray asked her without looking up from Anthony.

"Motor strip on the left brain controls the right side. Pupil is left is innervated by the left cranial nerve, oculomotor cranial nerve III. The light hits the optic nerve, #2, and the muscles of the iris are controlled by parasympathetic nerve fibers derived from the oculomotor nerve. "

"Wow! What were you doing last night?

"Studying my neuroanatomy. What were you doing?" Katie blushed and looked away.

Ray did not blink, "I was working on my future career."

"And what did that entail?" Larry continued, definitely overstepping the unspecified boundaries for students, but since he did not care about neurosurgery for his specialty, he decided to continue the exchange. "Did you decide on Sumo wrestling?"

"Basta, young man, I have not filled out your grade yet. Yes, this was a good day and there were more to come."

Anthony had definitely improved his rate of recovery. Over the next weeks his right arm and leg continued to improve, but the muscles on the left side were stiff and slower to return. The physical therapists changed their treatment plan to work on his left side and balance. He was finally strong enough to be transferred to a rehabilitation center where he could get all the therapies, physical, occupational and speech.

Fred and Sandy were elated at each step, still holding out for full recovery but accepting of anything as long as Anthony could leave the hospital. 'Reach his full potential' was their motto. They could not forget that a big piece of his brain was left at the scene of the fall.

Ray was always reassuring when he talked with them. "Children have an ability to rewire the brain and use part of the remaining brain tissue to take on new functions. Another positive for being young."

Katie continued to glow as Ray dated her at least once a week still respecting his abstinence vows.

• • •

Norman Oppenheim, a real estate developer and the newest member of the board, looked over the agenda for the Trustee's meeting:

- Financial report
- Compensation subcommittee recommendations
- 5 year hospital plan

He was interested in the details of the financial report as rumors in the community suggested that the hospital was having problems paying its bills.

The membership of the board of the CHUC was one of the most prestigious positions in the community. Most of the men inherited the post because for several generations, their families had supported the hospital. There were seats for local entrepreneurs with the anticipation that they would follow their initial contributions with additional funds. That explained Norman appointment. There were two women and 4 physicians, the president of the medical staff, the chief of medicine and chief of surgery and one elected junior physician but not any Black or Hispanic members.

The president, Clayton Pickering II called the meeting to order. His family had a sizeable real estate portfolio in the area as well as the main industry in South Creek that produced aluminum castings for the automobile industry. His father and grandfather were former presidents of the board of CHUC. "Lets get started; we have a lot to do. First, I want to address the rumors that are spreading about the hospital finances. I assure you I have gone over the numbers with Richardson and the Controller, Al Sharptee. We are in good shape and I will give you more details when we go over the finances. I was at the Early Bird Diner this AM where the chatter was so strong, no one would sit with me because they were afraid I could not pay the check." That prompted some polite laughter. No one had the nerve to tell Clayton that he was not funny.

"I thought you usually managed to fumble and let someone else pay the tab," chimed in Sam Rubinstein, the owner of the Mercedes agency and a good friend of Clayton Pickering, the odd couple they were called.

Clayton was also quite friendly with Richardson Beardsley, the CEO. Since Beardsley's arrival in South Creek, Clayton took him under his guidance to give him some polish in the way he dressed, showed him how to fish in Canada with a guide, and got him into the country club so he could learn to play golf and mingle with potential donors to the hospital. After all, Clayton was the main force in selecting Richardson to be CEO even though he did not have the usual credentials that the head of the hospital usually had. His undergraduate degree was from Montana State College, he started as a paper product salesman, moved into hospital supplies and after taking night courses, got a degree in hospital administration. Richardson quickly learned is to say the right things and network with the right people.

"Dick, can you fill us in on the hospital operations this month?" He called him Dick to indicate that their relationship was personal and solid.

"We had an exceptional month...... another exceptional month. The census is running 5% ahead of last year on a monthly average. Cash flow is sensational. Receivables are down as collections are up, thanks to our new computerized billing system. The usual summer slowdown is no longer happening; we are busy, busier than most months except January and February, the flu season months. Our new radiology equipment is supposed to arrive within the next fortnight." Back where Beardsley came from, if you said fortnight, one would think of a military camp after dark. But at the club, he learned the term; it sounded so high class to him that he could not avoid using fortnight to mean any time longer than a few days. "I will have more today about the finances when we hear from the CFO but believe me, we are in good shape. We have a new supply of resident physicians; we got the pick of the litter. Half of them come from Ivy League schools, a few from Stanford and UCSF and a few from the South. Good for diversity too. Our nursing staff is almost at 100% thanks to the good work of the Vice President of nursing, Jackie Lawrence. Unlike other centers, we do not have to close down beds because of lack of nurses. We have a new associate director of nurse recruiting to continue to seek new nurses and to retain the ones we have. Good job, Jackie."

"Speaking of retaining the present team, we are looking into a new form of compensation, benchmark, and performance based compensation. Each member of the executive team will get a base salary and a bonus based on achieving performance goals, such as increased revenue, decreased expenses, decreasing inefficiencies, and patient and employee satisfaction. It is my feeling that we should reward good performance but not award bonuses on an automatic basis, if the executive team does not make the hospital a better place to serve our patients and improve the margins so we will have resources to expand our services, we don't deserve a bonus."

"How does that work for you, Dick?" asked Norman Oppenheimer.

"I will have the same arrangement with the compensation committee; we will determine the goals for the year, the benchmarks, if you will. And if the goals are achieved, the compensation will follow." Beardsley was obviously annoyed at this question from this newcomer who had not yet come under his spell.

"Does that mean if you cut back on expenses, such as restricting hiring, the profits, I mean the margins, I must remember we are not for profit, will increase and you will be rewarded? That could lead to problems with staff support that, in turn, can lead to low morale. I know this is hard to document but I am afraid that this system could eventually create serious problems. Seems to me to be some kind of conflict of interest. How do you balance the cost cutting with the striving for higher margins?"

"We have the employee satisfaction factor in the formula."

"Will all the employees fill out the satisfaction form and how confidential will these forms be?"

"Look, if I wanted to make a lot of money, I would have gone into investment banking. Trust me, the system should work."

Norman was mainly bothered by the Beardsley eye movements. After he said something that might be challenged, such as his salary and his financial claims, he looked up and rapidly scanned the listeners as if to see if they were agreeing with nods or smiles or were shaking their heads or as Norman did, just staring ahead, non- committal. If the scanning showed the majority approved or did not frown or scowl, then he continued with his speech becoming more rapid and louder. He could also identify those who were not followers of his spin but may be asking deeper questions to find out if there was other information than what was fed to the board. This scanning eye movement was similar to the poker players' tell, the unconscious movements that indicated that he was bluffing or had an exceptional collection of cards. Was

Beardsley showing his tell or was he using eye contact to see if the board understood?

Norman leaned over to comment to Sam Rubenstein. "Sounds like one of your used car salesman. Strange thing about trust mistatements, they really mean "catch me if you can.""

"I am new here so forgive me for this naïve question. Have you engaged a consultant that specializes in executive compensation? I think that might be helpful."

"Good question, Norman. Of course, I have hired a compensation firm, Executive Strategies for Health Care. They do a lot of work in hospitals like ours."

"I never heard of them, are they local?"

"Another good question, Norman. No, they come from New York. We like to get a national prospective from our consultants and auditors."

I have to tap into the good old boy network around here, thought Norm. I know from the ethics courses I have my top management take at NYU that problems arise when the board is too closely aligned with the CEO who feeds them information that he wants them to know and scoots over problematic or bad news. This commonly happens on such a prestigious board like this one. The people here are so happy to be on the board that they spend the whole meeting thinking 'aren't I lucky to be here, Just think I am on the board of CHUC. I better not mess this thing up by making waves.'

Norman was not one of those people. He had no family connections to award him a spot on the board. He did not have good old boy network to get him here. He was interested in the hospital because his grand son was taken to CHUC for joint pains and after a long series of tests and treatments, he was diagnosed with a kind of psychological problem that expressed itself as pain. This diagnosis forced the parents to look at the problem in a new way and seek some family therapy. Shortly the grandson was back in school, playing sports and interacting with his classmates. The care he received was so personal and kind, Norman decided to get involved. Of course, writing a check for $250,000 did not hurt either. But he had the money and felt that good goes to good, as his grandmother told him many times. Norman did not need to be on another board nor did he need the ego boost that such a position gave others. He certainly did not need to add more meeting time to his weekly calendar. But he took the position because he wanted to be involved and wanted to help the hospital continue its magnificent work. Although his sense of smell was not the greatest, he thought he smelled a rat in this new deal of Richardson Beardsley. He would keep an eye on the plan and see what he could do to find another board member with whom he could align and see how he could get on the compensation committee to get more of the details. The real action happened in the committees, not at the board meetings since these were more of a show and tell.   Norman could already tell that the CEO and Leo Altime were good buddies. Fishing in Canada, playing golf at the same exclusive club, and now shopping for clothes at the same store, Chapel's Outfitters on King Street. Richardson was a fast learner about gracious living. He was sort of accidental bragger. He would complain that 'his elbow hurt, must have been when I banged it on the bar at the club or I turned my ankle when I was getting out of Leo's boat at the lake.' Just a human touch to the bragging. Poor Richardson did not realize that he was the only one who related such stories. The real members did not think anything about being a member of the club or fishing at the lake. That was the way they were raised.

So Norman made his own benchmark - find out what was really going on by networking and getting on the compensation committee for starts. He made a note to himself in his iPhone and set up a 3 month goal to get inside the action at the board. He looked around the room for people with whom he might align himself. He must make notes about who asked the kind of questions that suggested independence from the inner circle. He would have to listen carefully and promise to get to the meetings earlier to do a little socializing.

The auditor's report would be discussed at the next meeting. The rest of the meeting were reports from the parking lot committee, a few letters from appreciative patients and the report from the volunteer committee that announced that the annual meeting of the Children's Hospitals Volunteer will be held in Denver next year where Richardson Beardsley will be honored as the executive of the year. Everyone applauded as Richardson beamed. Norman thought that for an instant Beardsley was licking his lips.

Chapter 8

September Residents Meeting.

"Let's get started." Karl Strem, the chief resident, shouted to the noisy group of residents.

The group of residents was settling in to their medical role. They no longer choke on their introduction or response to a phone call when they said Dr. before their last name. Now it was "doctor" spoken naturally, without a pause. They were still enthusiastic and excited to be at CHUC but the long hours were beginning to make some of them a little short in verbal exchanges with the nurses. They dozed off during teaching sessions or weekly grand rounds when the actually attended the sessions rather than sleeping in the on-call rooms. But they were coping for the most part. It was Karl's job to see that they stayed on the positive side by intervening when a problem arose, that is a solvable problem; he could not arrange dates or pay off loans, two of the biggest issues for residents.

"First we have a memo from Mr. Edgar Grimely, assistant vice president for transportation.

To House staff CHUC
From Edgar Grimely, assistant vice president for transportation.
Re: Parking lots

Background. As you all know, the parking spaces are at a premium in the hospital area. We have organized an equitable allocation of parking spaces for our patients and staff. Because of increased patient load, we must reassign parking spaces. The following program will commence on November 1.

All residents who park in Lot 1-A will move to 2-B. Those with compact cars can park in spaces 22-49; those with regular sized cars will park in the spaces from 50 and up. If you have a truck, you will not be able to get into the lot because of height restrictions. Truckers will park on the street in any spot they can find.

I understand this is a hardship for some of you who are accustomed to parking in the main building but we need those spaces for the patients and key executives. In case of rain, you can take the shuttle bus from Lot 1-A.

Thank you for your cooperation.

EG/la

"Any comment" Karl asked.

"Who is this jerk, Grimely? Where does he park?"

"What happened to the elevator button survey?"

"I checked with Mr. Grimely and he was in the midst of appointing a committee to look into the research project regarding incidence of button pushing, demographics of the type of pusher, estimate of delay in elevator service among other things. He projected a completion of the committee formation in about 8 weeks and then 6 months of research plus one month of report writing.

"That should bring us almost to the end of the year, just in time to welcome a new set of elevator pushers. This is real science!"

"Some housekeeping details.

Charts have to be dictated within 48 hours of patient discharge. Most of you are doing a good job but we have a few people headed for trouble. Cal Painter has already 43 charts to dictate. This is hard to figure out since he has only had 31 patients but somehow 12 extra charts got into his to be dictated box. I will check with Margot Sullivan, who is in charge of making sure charts have dictations. Shirley Dent is next with 5 charts; the rest of you guys are going your job. I look forward to next month's report when Cal will lose the lead."

"There is room for a few moonlighters to fill in for the newborn nursery. Those on electives without night call can sign up for moonlighting. Those on call every fifth, can sign up for day three of five. Check with Eva Masters for assignments."

"There will be a softball game this Saturday against housekeeping in Centennial Park on Carpenter Street. Sign up after the meeting."

"Any one who found a black stethoscope with a yellow teddy bear on it, contact my office. Seems like Amy lost her stethoscope."

Any other questions?"

"Who gets to go to the Giants game this weekend?"

"See Eva Masters."

After the meeting, Jeff Collins, a third year residents leaned over to his fiancée, Barbara Magnusen and said "I may sign up for a few sessions. They pay $800 for a 12 hour shift."

"No we don't need the money that bad."

"What do you mean? With the wedding, trip to Bermuda and fixing up a new apartment, we need the loot."

"Apparently you don't believe the story how you get to moonlight. They don't call her Evil Eva for nothing."

"I don't believe those stories." I heard them last year but since we could not take moonlighting jobs, I never could find out if the stories were true. Now is my chance."

"Please don't."

"Don't worry, it will be fine. Now I can check out the rumors. They are just rumors."

"Why do you think girls have a hard time getting moonlighting assignments?"

"Do you know that for sure?"

"No, But if I had time I would check out the numbers. I have to get back to clinic."

The meeting was a great time for Felix to pursue the ice maiden, Beth Conover, the new resident that was working hard at avoiding any contact with Felix, especially when there were no witnesses.

"Hi, how's it going on the baby floor?"

"Just fine, I have moved to a new floor and have to get back to see my patients."

"What floor might that be?"

"The one in the patient care wing. Hi Jackie, walking back?"

"May I walk with you?" Felix sped up to keep pace with her.

"I think your beeper is going off"

"Can't be mine since I don't carry a beeper this month."

"Well it may be mine. Excuse me I will drop into the ladies room since the call may be from my finance." She hoped to meet a colleague there who could protect her when she came out of the restroom.

"OK, I will wait for you to come out."

"It may be a long time. We are discussing our wedding plans and I have a lot to tell him."

"I am in no rush; I am surveying all the new residents to make sure things are going well."

Beth hoped that there would be another door to escape from the ladies restroom but she knew that was magical thinking but she quickened her step a few beats to get into the security of toilets and washbasins. Felix made a note on his iPhone.

1. Check his sources to see if Beth was really engaged.

He had time and he had a lot to do. Off to the gift shop to check out the volunteers.

The gift shop, officially called the Toy Chest, was run by the volunteers, mostly blondes or gray haired grandmother types but once in awhile there was a junior league member or post debutante idling away waiting for prince charming or maybe a recently divorced doctor, hopefully, a well to do cardiologist or neonatologist. The Toy Chest had a variety of gifts, a few coke machines and the best calorie packets in the form of peanut brittle, licorice or chocolate chip cookies. The volunteer office was next to the gift shop so there were always a few of the ladies in the turquoise jackets that identified them as CHUC volunteers.

Felix scanned the room and the TV monitors to see what was doing behind the get well balloons. There was one volunteer there arranging the children's books. She was neither the grandmother type nor the cute young thing. Maybe 40 to 45 with a few extra pounds starting to show around her hips and under her chin. And sure, a wedding band and about a 2 carat pear cut diamond ring. Not the best color but 2 is more than 1. You never know, thought Felix. He had to make a quick decision since there were lots of areas to cover in the hospital. He almost finessed this one but the she looked up from the books and Felix saw hungry eyes. He could always tell hungry eyes; it was worth a try.

"Hi. Any X rated books for an overworked resident? None with big words, I have a reading problem."

"You are so funny. These are kids' books. I don't think they would have X rated books in the hospital."

"Well, then where can I find some? I would even take a DVD so I could save my eyes and pick up a few pointers."

"What kind of pointers does a man about town need?"

"This was going faster than I had hoped to but she is not backing off or blushing. It may be time to see if she is open for monkey business," thought Felix.

I am always eager to learn something new." As he said that, he tapped her forearm with his hand. *She did not flinch*- Felix took this as a positive sign.

"X rated DVD is not my area of interest so I can't help you with that."

"What do you suggest?"

"How about Emma Goes to the Hospital?"

"No I have had enough of hospitals. How about a new suggestion?"

"About what?"

"What ever you have in your wicked mind."

"How do you know I have a wicked mind?"

"I can see through your hungry eyes. My name is Felix."

"Diane."

Felix's philosophy was one for a thousand is better average than zero for zero. It does not hurt to try. "OK Diane, how would you like to be a real volunteer?"

"I am a volunteer. I have the jacket and two gold five year pins."

"I mean a real volunteer to boost the morale of tired residents."

"How can I be of service? I am here to serve. But not right now. Do you have a card?" She opened up her Hermes purse and pulled out a pink business card. "Here is mine." She placed the card in Felix's hand, keeping contact with his hand for a few extra seconds.

I better slow down. Maybe she is some big shot's wife, he told himself.

Felix allowed caution to take over but he did notice the new blush on her cheeks and the increased breathing rate.

Felix took the card, looked at the address- she lives in a very nice neighborhood. "I must go off and save a few lives."

Diane Kruger felt a warm glow after this rapid fire exchange. This was more like being 15 and getting a note during study hall from some oversexed teenager. The brief conversation was more fun than she has had in a few years trying to cope with her husband who was more interested in what was on HBO or ESPN than paying any attention to her. She would see how she felt in the morning but she already knew what she was going to do. "Don't use up all your energy saving lives upstairs. Nice to meet you, Felix."

"Ciao, Diane."

As he left the gift shop, he said to himself, take it easy! I don't want to get in trouble and ruin my chances for a fellowship in Boston. They are hard to get so I don't want to sacrifice my career for a hungry eyed volunteer. On the other hand, she gave me her card, and then it was her call, not my testosterone that caused the trouble. He noticed that he, too, was breathing fast and a little sweaty. After turning the corner towards the elevators, he stopped and laughed. "That is what I call a really big tuna. Lots of sushi in that catch. I was not sure my line could hold up, but it seemed to work. This could be interesting. How to make the next contact?"

Chapter 9

After a week, Felix had no news from Diane. "Thank goodness," thought Felix, "that was quite an exchange and it moved far too fast. This needed time to cool and change the playing field or even the game." He started to comb his hair. When he looked into the mirror, he usually talked to himself. "I was getting over my head, especially not knowing who she was other than a ten year volunteer. But then again, she had a lot of the signs-hungry eyes, past the big four O, bored and boring husband, she took my bait with lots of suggestive banter, even though that kind of chatting is misleading, you know all talk and no action- the motto of many of the nurses in the hospital." He left for the hospital, intent in avoiding the gift shop, for now.

No escaping her. At lunch time, his cell phone rang.

"Felix, dear?"

"Si" he knew who it was but the husky voice and the way the R was rolled. She had either been to Spain or she was practicing her accent.

"I have been away for a week so I missed my turn at the gift shop. Have you been checking for me there?"

"I have not left the book section except for a few forages to the candy containers. Loneliness makes me hungry for sugar. How are you? What is going on?"

"Same old, same old. Garden club meetings, volunteering and a few tennis games. Nothing new. How about you?"

"Still saving lives and trying to avoid hard labor. Working my shifts as usual. How did you get my number?"

"I have connections."

"Oops, that is what I feared."

"Feared what?"

"Connections."

"Yes. I have connections. I called the residency office and asked to be connected to Felix. You are famous. No last names, just Felix and here we are."

"Where are you?"

"At my tennis club in the hot tub. Would you like to join me? Do you play tennis?"

"I did before I injured my knee." Felix lied, not wanting to show his lack of that kind of athletic ability.

"Listen, I have to be in town for an art opening. If I come in early, will you be free to join me for a drink at the Pedro's. They have the best margaritas. I bet you are on call tonight, are you?"

"No night call for the rest of the week. I did my time on Monday. Where is Pedro's?"

"Across town from you. Next to the farmer's market on the Patriot Square."

"I know where the Patriot Square is. What time are you thinking about?"

"I am ready when you are. You tell me."

"6:30"

"Don't be late. Adios, Felix."

Now Felix is in full sweat and palpitations. "This lady could be 15 years older than I am and 14 years older than anyone I have pursued in my career. This could be interesting! "Now he had to con someone into hold his beeper for a few hours while he sneaks out of the hospital. With so many residents, it should be easy to get some help from a colleague.

After a shower and putting on a white linen shirt, he headed off to Patriot Square. He was not drooling with desire but the anticipation of the unknown fueled his race across town.

Felix continued to scheme. "Be cool, slow down, act as this is not a new experience, I have met older women many times," Felix thought to himself. "But then again, this may be a nice lady trying to kill time and show a poor resident how he may live some day. That is if the old man does not meet them with a shotgun or the detective who maybe following Diane gets the needed photo that will be used for the divorce. But how many married women have affairs. 30-40%? I will soon know which story is playing out. Maybe I should back out before I get that buckshot up my ass or even worse." All the while, the streets were being crossed and in about 15 minutes, he was pulled into the parking lot and could see the neon sign with Mexican sombrero flashing in three colors. Although margaritas were not his favorite drink, they will be for the next few hours. One never knows until the fun begins.

Pedro's was the typical northern version of a Mexican restaurant. Plastic cacti along the wall, serapes on the wall and a horno with fake fire in one corner. The rest was minimalist modern décor with an interesting bar with glass shelves, back lighted in blue. The bar was also glass with a paler blue lighting. A few very attractive women, sitting on high tan leather stools, looked at Felix as he walked in. They turned away when the sized up his non-designer clothes, Hush puppy shoes and non-Rolex watch. He looked around the room and did not see Diane. Maybe this was her version of a spook test. He took the bait and now he was locked into sitting in this probably expensive bar for the proper 30 minutes, waiting to see whether she would appear or be a no show. Well he was here and this is not the time to turn back. His father always told him to be nice to his elders, but that did not include elder 40ish women on the prowl.

He took a seat at a small table just off the bar and tried to look relaxed. He looked for a napkin so he could dry his sweaty palms. He was a mess but he tried to look cool.

A waiter appeared and stood still.

"I'll have a margarita."

"We have 16 different margaritas. Which one do you like?"

"What is the most popular?

"The seductiones"

"Fine"

"What kind of tequila do you want in it?"

"This is getting complicated. I am getting over my head."

"Excuse me?"

"Do you have Three Brothers?" After seeing a poster on the wall of three people around a bottle of tequila, Felix made up the title but figured the waiter would rebound with a suggestion which he would take.

"We have Three Generations, a very good choice."

"Fine"

"Five year or ten?"

"Five is fine for me." Now he wondered if he was getting into some high priced booze. At least he had a credit card if things get out of hand.

5 year was a good choice, he now had a warm feeling and time to plan his next move; should he wait for Diane, should he get out of this fling, should he go outside and wait for her to enter Pedro's and then trump her lateness with his pseudo-arrival? Lots of possibilities but no

one stood out. He wanted to be a player but was a little frightened. Stay cool above all, that was the motto his old roommate taught him. Thinking of roommates, where would he take Diane if things started to move along in the direction he hoped for. He could not go to his pig pen- too much mess and unpredictable roommate who comes and goes at strange hours. Last choice would be a motel but that seemed so tacky. A real hotel was not worth the expense because he was not sure of the cost and the return on investment. Whose apartment could he borrow? Taking out his Palm, he scanned through the addresses and found a few possible old friends' names. Ray Bartlett, that was perfect. He was always on call, so his place should be free. He seemed to be the kind of guy who kept a neat apartment. He must live alone.

"Perfect."

Felix dialed Ray's pager and got a busy signal. Maybe that means that Ray was being called back to the hospital for an emergency.

"Perfect" Felix said out loud.

"What's perfect?"

"Hi, Diane. Good to see you. Wow do you look good! Is that Calvin?" Felix did not know a Calvin from an Oscar but he liked the ads for Calvin Klein underwear so he tossed that name out.

"Close, it is last year's Donna. I am impressed with your fashion sense," she said as she passed her hands over her skirt to get rid of the imaginary wrinkles.

"Sit down; this place is famous for its Seductiones margaritas made with Three Generations tequila, Superb!"

"Boy, are you a fast learner! I have been coming here for several years and only recently discovered the Seductiones; it is made with fresh pineapple and lime juices. I am impressed. How appropriate! I thought you did not know about this place."

"I have not been here but I do know a good margarita when I drink one. I just got here; hoped I would not be late."

"I am the one who is late. I got a call from the builder. We are doing some work on the house and there are a lot of decisions to make. It is exhausting and quite stressful. Where is the waiter? I need a drink to calm down."

Just then, the waiter appeared. Felix signaled the order, one for the lady and another one for him. In his plotting his next move, he finished off the first Seductiones. He did not know that tequila is like a stealth bomber, it can attack before you are aware of its presence.

"I was surprised, but glad that you called. What have you been up to this week?"

"The usual, traveling to art shows, committees, tennis lessons and book club. Nothing exciting, just the routine. How about you?"

"Same usual, work and work and no play."

"I bet I can change that. You know what they say about too much work."

"I hope it does not give you cancer or an enlarged prostate."

The waiter arrived with the drinks and before he took three steps away from the table, Diane downed the drink, raised her glass and said "Mas." The waiter returned and Felix blinked. "This lady is tough."

"It's been a trying day. Do you have any plans for the evening? I am not sure I want to go to another boring art opening, especially for an artist that cannot paint, only emote through colors. What a waste. Where do you live?"

"I live near the hospital. I am afraid it is not the place you would like to go. A little unkempt and a roommate who are there tonight."

"Don't you have friends, this place is giving me the creeps and I have a lot of friends that stop by here."

Felix's mind was racing now. "This lady does not waste time. She wants what she wants when she wants it and I am here to oblige, if I can find Ray."

"Let me see if I can make a few phone calls." Felix redials Ray and enters his phone number when the page program asks for it. "I called a friend to see what the possibilities are. We have to wait for the call back. Felix was a little edgy being pursued; he liked being the hunter. "How was the drink?"

"Excuse me, I don't usually down a perfectly good margarita that quickly, I guess it was all the commotion this afternoon. I promise I will behave with the next one, when ever it arrives. Too many decisions and too much debate about each one. I should never have agreed to do this renovation." She bit off a piece of the lime and licked the salt from the rim of the glass. "Where is the waiter?" As if on cue, he arrived with the drink.

"Gracias" she smiled at the waiter and took a sip. "Perfect. When do you expect the call from the pager?"

"Any minute."

"Do you have a plan B? Is your apartment so bad? Can't you get rid of the roommate?"

"You are a lady of action. Are you sure you don't run a mega million dollar company? Let's give him a few minutes and then we can try plan B. Are you always in such a hurry?"

"No, excuse me, I have to get home at a reasonable time since the art gallery closes at 9:30 and I wanted to get to know you better. Remember you are the one who asked me to up my volunteering."

"Right you are, Plan B, here we come. Remember that it is not the Ritz. Let me check in at home." Felix dialed his apartment and said "fire drill—one--- I owe you"

"What kind of fire drill are you having?"

"Just a short hand for saying that I will be coming home shortly. My roomie is a bridge nut; he is out every night that he is awake, playing bridge with his friends. I am sure that he is away but this was just a signal to evacuate in case he was in the apartment. At a fire drill, all occupants have to leave the building."

"So you are the fire chief?"

"Not exactly but I do drive a mean fire engine."

"OK, chief."

The apartment was as advertised. Lots of dirty clothes on the chair, bed not made and dishes in the sink. There was a living room, of sorts and two bed rooms. The living room had a few chairs and an extremely bright light hanging from the ceiling. The only positive feature was the iPod hooked into the stereo system. Felix pushed the clothes into the closet, picked up the papers from the floor and turned on the iPod and selected a play list labeled 'night mood,' a collection of Barry White, Eva Cassidy, Linda Eder and Abba. That should be the right era for this lady, I am sure that she was not into Rap or hard rock. ABBA was at the end of the list with the anticipation that at that time their syncopation would be appropriate background music that is if things go according to plan. Felix had great planner skills when pressed.

"Barry White, Can't get enough of your love. I remember him. You like Barry?"

"My favorite-"

"Where is the bathroom? I think the drinks are coming through."

Diane laughed as she went into the bathroom and saw the condition of the place. She closed the door and started to sing along with Barry.

Felix was not sure of what was going on, there was no chase, no pursuit. "How am I going to make a move if that seemed appropriate? I don't want to be accused of rape; I don't know who this lady was. What was her connection? It was exciting and could possibly be a night of new experiences. I bet she must be 40, who knew what a 40 year old was like but I do remember reading that their sexual peak is late 30's so it could be different from the 20 year olds that he had been pursuing. What a difference 15 years could be? How am I going to get her into the bedroom? Do I let her take off her designer clothes? I am not going to rip them off like they do in the movies. Stay cool and see what unfolds. Yes, that is the best approach, be interested but not too eager. I wonder if she is on the pill. Where are the condoms? I bet she is worried about STD's."

Hearing the door open, he turned and there she was. High heels and pearls. She had released her hair from the tight bun. The rest of the outfit was skin.

"Nice pearls" Felix choked out as he surveyed her C cup breasts that were just beginning to lose their firmness. The rest of her body was trim. He did not see any signs of liposuction scars. She must do a lot of gym work. Felix smiled at her hair style. "Something about 40 year old women, they think that letting their hair grow long makes them look sexy and younger. The sad thing is that their hair is thinning out so they do not look like the news readers on CNN; they look like 40 year olds trying to look like a young news bunny."

"Why so dressed up? I bet you would like to be little more informal than you are. I am here to volunteer. Can you get rid of that awful bright light?"

"Out goes the light. Anything else, I can do for you? We treat our volunteers with respect and gratitude."

"Not too much respect, I hope. Let me help you with those buttons. Enough of this small talk. No need for a wrestling match for disrobing, I have to get home before my husband sends out the hounds."

The words 'husband and hounds' seemed to implode this passion, at least as far as the status of his erection bulging out under his trousers.

"My, what happened to pecker power? Are you OK? Let me see what I can do to help you."

"Oh my, you know just what to do. Experience, which is always the best solution."

"Speaking of solutions, are you OK with HIV tests."

"Clean as a whistle. And the good housekeeping seal of approval."

"Show me your stuff, big boy."

They continued with their aerobics for a few minutes. Diane started to unbutton the shirt between deep and frantic kisses. Felix was working on her soft buttocks as if they were fresh pasta dough that needed more kneading.

Just then the phone rang. Felix leaned over and pushed the speaker phone button.

"This is Ray answering the page."

"False alarm Ray, I took care of the problem. Thanks for calling."

Now Diane was working on the zipper, having just unbuttoned the waist. "There is something big and hard that wants to get out in the air."

The pants dropped to Felix's knees, stopping there as he had a wide stance to get keep his balance and get a good hold on her butt.

Just as her hand grabs onto Felix's penis, the front door opens, the living room light turns on.

Felix, tangled in his half mast pants, falls on his back. Diane tries to cover her crotch and heads for the bedroom.

Lester Martin, the roommate, who did not expect to find anyone home, entered the apartment and flipped the light switch. He looked up to see Felix with his flag pole extended to full size and a lady's cellulited derriere vanishing into the darkness of the bedroom, he knew he was not welcomed in his own apartment.

"My word! I guess this is really a case of being caught with one's pants down."

"Turn off the damn light!"

"Very sorry. I did not know you were in here. Where was the blue flag on the door?"

Diane, having picked up Felix's soiled sweat shirt from the pile of the clothes, screamed "What the hell is going on? Who invited him to the party?"

Lester, as if he had been programmed, ran out the door while Felix retrieved his clothes and went into the bedroom to see Diane cowering in the corner of the room.

"I thought you said he was out playing bridge."

"He was but something must have happened. By the way, the grunge look is out of style, miss fashion plate."

"I like the retro look. You better explain, something happened and nothing happened. I better get out of here and head home. This had great potential for an interesting evening but I guess that is why they have motels. Maybe next time."

• • •

"I need to see Judy Samuels in PR and get me Thomas Heatherson from the board on the phone," Richard Beardsley called to Ann Ranier, his secretary. Richard's routinely made contact with one board member each day, learning early in his training, that good relationship with a majority of the board members will assure him smooth sailing for getting approval of his initiatives. His job was to convince them that he was the only one who can lead this hospital, that he is under paid for all the work he does and to defend him when critics on the board question his projects or his compensation. Most of the board members did not bother to read the financial reports or could not understand them as they had accountants and Goldman Sachs's wealth management people take care of their trust funds; they only checked the bottom line. Richardson was good at making bottom lines look good. The buzzer on the desk indicated that Tom Heatherson was on the line.

"Tom, Dick speaking, how are you? I hope your family is good." Richardson learned that asking about the family was the proper thing to do. Even when he did not care, he always asked. He did not know that the wealthy board members did not usually ask about family; something middle management people did. "I am sorry I did not get chance to speak with you at the last board meeting, I have been spending a lot of time going over the possibilities of various MRI systems for radiology and I wanted to get your input on what you think the hospital should be looking at..... Yes I know I reported on new equipment arriving soon for radiology but this is another project a faster MRI with more ability to pinpoint activity of tumors. ...... 2.1 mil in that range. .... Yes that is the issue; I wanted to know if you would head up fund raising for this. Great potential for naming a room with this high powered machine.... We would be the second pediatric hospital to have this technology. The other one is on the West Coast in LA. Yes, we would be the first on the East Coast." Richardson knew how important it was to be first, even if it was a stretch by making it first on the East coast. "Of course, I would like you go over the specs and get your input on this project... of course, we need your valuable opinion, from the public perspective. I am sure you would want to know that we have a special deal from the company, a major discount since we would be a good reference for other hospitals that want to catch up to us." Thomas was on the hospital board because his wife's father owned a lot of land near the lake and has been developing summer homes on what was the old family farm and warehouse. His major job was to sit on boards and represent the family in civic enterprises. "What do you say about meeting for coffee some morning? What time is good for you? Super, How about meeting at the hotel dining room nest Tuesday..... Your house, that is better. I will see you then at ten."

Richardson put a check mark next to Heatherson's name and reviewed the list to see who had not been contacted this month. He planned to work on a few more this week so he could soften them up for the new compensation plan that should make him very wealthy if the board passed it. He smiled at the thought of the big payoff. "Who said that not for profits are not profitable?"

When he hung up the phone, Judy Samuels stood at the door way, waiting to be asked to come in.

"Hi Judy, come in. I wanted you to know that I was just named the CEO of the year by the national hospital volunteer group and I will be going to Denver in the spring to get the award. Mrs. Randolf was instrumental in nominating me and promoting the award through the committees. I was unaware of her nominating me, but now that it a fact, we should get this out in a tasteful way. The hospital needs all the good publicity it can get, especially with all the rumors about financial troubles and big budgets. Speaking of publicity, I did not see any pictures of the presentation I got from the community as the man of the year. I noticed a photographer there but I have not seen the prints. When will it get into the paper? Makes me sound egotistical, doesn't it but good publicity is hard to conjure up these days. That would make the hospital look good." As in most conversations with Beardsley, the flow of talk was from him to the listener. Judy looked interested and smiled. She was writing a book about hospital life so she would have her turn to speak some day.

Chapter 10

D irk Adman, dressed in a blue shirt with Electric Department written under the left pocket and matching blue Dickie pants, knocked on the door. He could hear the noise of playful children enthusiastically expressing their joy.

"Whose there?"

"Electric department, I am here to check your circuit breakers and do a balance of the lines. We seem to be having a voltage problem in the area.

Allen opened the door just enough to look Dirk over and decided that his rosy cheeks and nice smile were OK. "What do you want to do?"

"I have to take a few meter readings and check the outlets to make sure that the voltage is not too high. High voltage can ruin your TV. Can I come in? It is hot outside."

"I guess so. How long will you have to stay?"

"As long as it takes. Sometimes a half an hour and sometimes a few hours. I don't want to have you lose your TV."

The room was just about the same as the report described. There was a 32 inch TV sitting on an old 19 inch set. Toys were everywhere. Many were broken or wheelless. Several dolls were on the floor; a few needed major rehabilitation. Dirty dishes filled the sink. The book case had many DVD's and CD's plus an off brand stereo system. The soiled and worn sofa had a few pillows but mostly toys. The walls were marked with hand prints of a variety of colors and foods.

Adman took out a few meters from his tool box and began to test the outlets. The meter had a large bulb that would turn on indicating current. He took out his notebook and began to makes notes, presumably of the readings. The light turned on many times. He began that horrible sequence of "oohs" and "Oh's" just like the doctors do when they are going through an examination. As the "Ohs" became more frequent, Allen looked up and moved closer to Dirk Adman. "Anything wrong?"

"Not sure yet, this looks complicated so it may take longer than I expected. I have to call my boss."

Alan became alarmed because he was hijacking the cable signal. Another friend of his showed him how to hook into the cable to avoid the bothersome cable bills. The cable people have enough money, he rationalized and they overcharge for the premiums like HBO and Showtime. Adman picked up on Alan's interest and increasing nervousness. But he waited as he turned up the pressure. Dirk continued his survey of the outlets. As he moved towards the kitchen, he noted that Alan slouched back in his chair. It was becoming a game of battleships where you guess the location of the other players' ships and keep making moves until you get a direct hit. "No, it was not the kitchen," Adman murmured, He then went towards the bathroom, keeping his eye on Alan.

"OK if I go into the bedroom?"

"Sure."

The bedroom was neater than the kitchen and living room but not by much. Dirk stayed in there for a few minutes then called out to Alan. "The readings here are good, how is the cable reception."

"Cable? Oh, the cable. That is perfect. Not a current problem," Alan tried to reassure Dirk. But the pitch of his voice and the speed of the reply underlined the tension that Alan was feeling.

"A hit" Adman remarked, somewhere between the level he would use talking to himself but loud enough for Alan to hear.

"Say what?"

"Seems to be something in the TV line. I am getting a different reading." He switched the meter to flashing red light and continued his journey towards the so called entertainment center."

"I am sure it is nothing, but the meter is flashing red as I get to this area. Are you sure you have not had reception trouble?"

"No, perfect. The cable people checked the line a few weeks ago," he lied, "and said it was good. Real good."

"That's strange because I keep getting the red flashes."

"Maybe it is something from the apartment above."

"Good idea. I guess I will have to check them next Mind if I sit down and think about this?"

"Great. Sit here." He pushed a few toy cars off the seat and pulled out the chair.

"Feels good. I don't do well with this heat. What did I do with my water? It is the good stuff Poland Springs. Want some?"

"Sure, my mouth is dry. Never had Poland water. Where is it from?"

"Poland I guess, but then it could be from the city supply put into fancy bottles but I like it."

"This is the best water I have ever tasted. Thanks for giving me some. On my salary, I don't usually buy special water."

"What kind of work do you do?"

"I don't have a job, but I am looking. I have a friend that promised to get me a job at the gas station. So I am going there tomorrow. I hope it works out since I will lose my welfare soon. They have a new rule about single men living with girlfriends. They want me to get a job."

"It must be tough, not getting a paycheck. I have been working since I was 17. Now I am up for a promotion to supervisor of circuits and cable lines."

"What is the difference between cable lines and the other thing you said"

"Well, cable lines have a special framus in them that sends out a signal back to the cable company. That is how the meter people can track the sets and sometimes pick up the lines that are illegal."

"Illegal? What do you mean? Porno stuff?"

"No people who tap into the lines. That is serious stuff." Now Dirk knew what was going on but he was not sure how to use this information. So he went back to his fishing and baiting approach.

"So you spend a lot of time looking for work or staying at home."

"No I can't stay home, the kids are too noisy. They can get on your nerves if you are here too long. Besides only one is mine so I feel funny being with the other two. Them not being mine and all."

"What do you mean? I bet they are cute kids."

"Well they are cute but I get a little edgy, not having a job and getting short time with the welfare people. I want to get a job and get this place fixed up and get on a new page. You know what I mean?"

"So how did you meet your girl friend? What is her name?"

"Shana. She should be back soon. We met at church. My grand mom always took us to church on Sundays. So I continue to go even though she passed a few years ago. They have some cool music at our church. The lead singer sounds just like Tina Turner. Can't say anything if her legs are as good as Tina's since she wears a long purple gown. But she has the pipes and the moves. Real nice."

"So you met at church?"

"Yeah. We were walking out of the Sunday service and I bumped into her. She has the nicest smile. A few months later I moved in here and then all of a sudden she got pregnant. I don't use a condom but she said she was safe. I trusted her. Mistakes happen, you know. She is allowed to make a mistake, you know?"

"So what did she say when she found out she was pregnant."

"You should have heard the words that came out of her sweet mouth. Not the kind of things you hear in church. She was upset and blamed me, of course. She said she was safe so I fired away. And now it is my fault. Anyhow to say she was upset does not get the picture on the screen. She still does a lot of screaming at me, at the kids, at anything that moves. She can put on a good face, at church, when the case worker comes here to check us. Don't get me wrong, she is a good mother when she is not screaming."

"How do you handle the screaming?"

"Well, I used to get screaming back at her, but that did not work. So now I walk away. Sometimes she keeps up the noise, even when I am not in the room. When she gets the steam out, she is back to her old self. And then the make-up fuck. They are the best. It is almost better to let her get mad when there is a payoff like we have most of the time. It will be good for a few weeks and then the tension builds up and away we go again."

"It must be hard to live like that, with all the changes in personality."

"I get used to it. Part of why I stay is to watch my kid, Tamir. And the other part is that I have not found another place to go.

"Oh, my, it is getting late. I think I have almost found the problem but I need some more time. Is it OK to come back tomorrow?"

"Why not? I usually sleep late but Shana gets up early with the kids."

"Good, I will see you tomorrow."

Dirk Adman smiled as he packed up his meters and tool box and left the house. He felt that he really got a good start on the investigation. Taking out his cell phone from his pocket, he called his report to the dictation service at the hospital.

"It seems that Shana is not the saint that she appeared to be in the interviews at the hospital. That is the reason I am making home visits," he mused. "Catch them off guard and not on the party manners. Allen was talking a lot but still nervous about my being there. He tried to divert the discussion to Shana. I appeared to take the bait but I remain suspicious. I cut off the discussion with the hope that Shana will be there tomorrow so I can get her alone. Since Allen sleeps late, I will get there early. It is also a stressful time trying to get the kids ready for the day. Maybe she will talk."

The next day.

"May I come in? I am from the electrics; I was here yesterday to check the voltage and lines. Did Allen tell you that I was here?"

"Yes, he did. This is not the best time as the kids are just getting up. But you are here, so come in."

"Cute kids, how old are they?"

"Six, 18 and 30 months. The middle one broke his leg so he has a cast. Otherwise, he would be chasing around more than he does."

"I will stay out of your way, just checking the voltages. Look Sam, see the light blink."

"His name is Sam-ear", she emphasized the second syllable.

"OK Samir, see the blinking light. No, you cannot have it. It is not a toy."

After keeping busy for about 15 minutes with his bogus searching, Dirk stopped to watch Shana ride herd on her kids. She got the two older ones to sit down in their chairs and the baby was placed in the high chair. Pop tarts were given to two older ones and she put on the TV so they would be quiet as she tried to clean up the room and straighten out the kids' bedroom. A bottle sat in front of Tamir. Not much free space when there were five people in a very small two bedroom apartment. Alan, as promised, was asleep in the other bedroom. Shana wore low cut jeans and a silver halter top. Her naval ring indicated that three kids were not going to turn her into a matronly mother. Her slim waist belied the fact that she had three kids in three years."

"Here, let me help you feed the little one. His name is Tom?"

"No Ta-MIR."

"Sorry, what is he drinking today?"

"Formula from the WIC program. The WICs give us free formula so our kids get a good start in eating good food. He is a good eater. Thanks for the help. This is a busy time.

"I don't know how you do it. Three kids, you must be 18 or 19."

"No she smiled. I am 23. I guess I have not lost my looks. "

"I guess not. How do you handle all this?" It must be hard, a real responsibility."

"I do the best I can. I got myself into this mess so I have to do the best I can. Some days it gets to me. If I had someone to help me, it would be better. My mom is no help. She has her own problems. With drinking and some crack now and then. Actually I would not trust her with my kids. And my sister has her own pack of kids so I have to do it alone."

"That must be hard," he repeated.

"You should only know the truth. They can get to me. Do you have any kids?

"Two."

"Then you know what I mean. It is a lot of work."

"I will second that. But how do you do it? The kids look so good and they seem to be well behaved."

"That is just because you are here. They must like that red flasher thing. Yes, they are good most of the time but they do get on your nerves sometimes."

"What do you do then?"

"Sometimes I yell and sometimes I scream."

"Does that help?"

"No but it gets some tension out of my system. I know yelling is wrong but I cannot help myself. It kind of gets to me."

"What about Allen? Does he help?"

"Allen, the sleeping king. He will watch out for Tamir, that is his kid. But not the other two."

"Do you get support from the other fathers?"

"How do you spell support? I have to go to court to get something out of those bums. I was good enough for them when they were looking for some good ass but when I got pregnant, they did not know my name. Now I am more than careful. But it took me three strikes to get the message. I know the people at the clinic told me about birth controls but I did not like the idea. My church is against birth control but they do not have to care for the kids like I have to. I thought I was hot stuff with having a kid. I held out longer than most of my friends. Back then, I was having trouble with my mom so I figured a baby would solve my problems."

"Did it help?"

"It seemed to help at first when the baby was small. All I had to do was fed her and change the diaper. But when she started to crawl and get into things, it was all work and no fun no more. Then I met Junior. He is from my school. What a sweet talker he was. I was in bed before I knew it and bam another baby coming. I felt good when I was pregnant so I did not complain but when the baby came. It was different. They say that two kids are more than one plus one. I did not know what that meant until I had two. It is more like one plus one is ten. Junior is in jail now; they caught him stealing from the dollar store on Maple Street. He had a record so they but him in jail."

"How often do I have to burp Tamir? He is almost half way through the bottle."

"Now is a good time. Hold your ears because he is a good burper."

"You must be organized to get all three kids fed and washed and what ever you have to do."

"I guess you can say I am organized. At least most of the time. It helps that Aziza is going to day care at the center. That gives me a break."

"So what do you do with your spare time?" He asked with enough of a twinkle in his voice to let her know he was not serious.

"Right, lots of spare time." I wish I had more time to read books to them and even read some books for myself. I want to get my GED, I plan to go to community and study nursing. I always wanted to be a nurse."

"Maybe someday. So how did Sam, I mean Samir, break his leg?"

"I wish I knew."

"What happened?"

"I was home with the kids. After lunch, Allen said he would watch them so I could go to the store. I got back about 3PM and sat down for a few minutes after I unpacked the grocery bags. Food stamps are a great help to me. Allen took off so I waited for the kids to wake up from their nap. Praised be the naps! Amen. Samir was in the crib. Aziza got out of bed by herself and was running around. I got Tamir up and changed his diaper. Then Samir was crying a lot so I went over to him. He would not stand up. So I knew something was wrong. I wanted to call 911 but there would be no one to take care of the kids if I went to the hospital with Samir. I had to wait for that bum Allen."

"Why do you call him a bum?"

"Because he is. He sleeps late, goes out to look for a job, right! He goes out and probably chases a few girls at the corner where they all meet. Then he comes home and wants to get me in bed for a quickie before dinner. That is impossible with all these kids but I must admit it is tempting at times. I don't know why I am telling you all this, I hardly know you. What are you doing here anyhow?"

"So how do you think Samir broke his leg? Allen is the only adult here. Do you think he would do this?"

"I am sure he would not hurt Tamir and probably not Samir. He gets a little edgy when the kids cry too much. I was away so I don't know if they were crying a lot while I was gone. But maybe it was Aziza, she is very jealous."

"How could a three year old do this?"

"I saw her pull his leg, when he slips it through the slats in the crib. Maybe she did that. I don't know, I just don't know." Hey, I have a lot to do. You know talking to you makes me feel better but I have to get back the kids before I get so far behind that I will be lost for the rest of the day."

"You're right. I may get fired if I don't get this done. I will be only a few minutes more."

Dirk continues the technical charade for a few minutes and then announces that he has found and fixed the problem. "There should be no more problems with the voltage but will have to have the cable people come and check the line as I am getting some weird readings."

• • •

Note to file:

"Visited today with Shana. She is trying to be a good mother and when I was there, she seemed capable of caring for the three kids for most of the time. I can see how she can get overwhelmed when she is stressed with all three kids hitting peak energy and demands at supper time when the kids are running on fumes and hungry- a set up for loss of control. She seems desperate for someone to be a friend and helper. My gut feeling is she is not the culprit.

She did mention the oldest child is still jealous of her sibs. It is possible that she hit the leg while it was sticking out of the crib. That may be a diversion by a crafty lady who wanted to get off the spotlight of possible perps. Just a thought.

Because the visit did not produce any new information, I think we need to convene the committee and then hold a hearing with Shana and Allen."

FALL

We have various images of ourselves- the one that others see, the one that we think is our image which we confirm by looking into curving mirror at the fair grounds and the real one.

S. Black

Chapter 11

Carter was back in the OR to operate on a patient who had a lacerated spleen after an auto accident. This was a routine splenectomy case but he had the usual pre-op jitters. As usual, he began with a prayer then he turned to the team, moved to the OR table and began the deep breathing exercises. That is what he called the last check to see if the patient was identified, the blood type rechecked and all the permission papers were signed. Even though the recent literature indicated that close observation instead of splenectomy was an appropriate management plan, he elected to go ahead with the surgery since 'in his experience' it is the best approach. He did not need that fancy new evidence based research; "in my experience" was enough of a decision maker. The resident had scrubbed the abdomen and directed the proper placement of the clear plastic sheeting on the skin and then covered the abdomen with green drapes.

"Let's go" The scrub nurse standing over the instrument tray gently but firmly slapped the scalpel handle into Carter's palm. The resident stood by with an electric cautery to burn the edges of small vessels in the fat under the skin. The other assistant held suture material to tie off the larger vessels. "Let's review this case. Where is the extern? I want the extern at my right side, next to the anesthesiologist. Tell me his story, son."

"This is a 7 year old who was in a car accident this morning. He was taken to the Emergency in shock, pale, rapid pulse and BP 70/30. His signs returned to normal range after two liters of fluids. They tapped his belly and found blood. An MRI with contrast showed a small blush of contrast, indicating bleeding."

"Is that why he is here in the OR?"

"Yes. Can I ask a question?"

"I am the one who asks the questions........ Just kidding. Go ahead son."

"I read that the blush is not an indication for surgery. In Pittsburgh, they reported that hemodynamic stability is an important factor. His BP and pulse are back to normal range after fluids."

"Pittsburgh is the home of the Steelers. Would you believe anyone who supports that team?"

"I am from Johnstown; I have always been a Steelers fan."

"Listen son, if you want to pass this course, you must change to Giant Blue. How loyal are you?"

"I am applying for law school when the operation is over."

"I like your spunk. In my day we would never talk to the chief like that. If I had said that to old Dr. Montague, I would be hamburger on the floor. See how modern I am. You are still alive and I am not screaming …..yet"

Peter Bird, the senior surgical resident assisting on this operation, watched this interchange with some fear. The student was right and the boss was wrong. He was about 15 years out of the loop of modern surgery. There was no evidence that this young lad needed an operation but he was not one to challenge the chief. He had to complete this year and he would be gone from the training program. The future jobs and passing the surgical boards were ahead of him. He needed a good letter from his chief to take the exams and get interviews at the best children's hospitals. He decided it was best to keep his mouth shut and keep store the surgical literature in his brain for future use. Fortunately, the spleen will be sent to pathology where the pathologist will examine the tissue. Then the case will be presented at a surgical pathology conference where, no doubt the question of surgery versus observation will be discussed. Depending who attends the conference, there could be some interesting exchanges between those who would not have removed the spleen and Carter. Unless he can make a good case for defending surgery, he may be exposed for not keeping up to date. Carter was born with an extra large ego and ability to argue effectively in an unrehearsed dialogue, so he might convince the group that he made the right choice. Right now, Peter Bird had to help his boss with this case.

The first phase of the operation consisted of repetitious cutting through the skin, muscle and fat prior to getting into the abdomen. When a vessel was isolated, the surgeon clamped down on the bleeder, the assistant would pass a suture behind the clamp and tie a knot. At the command of cut, the student would cut the excess suture.

"Too long," bellowed Carter, seeing the excess suture material.

"Sorry."

The next bleeding point was identified. The edges clamped. The student cut the excess suture.

"Too short." The suture end was dangerously close to the knot, potentially allowing the knot to loosen and massive bleeding to occur."

"Sorry."

When the student was ready to cut the next suture, he asked "Do you want me to cut this too long or too short?"

"Your choice."

By now tissue snipping and ligating the bleeders continued until the incision was complete and the abdominal cavity was ready for opening. Before getting to the spleen, the rest of the abdominal contents were examined to see if there were additional injuries. The spleen, situated in the left upper quadrant, was bruised and a dark clot in the middle. No active bleeding was found. The tension eased so Carter went back to the teacher mode.

"Did this lad have a seat belt?"

"He did have a seat belt."

"Did you see the article in the New York Times that seat belts did not save lives? These guys reviewed many years of reports and showed that seat belts were not protective." This bit of iconoclasm suited Carter's libertarian bent, as it supported the individual making choices without government influence.

"We discussed that article in our Evidence based Medicine course. It had so many problems with selection of cases that it was next to worthless."

"What do you mean?"

"For starters, they selected only cases where there was a death. They did not include those accidents where proper booster seat and shoulder restraints were used, thus preventing deaths. Our instructor was livid that such an article could be published, giving people an excuse not to use seat belts plus booster seat and shoulder restraints."

Carter was wise enough to stop his bravado review of the New York Times and listen. "I feel the same way as your instructor. I don't know how the paper got published. You would think they would have the article reviewed."

"They were so busy playing with the numbers that their data is misleading."

"Data is misleading?"

"Yes, sir"

"Tell me son, in you education, did you take Latin?"

"In sixth grade for 5 months."

"Did you learn about singular and plural nouns?"

"I may have."

"Did you learn datum is singular and data is plural?"

"I am sure I did."

"Well data is the plural form so you say data are, not data is."

"I kind of remember that but on the news they usually say data is disturbing or data contradicts the findings."

"Do you think those news readers took Latin"

"I don't know but it seems to be common usage. And common usages allow us to use what was formerly incorrect."

"Not in my OR."

"So let's finish the case and go on to save other lives. You were so good today, I will let you sew up the skin and I will cut the sutures either too long or too short. Your call."

"Sounds good."

Carter Randolf III left the operating room, put on his overly starched white coat and headed for the parent's lounge. No one could figure out how Carter's jacket never wrinkled. Others developed creases as they were worn, but not Carter's jacket. He found Mr. and Mrs. Pepper sitting near the television set, watching the news program on CNN. They stood up when they saw the white coat enter the room. They recognized Dr. Randolf from the brief discussion they had with him prior to the surgery.

"Dr. Randolf, how is he?"

"He is doing fine. Just fine. We had a beaten up spleen from the accident and now it is out and will not bleed anymore. Thank the Lord. The operation went well and after a few days of watching him recover, he should do just dandy. We have to keep him hydrated with intravenous fluids, watch his temperature as a sign of infection and wait for his bowel to restart its work. When we go into the belly, the bowel gets pushed around and it is temporarily paralyzed, so in a few days and we should get him back to normal bowel function. Right now, we pray for gas, intestinal gas that is. Speaking of praying, would you mind if we pray for your son?"

"Sure"

Carter Randolph got down on his knees and closed his eyes. "Thank you Jesus for looking after this young man and helping him get through this operation. We pray for his recovery and good health. Amen."

"Amen."

"Do you have any questions?"

"When can we see him?"

"He will go to the recovery room and then to the intensive care unit on this floor." His nurse will call you when he is ready. It should be in about 45 minutes to an hour. Dr. Bird, my assistant will be around to speak with you. I have to get to my own doctor for an appointment. I will see you tomorrow. I am off the TV station."

"What a wonderful man. Did you see how he prayed? A real saint."

Carter has a date with the local TV station to do a public service piece about male sterilization He was   adding his crusade for limiting family size for married couples and his abstinence stance for teenagers to his anti-abortion campaign. His new attempt at humor produced this response to critics of the abstinence approach. "Just say no, it's easy. My wife says it all the time."

Privately, Carter was aware that he was entering the twilight of his career but one would never see it in his public image. He took the lead from the Republican party when it came to family planning and teen sex. Abstinence, just say no and the sanctity of marriage were his approach to teen age hormones. "I feel that large families that could not be financially or emotionally supported could bring on social problems" he frequently told his group of supporters. "I have personalized this feeling by now advocating vasectomies for men who did not want to have more children, such as myself." Loving publicity, he became the poster man for voluntary vasectomies by having his operation widely publicized. He had the cameras follow him to the Day Surgery Unit, then he held post op interviews. Showing uncharacteristic modesty, he did not have the camera in the procedure room. Now he was at the urologist's office to televise his follow up visit to see if the vasectomy did indeed block sperm cells. Consistent with his modesty about private matters, he did not plan to have the production of the specimen televised. His wife refused to be part of this publicity, afraid that she might slip and say that there was no need for him to go through the operation as far as she was concerned since they had separate bedrooms and had not participated in any sex acts for several years. His call, not hers.

• • •

"Do I need makeup for this shoot?" Carter Randolf asked the producer of the vasectomy series.

"I think you could use a little powder on your nose. Other than that, you look just fine" replied Candy Mandelo.

"What is the plan for today?"

"We want to get the point across without all the gory details today. So we will show you going into the urologist and then having a discussion with him on the minimal side effects of your procedure. He will also ask you about side effects, pain, swelling, you know the usual post op problems. And then you will get the silver clip pin to signify that you have been successfully clipped."

"And sterile. You know we surgeons are always worried about sterility."

"You have to talk to your doctor about that. Are you ready for the cameras?"

"I never refused an opportunity for good publicity. The public ha a right to know. Let's go."

This was a simple shoot. He walks through the office door. Stops at the reception desk and is ushered into the consultation room."

"How are we today?" asked Harold Shifflerson, the urologist."

"I am doing just great, just great."

"Did you have any problems since the procedure?"

"No, the usual redness and swelling but nothing that a few ibuprofens and a little Talisker single malt could not cure."

"Cut! Remember Doctor, this is going out to the public and we don't want to offend those who do not approve of single malt Scotch, or alcohol of any kind. We will erase the voice."

"No the usual redness and swelling but nothing that a few ibuprofen could not cure. I feel fine."

"Well. Things look great." That was not the truth as the doctor had no time to get the results of the test but since the TV crew was in a rush. This was a bit of acting.

"I think they want you to be careful for a little longer. But you are almost sterile is what I think they say. In three months you can hang out the all clear flag to be sure that your system is clear of sperm cells."

"Great. I think this is such a minor procedure; I encourage others who were thinking about having a vasectomy, to speak to their doctor and not be afraid of the operation. It is a breeze to go through. Thanks for all you have done."

"This concludes the vasectomy story. Dr. Carter Randolf III, chief of surgery from CHUC has volunteered to share his experience with our viewers to show that vasectomy is both a brief and safe procedure. It is one of our series on family planning and birth control presented by WLBB, your station to watch for medical news."

"Did you have to mention birth control? I don't like that term associated with my name. But then again it is not that kind of birth control that I am against. So I guess it is OK."

"Sorry Dr. Randolf, I did not know of your sensitivity. We can erase the voice in the part and do a voice over about the procedure. OK"

"I don't want kids going around having sex before they were married. Abstinence is the answer!"

"Wonderful and thanks again for participating in this public service program. I think a lot of people will follow your advice. We need more doctors like you who do not just talk about solutions to our problems. They participate. Great! And thanks"

• • •

Karl Strem calls the monthly meeting of the house staff to order. "Welcome. Let's get started. We have a few things to cover. A new program, records to be dictated and a report from Mr. Grimely. Let's go in reverse order.

From E. Grimely
To House staff
Re: Elevator button survey.

We are pleased to announce that the committee has been formed and has begun its survey. We have an incidence of double button pressing of 15%, on average. The areas surveyed were the main entrance elevators, the staff elevators in the patient wing and the emergency wing elevators. There is a trend that in the evening there is 45% more double button pushing than in the morning. The location does not seem to be a factor. We are now doing a cost analysis of what this double button pushing does to the hospital bottom line.

We will begin an education program after we get this data and then benchmark the changes that training will do to decrease this bothersome activity.

The parking situation has changed. Now residents whose names start with A-M will park in lot 33. Those whose names start with N-Z will park in lot 47. Please check with Ann Ranier for new parking stickers.

EG:bw

"OK…….. Mr. Grimely rocks!!! Now to the new program for the first year residents. We will begin a rotation in pediatric surgery. This will be a trial to see if participating on the surgical service will add to your education. A hands on experience. The planning committee has worked on this program for about 4 months and has come up with an exciting experience that hopefully will add to your knowledge and awareness of pediatric surgical problems. We put all the names in a hat and selected the first person to begin this rotation next month. I am happy to announce that Adrianne Cunningham won the honor. Let's hear it for Adrienne!"

"Shit! I don't like surgery and don't want to be part of that life. Early rounds. Late sign out. Long hours in the OR. Not for me," muttered Adrienne.

"Don't worry, it will work out. They try this every 5 years and maybe someday it will succeed. After the meeting, lets talk and I will give you a few hints." Lester whispered back. "I know how to beat all the problems."

"Report from the record room regarding unfinished charts. Seems like Jeff Marion has the title of most undictated charts. After a few months off the list, probably because he was on specialty services, he has returned to clinical medicine and now will be on our watch list. This year the administration has instituted a new policy as we are being evaluated by JACHO. The new plan is those with more than 10 undictated charts will be suspended from duty without pay and will have suspension removed when charts are dictated. Those with more than 20 charts will lose vacation days. I know that this is tough but we don't want the hospital to lose accreditation because of our failure to dictate. So get to the record room. Jeff, I know you need the money so you can't afford to lose your pay."

"That is a bummer" sighed Jeff. "I have tried bribery, candy and promises of unrestrained sex but I can't get the record room ladies to lose the charts that are in my undictated box. I guess I will have to get down there. Have they moved the dictation room since last year?"

"Finally, we have a ball game on Thursday night. Please let Eva Masters know if you are will show up for the game. We play shipping and receiving, they are tough."

Felix was not at the meeting so Beth Conover was free from his lustful advances. Lester caught up with Adrienne to give her advice about surgery. "Let's go over to the coffee shop and I will help you make the most of that month. It will not be too bad but there is so much down time standing in the OR that I want to tell you what helped me in medical school."

"Anything. One of the reasons I went into Pediatrics was to avoid the OR. So much ritual and so much to do with surgical personalities and one upmanship. Tell me anything. I won't listen to Karl who told us not to follow you and your example of not dictating charts."

"Oh him. I have a whole file on him. One more public embarrassment and I will release all the information about Karl and how he took extra sugars in the cafeteria and he did not wash his hands after he left the men's room on more than one occasion. No one is safe from my revenge. You know the movie. Revenge of the Nerds. That is my bible."

"So how do I cope with the operating room?"

"Do you now how to dance?"

"You ask a black girl if she knows how to dance. I was the double Dutch rope jumping champ when I was 8, I won the IceT karaoke contest in high school. My cousin was a Florida State cheer leader and you want to know if I know how to dance. Rest assured, brother, I can dance."

"How about the OR," Macarena?

"The Oar-Mac what?"

"Macarena. You know the pat, pat down to the butt and turn, Macarena. And adapt it to the operating room."

"Oh that – sure I know how to do that," Adrienne begins to clap her hands on her hips.

"Well here is how it goes—you know you have to wear sterile gowns in the OR."

"Right."

"Well, in their rituals, they have rules about breaking sterile conditions. If you are next to the drape that divides the surgical team from the anesthesiologist, and your elbow happens to lean on the drape, the OR nurse in charge of sterile conditions will call a foul on you and you have to go outside and change gowns after scrubbing for 2 minutes. I am not sure why you have to wash your hands when your elbow crossed over the divide. But that is the rule. If you have broken sterile technique with the elbow and then touch your gown over your abdomen, you have to leave but the scrub is now 5 minutes. If you move your elbow over the line, touch your gown over your abdomen and then touch the mask over your nose and mouth, you have to go out and scrub for 15 minutes. Are you seeing the steps of the OR Macarena?"

"I think I get it. Elbow, elbow, belly, mouth. Walk, walk, walk, scrub, scrub. I like it."

"That is the basic step but if the Sterility Nurse does not see your first elbow. You have to subtly repeat the elbow motion until she starts the music. The first time just do the elbow part. Go out and come back. The Sterility nurse will be watching you like a hawk. I think she was trained by the KGB. Then you can do the rest of the sequence. It is natural for someone who makes a mistake to hold their hands on their abdomen or even reflexly cover their mouth as in 'my word, what did I do?' I recommend starting the dance after the best part of the operation is over. That way you can get out of the OR early. They won't mind since when you are gone, they can tell their dirty jokes. You might inhibit them until they get to know you better."

"I like that dance. Where did you learn it?"

"I made it up. In medical school, I hated surgery and they hated me for I was always late and they could tell that I did not want to be a surgeon. I was in the OR in a cardiac case. The boss surgeon always had the medical student crammed between him and the drape that separated the operating field from the anesthesia workplace. That way he could always know where I was and kept me from getting in his way. By accident, I rested my elbow on the drape. That was the start of the expulsion from the OR. They rest of the moves were trial and error. When the Macarena became popular, I said, "hey that looks like me in the OR!" It is not 100 % because you may not get the right spot at the OR table or the nurse may miss your indiscretion. If that is the case, you can cough and cover your mouth. No dance then, hit the mask and you are out, out, out."

"What else?"

"Oral war."

"Does that mean I bite the chief resident?"

"No, not that. You know how the surgeons make rounds. Stop at the bedside. Say less than 30 words about the patient, ask them "how are we doing?" and move on. Well, start to tell all you know about the patient. How the night went. List a few physical findings, especially what was normal. What the labs were and what new tests you want to order, especially non-essential ones. You then explain that you ordered the test just to see how things are going or as a baseline test. Talk for at least 2 minutes. They will go berserk and will maneuver you out of presenting the case so when you don't show up for all rounds, they will be relieved and not think badly of you."

"You have this down to a slacker's science."

"You are looking at a member of the slacker hall of fame, a charter member. By the way do you play bridge? I am looking for another bridge game."

"I don't play bridge but when I get better adjusted to this place, maybe you can teach me."

"Sounds good but I am not the best teacher as I am impatient. Let me know how your dance routine is working. You will have an experience especially when working with the chief of surgery. Saint Carter, the evangelical."

Carter Randolf III was sitting in his office continuing to think about what he could do to boost his ego and image as he was feeling the pressures of the aging surgeon in an increasingly technical specialty. His mind wandered across many topics. New imaging tests were taking the mystery out of clinical medicine. In the old days, he could put his hand on a patient, claim to feel some mass and then go to the OR to see what it was. Today, MRI, CT or ultrasound helped make the diagnosis and demonstrate the size of the mass, if one were there. The computer could play with the images by rotating the lesion and then show the vessels that brought blood into the mass. Guess work went out when MRI's came in. Then laparoscopic techniques reduced the OR time and size of the scars. Unfortunately, Carter could not master the laparoscopic moves of looking, not at the patient, but at the TV console while moving the instruments; likewise he could not master videogames in the children's wards. Robotic surgery, the latest challenge to his skills, is now becoming standard treatment for some of his favorite operations; he was just too old to learn that system. He liked the old way when you looked directly at what you were doing while the assistants held retractors that kept the incision open wide enough to see what you were cutting out. And the antibiotics were hard to keep up with. There seems to be a new cephalosporin each month. Fortunately, the young ones knew the names so he would allow them to direct the therapy when there was an infection; it went against his macho persona to get an infectious disease consult. After all the surgeons were the complete docs, they saw, they diagnosed, they cut. Not like the pediatricians, who saw, diagnosed and referred to a surgeon to take over the case to fix the problem. But if he retired, what would he do without the OR and the locker room chatter?

Fortunately, he had his societies. Council of Pediatric Surgeons, International Society of Pediatric Surgeons, Association of Academic Pediatric Surgeons and the Academy of Pediatrics Section on Surgery. Since the number of pediatric surgeons was relatively small, there was a good chance that the members could be president of at least 2 or 3 of them during their active career. He was already president of two of the groups. But the young people were taking over the leadership roles.

The first Carter was the son of a furniture maker who came to the US from Germany to work in a factory in Rhode Island. His son Carter Jr., followed his father in the factory and raised his family in the same Rhode Island town until the factory closed. He left the East and moved to Montana where he bought some land and raised cattle. He had a daughter and two sons who did not continue the Carter name. However, his son married a girl from Virginia whom he met at University of Washington so they stayed in Seattle where they were both school teachers. Tradition was important to her so when she had a son, she named him Carter III, sounded so old family. Carter III was a bright young man who did well in school and played football until he hurt his knee. This allowed him more time to study so he got an academic scholarship to Johns Hopkins where he majored in biology, graduated with honors and progressed to Johns Hopkins School of Medicine. Having two last names with the trailing III fit into the old school image as many of his classmates were juniors, III or even IV. He continued on at Hopkins for his surgical training. He loved the surgical life, the bravado, the locker room humor and the unmerciful sarcasm. At that time the residents were on call 7 days a week, some nights they had first line call and some nights they were backups, allowing them a few hours of time away from the hospital. The total immersion of surgery toughened as well as scarred them so when they progressed along the years of residency, they were able to maintain the sarcasm, the shit trickles down approach to those under them keeping the tradition alive. Hopkins' prestigious surgery and pediatric programs made it an attractive place to do pediatric surgery training. Carter had the famous quote of Sir William Osler, one of the founders of the school, set in needle point and placed behind his desk. "In the physician or surgeon no quality takes rank with imperturbability...coolness and presence of mind under all circumstances, calmness amid storm, clearness of judgment in moments of grave peril."

Although Carter did not think about it when he was in training, the farewell speech that Osler made when he left Hopkins for Oxford was now haunting him. Osler made a pitch for clearing faculty positions from those over 40 so that the young ones could have a chance to be innovative. He also suggested that 60 be a retirement age. Those words were now beginning to catch up to him as he felt he was on the downside of his career but had too much surgical ego to admit that he was no longer the leader of leaders. He had done well at Hopkins, then left for a stint at London's major children's hospital on Great Ormond Street where he worked with Mr. D.I. Williams in pediatric urology. It was there where he learned about 'shedules', firms, and operating theaters. Although he was only there for 6 months, he made it sound like it was 6 years as the experience was so frequently quoted, no matter what the topic. He was never allowed to refer to nurses as 'sisters' as they were called in England-sounded too familiar and degrading for the modern U.S. nurse. So he returned with an English hair style, long on the sides and combed across the top of the ear, a penchant for afternoon tea and referral to a PRO-cess. He had arrived. He was Carter Randolf III but was really the first edition.

He began to think about his legacy. At a recent funeral, one of the speakers mentioned that the books that the deceased had at his night table next to his bed. So Carter, worried that one of the people giving the eulogy at his funeral would use the same technique, went to Amazon and ordered a series of books, Shakespeare, Will Durant's History of the Roman Empire. James Joyce's Ulysses and Michael Lewis's Money Ball about the Oakland A's use of statistics in making baseball decisions. This would work as long as they did not take finger prints on the inside pages. To insure he had a good list, he hired an English professor to review the book titles and then added Walter Issacson's biography of Benjamin Franklin.

His musings continued. "Maybe it would be better to step down before I get exposed. I am getting close to the 60 mark that Osler talked about. Not usually a fan of the left, but I am glad that those do-good liberals fought forced age based retirement in the name of age discrimination. I was never a quitter but I have to be realistic. Maybe I can cash in on some of my contacts, start an Institute of Surgical something or other. Ethics of surgery sounds like a good idea. It is really true that surgery at my level is a young man's game. What to do? What to do? Institute of what? Maybe medical history, maybe I will write a history of surgery. I think it has been done and I cannot write well. But that is why they have ghost writers. No, I like the institute pathway. More travel and more write-offs. If I had not battled Beardsley so much, maybe I could be appointed vice-president of the hospital. I am good at fund raising and working with the board. I think it is time to build a legacy before I retire. Maybe, I will have a reunion of all the surgeons that I trained. Maybe they will start a foundation or endow a chair in my name. Maybe….."

If he were truthful, it would be the adulation of the patients that he would most miss most. The musing was interrupted by his secretary," Time to head to the airport for your trip." Carter was off to Cancun for the 3 day meeting of the Central American Society of Pediatric Surgery.

•••

The hotel was lavish; the weather perfect, but despite drinking bottled water, he developed a bad case of turista, not at the hotel but on the plane coming back from Mexico. Fortunately he had a seat near the toilet facilities which he used about every 25 minutes. Despite filling up with water, juice and Coca Cola, he was weak and tired when he got home so he went immediately to bed. About an hour after he fell asleep, the phone rang. It was Peter Bird, his resident.

"Sorry to bother you sir, I know you just got back from your trip. I hope it went well."

"Thanks for the welcome, Peter. I am sick as a hungry squirrel with a tooth abscess. Did something happen to the department while I was gone?"

"Not that bad, sir. I know you are not on call but Enzo Romanesco, the local mafia boss is at the hospital with his grandson, Ernest Romanesco, who has abdominal pain."

"Sorry to hear about that but why the call?"

"It is a classic appy deal. We verified it with an abdominal CT. I went to see Mr. Romanesco and told him that this was most likely an acute appendicitis. I told him it was a serious problem, but easily fixed with surgery, as long as we got right to it."

Mr. Romanesco, in the most polite manner, suggested that I call you and have you come immediately to the hospital. This is what he said. "You tell this Dr. Carter that I would appreciate his attendance and added that it would be quite profitable for the hospital to have Dr. Randolf be present in the operating room and, depending on the outcome of the surgery, every one would be taken care of. You know what I mean?"

"I told him Excuse me, for a minute. I will call Dr. Randolf and tell him. I told Mr. Romanesco that we want to get things rolling as you can't tell when the appendix will burst, sending pus through his abdomen. That is a real problem that requires a long hospital stay and many doses of antibiotics. We have to get moving."

After hearing Peter's version of the story, Carter told him, "I have been hit with the turista. I have been in the head every 20-30 minutes and finally fell asleep. I am in no shape to operate and could even do harm, no way can I get to the OR."

"I understand but I will have to get you here some even if you don't do the surgery. After all, many a medical student or navy corpsman has performed an appendectomy. I can poke the laparoscope into his belly and it will be done in minutes. Then you can go home.

Carter cringed when he heard "laparoscope."

"Glad to have you on my team, old man. Did I ever tell you, Peter, how much I appreciate your help? Especially when I am as sick as I am."

After 8 years of surgical training, Peter knew that he could handle the case. The pressure of having a mafia boss looking over his shoulder frightened him.

When Peter told him "Mr. Romanesco had promised a major donation for the surgery department, Carter replied. "That gives me new energy; I am feeling better already."

Peter put his phone down and went to the cubicle where Ernest was resting quietly now. "Fortunately today, Mr. Romanesco we do the operation with a laparoscope that, when successful, speeds up the recovery time as we do not have to cut through the abdominal muscles. I have talked to Dr. Carter who agrees with the plan. He has just returned from a trip abroad so he told me to go ahead and get started. We better get the appendix out before it causes more trouble. When Dr. Carter arrives, we will have your grandson prepped; time is important so I will take him to the OR now. Is that agreeable?"

"I like your style doctor. I wish more people in my organization were like you. Thinking ahead, using your head. You are a good man."

Peter called Dr. Randolf back. "We are ready to go. I am sending an ambulance and a resident to your house with an i.v. to hydrate you with some sugar and saline infusions so at least you will not faint from de-hydration when you meet the Romanesco family."

"I don't think I will need that but if they are already on the way to get me, OK. I am not sure I would trust myself driving into the hospital."

In about 15 minutes, the ambulance arrived. Randolf was in no shape to argue with the transport team. He did not like being strapped down but went along with the rules. Safe in the ambulance, he felt bet-ter as the IV fluids ran into his system. "At least, I will be able to stand erect when I get to the hospital to discuss the surgery with the family. After all, if things do not go well, I will be wearing cement shoes when they toss me into the lake outside of town, I can say I was present for the surgery. Hopefully the hospital will have a new surgical endowment instead of a water logged dead surgeon."

The transport team laughed respectfully.

The plan worked out well. Carter, still looking a little green, met the family who were quite nice. Enzo Romanesco was soft spoken and gra-cious. It was hard to accept that he was a mob boss with the obvious past history of deeds that were chronicled in the local paper. Carter's only fear was that he would not vomit or pass flatus while standing next to him.

"Thanks a lot for coming in tonight, I hear that you were away and just got back. Where were you?"

"Cancun, Mexico."

"I know where it is, I have some business interests in a hotel there. We did some of the concrete work for several of the new hotels. I hope you did not drink the water."

"Absolutely not, I did not want to get the turista, if you know what I mean. Ha Ha."

"It is hard to avoid, even when you drink bottled water. Sometimes they don't wash the lettuce well."

"Interesting. It is a pleasure to meet you, Mr. Romanesco, Time to fix the young man. It was a pleasure to meet you. Why don't you go to the parents lounge and I will meet you there when we are finished."

"Likewise, I agree." Mr. Romanesco liked the brevity of the conversation.

"This guy really knows what he has to do and gets down to business without a lot of bullshit."

Carter made a bee line for the door as he had one more visit to the men's room before going into the OR. Peter Bird did the case while Carter sat on a chair with an emesis basin. The laparoscopic procedure went well. Peter isolated the appendix, clamped it off and secured it into a plastic bag that he pulled out of one of the puncture sites. As Peter put the red and swollen appendix on a metal basin he added "get your red hot chili peppers!" with that announcement, Carter threw up all over the equipment table. Peter was quick to respond. "Good shot, Dr. Randolf, Fortunately we don't need the instruments any longer. Are you OK?"

"Oops. I never liked chilies before this trip and now surely, they are permanently removed from my menu. I prefer French food." With the mention of food, he threw up again. "Turn up the juice, I am getting dehydrated. I don't want to go into renal failure. I should be home in bed."

Carter and Peter went to the family lounge to meet the parents and grandparents. Before they arrived, Carter messed up his usually perfectly groomed hair, took off his starched white coat and rolled tightly to get some creases in it. He dropped his mask from his face so he looked like Alan Alda in Mash.

Then he pushed open the door to the parents lounge. "Great news, we got the mean appendix out of your grandson. The procedure went well. No complications. We are pleased with the whole result."

"Thanks Doc, how is the little guy?"

"Oh he is fine. We are keeping him in the recovery room until he wakes up and we are sure that his vital signs are stable. "

"Tell me, doc. What exactly does the appendix look like?"

"Well it is about three inches long and swollen because of the inflammation."

"Like a juicy worm?"

"Well more like a red hot chili pepper. Oops excuse me for one minute, nature calls."

Carter ran out of the room and did not make it to the men's room. He bent over and gagged several times. Fortunately it was just nausea this time so there was no need for the clean up crew. "Why in hell did I mention chili? Damn Peter and his food stories." He returned to the waiting room.

Excuse me, Mr. Romanesco. Back to the operation. We had some issues to deal with during the procedure but fortunately, this being a children's hospital, we have a lot of experience because we see so many unusual cases. I would put this case in one of the most difficult ones I have ever operated on. He did well and I expect no problems but we are on alert for any clues that things are not going according to plan."

"I appreciate all you have done, Dr. Carter. I won't forget what you have done to save Ernest's life. Believe me."

"Now to get back and cure some more children. Busy night. Excuse me, must get back to recovery. It would be nice if we had more surgical fellows, but that take funds for support."

"Maybe I could help you with that."

"Let's talk, maybe we can have lunch." Carter learned from the fund raisers that the way you get funds is to ask for them.

On the way back, he finally thanked Peter for all he had done. "I won't forget you."

The next day Mr. Romanesco appeared at the hospital main door with his entourage. The volunteer at the reception desk greeted him and asked him how she could help.

"I want to see my grandson, Ernest Romanesco."

"Then you will have to have a pass. Here is one for you and you get one more. We have to limit visitors to two people at a time." She looked at the four men that came with Mr. Romanesco. Although it was sunny and warm outside, the four men had rain coats draped over their forearms.

She looked at them and the raincoats and asked, "is it going to rain today?"

"Not if we can help it but you never know this time of year."

Romanesco, not wanting to make a scene at the reception desk, told his men "You guys split up and each get a pass for Smith or Jones. There must be a few patients with that name in the hospital."

Enzo relaxed a little when he entered the private room and saw Ernest was sitting up in his bed watching TV with his two private nurses.

"Anything I can get you, Ernest? A pizza? Some peanut butter and jelly?"

The private duty nurse waved her finger, Enzo knew what that meant. "Sorry, Ernest, we have to wait until the nurse says it is OK to eat. I did bring you a few new games for your computer game thing. You like it?"

"Great pop pop. You are the greatest. Every kid should have a pop pop as nice as you. I feel great, just a little sore."

Before he left the room, he took three boxes of doughnuts to the nurses' station, handed out gift certificates to the staff for dinner at his restaurant, Palermoama and left two bottle of champagne for Dr. Randolf. His associate, Bruno surveyed the room and for a few mementoes to slip into his overcoat. He tried to get the electronic thermometer into his coat pocket but stopped when he realized that it was connected to the box on wheels. He did lift a pack of vinyl gloves and two boxes of tissues.

• • •

"Sorry to interrupt, but your wife is on the phone."

"Oh, yes, thank you." Carter returned from his wandering thoughts. "Hey Babe, what's going on? No, I did not forget the dinner," he lied. "7 sharp."

Carrie Randolf was the perfect social wife. She got involved in the cultural life of the city, worked her Southern charm to earn an inside track to several leadership roles on the most important committees such as the opera and modern art museum. People would kill to get on one of them. With all that social climbing, she also took on leadership of various dinners so Carter, even with his begging off because of clinical duties, had at least one dinner a week to attend as the interested and involved spouse. He was bored and annoyed that he did not command the awe and admiration that he had in the OR. After he declared his opinion on a topic and topped it off with "we surgeons would approach the issue in this manner," he got a sense that it did not carry much weight with the audience of law firms managing partners, CEO's of several electronic plants, founders of mutual funds and venture capitalists who were not impressed with this egotistical mouthful. These men, more wealthy and more powerful than Carter did not like sharing the spotlight either.

Carrie had endless energy to the outside world but at home, she was tired and preoccupied to bother with intimate times with Carter. At first this coldness bothered him but he has adjusted over time. Although he was married to surgery, he still lived with Carrie. His pleasure came from cutting, sewing and the camaraderie of surgeons. Her pleasure came from heading committees, seeing a full house at luncheons and sitting at head tables of the important organizations where she could enjoy her power position. She, like Carter, thrived on power trips; in this case, Carter provided the vehicle. Having headed up the most of the local organizations, she is now going national. Her latest target is the National Organizations of Children Hospital's Volunteers, NOCHVOL, the group that is awarding Richardson Beardsley its Executive of the Year Award next spring. She did not care about Richardson's award but it gave her exposure to the board members of NOCHVOL. Meeting the president of the board at the award ceremony did not hurt her campaign either. It did not bother Carrie that no one in South Creek heard of NOCHVOL and even no one cared about its functions outside of the members who, like Carrie, needed a national organization as a new playing field. She would not admit it but traveling to meetings gave her a break from Carter's bullshit.

Carrie arrived early for her meeting of the committee to plan a garden party next fall so she checked her iPhone for any email.

Dear Carrie, Sorry to take so long to answer your email from July. You know your sister- never prompt with anything except for getting to sales at Neimans. I hope things are better with Carter, maybe you were having a bad day. I have plenty of them out here. You should come visit and we can share stories. I don't want to put mine in writing for one never knows when someone may take my computer and look for evidence. I haven't done anything lately that could be incriminating but that may change. I did see someone of interest at the pool this past weekend. Kind of got my juices flowing again, a rare event. I haven't had an affair since Alex and I broke up. I think that fling made me look 5 years younger. Send me a recent photo and I will see if you could use some anti-aging treatment. I know I shouldn't be saying this to you, sis, but a little fling may change your outlook on a lot of issues that seem to be bothering you.

When are you coming to visit? I miss you.
Love
Liz ☺☺☺

• • •

In the medical service suite, Bob Farmer is continuing his afternoon session. Mia, the medical student, is still working with him and starting to get the feel for how a doctor makes a diagnosis by asking good questions and allowing the parents and patients to tell their story. Her head is pounding with the excitement of being a real doctor for an afternoon. Then the phone rings. It is Ralph Trigent, a family doctor from a small town in Union county.

"Hello Bob, How are you? And the family? Keeping busy? Say, I have an interesting case for you. I need your brain for this one. Do you have a minute?"

"Great, tell me about him." Bob Farmer had great relationships with the referring doctors, the source of many interesting cases and unfortunately, many weekend dumps.

"We have an 8 year old boy here who is having trouble in school. Overactive and keeping the noise level up in class. We are working him up for ADHD so I ordered a CT the head. Our machine is down so could you take a look at him and get the study done at your place? I think there is something there; he is not the usual ADHD. Is it OK if I send him over to you? Thanks buddy. I have some more kids that I may be sending to you too. Great cases! Thanks buddy."

Along with Mia, Bob Farmer was in his office with Keith Aaron, the resident who was on general pediatric elective this month. For Keith, this chance to be with Bob Farmer was an honor for he was the best diagnostician from the old school.

As Keith tells the other new residents, "Bob works up a patient in the classic manner. Thorough history, following up clues in the history, being very curious about those aside comments that parents make and doing what pediatricians do, talking to the child as well as the parents. Then, a hands on physical examination following the inspection, palpation, percussion and auscultation sequence. At that point, he might order tests to confirm his diagnosis. He is not like the young docs who zip through the history and physical and then order batteries of blood tests and end up with the choice of scans, MRI or CT with or without contrast. I like the old fashioned way."

Bob hangs up the phone and smiles, "It must be Friday. I always get a phone call like this on Friday. A doc has a case that he has been working on for a few visits and has not come up with an answer. He reaches Friday, the Friday before his vacation, and cannot sit on it for a week so he sends the patient to me for a consult. I bet if I call him back in a few hours, I will get a message that he is away for a week and if this is an emergency, call Dr. X. Anyway, if I see him today, I can use him to teach Mia some physical diagnosis. You stick around; you never know when this guy will send in some interesting patient with an unusual physical finding."

"Why would they order a CT for ADHD?" asked Keith.

"I am not sure but maybe they had time on the schedule. There is a tendency to over use a new test but CT has been around for a long time. So when the family comes in, we can ask them. There must be more to the story. Let's go and see the next patient while we wait for the mystery boy."

Every hospital has or should have an all around physician with enough intelligence and experience to be a master diagnostician and knowledge of treatment options to tackle difficult problems. These skills, combined with a heavy dollop of common sense makes him the go-to-guy when a difficult case comes the hospital or when a demanding family will intimidate those with less confidence. He's the doctor's doctor. Many in the hospital think they are that unique individual and some of them come close to but cannot match Bob Farmer. Bright, unflappable and streetwise, he has slightly rugged features that suggest either a former boxing career or a car accident. His always trim gray and brown hair and conservative outfits add to his image of confident power.

"I wonder where the little boy is that needed to be seen right away. So we have a few minutes to take a break before the transfer patient gets here. Come into my office and we can chat a little or maybe you would like to take off now since I am not sure when they will get here."

Mia declined but welcomed the chance to get off the hot spot of thinking on her feet about medical topics. She started with the questions. "How many patients do you see in a day? Who sends them to you? How did you decide to go into pediatrics? How did you come to this hospital?"

"Whoa, again. First let me get some coffee." Farmer went over the Cuisinart machine and turned on the bean grinder. "My secretary did not make me coffee but she does keep the machine loaded so I can get fresh hot coffee when I am ready. You pick a specialty for many reasons. Money is the wrong reason but many people do select a high paying subspecialty because they like the money to live well and catch up with their college classmates who are already vice presidents of some company They need money to pay off loans that have been building up since college and medical school. I bet your loans are over 100 thousand, right?"

"Not yet, but I am working on it."

Keith added, "It is easy to hit 100 grand in debt. I hit 135 when I graduated."

"A common reason for selecting a specialty is you like working with people in that field. You have a feeling of comfort when you are with one specialty and conversely, there are groups that you would not like to be with in your work. You may like the working environment whether it is the office, the OR the radiology room. You may have some family experience like a parent or relative dying of cancer or a mother or father who is a physician and you want to follow the family line. What about you? Why did you pick medicine?"

"It was a long road to get here. I graduated from Swarthmore as the most liberally educated person. I majored in Chinese culture and language. With that degree I went to St. Louis to follow a boyfriend and worked in a Chinese restaurant as an assistant chef. Then I moved to Seattle and worked in a coffee shop while I wrote Chinese poetry and studied drumming with an expert from Mali. I competed in drumming marathons for a few years and then decided to attend community college in the premed program."

"Your poor parents." frowned Farmer. What did they say?"

"They were relieved that I was settling down and maybe following them."

"What do they do?"

"My mother is a doctor, an OB/GYN, my father runs a head hunter company for placing doctors in the pharmaceutical industry."

"Help me understand what was going on in your head to do all these things and bother your parents while you were doing it."

"I guess I did not want to follow them. I wanted to go into medicine but did not want it to seem like I followed them. I needed the space, as they say. In retrospect, I always wanted a medical career but I wanted to come in through my own door."

I guess you are what they call a well rounded student that adds diversity to the medical school class."

"Oh yes, we have a lot of people who seemed to have different entrances into the field."

"And why do you come through with so many questions at one time."

"I always did that. When I was young, my parents called me Mia the quizza."

"Ok, Quizza lets go back to work. Maybe we will be lucky and the young boy with ADHD will be here. Remember this is physical diagnosis time."

Fortunately, the patient did arrive. Henry Barksdale was a nice looking boy. He was wearing a NY Yankees T shirt and baseball hat with the NY logo. "Hi doc, how are you?"

"I am fine. But just a minute. We have a special room for Yankee fans. That is in the garbage room down the hall. No Yankee uniforms in this office."

"What are you, a Mets fan?"

"No, I am part of the Red Sox nation. Although I am not from Boston, I was always a fan. Maybe I felt sorry for the Babe's curse on them. Finally a few World Series wins. Finally." He turned to the family and offered his hand. "I'm Robert Farmer, Glad to meet you. Did you have any trouble finding this hospital?"

"No, thank you. I am Don and this is my wife Sara. We are pleased to meet you and thank you for seeing us on such short notice."

"Your doctor was anxious for me to see you so I thought today was as good as any. The waiting list for new patients is not too long but it worked out that I could put you on the schedule at the end of the day. This is Keith, a resident here and Mia, a medical student, who is with me this afternoon, trying to learn physical diagnosis. So if it is all right with you, she will be helping me check over Henry. Can you tell me your concerns about Henry?"

The family went over the usual material for someone suspected of having Attention Deficit Hyperactivity Disorder. The history included the inability to stay focused, distractibility, and constant motion and in his case, talkative to a point of annoying those around him. Obviously these traits did not bode well for sitting in class and doing assignments so they consulted their family doctor who ordered the MRI for some unclear reason and then the referral. After the rest of the history was completed, Bob Farmer stood up and spoke to Henry.

"Now is the time to check you over, will you take off your shirt and hop up on that table, I will be right back."

Outside the room, Farmer took a deep breath. "One more example of ordering the wrong test and starting a cascade of extra medical expenses. The doctor always referred cases to me, hoping I would sort out the problem and get him to the right doctor if I am not comfortable handling the patient. Let's go in and see what we can find. So far, I have no sense of this case."

Looking at Mia, Farmer begins his famous bedside teaching. "When someone comes for a physical we start with the vital signs. Temperature, Pulse, Respiratory rate and blood pressure."

"Blood pressure? Aren't they young to have the blood pressure taken? I never heard of high blood pressure in a child."

"Oh Mia, we take blood pressures on children over three years of age. Right Keith? Once in awhile we see hypertension in a child. It is important to find it early since untreated high blood pressure can cause a stroke, heart failure or kidney damage. Have you taken a blood pressure on a child?"

"No."

"Well let's get started. You go first and I will follow."

After getting the blood pressure cuff around Henry's arm, she pumped the bulb that inflated the cuff. Unfortunately, the Velcro did not hold and the cuff popped off the arm.

"Here let me show you. Henry this will feel tight for a few seconds. Then it will release and you will be fine."

Farmer reapplied the cuff, smoothed over the two facing Velcro pieces and pumped up the bulb. He noticed that the electronic read-out showed that the pressure reading went up past the usual 150 range before coming down to detect the actual reading. The look on his face indicated that something was wrong here. The reading was 160/110.

"This is strange. Let me do this again." Farmer repeated this again and it was 162/110.

"His reading is high today. Has he ever had his pressure taken before?"

"No, this is the first time. Is there something wrong?"

"Many times a high pressure reading is caused by a person's being excited or nervous when a doctor is near. Let me finish checking him and then we can discuss what that means."

After Keith looked into Henry's eyes, Farmer showed Mia how to use the ophthalmoscope to look into the eye to check the retinal arteries and veins and the optic disc. "See the optic disc has a sharp outline and the arteries follow a normal pattern. In severe hypertension, the disc edge would be blurred and the arteries would be thinned and curly. There could be small hemorrhage in the retina. He does not have this.

That is good news. Let's move down the head, ears and throat, and then he pulled out his stethoscope to listen to the heart. "You go first."

Mia spent the required time listening to the heart but seemed lost in the exercise. "OK my turn." Listening to the heart at various areas he listened to the chest and then turned to Mia and asked, "What did you hear?"

"The heart was beating so fast, it was hard to hear anything. I don't think there was a murmur. Was there? How did I do? Did I miss anything?"

"No, you did fine. OK, Keith, you go next."

"I hear a lot of loud sounds but no murmurs."

"We will discuss it later. When you examine the abdomen, you need to listen before you feel for his liver or spleen. You are listening for the squeaks of bowel sounds. The air moving through the intestines makes high pitched sounds. We are not very concerned about bowel sounds today as he has no GI symptoms. But let's listen anyhow." Mia went through the motions of listening but her blank face indicated that not much was getting to her brain. Keith, getting annoyed, as usual, seemed irked that he was being grouped with a medical student, put the stethoscope on the mid abdomen and said "mmm."

Farmer ignored the resident's displeasure, put the stethoscope on the abdomen to the left of the belly button. "Just as I thought."

"Thought what?"

"He has a bruit right here."

"A what"

"Bruit – spelled b r u i t but sounds like broo-ee"

"Sounds French. What does that mean?"

"It is a sound from the blood pushing past a partial obstruction. Like the noise you make when you put your finger over the end of a hose. You hear the water flowing past your finger. Turbulence."

"Let me listen." She put her stethoscope over the area where Farmer heard the noise and her face lit up. "I hear it. I hear it. What does that mean? Is it bad? Can it he fixed?"

"He has a block in the renal artery. This decreases the blood flow to the kidney. The kidney senses it is not getting enough blood and decreased pressure right so it signals the heart to pump more blood, angiotensin hormone, do you remember that from physiology?"

"Angiotensin, yes I remember that. Amazing to think that people really have problems with angiotensin. Oh my goodness! Oh my goodness! Let me listen again."

Then she moves the stethoscope across the abdomen to the right side. "Wait a minute. He has one on the other side. Maybe it is a normal finding. How could he have it on both sides?"

"Because he has arteries obstructed on both sides." Farmer responded nonchalantly even though he had never seen a patient with both arteries involved. Obviously, he had read about the condition but this the first real patient for him. One would never know that this was a novel experience by his cool and calm demeanor. He was good at poker for he same reasons. Bright and cool. Unflappable.

Now Keith finally showed some enthusiasm and asked Henry. "May I have another listen to your tummy?"

"Well, well, well." Farmer turned to the parents. "Henry has a major problem. He has high blood pressure. I heard abnormal sounds in the area of the renal arteries. Of course we have to do some tests but what it looks like is he has narrowing in the arteries going to his kidneys. As you heard me tell Mia, this causes his heart to beat harder to get past the narrow obstruction in order to deliver more blood to the kidneys. That leads to high blood pressure. Of course, this is my first pass on this diagnosis. Fortunately we have amazing machines that will show exactly what and where the problem is. If what I said is true, then we can talk about fixing the problem. In the meantime, we need to keep him in the hospital and treat his blood pressure. Let me stop for some questions."

"How did he get this? Why was it not picked up before?"

"It is not clear why he got this. Maybe a virus, maybe something in the genes. The usual case involves the walls of the arteries that slowly close down the artery diameter. It takes time for this condition to develop so when there is a small amount of narrowing, the blood pressure will be normal. When the narrowing increases enough to prevent blood getting to the kidney, the blood pressure will then begin to rise. Listening to his heart and looking into his eyes, I suspect that the high blood pressure has not been here for too long a period. "

"What is next?"

"We need to get some experts to help diagnose and fix the problem. I will be here to coordinate the workup and treatment but will be part of what will eventually be a large team. Let me warn you, this is a teaching hospital so you will hear a lot of dialogue about things Henry has and things he does not have but are being considered. So if you hear something that concerns you, talk to me or one of the members on the team before you worry yourself. You have enough concerns just getting through the admissions and into a bed. It is getting late so we better get things moving on. I will turn you over to my secretary who will make the calls and get you admitted so we can start the treatment tonight. In the meantime, I will talk to the radiologist to see if we can expedite the tests to check his arteries. Any questions?"

"Yes. You seem to work backwards. On TV the doctors go for a test and then examine the patient. You figured out the diagnosis without a test. I guess you are what they call an old fashioned doc."

"You might say that but I came into medicine before they had all these tests so I rely on the history and physical exams as the first step."

When the parents left the room, Farmer sat down in his chair, losing his cool façade. "Wow! What an afternoon! Not every day is like this"

"What do you mean? This was a real lesson in physical diagnosis and pathology. You don't do this every day?"

"Not hardly. Most doctors will not see cases like this in their lifetime. That is why I like to be a big referral center where you get the chance to see unusual cases. There are a lot of routine problems to me but not to the parents. The challenge is to sort out the rare conditions from the common one. At a place like sometimes when you hear hoof beats, it may be a zebra. That is the challenge." Farmer face was flushed with the excitement of detecting a problem that can save this young man lot of trouble as he ages if it were undetected. "Great hospital, what a great place to be!" He dialed John Spirito.

"Hey John, I got a hot case for your department. Major hypertension. I turn him over to you for the best tests to see his renal arteries. Yes, big time hypertension, 160/92, bruits in the belly, has to be renal artery stenosis, but with a twist. He has the bruit on both sides. Great, I will get one of the parents to admission and send the other with him to you. I don't think I need a plan B for this case. This is a hot one."

"I have a board sub committee meeting but I will get the Doppler people to do the test and I will be back later to give you the report. Sounds like a hot one."

Chapter 12

"My time flies. Here we are again at the operations committee. Let's get started." Richardson Beardsley called the meeting to order. "I see Carter is not here. I understand he had success with young Mr. Romanesco's appendix. Our Development office has been in touch with the family because we are looking to open additional beds in the neonatal unit. As you know, these beds have the highest return on investment of any of the beds in the hospital. More procedures, more studies, higher daily rates for the beds for all the nursing and support staff that these little critters need."

"What has been the occupancy rate in the present beds?" Asked Norman Oppenheim, the new board member.

"We are running about 60% year to date with some better months in the winter when the RSV infections bring in the premies."

"So why the rush to build more beds?"

"ROI- return on investment," Richards brusquely responded.

"We are short on beds for asthma and GI infections, What about building up that service?" asked David Grunberg, chief of Pediatrics.

"Same answer- not a good return on investment. These patients are mainly on medical assistance and you know the reimbursement for these cases is low, immorally low. We can do better with better payouts if we send these kids to go to the religious hospital- St. Andrews should take them."

"But that hospital is on the other side of town and the transportation to get there is poor. I thought our mission statement is we serve the community. Have you thought about what you will do when the community activists see this trend towards profit and away from meeting the needs of our patients? They are getting agitated about the wait for appointments, the lack of services for disabled children and the social problems like teen pregnancy."

"Those are important issues that we are working on. My staff is on this right now. The community is our high priority; I think we are doing a good job servicing their needs but we serve some better than others.

Listen, it is too premature to talk about allocating resources for community services as we have not gotten a commitment from Mr. Romanesco. Give us 6 months to work up the final plan."

"I heard that Romanesco was going to create a fellowship in surgery."

"Rumors, just rumors. The final decision about donations comes from administration. I am sure when I talk to Mr. Romanesco, he will see the benefit of an expanded neonatal service. His name over the entrance to the unit is hard to resist."

"This guy is too much," mumbled John Spirito to Norman Oppenheim. "He does not know about anonymous gifts. How could a man like Romanesco, who claims he is a salesman for office supplies come up with the money to build a new unit? When they give money, rare as it is, one would never know the source. But Beardsley does not get it when it comes to practicalities. He is blinded by MBA bullshit. ROI, margins, market penetration. When does taking care of patients' needs take precedence?"

"Let's get back to unfinished business. At the last meeting, we discussed the new financial plan that links benchmarks and remuneration. At the beginning of the fiscal year, there will be goals for profit, excuse me- margins and volume goals. We are not-for-profit, as you all know. When we have the right volume and margins, we all gain. When we do not meet these goals, the personal gain is less. That way we are all focused on the bottom line. We do what is good for the numbers and make decisions in a way to maximize the payout."

"I don't think we discussed this matter in this detail," John Spirito spoke out with a calm voice but his red face indicated his true feelings. "I remember that the idea was briefly mentioned, I think you called benchmark, performance based compensation."

Beardsley's head turned to Spirito, his eyes flashing the anger that his voice echoed. "You have a good memory John, since the last meeting, the CFO, COO and I have tossed things around. It made sense to us as we are about to embark on a major expansion and need the funds to build up our bond rating so we can issue bonds at a AA or better rate. It seems logical that we reward those who are bringing in the profits and not those who are negative profit centers. "

"When did we decide to expand and issue bonds and reward those who bring in the profits, the CFO?"

Beardsley ignored the second half of the questions. "When we decided to be the number one children's hospital in the U.S. We will only be number one when we are bigger and have the best facilities to attract the best staff and the most research grants. In our present configuration, we will not be about to overtake our competitors in Boston, Philadelphia or Baltimore or Cincinnati."

"I know I asked about this at the last meeting but since this seems to be moving along, I will repeat the question. When the margins go up, your pay package goes up."

"That is one way to look at it, Norman."

"Well, then it is to your advantage to push programs that will be profitable even when they do not meet the mission of the hospital or the needs of the patients. Seems like something of a conflict."

"I am not in this for the money. I could make a lot more in big Pharma or Wall Street. You know this job has no stock options. This is not about me. It is about being the biggest and the best. Don't you think we should be the best?"

"I think we should take the best care of our patients and not worry about who is the best. Who is to judge who is the best?"

"U.S. News and World report issues a list each year

"That is what I was afraid you were going to say. My cousin works there and tells me that there is a lot of PR that influences the listing. Those hospitals that take the time to fill out the forms and work the newspapers and TV stations have a leg up."

"I am proud that our PR department is doing its job."

"That is not my point. It is that fickleness of ratings based on PR. When someone else gets a better Madison Ave. type we are at risk of a lower rating. And who tells me bigger is always better?'

"I am told by some that size does matter." Richardson chuckled. No one else in the room laughed.

Spirito silently mused that men with small dicks drive a Porsche and proclaim that size matters. He has seen Beardsley pull into the executive parking lot in his 911.

"Anyway this is a board level decision, I am just filling you all in on the early thoughts that we will be fleshing out at the board level. Right, Norman? This group is here to communicate between departments and administration. For the record, I am communicating. Let's go around the room and communicate. John?"

"For some reason our MRI's are not fully booked. I am not sure if this is a blip or a trend that the HMO's have cut down their approvals. As you all know, we have 3 MRI's in house. The radiology group from

Victory has opened up an independent unit near the mall and the National Cancer Centers have an MRI in their outpatient units. I have gotten a list of their charges so we are about 30% more expensive than these units. I know our radiologists are better but are they 30% better? Anyway the HMO is not concerned with such nuances as quality of interpretation. I know there is some discussion about new machines. I have to admit that our machines are fast but the news ones are 5% faster, they have a built in viewer rather than an independent screen and a closed circuit TV for security is included in the deal, no extra charge."

"I would think that you, more than others would like a new toy for your unit, John."

"I did not ask for a new unit and told you before, I am opposed to spending hospital money for this."

"I don't have the same memory that you have John. You never seem to forget a thing, a real elephant, you are." Richardson smiled.

"Again no one in the room smiled except the CFO, Al Sharptee.

"What I was getting at, I don't think we need a new MRI at this point in time."

"OK John, I hear you. We have been promised a good deal by National MRI systems. They are the local dealers for MRI's. Since we have been such good customers, they are giving us a major discount. But let's not worry until we get more data from usage and of course profit margins. David?"

"I am concerned about the staffing of the community clinics. We have a 5 week waiting list for appointments. The acutely ill kids are being sent to the ED where they create a long waiting time for emergencies. We could unclog the system with some more help, doctors, nurses and aides. That's what we need."

"Submit a proposal, a business plan that shows the costs, reimbursements and projected profits. You know how low the reimbursements are for regular visits that don't involve procedures or studies."

"I understand that this will not be a profitable expansion but we have an obligation to the community. Isn't that what our fund raising is supposed to support? We have an obligation to the community."

"An obligation to stay afloat and not lose money doing our work."

"I'll see what I can do."

Spirito patted David Grunfeld's arm, "Same old, same old. Talk to the public about community service and caring for our neighbors but not supporting the chatter with any program that is not profitable. But they are eager to tell how much uncompensated care we give to the community when it is time for fund raising. What happened to the good old days when we did our job and it all seemed to work out? How do we get out of this mess and go back to doing our job?"

"Greer Messic, we have not heard from you. How is the laboratory doing?"

"We are doing more tests than last year. We have some special tests for rare metabolic diseases that seem to be working out. Casey, the head of chemistry has taken the lead on this and it seems to be close to being implemented."

"Casey?"

"Jack Casey, he is the PhD that runs chemistry. Doing a great job. Knows all about the new automatic analyzers for routines and devotes his time to these special tests that come up every so often in this place."

"Why a PhD? Don't they cost a lot? Where do we stand on out-sourcing the lab?"

"Not a good idea, Richardson. I have talked to colleagues in Chicago and St. Louis where they outsourced. The quality has gone way down. Long turn around time for special tests and then no quality control to make sure of the results. Not good."

"It could save a lot of money. We will have to look at your bench-marks."

Messic continued. "A number one hospital should have a PhD running the lab; in fact, we need one for microbiology too..... Yes, I will submit a proposal to you for that. Not sure I can make it look good for the benchmarks but it will improve our quality in the labs. With all these new viral infections and resistant bacteria, we need to upgrade our capabilities for diagnosing serious infections."

"Great. I look forward to reading your proposal."

"Is waiting for a proposal, the kiss of death" asked John Spirito. He was thinking of past times when Beardsley would look at a proposal and file with the comment that is it quite interesting and it will forwarded to the board. This guy does not get it. He does not understand quality, he just talks about it. It was time to jump in trying to calm some of the tense exchanges. "Maybe it would be helpful to go back to our famous mission statement that we took so long to create. We talked about service to all children, the need to respond to the needs of the community and our academic obligation to create new knowledge and translate this information to medical care. Making money and supporting profitable specialties are important but not our basic mission. I know money allows us to fulfill our mission."

"That is what I have been trying to say, we need to have the resources to fulfill our mission."

Spirito sensing some compromise rejoined." It is not an either or thing. An institution of our stature can do both. We need to keep a balance."

"Well said," sighed Beardsley. "That seems like all we have today. Any more comments or questions"

"I do have a comment." interjected Carter Randolf. "There seems to be a little tension in this discussion about financial concerns driving the program. I am sure that Richardson does not mean that. We are here because we want to help children and their families with the best people and up to date equipment. We have to work as a team to do the best we can for the families. This kind of dialogue is good for us so we know the issues and the problems. I am sure the board will do what is best."

"See you next month."

"What was that all about?" asked David Grunberg

"Carter has started a campaign to get on the good side of Richardson so when he wants to expand his program or more likely, get a good position when he steps down as chief of surgery, he will have an ally in the administration. No one could accuse Carter of not having an exit strategy," replied John.

"Any other new business?"

Norman raised his hand, "What about the auditor's report?" He noticed how Beardsley was keeping the discussion away from the promised auditor's review of the hospital's finances so he suspected something was being hidden from the board. "You mentioned at the last meeting that we would hear from them this month."

Beardsley head spun around towards Norman Oppenheim, "The auditor's report?" He coughed nervously as he went through the pile of papers in front of him. "I have it right here, somewhere. It just came in a little later than expected. "I will read the summary statement- We have found the auditing principles to follow standard methods, the hospital balances are correct and the surplus as stated in table 1. We found no problems."

The group nodded in approval. Norman did not say anything but remained suspicious as no group as large as the hospital gets such a sterling summary. He runs his business with a strong internal auditing team and an active board who watches all divisions carefully. They always get a few comments from the outside auditors that systems should be changed in one way or funds should not be placed in one account but in another one. He always thought that was a way to justify their bills and importance. This needs further investigation. He made a note to himself that wanted his auditors to go over the statements when we get them. Beardsley put on his artificial smile that he used when he thought he was pulling off a deal or when he felt that he had successfully obscured some of his financial magical tricks. When he got in the hallway, he thrust his fist in the air and mouthed his victorious – "Yessss!"

• • •

While he was celebrating, Malcolm Harlyn, the district attorney of Union County, was also giving the same victory signal. He had just finished a phone call with Bill Ryan, the DA from Cincinnati. Malcolm turned to his two assistants. "I think we are ready to go. Ryan in Cincinnati has just told me that his case against Wally Finley, the CEO of the UPS Children's hospital in Cincinnati, for insurance fraud has resulted in a guilty plea from Finley. He has agreed to cooperate in our case here against the people at CHUC. He has implicated our friend Beardsley as well two others in South Jersey. The usual stuff about reduced sentences was offered to this Finley creep but that will be up to the judge. Let's get to Judge MacManutter for a search warrant so we can take the computers from the hospital and see what evidence they hold."

"Hey Chief, what are we going to charge him with?"

"Insurance fraud, unauthorized entries into the medical records, conspiracy, misuses of the public trust- the usual add-ons."

"Why in the world would he want to alter the medical records?

"Because his father was a tailor and he told him there is money in alterations- get serious. The bird in Cincinnati admitted to 1.5 million dollars of fraud and his hospital is much smaller than this one so we are talking about 2 mil or more. Seems that they have a deal where they get a bonus on profits. Believe me, this is not the only thing that he did here. He could make a lot of money in his alterations. Let's get the warrant and head out to the hospital before this news leaks out and they destroy records or lose a computer, if you know what I mean.

"I called Judge MacManutter and told him that we would be over in 10 minutes."

"Let's go."

• • •

"And what do we have here? This cute baby looks so happy in your arms. What brings you in today?" asked Sarge Cranford as she greeted the next family in the triage booth of the ED. The Sarge was doing double shifts today but her energy level was the same as if she had just come to work.

"She won't stop crying. I think there is something wrong with her. She must be in pain."

"How long has this been going on?"

"She has always cried a lot but it is getting more intense."

"How many kids do you have?

"She is the first."

"First one is the hardest. I always said you should have your second child first."

"What? How do you do that?"

"I guess you start by not worrying so much and getting more rest. Let me take a listen and then get you into a room. How is she eating?"

"She is a good eater and she sleeps well, once she gets to sleep. I am not such a worrier. I had three younger ones in my family so I had a lot of experience with kids."

"But when it is your own, you see things differently."

"I guess you are right. I know that I should have waited for the morning to check with my doctor but the crying got so bad after Rebecca's night time bottle that I knew something was wrong and that if I called my doctor, the answering service would ask me to wait until the morning or if it was an emergency, I should go to the hospital. So here I am, not knowing what to expect but I need some comforting some even if you say it is nothing. I have talked about the crying with my doctor before but it was all assigned to the first baby syndrome and a young mother with a husband that was working two jobs so, except for weekends, he was not around much to give her a rest."

"Don't worry; we have lots of new mothers come in here. We take care of cuts and breaks as well as crying babies; that's our job. But dear, you baby looks good now; the chest and heart sound good. She is not having any breathing problems. I think she will do fine going to the quick care section upstairs, away from all these emergency cases. The doctors are nice there and will help you."

"Thank you, you are so kind."

Elise Marquis picked up the diaper bag and toy bear and took Rebecca, her 6 month old, to the second floor where she checked in with the clerk and waited to be called. She looked around the waiting room where the seats were mostly occupied by young mothers, a few fathers and a scattering of older women probably grandmothers. The receptionist, a stylishly dressed young woman was the greeter of the unit. "Welcome to our unit, please have a seat and we will call you when a room is ready. I guess there will be about a 15 minute wait, maximum. We will call you." Rebecca had calmed down so Elise was more relaxed and glad to have a few minutes of peace.

"Ms. Marquis"

"Yes!"

"Please come in. You are in room 4"

Elise took Rebecca and the diaper bag into room 4 and began to take off her jacket and pink outfit. Miss Wiggins, the practical nurse, took her temperature and put her on the scale. "16 pounds, even. And no fever. The doctor will be right in"

This part of the Emergency Department had a resident seeing the patients and then a staff doctor would check over the history and physical and approve or change the diagnosis or treatment as necessary. Tonight the resident was Jeff Marian. This was his sixth hour on duty so he was getting ready to leave. He had already seen 20 patients who either had a cold, an ear infection or loose stools. Not very exciting night but what they call bread and butter pediatrics; the cases which pay the rent.

"Hi, I'm Dr. Marian. How are you and Rebecca?"

"I'm fine. Just worried about her crying. It is getting worse and worse."

"Worse in what way?"

"Just louder and louder. She cried a lot since she was born but now this is stronger and she looks like she is in pain."

"Pain?"

"That is how she looks."

"Is she eating?"

"Yes she eats but now she is not eating as much as she did before."

"Is she gaining weight?"

"Yes she is 16 pounds tonight."

"Does she have diarrhea or constipation?"

"No"

"Is she sleeping?"

"Once she stops crying, she sleeps pretty good."

"So it is the crying that bothers you."

"Right the crying. She seems to be in pain"

"Yes--- the pain. What seems to make it worse?"

Nothing I can tell."

"What makes it better?"

"She seems to wear herself out and the crying stops."

'Do you have other children?"

"No this is the first."

"Married?"

"Yes."

"What does your husband think is wrong?"

"He is not around much. He has two jobs and is either working or when he comes home, she is sleeping. He says she looks good to him."

"She looks good to me too; do you think she looks OK?"

"She looks fine when she is not crying."

Jeff does a physical exam and does not find anything wrong.

"Her physical exam is normal. That is good news. No lumps or bumps. Nothing but the crying. I want to check with the staff doctor. I will be right back."

Tonight the staff doctor, Donna Barstow, was in room 3 checking another patient. When she left that room she looked at Jeff and asked, "what do you have for me?"

"A new mom with a crying baby. 6 months. Cries a lot. Mother says she thinks the baby is in pain. What else is new? The history is normal, good weight gain, nothing unusual in the review of systems and a normal physical"

"So what do you think is going on?"

"First child syndrome. Worried mother, crying baby, father working two jobs, no support from him."

"Sounds like you took a good history for this unit. What do you want to do?"

"Reassure her and send her home."

"Crying babies, that is my specialty. Let's go take a look together."

Jeff sighed to himself figuring Dr. Barstow wanted to make a teaching case out of every patient even the last one of the evening. "She never lets up. A crying baby is a crying baby is a crying baby."

"Hi Ms. Marquis, I'm Dr. Barstow. Nice to see you. What can you tell me about Rebecca?"

Elise repeated the history including all the information she told Jeff.

"Great! Now let's go over some of the details. Does she hold her breath or stop breathing before or after she cries?"

"No"

"Does she cry more in the day or night time?"

"She sleeps mostly at night so I guess she cries more in the daytime."

"Does she cry before feeding, during feeding or after feeding?"

"I guess it is during feeding. After she takes the bottle is when she cries the most."

"After about how many ounces does the crying start."

"I don't know, I guess it is 3-4 ounces."

"How much does she finally take in?"

"When she starts crying, the feeding is over; she never finishes a 6 ounce bottle. Do you think she is getting enough?"

"No, you are doing fine. Tell me about the last episode of crying. When was it? Describe how she looked."

"It was tonight at about 8PM. I was getting her ready for bed and gave her the last bottle. We were sitting in the bedroom, in a rocking chair. She seemed hungry so I started to feed her a bottle. She took the first two ounces like she had never eaten before. Then I burped her which she did not like. She was a little fussy so I gave her the bottle again and started to rock her. The next two ounces seemed to do her in."

"Do her in?"

"Yes she started to scream again."

"Tell me how she looked then."

"She was bright red. She would not calm down. She looked like she was in pain. Maybe she was having a cramp. She did pass a lot of gas then but she continued to cry."

"I can see why you were so worried. What do you think is going on?"

"I don't know. That is why I am here."

"Does your mother know about these crying spells?"

"Yes. She says that I am a nervous mother that I cried a lot. It was just the colic and she would grow out of it. Do you think it is the colic?"

"Does not sound like the typical case. Let me take a listen to her chest and look into her ears."

Jeff perked up. He thought this was the colic but did not mention that term because he knew Dr. Barstow did not like using that word. She liked to make a more definite diagnosis or try to calm down distraught parents when the crying was normal but the parents were worried about ominous conditions. He looked at his watch and thought that he was not going to get an early exit from the Quick Care unit.

Dr. Barstow checked Rebecca and agreed with Jeff that the physical exam was normal. It did not seem to fit the usual pattern of crying babies. The only clue was the feeding- crying link. So she did decided to create the situation right here.

"How about giving Rebecca another feeding so we can watch what is going on."

"You don't believe me?"

"Oh, I believe you. If I did not I would have sent you home already. Let's go."

Elise got out a bottle from the diaper bag and started to feed Rebecca. Just as described, the first few ounces went down easily then the fussiness and then the screams and the squirming.

"Look at that!"

"At what?" the annoyed Jeff asked.

"She is sweating!"

"She is what?"

"See the moisture on her forehead. This pain is severe. She is hurting. I don't believe it."

"Believe what?" Jeff was now officially annoyed at this colicky baby, her nice mother and this overreacting doctor. "You're in a sweat about sweat?

"Get an EKG! I need to see her ST segments and T waves."

Jeff goes out to find Miss Wiggins and comes back with her and the EKG machine.

"Let's hook her up. It will be hard to get a tracing since she is crying but we may get lucky."

They attach the EKG leads to her chest, type in her name and wait for the machine to spit out the tracing.

Jeff is the first one to admit that EKG interpretation is not his strong suit so he cheats and looks at the interpretation printed at the top of the EKG. "This is crazy. It says she has an ischemia pattern. Who ever heard of a baby having angina?"

"Look at this. Depressed ST segment, Inverted T waves. Just as I suspected. Her heart is not getting enough oxygenated blood. I bet her coronaries are mixed up. Anomalous coronary artery is what it is called. Wow! I have not seen one like this for at least 20 years."

Now Jeff is getting interested. "Slow down. Let's get an instant re-play. We need a TIVO here."

"Mrs. Marquis, the EKG shows that the blood is not getting to her heart muscle. I suspect that the arteries that feeds the heart muscles, the coronary arteries, are not hooked up in the usual way. When there is not enough blood with oxygen feeding the heart muscle, she gets pain and then she cries. I will need some more tests to be sure of the diagnosis. Taking a bottle for a little one is like you climbing up a flight of stairs; the heart has to work harder. That is why the crying occurs during feeding. In similar cases like this where there is no heart murmur and otherwise normal exam, the first condition I think of is a problem with the arteries that supply oxygenated blood to the heart muscle. Wait a minute. Let me back up." After getting a clean sheet of paper and draws a few lines. She continues "Here is a drawing of the normal arrangements for the coronary arteries that supply the heart muscle. These two tubes come out of the aorta which is the main artery that starts at the heart and sends blood, full of oxygen to various smaller arteries that go to the brain, the arms, legs and abdomen. Let me fill them in with red ink. Now if what I suspect is true, there is one coronary artery that is the same in the first drawing. Red blood going to the heart. But here is the difference. One of the coronary arteries comes from the pulmonary artery that has blue blood in it. This one feeds blue blood or blood with low oxygen to the heart muscle. That is not good. So when the blue blood gets to the heart muscle, there is not enough oxygen so the baby has pain. The harder the heart beats as when she is feeding, the more pain she gets. That is why the pain goes away when she stops feeding. She knew how to treat herself, at least temporarily. She stopped eating and the pain was gone."

"What we have to do is get a hold of the cardiologists and run some more sophisticated tests. They will do ultrasound tests to see the arteries and then depending on what they see, they will do more tests. I know this is fast and not what you expected but at last we have a clue about what is bothering Rebecca. Because you were so observant and gave a good history about what you saw, we were able to move along. Often because these problems are so rare, it takes many visits to finally come to the diagnosis. Questions?"

"Can they fix it?"

"Yes they can, with surgery. These operations are difficult because of the size of the baby, the tiny arteries and heart but they have ways to do it. They will discuss this with you but right now we need to get you in a bed and get the tests started. Do you want to call home and tell your husband where you are?"

"I will call and leave a message for him. He gets home at 11."

"Get your things together, I will make some calls and then Miss Wiggins will get you over to the admissions. It is on the main floor."

Jeff was awake and energized. "Good old Dr. Barstow, she knows the right questions and the right way to get the parents to tell him what is wrong. I would have looked like an overcooked turkey if I had sent her home with a colic diagnosis. "Hey Dr. Barstow, I am ready for the replay. Do you have time to tell me what and how you did this? What made you think of this?"

"Good let's sit down and chat. It is not so busy here that we can take a few minutes. That is a wild one. Come into the conference room over here."

"What made you think of that EKG and the diagnosis?"

"Time for a war story. I love to tell war stories but it is hard to be brief. As I get older the stories seem to get longer. Let me know if I need to pick up the pace. About 30-35 years ago, I saw a patient that had just moved here from Detroit, something about a job at GE. Anyway they told me that their son had been diagnosed with anomalous coronary artery but there was no treatment for it at that time. Microsurgery was just beginning but most places did not have surgeons trained in operating on such small arteries. So she was going to die and the family seemed to be adjusting to that sad news. They had some connection in their family with a cardiologist who confirmed the sad prognosis. For many reasons, they raised him in the most permissive way, taking each day as a gift. The little boy was a holy terror. He took my office apart in a few minutes, like a tornado. This did not register at first that he was full of energy and did not seem to be in any pain. I was trying to remember what an anomalous coronary artery was. We did not have Google then. After a few visits, I was a community pediatrician then, it dawned on me that this boy was not in pain, he was not having angina. Something had changed. So I sat the family down and told them about my new thoughts about the prognosis. He did have the problem but I thought that something had changed. I suggested that they see our cardiologist who would re-evaluate them and then decide if there was something else going on inside. They agreed and went to see Dr. Williams in cardiology. He was an expert in doing cardiac catherizations so he skillfully got a catheter into the coronary arteries and outlined the blood flow. Sure enough, the blood flow had changed because new vessels formed in response to the lack of oxygen. The old problem was gone but now he had a new problem."

"Could they fix it back then?"

"Yes, the patient needed to have surgery. I did something that I had never done before. I told them that the heart surgeon that was here at the time was not the one to do the operation as he did not have experience. We asked Dr. Williams who agreed with the outsourcing plan and suggested sending him to the Mayo Clinic where coronary surgery was being done in adults and recently they were starting to do kids. So off they went. I got a call on the third day post op, fearing the worst. The mother was upset, complaining that the doctors there would not let her son ride a bike. Imagine wanting to ride a bike three days after coronary artery surgery. That was her only problem. After 30 years, I still get cards from the family. He is fine and working in venture capital in California. Cases like that you don't forget. It was the original presentation that the boy had, sweating while eating that I have always kept in mind. Tonight was the right situation, the right history and my gun was ready and loaded. One shot and bulls eye. Wow!"

"I can see why you jumped on this. What a night!"

"Now to be honest. I have thought of it about 500 times in the last 30 years but now I am 1 for 500. But to you it looks like one for one, a good one to put in your holster."

"Do you have any other bullets in that gun?"

"I have a few favorites. But not tonight, we have to get back to work."

"Work? This is fun!"

Chapter 13

"Will you ask Caroleen to please come in my office?"

"Yes Mr. Beardsley. She is right across the hall. Should she bring anything?"

"Yes, the file on the MRI purchases."

Caroleen Columbe, the assistant chief financial officer was tall and naturally blonde, with a pleasant and authentic French accent as she was originally from Lyon. Beardsley had heard that she is single and quite popular at local coffee shops and book stores where young people gather to meet people. She has many friends but no special relationship. He hired her because the president of the water company had a French assistant so Beardsley thought she would give an international touch and because she had an amazing chest and narrow waist. Even if he could not get her in bed at least he could fantasize about being with her. So far, she gave no indications that she was interested in him but one never knows when the situation will be right. He was hoping that she would have a breakup of a romance, come to him crying, he tries to comfort her and he puts his arm around her, she snuggles up against him, pressing her boobs into his side while he drops his hand to her derriere, she turns towards him and…

"Here is the file on the MRI. Mr. Stevenson, the rep, called this AM and said he would call back."

"Timing is everything." Beardsley opened his eyes and there she was, all 5 feet 8 in her light yellow sweater, brown skirt and her hair in a French twist. That must be cashmere she is wearing, it looks so soft. I better keep my hands in my pockets so I don't get into trouble. "What did Stevenson want?"

"He wanted to discuss the details and see if you were making headway into the purchase."

"When we are done, I will give him a call. Let me see the spread sheet on the MRI usage, the one on reimbursement from the insurance companies and the various financial terms." He hoped that she would bend over so he could get a glance at her cleavage but no luck; she was now holding the files against her chest and dropped the files on the desk without doing any bends. "What do you think of the offer, Caroleen?"

"It is only one bid, I thought there needed to be three bids on such an expensive purchase."

"Right you are. The other two are coming in shortly. I wanted to make sure that there was a need for a new MRI. We have to justify the purchase on basis of usage, time to get an appointment and competition in the area. I needed the spread sheets that you developed so I can make the case for the purchase."

"Here are the figures. The MRIs are used about 62% of capacity. There is down time during weekends and evenings. During the day the schedule is mostly full. The two new radiologists read most of the studies as Dr. Spirito sticks with the old fashioned x-ray studies. The tests are ordered mostly by surgery, Emergency, neurology and orthopedics. General pediatrics and dermatology are the groups that have a low requisition rate. Compared to similar children's hospitals, we are about in the middle of the group for number of studies per patient bed, our schedule openings are slightly more than average and our charges are almost at the top of the list. From these numbers, it would be hard to justify adding on a new machine."

"We were not thinking about adding but replacing the old monster with this new slick one, much faster. Better for the patient, you know, less radiation." Beardsley wanted to keep the conversation going so he could leer a little bit longer but he had to move on. "Great, that is all for now." At least he could get a look at her rear as she left the room. "Someday, someday"

"What did you say?"

"Have a nice day"

"Yes, you have a good one too."

"Just a minute, Caroleen, I have one more thing."

"Yes?"

"I would like you to do some snooping for me."

"Snooping?"

"Not really. Come back and sit down. I am concerned about the flat income from surgery. I see their operations and visits are up about 3% but the expenses are higher. I am not sure what is going on. Figure out a project or problem that will allow you to spend some time in their offices so you can get a fix on their operations. Maybe it is just inflation

175

of supplies and new equipment to keep up with their surgical advances but then maybe they are playing games with the books. Since I took financial control of their practices, the profit drive may have decreased. I know that is a risk when doctors no longer have control of their destiny, I mean practice. Can you do something?"

Caroleen, flattered that she was asked to do this detective accounting, blushed slightly, agreed to come up with some project. "Should I put on a wig and wear dark glasses so they won't recognize me?

Beardsley liked her sense of humor, unusual for someone in finance. "I suggest you start with making an appointment with Dr. Randolph, the chief of surgery. Thanks, Caroleen."

He now had to generate two more bids with numbers that would allow him to choose Stevenson's bid as being the lowest, even though it included a nice kickback. When you had the Board in your corner, you could get little things like fake bids presented without much question about the veracity of them. The low bid would be so attractive that the board would assume that they were all Kosher. Then there was the maintenance and insurance that also had his incentive built in. He would have to juggle the numbers that Finance gave him to show less down time and more favorable numbers for tests per bed so he could look better in the comparison with other children's hospitals.

Great business this health care, Beardsley smiled to himself. No one caught me when we were doing the renovations. That time the contractor that was eventually selected did submit the lowest bid but did not include the required electrical work that was then listed as a cost overrun. The other bids did include the electrical updates required by the new power demands. Of course the wining firm would not get hired again because of the huge overruns but Beardsley came out all right. Now Beardsley had to get that Spirito off my back. He is really right this time, we do not need another MRI but I need a new kitchen or maybe that new Maserati that I just had to cancel, so we need a new MRI.

"Ann, get me Dixon McIver on the phone."

"Dixon, this is Dick Beardsley, How's the family? Good …. Listen, I wanted to get you up to date on the new MRI plans. I discussed this at the operations committee and the staff seems to be in favor of it, especially Dr. Randolf. He is always glad to get faster images so he can get to the OR quicker. You know those cutting guys. There was a lot of favorable comment on the new compensation plan where we grant bonuses on basis of performance. Of course some of those "academic" types who don't see a lot of patients were not happy. But with all the money we pay them, they should be more productive. You know the one with the chalk on his suit coat. He sees about 10 patients a week."

"His patients have rare diseases, mostly chemical or nutrition ones they do not generate many lab tests or billable admissions since they are on some sort of research studies. We need experts like him to take care of other sick kids."

"They must generate some cash. We do OK with them but not like the neonates. They are cash cows. Lots of tests and intensive care rates. We love them. I don't know what to do with chalk suit. He has been here for ever and is the best teacher in the group. But again, teaching does not bring in income, it costs us."

"Yes, he helps with the hospital prestige."

"But one cannot buy new MRI's with prestige, Ha ha. Oh, I would not think of getting on his case, I know he diagnosed your grand daughter with that rare disease and got her treated with the new research drug that helped her recover. We owe him a lot, don't we? Great guy. I think the world of him."

Beardsley was glad that he did not have videophone so Dixon could not see him sweating and squirming in his seat. How could he forget about Al Barnes doing that amazing job with Dixon's grand daughter? Maybe I am getting ahead of myself. Slow down and don't be so greedy, Beardsley.

"Just wanted to keep you up to date and have no surprises at the board meeting. Best wishes to Abigail."

He then looked at his list of board members and realized that he had ignored Bunky Peterson, daughter of Hal Lurentze, who made a fortune in junk metal or reclamation engineering as he referred to his business. Bunky was one of the few women on the board and very outspoken when it came to status of nursing and advancement of women in leadership roles, both of which the hospital had a major problem as it was still dominated by males, white males mostly but not entirely WASPs. Bunky' father turned over his foundation to her and fortunately, she was generous with her father's money. But like the new breed of donors, she wanted her say in how the money was being spent. It was easy to see why she was on the board, even with her diversity kick. She was always pushing Blacks and Hispanics. We have to do something about that to preempt her from making diversity an issue regarding the MRI purchase. What we need are a few token blacks that will not get in our way. It is really hard to find them, especially if you are not looking for them.

Although he dreaded talking to Bunky since she was so astute that she would catch him if the lies were too blatant. He would have to think of how to get some diversity aspect to the purchase plans. That was a hard one but he was sure something diverse would pop into his head. Why didn't they hire that black candidate for radiology? That would have been better for this case.

"Ann, please get me Bunky Peterson on the phone. Thanks."

"Hey Bunky, Dick Beardsley here. How's the family? .... Good Good .... Say Bunky, I wanted to keep you in the loop about the new MRI. ...Yes, we did get one last year but this one is faster and better for the kids. You know, the price of men's toys things. This one is more expensive but it is really slick. We can replace the old model T that is 3 years old and keep us competitive with our sister institutions. Advantages, oh yes, the advantages. It will show more definition because of the pixel count. We are planning to use it in the ED cases where small fractures may be missed and we will be able to detect traces of lead in the children's' stomachs. Those inner city kids are still getting exposed to lead and we want to catch them before the brain development is affected. You know our primary care is directed to these inner city kids. I also have quite a deal worked out with the cooperative that does our purchasing of big items. They are giving us a monitoring system so we can have full security in that area as well as monitor the usage. One monitor at the MRI, one in security; another one in my office. I want to see what goes on there and make sure that they are processing the patients in an efficient way. Quite a deal. I hope to see you at the next board meeting where I will give all the details. Ciao!"

After he hung up, Beardsley's artificial smile that went along with his manipulation of the systems was interrupted by a knock on the door.

"Mr. Beardsley, there are some men from the DA's office to see you."

Beardsley jumped up from his chair, slid the file about the MRI under his newspaper and ran his fingers through his hair. "Good day, gentlemen, what can I do for you?

"Mr. Richardson Beardsley?"

"Yes, that is what my mother named me."

"I am Malcolm Harlyn, District Attorney, and these are my assistants, Paul Jameston and Charles Phillips."

"Pleased to meet you all. Is this something I should call my lawyer, you all seem so serious."

"Mr. Beardsley, we have a search warrant signed by Judge MacManutter, to take out your computer and files."

"All my files? I am running a big operation here. I would be shut down without my records."

"Judge Macmanutter realized that and he authorized only the records that pertain to billing and dealing the insurance company correspondence regarding charges and bills. We also are going to the medical records and finance to get copies of the computer records regarding billing."

"How long will you keep them, Excuse me but I don't know much about DA's and hospital records. I am happy to cooperate with you in any way I can. Can I get you something to drink, some water?" Once again, Beardsley flashed his smirky smile, knowing that he destroyed his old computer and never used his new computer for email or for any reason and the server that handled the billing had been destroyed by IT after he got the call from Finley last summer. He was going to be Mr. Nice Guy and pledge full cooperation with these legal jerks. "Ann, show these men where my computer is and then take them to the other places that they want to go. Is it all right with you gentlemen? Then I leave you to your business. I have a conference room of people waiting for me. You know we have one of the best children's hospitals in the country."

"Fine with me, Mr. Beardsley. We will not be too long. I know about your hospital. My son was here for a hernia operation. That was many years ago. He is almost 40 now."

Beardsley left the room heading for the executive conference room a few doors away.

"He seemed like a nice guy with nothing to hide." Remarked Paul Jameston.

"Nice like a crook, did you see his nervous eyes. His palms were so wet I need a towel to dry off before the sweat drips on my Dockers, even though they are waterproof. I bet his sphincters were tight as a lid on a jar of peanuts when you are famished."

"What kind of peanuts do you eat? Mine are in a paper bag." Paul replied.

"Let's go and get the evidence and get out of here. I don't think we will have to look too far. Paul, get one of your guys to apply for a job in housekeeping at the hospital so he can snoop around. Once we get a look at what is in the computer files, we can make a plan for the rest of the investigation. Having a secret agent on site will help us a lot. We have a live one here and I know the publicity will not hurt me when I run for Governor in a few years. I don't know how the people stand working here. All these poor children."

Before he went into the conference room, Beardsley went into his private bathroom to call his lawyer.

"Bill, old buddy, how are you doing and how is your golf game? I want to give you a heads up on what just happened. I had a visit from the DA. … Yes. ..DA as in Malcolm Harlyn. Seems that he got a call from another DA in Ohio that I may be part of a billing scam against the insurance companies. They had a warrant and took my computer.. The assholes do not know that I never use the computer, don't send email and don't write anything down….. What? Do I receive email? Of course I can't stop that part of the system. I get over 100 emails a day but I don't respond to them; in fact I don't even read many of them. I never thought that the computer would keep emails that I did not write. But there are no emails about billing or references to insurance billing. I do remember the CFO writing emails about accurate billing for all procedures. But I did not write them. ……OK we will talk next week. I will come to your office. Maybe they bugged mine so I will be careful. Thanks Bill."

• • •

Adrienne, the first year resident, had survived the surgical rotation. She actually liked the change of pace but not the hours. Not that she had anything that competed for her time but if she had a social life, getting up early and staying so late would have caused some tension. Now she was on elective and covering the well baby nursery when needed, that was a welcome change of pace. Better hours and less testosterone. She even had time for a coffee break so she migrated to the cafeteria to get some Seattle's Best. The coffee was good but she had a tinge of guilt about spending that much money for a cup of coffee. Especially one with $125,000 in loans to pay back. But coffee was her one treat. The other residents and nurses that congregated there served as her hospital family and her group therapy. Someone always had a problem and someone else had a solution that rarely made sense to the one with the problem but it was an ear and also provided a perspective that the situation was not unique. As usual, Felix was there along with his roommate, Lester. Their skills at getting an easy schedule and finessing work allowed them maximum time at the cafeteria corner. Although doctors and nurses were not allowed to have an assigned section in the cafeteria, everyone who worked at CHUC for more than a week knew which tables were for the doctors and which one for the young nurses to hang out. So Adrienne headed for the corner to see who else was there.

"Hey Babe!" Lester greeted here. "How's things?" Lester was a bright fellow but lacked most social skills. He knew a lot about many topics but was not too strong on relationships and small talk. Felix was his role model as he was strong on relationships but weak on detailed knowledge. Felix had coached Lester on how to be cool. He taught him to say "Hey babe and how's things?" But with Lester, the emotion was missing so he sounded like a talking doll. Every one agreed that Lester was getting better with interacting with peers. No one could figure out how the odd couple, Felix and Lester, would buddy up enough to share an apartment but they did and it proved to be successfully so far.

Seeing Sevasta Patel and Sara Wright, Adrienne felt relieved that someone besides Lester and Felix was sitting at the table. "Hey Guys, glad to see you. What are you doing?"

"We are debating the merits of the various dating services. Have you ever tried to use the internet to meet someone?"

Adrienne blushed "Who me? Of course not, have you?"

"We are about to start. For the first few months of the residency, we were so uptight and exhausted that dating was not even low on our list. But now things are settling down so it is time to hit the hair salon and get back into society. Linda in the well baby nursery got us thinking. She went to eHarmony.com and met a perfect match. She looked at 27 recommendations and picked three. Her first choice had matched with 53 women but he picked only one, Linda. End of story, she is getting married June 11. This was not her plan but Roy seemed like the right one so why play games? So we are looking at the various plans. eHarmony seems to charge more but that scares away the budget minded and cheapskates.

Lester chimed in. "What is wrong with local people? Just go to the Whole Food Store and hang out. Or to Borders. That is what I do."

"And how does that work out?"

"I get good food and read a lot of books."

"My mother would kill me if she found out that I did this."

"Just another reason to kill you if she found out all the things you did."

"Not me, I am the good one. But how do you sign up? Enough of this dedication stuff. I look at my friends that are not doctors and they seem to be doing just fine."

Lester warned the group. "Beware of the perverts and married men. They are looking for desperate house officers or anyone with XX chromosomes. But I guess that going to the internet is safer than sitting in a bar, waiting for some drunk to attack you."

"What should I put down on the form? Bright, well educated young black female with good future, pleasant personality, love of sports and music with $125,000 in debt looking for cultural exchange, send photo."

Lester butted in "Why do you have to put in black? I thought all people were created equal. Anyway you are as far from being black as I am being a sumo wrestler. Look at your arm and my arm. My skin is darker after a few days in the sun than yours. Who's your daddy?"

"Actually my mother is half Irish and half African American. My father was Spanish."

"How did your parents meet?

"My father was a jazz player and my mother was a groupie."

"So why does that make you black?"

"That is the way it is done."

"Sounds racist to me."

"I, a racist?"

"Call yourself whatever you want."

"Why do you care?"

"I remember from Holocaust studies in college. If your grandparent was part Jewish, you were Jewish in the Nazis view. The whole thing was wrong but the tilt towards labeling was an additional wrong and racist. When we mention black or white when referring to people, we reinforce the need to think about race, when it does not really matter. Do you agree?"

"I never thought of it that way. How about "of color""

Lester who gets the prize for being most laid back or in some people's eyes, most out of it, for the first time showed some fire in his eyes. Something was bugging him.

Adrienne tried to change the subject. 'So what am I supposed to say about myself?"

Beth interrupted, "You fill out the form and the computer matches you with people that the psychologists say are compatible. Then you get directions for contacting them by email and the rest is up to how well the chemistry evolves.

"How do you know so much?"

"I am on five different lists and have had fun sorting through the perfect males."

"And?"

"And I have had some special dates, nothing to move to marriage but some wonderful times. In fact, I am meeting someone new tonight for a drink at Farmacia, the new place on Third Street, near the post office. I am not ready to settle down but I want to travel and pay off some of the debt. Internet dating is fun and better than staying home or sitting in bars fending off predatory males."

"My mother would kill me. She would be so embarrassed. But another few weeks of this and I will be ready."

"I don't have to bother with all that" piped in Sevasta. My father puts in the ads about Well Educated Indian Doctor with no debts vabom, vabom, vabom."

"You mean he arranges your marriage."

"He thinks he does but he does not know that we are now in America and we don't have to do arranged marriages. So far, he has turned nothing up so I will let him think he is the big arranger but I will do some of my own looking. There are so many Indian doctors, I should not have a problem, except most of the ones around here are either geeks or they are dating white girls. I am in no hurry."

"So what's the gossip?"

"I hear they are going to change the parking lot assignments again."

"No, I mean real gossip"

"I heard that they were going to outsource residents and bring in a lot of foreign graduates who will work for half our meager pay."

"Where did you hear that?"

"From Eddy, the shoe shine man. He gets all the news when he goes to the executive offices to shine shoes. He is never wrong."

"He was wrong about the pay raise rumor."

"Just a little mixed up. There was a pay raise but it went to the administrative staff, not the house staff. Eddy gets things mixed up at times. But he heard this first hand."

"Forget it, it will never happen."

"Don't be too sure. Look at the pencil plant in South Shore. Gone to China. And the lighting factory on Alpha street. Gone to China. So it can happen to us."

"They would never send up to China."

"No but they could send Chinese here. They would love it- getting a BTA degree to add to their MD."

"BTA?"

"Been to America. It is the magic card that gives them unlimited prestige when they get home."

"I thought that when they come here, they stay here."

"Not for Chinese. They can go back as Americanized doctors and take advantage of the new millionaires in China without the hassle of the HMO's and the malpractice. China is the place to be."

"This is getting too serious for me. What about the dirt?"

"Margaret on 5 west said she saw Frank Winston and Melanie Katcher going into a restaurant on River Road."

"Now that is gossip. I saw those two at a staff meeting and they did everything but pull out a gun and fire away. They hate each other. Winston is the oncologist that thinks chemotherapy is the answer and Melanie is the surgeon who wants to cut anything she can get her scalpel on. Cut first and ask questions later is her motto. Even if it were true. They could not agree on a restaurant or who would drive. Oil and water those two. Believe me."

"How do you know so much?"

"I have been on oncology for two months and have seen them in action. Bad blood. Try another rumor."

Chapter 14

Henry Barksdale was sent to the intensive care unit for control of his high blood pressure while the various doctors discussed his case and planned the next steps, most likely an operation to open up the constricted arteries. But first he needed medication to control his pressure. He seemed to like the monitors and activity of the ICU but did not relish being kept in bed. Since his parents could visit most of the time, he rather enjoyed all the attention. After the nurses hooked him up to all the monitor leads and started an i.v., he was allowed to watch television as much as he liked. "This was going to be a great place. They even let you pick out what you wanted to eat."

The intensivists came by on rounds, heard the history and listened to his heart, chest and abdomen. They wanted to hear the bruits in the belly that Dr. Farmer detected in his office but they were more interested in numbers, monitor readings, which lab tests to order, and the fluid ins and outs.

"Sounds like Niagara Falls" concluded Elisa Blackstone in her Alabama drawl. "I reckon that we all better get him some of that good juice to get those there numbers down. An ace inhibitor and a diuretic make good sense to start. And we need to cut out the sodium on the diet." Elisa wearing a light blue sweater over her ample torso and black slacks. The tight leather belt indicated that she had just lost a few pounds that she felt justified showing off her new waistline. To others, she was still rather portly.

Poor Henry, he did not know the meaning of cut out the sodium, not aware they meant salt that strongly flavored his favorite foods, pizza, chips, pretzels and French fries. He would soon sadly learn about how unsalted food tasted when the meal tray was served. Now the parade of studies was to begin. First to the x-ray department.

Radiology bumped an elective procedure so they could get a look at Henry's arteries using a color Doppler to show the blood flow to the kidneys. Keith Aaron continued to follow the patient as best he could, luckily,he arrived at the radiology suite just as they were starting the test. Sensing a neophyte resident, the ultrasonographer described what he was seeing. "The Doppler is a radar type test where there are waves that bounce off an object and return to the instrument. When they are looking at the blood flow at the renal artery, the artery going from the aorta to the kidney, the color red shows the movement away from the Doppler while the color blue shows the movement towards the Doppler instrument. If needed, we will follow with an MRA. The MRA is like an MRI but it shows the arteries more clearly. Look at this! Amazing! Both renal arteries had a severely constricted narrow segment. The right renal artery was constricted near the aorta; the left artery had a constriction midway between the aorta and the kidney. Save this beauty for the teaching files!"

Henry Barksdale was not sure what all this meant but sensed he was going to be a star patient for the next few days.

Communication between different disciplines was one of the features of a specialty hospital like CHUC. The various specialties planned to get together at 6 PM to go over the possible treatments and come up with a strategy. Elisa had arranged that meeting so the team developed a plan that they jointly developed, thereby limiting the arguments between the various specialists. A group meeting was better to get all these things on the table rather than have a lot of murmuring about wrong treatment, why didn't they do this or that. Fortunately, Henry's pressure seemed under control so there was calm in the ICU until the 6 o'clock conclave.

In this meeting, Dr. Randolf, chief of surgery who considered himself a vascular surgeon, Dr. John Spirito, representing radiology, Charlie Hollis, intervention radiologist, Elisa Cunningham, intensivist, Robert Farmer, general pediatrician and Briana Testade, renal service. As usual, Dr. Randolf sat at the head of the table and called the meeting to order since that was what surgeons think is their right and obligation. The rest of the group except Dr. Testade, the nephrologist, did not care who was in charge so they allowed Randolf to be the leader. Dr. Testade, all five feet three inches of her liked to sit at the head of the table and control things too. Soon the two control freaks were destined to clash on some point, probably a minor one.

"It looks like a typical case of bilateral stenosis," Randolf stated, as if this was an every day occurrence. This was the 15th such case that he had seen in his three plus decades of practice. Most of the 15 were not taken care of personally but he was around when the patients were in the hospital. This was more experience than the entire group in the conference had so he was the local expert. "I see snipping out the constricted area and curing this lad. What do you think, Charlie?"

"The right side is quite tight and hard to put a catheter through it. I think I can balloon out the left one and maybe save him some hours of surgery. Since dilatations have a higher percent of restenosis, maybe it would be better to operate on both sides while you are in there. I would be glad to give it a try."

"No fight from surgical side. Maybe you should give it a go as I have to be out of town for a few days and would like to give the medicine time to bring his pressure down towards normal." Carter Randolf was obviously seeking a delay so he could take his trip.

Elisa wanting to generate some interspecialty warfare jumped in. "What do you mean, no fights?"

"Well this is a tough one and not worthy of a fight just to fight."

"When do you expect to be back home?"

"In about 3-4 days."

"Anything else. This was brief, I guess since so many of the same people argetting gray hair, they are trying to act mature for a change." Now Testade was ready to make her move from the other end of the table. "While we are here, let's go over the medication for hypertension. As you know, nephrology takes care of hypertension. This case can be tricky since both arteries are involved. Does anyone have a problem with renal taking the lead in antihypertensive therapy?"

Elisa Cunningham, the junior member of the team turned a little red but kept quiet. She wanted to be involved but she did not relish a turf battle with the senior staff. She hoped that sometime in the future she would have her chance. Or maybe when Testade was away on one of her frequent lecture trips.

Testade, seeing she was unchallenged, chimed in "OK, I will take care of medications, Charlie will have a crack at ballooning the left artery, Carter will be away for a few days and then will come back and do either one or two arteries, depending on Charlie's success or failure at blasting the stenosis and Little Liza will take care of the fluids, nutrition etc while the patient is in the unit and Farmer will make sure we all do our jobs. Right?"

"I will be away for 3-4 days but my chief resident Peter Bird will see the patient daily for our service."

"Sorry, Carter will be away for 3-4 days, not a few days as I originally stated."

"And Peter Bird will stand in for me."

"Right, Peter Bird will stand in for Carter."

"I think we have a great team and I am proud to lead it in this tricky case."

"No offense Carter, my man, but you will be out of town so you are not the leader. Since I am taking on the medications and I have a full renal team with me, I think I should be the leader of the group up to the time of surgery."

"I don't think it is fair to the parents to have a change of leadership before and after surgery."

"But how will you be a leader when you are in Peoria."

"Phoenix! I guess you are right."

"Ok I will be the leader."

"Right, you will be the leader."

It took a few rounds of this to realize that surgeons have to have the last word and they would be playing Abbot and Costello until Carter had the last word. This was so-called grown up version of five year olds saying "is so" followed by "is not" followed by "is so."

When Carter sat back in the last word triumph, Testade piped in with "and Marquis you will do the cardiac workup to check on LVH."

"Good idea" Carter came back. "We do need a cardiac workup."

"And don't forget me, I will order the yellow shirt that says LEADER so the whole team will know who is in the lead role, just like the Tour de France," concluded Elisa.

• • •

The first few days in the ICU went well. Carla Allen, the ICU nurse, took the Barksdales under her wing and did her usual great job of providing her holistic care to both patient and family. The blood pressure started to come down but Henry continued to rebel at the low salt diet. Testade came into the ICU with her team and managed to exert control over the treatment. If the resident ordered 62.5 mg of a drug, Testade changed it to 65mg. She even changed the vitamin from one tablet in the morning to one vitamin with extra vitamin E in the evening. She quoted an article from the journal International Pediatric Nutrition that recommended this vitamin routine, saying it with such authority that no one bothered to check out the journal. It did not exist. The new people on the team did not know that Testade was a master of quoting a non-existent journal. This ploy worked on the young doctors and students but the old timers just smiled and if it did not matter, like the dose and content of vitamins, they went along with her fragile ego. After going over the vital signs, the fluid Ins and Outs, and the blood pressure, she noted that the urine output seemed to be less each day. Carla swore she measured Henry's full output. "We need to watch this" proclaimed Testade as if they were not going to watch his I's and O's; that is what they do in intensive care, especially on a patient on the renal service. "Yes, Dr. Testade" we will watch it."

"When is the balloon attempt scheduled?"

"He is on call for tomorrow in the AM.

"Good. Let me know if there are any changes in his condition. I am in charge of the treatment, you know." Reminding those present that she always had the last word, the team took off to share her vast knowledge to the people on the 4th floor.

The usual calm Carla sat down in the chair at the nurses' station and exhaled loudly. "She is a real package. If she were not so smart, I would not put up with her Napoleon complex. I bet she even wears elevator shoes. She is so busy being in charge and controlling things. She must be upset that the air traffic controllers have a union and national recognition while her group, the medical team controllers don't even have a website. Besides, she treats us as if we are stupid."

"Wow! What's bugging you?" asked Katie who had just come over to chat during her break.

"Me? Why do you ask?"

"I never heard you say anything about anybody. She must have crawled under your finger nail."

"I did not think it was that obvious."

"Sounds like PMS to me."

"No PMS I just had my period."

"That means you are not pregnant?"

"Right. I guess the tension of getting pregnant is getting to me."

"Well my advice is to stop trying and call an adoption agency."

"What!!! I am not a quitter. Why do you give such bad advice?"

"When you quit trying, I mean quit trying to time the ovulation and all that stuff, your chances for pregnancy goes up 25% and when you call the adoption agency, it goes up another 25%. When I say stop trying, I don't mean stop going through the motions. Just take the goal seeking behavior away. Diane went through the same thing and believe me, when she finally called the agency for an appointment, she felt so relieved. She said she could feel the egg pop out of her ovary; I think it was the left ovary that time. Take off the pressure- defuse the situation. You will never conceive when you are under such stress to perform. If my advice does not work, then get a ticket to Hawaii or Jamaica and that will work, I guarantee it."

"I think you are right. There is too much tension in my sex life. The pressure here is not helpful, but I love my work."

"I can see that. You are the best and you know that from your patients telling you."

"Thanks for the therapy; I owe you a double skinny latte at Tom's. Anytime... Thanks."

Dr. Testade's concern about the urine output was real; the output measurements were lower than the day before. Elisa confirmed this observation noting the BUN and creatinine she ordered this morning showed were rising, indicating that renal function was getting worse. She was tempted to comment that she has never seen renal failure develop during treatment but she caught herself since she had never seen a case of bilateral renal artery stenosis before.

"Time to do some reading." She marched right to the computer in the intensive care unit's conference room to access the National Library of Medicine. She first tried Google and was lost in all the hits it returned and none were about this rare situation with both renal arteries involved. In about 30 seconds, the NLM informed her of several cases of renal failure when ACE inhibitors were used in these patients. She called Testade and told her she was stopping the ACE inhibitor and switching to calcium channel blocker along with the beta blocker and the diuretic. This was getting complicated but that is why she was working at CHUC. Great cases and great challenges kept her here but surely she was not here for the money as she thought of her student loans that still needed repayment.

Testade seemed surprised by the news. "The shock of hearing this jolted my memory. I had read about this but I had not taken care of such a patient either, so this fact slipped by. I wondered why the computer did not red flag this order but maybe the computer has not seen this before." Testade recovered her composure quickly to regain control of the case. "Have you replaced the Ace with Calcium channel blocker?"

"Good idea. We did that immediately. I hope that his kidneys do not shut down;'

"That goes for both of us. I will immediately come over and talk to the kidneys and tell them to stay awake. We are under control."

Unfortunately, the urine output continued to decrease. Both Carla and Elisa informed the parents that Henry was having a reaction to the medicine which they had replaced with a new type of medicine to treat the hypertension. Although worried, they thanked the two women for catching it early and expressing their confidence in the care that Henry was getting in the ICU.

That is not how Henry's uncle took the news. Doug Barksdale was a roofer, which means he is a tough guy, the kind who joined the infantry in the army and was the first to jump out of the foxhole and fire away at the enemy. When there was no war, roofers congregated at one of two bars in town where they acted like three year olds at a birthday party. Lots of noise and wild man activities. Abstract thinking was beyond them; they could only talk about what they saw and touched. So when Uncle Doug heard about his favorite nephew Henry's kidney failure, he reverted back to the roofer's motto. 'Yell, scream and hit someone.' So he rushed into the hospital and started to flail away. "How come? How come? What the hell did you do to my Henry? Who is in charge? I want an explanation."

"May I answer your questions, sir?" volunteered Elisa. She tried to explain. "His constricted arteries stopped the pulsatile flow to the kidneys. This caused the kidneys to produce extra amounts of renin, a hormone that will raise the blood pressure. Unfortunately, the medicine we used to treat this condition caused additional problems with the perfusion of his kidneys, we have discontinued the medicine and given a few days, the prognosis should be better. I take full responsibility for the problem."

Don Barksdale tried to calm his brother but gave up as he saw Doug was in a different zone to pay attention.

Having no respect for women, he pushed Elisa aside. "I did not understand one word you said. I'm looking for the man in charge." Doug was not ready for the number of women on the physician's staff. Before they could explain about 21st century diversity, Karl Strem, the chief resident, who had been chatting with a nurse a few beds away came over to find out who was making all the noise.

Doug stood at the bedside to block Karl's passage and shouted at him. "How come my nephew came in here when he was not sick and now you guys have made him sick? His kidneys were fine a few days ago but now they are dead. He will need a transplant and maybe die. How come you guys screwed up so badly on my Henry? How come?"

Karl went over the same explanation that Elisa did but Doug was having no part of it. His voice got louder and his face got redder as he moved closer to Karl's face.

Carla slipped away to the nurses' station and called security.

Karl, raised in a tough blue collar town, would not shy away from a good fight even though Doug stood about 6 inches taller than Karl, full of muscles just waiting to flex and do some damage to someone's teeth. The skull and bones tattoo on his arm added to the image of a tough guy. Karl stood his ground and pointed to the hallway outside the ICU. "Why don't you come out in the hall and we can settle this."

"Where is the security when we need them?" asked Carla. "We need that 300 pound lineman guy, Nate, who is always checking our ID badges when we come in to work. Where is he?" Carla was also worried about Karl, He was athletic, having played baseball in college but that was a few years ago. "Karl could get killed in the hallway. What a guy, trying to protect us and now he is going to lose his teeth. Or more."

In about two minutes, just as the breathless security guards arrived in the ICU, Karl and Doug come through the doorway. Karl, smiling, and Doug, looked like a sad poodle at the dog show who was just eliminated from the competition, Doug came over to Carla and said "Sorry, I was a dope." He looked at Elisa and said "Thanks Doc, you are doing a great job. He then sat in the chair and held Henry's hand.

What happened, Karl?"

Karl pointed to the hallway again and motioned them to come that way.

"I just pointed my finger and said "you son of a bitch, who the hell do you think you are coming in our place and acting like a total jackass. If your nephew was not such a nice kid and your brother a great parent, I would kick the living shit out of you. If you ever, ever, ever do that again, I will not hesitate to kick you ass all the way out of the hospital and into the sewer where you belong. Do you get me? You son of a bitch. This shocked Doug but I spoke his language. No fancy words, just words that he could understand. No logic or hypothetical examples. Then I said in simple terms. The artery is too small. That makes blood pressure rise. The medicine brings down the pressure but in this case, it caused problem in the kidneys. It is a side effect. Like when you drink too much beer you get a headache. When you take ecstasy you get thirsty. A side effect. Get me. No one's fault. Just a side effect."

"Why didn't they tell me this before? I see your point, Doc. I read you clear. Side effect. Cool."

"OK get your ass in there and say you're sorry. NOW!"

The group stood silent, surprised in their chief resident's choice of words and bravado.

Karl continued, "That simple. Keep it linear and speak their language. We now have uncle pussy cat and I am sure he will be a help to Henry. Let us pray that the renes open up with more urine."

The next day there was no change in the urine output.

"Is it time to worry?" asked Doug.

"Keep the faith, brother. Our day will come." Elisa tried to reassure him but even she was beginning to have doubts.

It took a few more days for the kidney to regain their full function. In fact, they started to put out more urine than before the new medicine started. This is a stage of healing.

"Tubular flutter" proclaimed Testade. "Not really shut down but a fluttering that disrupts the function for a short time. I am glad I caught it in time. Good job, Elisa and Carla. How is the BP?"

"About the same. The balloon did not open up the artery. I think we are ready for surgery. When is Carter coming back?"

"He is not due back for 2 days."

"We better get him fixed before we succeed in killing him as we try to help. How is the urine output?"

"The volume is large but the quality is not great. BUN coming down ever so slowly. In a sense it is piss poor."

"Keep that pun to yourself. That was awful."

"Well. Carter will not go after him until he is putting out good urine. Maybe we can give him a shove or do a rain dance. I took rain dancing lessons when I was in the Air Force in Nevada. Never fails."

"I'll keep that in mind." Testade actually smiled.

For the next two days, things seemed to be stable or improving. The blood pressure was not any higher but was not coming down either. The urine output slowed down to normal rate as the kidney was able to remove the toxins that had built up in the blood. Of course when Carter came back, he was all upset that the vital signs were not perfect. As any control freak would, he nit picked all the decisions that Testade made.

"Why did you use nifedipine instead of Adalat?"

"I think they are the same drug, Carter. Elise replied.

"I don't like using hydrodiuril either. And change that 50 mg to 40 of lasix. Who ever wrote down the vital signs this way?"

"That is the download from the monitoring system," Replied Carla.

"My, My, aren't we pissy today. And you don't even have on the yellow leader shirt. When are you going to schedule surgery?"

"Tomorrow."

The parents were relieved that finally they would get the needed removal of the obstruction.

"Whoopee, now for some real blood and guts surgery. Get 'er done." yelled Uncle Doug.

At 6 AM the next day, the staff was busy getting Henry ready for his trip to the OR. All the IV lines were replaced with new ones, his pre-op sedation was given and the ICU staff kissed and hugged him as the transport team took him out the ICU doors.

The OR staff was also busy with getting all the equipment, catheters, grafts and medications lined up on the prep trays. The room was chilly so Carla had put an extra blanket on Henry so he would be comfortable. After the usual banter and one-up talk between the Thor Norton, the anesthesiologist and Randolf, the case got underway. The operation started with scrubbing of the skin and covering the body with a series of drapes so only the area to be cut was exposed. The long incision along the bottom of the rib cage provided a good exposure to get to the renal arteries. . After a lot of clipping small arteries as the opening was enlarged, the aorta and renal arteries were finally exposed.

"There is the criminal, See that narrowing on the renal artery. That is the problem. Notice that the area after the stenosis is larger from the jet stream of the blood blasting past the narrow segment, just like the MRA showed. How is the blood loss so far?" Carter's voice reflected his internal excitement.

"About 50 cc's., vitals are good" replied Thor Norton.

"OK. Let's move on. The plan is to open the right artery at the site of the constriction and put in a patch to achieve a continuous caliber of the artery from the aorta to the kidney. On the left, since the stenosis is so close to the aorta, we will put in a Dacron graft from the aorta and attach it to the renal artery after the constriction. Should be a piece of cake. We have to make sure that the blood flow to the kidney is not cut off too long. Otherwise we will kill the kidney that we are trying to save. Follow me?"

"Right Dr. Randolf," agreed Peter Bird, the chief resident who was his first assistant and also his sounding board.

These arteries were about the caliber of a cocktail straw so both surgeons were wearing magnifying glasses to get a clear view of the three arterial layers. "I decided to use a graft from a vein and wrap a piece of Dacron around it and the renal artery for extra support. They got very quiet as Peter salvaged an unimportant vein from Henry's leg to serve as the patch. Carter stopped for a minute to review his approach.

"The vein was ready." Peter reported.

Carter took over. "Give me clamp time and call out the minutes that the blood flow is stopped." The scrub nurse slapped a small sharp pointed scissors in his hand before he could ask for it. Anticipation, preparation and smooth moves were the hallmarks of a great scrub nurse. The degree of slapping instruments was directly proportional to the anger in the OR. If there were a lot of shouting, the slaps became stronger. It was the unwritten way of communication. Strong slaps mean get control of yourself and stop screaming.

The thickened narrow piece of renal artery was removed and the graft sewn in.

"Eight minutes clamp time."

"Done- Dacron wrap with embedded fine titanium wire was sewn over the graft. We have learned the hard way that vein grafts tend to weaken over time to form an aneurysm and possibly rupture. Now we put in this safety feature to all grafts. We don't want any surprises in a few years."

This part of the operation took 90 minutes but their intense concentration on the operative field made it seem like seconds.

"How are we doing, Thor?"

"Things are moving along well. The BP was a little rocky when you were working on the artery but it is stable and still elevated."

"Blood loss?"

"250cc's. we have blood here, ready to infuse."

"Urine output?"

"Still about 1cc per minute. Stable"

"Ok Lets go for the other side. This should be similar to the right except the graft will be all reinforced Dacron and we will have to clamp off the aorta for a brief time. Let me see the graft. OK let's put in the stay sutures and have them ready for connection. We will do the graft into the artery first. Peter, you get that started while I get the aorta ready for the other end."

Peter did his part quickly getting the graft onto the renal artery. Carter seemed puzzled by the aorta.

"This aorta feels like someone stomped on it with hiking shoes. It is not holding the sutures well. The intima is like wet toilet paper. I'll have to use 6-0 suture to see if the smaller material will hold better."

"It is better but not great. Let's push on how is the aorta clamp time?"

"4 minutes"

"Let's get moving." Now the sweat was building up on his forehead and arm pits. Actually he was drenched but no one could see his scrub shirt as the sterile gown covered him well.

After more sewing, he finally got the graft attached to the first layer of the aorta. Then he went for the next layer which seemed to be slightly in better shape. He finally completed the microsurgery, stood back and told Peter to remove the clamp.

Niagara falls in red. Blood shot out all around the suture line. The diseased aorta was not holding the sutures. "Clamp the damn aorta and get me some packing."

He quickly stuffed the   packing around the graft. Release the clamp. This time it was better. Just some slight oozing.

"We are going nowhere until we make sure that the oozing stopped. Give some damn blood."

"Already taken care of, Carter."

"Good. I am not happy with this graft. I hope it holds."

Just then another gusher appeared.

Carter snipped it with a small hemostat the stopped the bleeding He looked over at the kidney which was a good pink color indicating that at least, the blood was flowing to it; the blood loss could be matched with transfusions.

Carter was getting more and more agitated that this delicate surgery was breaking down. "Oh Lord! I need your help! I can't stay here all day waiting for the diseased aorta to spring leaks."

Peter was feeling that Carter was getting over his head and now.

"The whole thing could blow up and the boy could die. I can't go backwards and remove the graft. I needed a plan B."

It was obvious a new approach was needed but Carter was too far along in panic mode to think clearly.

Peter was thinking, "No wonder they say that this type of surgery is a young man's sport."

"Jesus! Where the hell is Kirby?" He was now looking for Kirby Jackson, the cardiovascular surgeon who has done far more operations than Carter on these small arteries. "I guess I should have had him in here with me," knowing he did not mean it as then he would have to share the glory with the anticipated excellent results. "Has anyone seen Kirby?"

Peter replied "I saw him on rounds early this AM." Babette the circulating nurse called out "I put in a page for him. I am looking up his office number."

Kirby was indeed in the hospital. He had finished rounds about 7AM, had coffee with his team in the cafeteria and then mentioned to Mary Ann, the cardiac surgery Nurse Specialist. "What about Amkey? She replied. "I think that is a good idea."

Depending on the time of day there was the portmanteau; Amkey was Am-nookie, Noonkey- noon nookie or pee-emkey for anytime in the PM. In case you are not sure of the time, you can just grab your crotch. Since this was 7:30 in the morning, Amkey was the appropriate word. Kirby had a bed in his office suite where he could sleep when he was staying late in the hospital, when there was bad weather that would prevent him from getting home or to the hospital in the morning or for nookie. He and Mary Ann headed off to the office for their tryst while the rest of the cardiac surgery team went on to do their patient care.

"When are we going to do this in more luxurious environment? Once a year trip to Antigua is not my idea of the good life. You know sooner or later someone is going to walk in to your office and catch us."

"I know, I know, I am working on it. I have a plan. But not today. Let's go"

They took the elevator to the fifth floor, walked by the secretaries in the front room and went into Kirby's private office. There was an additional door which let to his apartment, a bed and a bathroom. Double locking both his office door and the door leading into the love nest, he hopped on the bed.

Thank goodness for scrub suits, saves time. "Do you mind if I keep my shirt on. This had to be a real quickie."

"As you like, chief, you can keep on your socks too. Never know when you will be paged for an emergency."

"Not today. I have a light day after yesterday's 5 operations. I need a break."

Mary Ann took off her white coat, her blue scrubs, bra and panties. "How do I look, I have been on LA weight loss, trying to get rid of a few pounds."

"You look great. But I think I am losing my eyesight. Can you come a little closer? As she danced over to the bed, Kirby grabbed her by the waist and pulled her down on top of him.

"This is almost as good as than standing all day in the OR and fixing little hearts. Now little girl, where is the problem?"

"You almost have hit it. You are a little high and to the right."

"Listen babe, that hard thing down there is not an endoscope with a television camera."

"The way you are pulling on my boobs, you would think these knobs are controlling the camera's position."

"Sorry, was I too rough, you know surgeons, have to keep their hands busy."

"No, not rough enough. It has been a long time."

"Bang,Bang"......

There was a knock on the door. "Dr. Jackson, Dr. Randolf wants you immediately in the OR. Sorry to interrupt. But he said it was an emergency."

"He has an emergency; I hope it is better than my problem at this moment."

"Sorry Babe, The boss calls."

Kirby arrived still breathless, even though he had to come down one flight of steps from his office to the OR.

"What's up?"

"I have a double renal artery stenosis. One side has a venous graft with a wrap but the other side has half of a bypass graft around the block but I can't get the sutures to hold when I sew it into the aorta. Things were temporarily under control. I had plugged up all the leaks but I needed a permanent fix to the getting blood through the rusty aorta. I could not trust any suture line."

"The old rusty aorta problem. Hold your finger in the dike while I scrub up and I will look things over."

The scrub seemed to take hours but in 10 minutes he was back at the operating table, ready for action. "Almost better than sex."

Carter smiled because he had the same dilemma, sex or surgery- which one was better?

Kirby felt the aorta and concurred, "You will not get a good suture hold in that rotten aorta. The same disease that is in the renal arteries is in the aorta in the mid-abdominal region. We will have to do a major by-pass. OK if I step in?"

Carter, totally spent, would have welcomed the tooth fairy if she could get him out of this problem. "Be my guest!"

Kirby was the best under pressure. His steely outward appearance hid the adrenaline pumping inside. His BP must be 200/150. Talk about internalizing stress.

"Get me three feet of aortic Dacron graft and 2 one foot pieces of regular arterial graft. Soak them in heparin and get me some vascular clamps and scissors. Adjust the light and raise the table about 6 inch- es." This last order was another dagger in Carter's side as he silently acknowledged the order to raise the table. That bothered him for it high lighted the differences in their heights.

"Here is the plan; I am going to put the graft into the higher up on the aorta where the tissue is normal. Then I will bring it down to put the other end in the artery near the leg. That artery should hold the sutures. Kind of a beltway around the problem, just like the 495 by pass around South Creek, you know. Then I will put a side graft from this large one into the renal ar- tery. What matters is that the blood gets to the kidney without the block."

"Just what I was thinking."

Kirby's innovative solution was hard for Carter to visualize imme- diately but he deferred to Kirby, a real cowboy but a genius in battle conditions. Kirby acted like he did this every day but this was his first such operation in these conditions although he had done numerous grafts and bypasses. It was the rapid way he came up with this solution that amazed Carter. Even usually silent Peter Bird shook his head in amazement. "You are like the Lone Ranger, galloping in from the mountain and firing your silver bullet."

"Thanks, Pete, I was not in the mountains but I am fully loaded. Let's go. Do you have the graft ready? Let's get some good country music playing." Country music was the only thing that did not go along with this urbane façade. But it seemed to work.

The next two hours were spent listening to Brooks and Dunne, Reba and Hank Williams while they exposed the aorta so that the graft could be inserted.

"Now let's do the same thing down in the iliac artery."

"I'll drop out and go talk to the parents. What was their name?"

Carter first headed to the locker room to take off the bloody OR gown and put on his white coat. The face mask dropped below his chin. All part of the image. He told them what was going on and how the operation was different from the original plan but it was working.

"I called in a vascular surgeon to work on the new approach. Right now we should stop and pray for Henry's good outcome. Let us pray."

The parents thanked him for all his concern and help. They knelt down, held hands with Dr. Randolf and prayed for a successful outcome. When Carter left, Mr. Barksdale remarked "Dr. Randolf had such humility. Another surgeon would not be so self assured as to ask for help. Thank goodness we came to CHUC."

But Uncle Doug piped in. "I bet he got over his head and could not fix the mess he made."

Kirby Jackson was the genius that he told everyone he was. He put in the grafts watched the color of the kidneys pink up and saw the clear slightly yellow urine come pouring out of the bladder catheter.

"How is the BP?"

"Still elevated."

"That is OK it takes days and even weeks for the kidney to calm down and the body adjust to the new blood flow. It should be easier to control his pressure. Good job, team Where is Carter?"

"I'm here. There can only be one captain of the ship so I did not want to get in your way. You are amazing Kirby. I am so glad that you were here. I have to admit that I would not have come up with your solution."

"I am here to stamp out disease and cure little children. Just my humble aim in life." As he took off his gown and threw it into the dirty laundry basket, he realized that this was better than sex, better than a whole day of sex. But he had to figure out how to make it up to Mary Ann. These quickies in the office bed were not fair to her, even though he did not mind cutting out all the preambles of dinner, wine and music before the big event.

Chapter 15

"You look tired, Lester. What is up?" asked Adrienne who was having her morning whine with Sara Wright .

Lester, taking his seat at the corner table in the cafeteria with other house officers, said "It was another late night. Felix had the blue flag outside the door of the apartment so I had to sit out on the street until the coast was clear."

"How did you hook up with Felix? You are so different."

"It seemed like a good idea. With both of us on call so much between the hospital and moonlighting at the Good Samaritan, it seemed like only one of us would be in the apartment most nights. But the schedules are not that coordinated so there are many, too many, nights when we are both not working at the hospital. I spend a lot of time in Starbucks across the street waiting for the all's clear signal."

"Why don't you get your own honey and there will be fair competition for the room?"

"I am not good at this dating thing. I can memorize pages of information. I remember all the data about my patients but when it comes to small talk with someone I don't know, I am at a loss. I learned how to say, "Hey, Babe. But not much after that."

"You need a coach."

"A coach? I was never good at being an athlete."

"This is not that kind of sports coach. A talk coach. A coach will help you with the script. You memorize what to say and then become an active listener as she talks on and on."

"Do these people exist? Where do I find one? You know I can't afford to pay a coach, I am still being bothered by my loans and buying food."

"I see you are not spending much on clothes. You wear the same things day after day. Maybe I can be your coach. I love to talk and I have, unfortunately, a lot of free time when I am away from the hospital." Adrienne volunteered.

"You do not want to tie yourself with my socializing skills."

"Why not, you helped me a lot getting through surgery."

"What happened to the eHarmony thing on the internet?"

"I got a few hits from some red necks in Alabama. Even though I am light skinned, they would see that I am black if they ever met me."

"I thought we settled it, you are not black; that is a racist view of your mixed heritage."

"I don't think we are going to change the world view of that issue. Let's get back to coaching."

"I don't know what I am going to do. This sitting at Starbucks or on the curb, outside my apartment is not working. I may have to rent another apartment, even though it will kill my budget. I am running out of options."

"Wait a minute. I have another idea. Why don't you move in with us? We have an extra room and you could be our guardian angel." Piped in Sara.

"What! Move in with two girls?"

"That is safer than moving in with just one of us. People would talk."

"Don't reject that idea. As the cold weather and early sunsets continue, you will be out on cold streets instead of a cozy apartment with two lovely girls scanning the internet for the perfect man."

"I will see how it goes. Maybe if Felix stops gulping down testosterone pills or if, hard to believe, he gets worn out, I will be able to get equal time in the apartment. I am not saying no, just on hold. I am more interested in the idea of a coach. Let me try you out, if I cannot get a real coach, I will hire you. What do I do after I say Hey Babe?"

"Why not try to look her over and notice a pin, a ring or even a logo on a shirt."

"What do I do with that information?"

"Say. Nice pin, where did you get that? People will like that you noticed and will be glad to relive the purchase if they bought it or think of the person who gave it."

"What if they say their boyfriend gave it?"

"Well then you know that they have a boyfriend. Better to find out early than later."

"You have a point there. But what if they bought it."

"Then you say where is that store or I know that store. Girls like to connect an object with a store where most boys just want to get their new electronics and watch it or listen to it, not caring where it was purchased."

"What next?"

"Maybe if you seem interesting to them, they will ask you a question then you answer and on and on you go.

"This is fun. Just like a computer program, If this, than that. If not this. Then try that. I see what you are getting to. I think you are hired as my coach. When is the next session?

"See you tomorrow at coffee time. Have to go back and check some labs."

• • •

Richardson Beardsley opened the operations committee meeting. "Welcome. We have a lot of things to go over. Is Carter coming? Does anyone know?"

"He had a big case yesterday and spent most of the night in the ICU.

"Well then we can get started. First item is the new MRI. We have ordered it and expect it to be here in June."

"Hey. Wait a minute Richardson! Another MRI? I thought we were discussing the need for another one."

"Come on John, we talked it over and the board agreed that if we are to be number one we need to show the public that we have the most and the latest."

"We have three MRI's already. I checked with my colleagues in the other major hospitals. Three is the most anyone has."

"That is my point. Number one has the most and the latest."

"What does this one do that our old ones don't do?"

"Well the new one prints out the report and sends copies to at least three different sources like the referring doctor, the family doctor and a consultant."

"How much does this beauty cost?"

"The retail price is 2.5 mil but I arranged a big discount."

"We need a digital x-ray set up."

The mark up and reimbursement of regular x-rays do not compare with the MRI. For Medical assistance, we actually lose money on x-rays while when we use MRI fully scheduled, we can get about 200 or more over costs for each study. Some even over $500 over costs. That makes good business sense."

"Who is going to read these additional studies?" You know MRI's are not my specialty. I like the good old chest x-rays and broken bones."

"I know that. We have to recruit some hot dog MRI specialist who can churn out the studies."

"I thought we were going to hire another general radiologist. We need one to keep up with the demand. There is such a long waiting list for people to get their studies done and read."

"In today's market and reimbursement rates, it does not make sense to build up routine radiology. I am looking up the possibility of outsourcing some of the interpretation to a service in India. You know they work when we are down for the evening so we can have a fresh batch of reports first thing in the AM. I have a few leads on possibilities."

"Slow down! How do we know their ability? What about their malpractice if they make a mistake. I think this type of decision should be discussed in a meeting with the radiology staff."

"I was just tossing this out. No decisions have been made. Just giving you a heads up. We have to be constantly updating our services; the old way is not the new way. The adult hospital has an arrangement with a group in Israel to read x-rays at night. It is day time over there so it provides 24 hour coverage for radiology without overwhelming the staff here. You don't want to be overwhelmed, do you John?"

"I know about that. The radiologists have been trained and boarded in radiology in the U.S. that is different than a company in India. We don't know the quality of their radiologists. I can't understand the computer help desk people, whatever country they are in."

"We will discuss this further. Now about the upcoming Joint Commission on accreditation's inspection of the hospital. You know that the best hospital in the US should have the merit award from this group certifying we are tops I have hired a new vice president for inspections and quality. She comes to us from Stanford where they have had great success with their JCAHO inspections. She will start in June and report directly to me. Anything from Pediatrics, David?

"We are having a good recruiting season for next year's first year residents. The number of applications has gone up 10%. We interviewed 120 people and accepted thirty. That is about as many as we can effectively handle. We are using hospitalists and nurse practitioners to take up the patient load. Above 30 interns, the supervision gets spread out too thinly. We still need some more coverage in the community clinics. Since these units refer a number of patients to the labs and x-rays, maybe the hospital can fund some of the community doc positions."

"Not right now, we are pressed for funds, you know. You have to understand that community service is a drain on our resources. We have to stay with our business plan. Any awards or honors I should know about?"

"At this point the medical group was so annoyed with the emphasis on money and margins, that they took the silent way to indicate that they wanted to end this painful hour." Beardsley, as usual, ignored this silent treatment but thought that he had overwhelmed them with his management style so he showed his evil grin and ended this meeting with "Nothing? So see you next month." He went back to his executive suite to meet with the finance staff.

Beardsley liked to have his meetings in his office where he was the boss and did not have to subject his decisions to the medical staff. He liked to look at the walls full of his diplomas and awards. Last year he had a new wall constructed so he could hang up more of his framed documents. When others talked, he counted his awards to make sure all of them were still on display.

"How is your son doing, Al? I hope the docs are taking good care of him."

"He is doing so-so. After he healed from the car accident, he had many complications from the surgery plus a mild pneumonia. That thank the Lord, is over but he still has a lot of rehab to do. They say about 1 year plus before they will know what he can recover. We take one day at a time. Thankfully the insurance is taking care of it until we settle with the driver. That takes years, I am afraid."

"Yes we take care of our own. We have the best medical coverage. A perk for being in the administration. Give your wife my best."

He turned to the new COO, Eugene James. "Are you getting settled in your bachelor quarters? I hope you can devote the time to your COO position; we need all the players to give 110%. I know divorces are messing things and are very costly. I have been through it several times. The child support killed me. Those kids that put me into poverty don't even talk to me now. Glad I have a new set of kids. They are so cute but I feel like a grandfather around them. Maybe that is why they still talk to me. They are raised by a nice nanny most of the time."

"And Caroline, how things. I hope you are saving some of your huge salary to pay back your loans. And not overdoing your credit cards."

"You bet! I am working on the repayment. The credit cards are a different story. It is hard to get the balance down. Maybe I will just cut them up and go cash only. That will be hard. There are so many sales now of things I desperately need." Realizing that she was already saying too much, she stopped talking and opened up her notebook that she carried at all times so she would remember who said what and when. Actually she hardly ever read the notes but it made her feel better to be writing than trying to listen to all the chatter at the seemingly endless meetings that went along with her job.

"Nothing is desperate. Self control--self control. Now let's get down to business. We need to come up with a revised business plan for the hospital. As you know, the board is cutting out the automatic bonuses and putting us on a performance reward system. For the medical side, it is productivity- how many patients- how much are the charges and collections and how good is the patient mix. They will have to see more, especially patients with good insurance. But for us, it is cash flow; charges, uncollected charges and timeliness of billing- the time it takes to send out the bill after the services are provided. That is the game and we are the players. You are my finance team so if you want a good bonus, you have to work harder to get the good numbers up and the bad numbers down. Get it."

"I thought we were doing a good job with the billing and the collections."

"You are. The one variable is the charges. There is a lot of unmined gold in those hills and we have to be creative to get more out of the reimbursement people. Unbundling the charges so we can bill more for the same amount of work."

"What do you mean? I thought we had done a good job with what you might call a little padding to the bills."

"Please don't use that word; we might have a hidden tape recorder somewhere in the room. Ha Ha."

"For example, we are approved for a minimum of one hour of OR time for each case. The simple operations like hernia repairs and tonsillectomies don't take an hour. Most of the down time is cleaning up after the operation and setting up for the next case. If we can speed up those two functions, we can squeeze several more cases a day and still get OR charges for one hour for each case. Look at Southwest Airlines; they have the shortest on ground time between landing and the next take off. They can more traffic through each gate compared to the older airlines. If we work it right, we can get 12 to 13 hours of billing for an 8 hour day. All it takes is an extra housekeeping person, oops I mean environmental services person. It would be worth the extra 12/hr person to collect 300 bucks for the OR rental. The other option is to skip the cleanup and hope that there are no germs in the OR. "

"Is this legal. 12 hours of billing for 8 hours of clock time?"

"Now Caroleen, you know we are always on the good side of legal questions. The insurance companies OK'd the one hour minimum payment. We are just being more efficient. Like the car rental business. You return a car early in the day, you get charged for a day and if they get it cleaned quickly, they can rent it again and get another day's rental from the next client. No one complains about that. Perfectly legal."

Caroleen dropped her head and went back to writing in her notebook.

"Next we need to discharge patients earlier than we do now. There are too many patients sleeping in a bed and then going home the next morning. If we send them home at night, we can have an open bed at 7 AM the next day awaiting the new patient. They can get attended to earlier and more tests or whatever done on the day of admission. Now the family wanders in when they like and the bed is not ready until 2-3 in the afternoon. I am authorizing a new position of vice president of discharge planning whose job is to get the discharged patients out of the hospital the moment the discharge order is written."

"Isn't it dangerous to send people out at night in this neighborhood?"

"That is their problem. This is the only way I can see to get thebeds open for the early morning admissions. Just look at the allowable charges, when an injection is given, there is payment for the injection. When they take a pill, there is no extra payment. We need to encourage injections. I have a report from a survey Max did for me about the difference in prices for generic drugs and patented drugs. We are missing opportunities of dispensing generics and charging for patented drugs."

"I don't think that is legal, is it?"

"Now Al, we would never do anything illegal. This is what I call creative patient care."

"I still have a problem with it, what ever you call it."

"Just how do you think we afford the great insurance that pays the costs of your son's treatments? Try to find that type of coverage in another job! Get the picture, Al?"

"Right, when you phrase it that way, it sounds very appealing to me."

"How about getting the billing people to upgrade the level of billing. I think we have too many level 3 cases that with a little review can be made level 4 with higher rates of payments. I hear there is a computer program that can review the record and the bill and tweak the record to make the case eligible for level 4. There is gold in those tweaks. The program does not cost that much. It can pay for itself in 2 months or less. I will get the IT veep to look into that and get it implemented on the inpatient and outpatient units."

Beardsley hit the table with his fist, "that would be illegal to alter the medical record. We have to keep this plan within reasonable legal parameters. I also want to remind you that this is highly confidential. If word of this gets out, we are cooked. And none of us can afford to be caught and be out of work."

"Now is the time for real brain storming. We have a big difference between our charges and our collections. Millions. In our finance reports there is a column for charges and another column for expected payments; In the third column, called the reserve is the amount of money that we don't expect to collect, since we never can recover all those charges. When the insurance company issues a payment, we record that as income then adjust the reserve amount. We use the amount of uncollected funds as our contributions to the community, a good will gesture, which is providing non- compensated care to the poor. It is sort of accentuating the positive accounting. Our bonuses are partly calculated on income. So you get together and see what you can do to make this figure larger. On the other hand, we do make a profit, no, not a profit but a positive balance. That cannot look too large because our contributors cut back when they see how well we are doing. A piece of the excess is transferred to the foundation. No we are not talking about an account in the Bahamas or Zurich, but the hospital foundation. Then we can cry poor mouth because cash on hand is not good and the contributors fork up more. The contributions will also be a positive on our performance and bonus."

"This sounds a little confusing. So depending on the game we are playing, we are either rich or poor."

"That is a little harsh but you are getting the idea. Since you felt confused, I think it is a good system. For some reason the auditors and accountants do not have a column for realistic anticipated collections.

So even though we know Medicaid will pay 50 dollars we can use our 250 charge so it looks like we are making a lot of money. If we had to list the income as 50, we would never get a bonus. Fortunately, the system is so complex, that only skillful auditors can read through all these bullshit numbers. I love to play the game. You make up the rules and I will be able to develop a creative accounting system to help our bonus. I will share some of this with the board- bringing more efficiency to our management team but not all of what we discussed. We have too much at stake to mess this up. Right? We don't want to lose our income, insurance and bonuses. Not with all the obligations we have right?"

"Right boss, we are with you. Creativity."

"You said it, creative. Look I provide the vision and you two write the code for the program."

Caroline remained quiet but her smile covered up the silence. One of the good things about being labeled as quiet or shy is that people don't expect much noise from you so silence is the natural response. She picked up her notebook and started to leave the room for her office and the load of emails that she had not yet cleared from her in box.

"Oh Caroleen, can I speak to you before you go?"

"Of course,"

"How are you doing with the surgery caper?"

"It is going quite well. Very well. I spoke to Dr. Randolf about working up a list of equipment and office improvements that he may want so that when a big donor comes forth, we will be ready with the list, the options, potential uses and costs. He jumped at that idea. When I was there, I noticed a lot of duplication in the mechanics of billing, too many hands touching too many papers, just to get a bill processed. Even though it eventually gets to the computer billing system, the lead-in is cumbersome. And I suspect there are a lot of dropped charges for supplies as I see a lot of disposable supplies for wound care, for example, that are not being recorded on the charge sheet. A perfect set up for a scanner system like the supermarkets have. Scan the name of the patient, scan the supply and it is in the system, no paper, no time lost. He liked that idea of freeing up his staff from billing and invited me to come back and look around for more areas that would save money."

"Great going Caroleen. You were very creative and clever. I am so glad that you got along with him. Sometimes he becomes too preachy."

"Well he did invite me to come to his church. Actually the church is near my apartment so I went. It is a very nice group and the pastor is full of passion."

"Hearing the word passion energized Beardsley. He was not going to be able to control himself if this discussion keeps going. "Did you find anything about his expenses?""

"Not really, he seems to be working long hours and not going out for long lunches or meetings. He loves the OR and surgery. Same for his staff. It seems from the outside to be up and up. I will still keep looking."

"Great job Caroleen." He had one more chance to see her walk out of the room and imagine what it would be like to take her on one of his trips. Sorry to cut this short."

• • •

The next month, in the executive suite, President of the board, Clayton Pickering looked around at the group and began.

"Let's begin today with a few announcements. We are happy to announce that we have secured a generous donation from Mr. Romanesco for the funding of a new MRI. Hats off of Richardson for negotiating a great deal from Dynamic Imaging, the supplier of our radiology equipment. Thanks Dick. Great job!"

"We have also been negotiating with a NFL coach to be our Man of the Year awardee for the First Trust Ball to culminate our fund raising week in June. Mrs. Randolf is doing a bang up job heading that affair. I don't think she is here but thanks to Carrie where ever you are."

"We are hiring a new accounting firm to replace the Patterson group that can no longer take care of our job as they have decided to get out of the health care business and focus on the security field. There many other companies who have submitted bids to take over our accounting."

"I am pleased that we are doing such a great job in the financial area but will not steal Dick's thunder. So Dick why don't you take over."

"Yes we have had a great quarter. Admissions are up 6%. Patients days have held even compared to last year and billing is up 15%, Yes 15%. We have had a great quarter.

"How did you get the billing up so much?" Asked Norman Oppenheim.

"We did a little of this and a little of that."

"What does that mean?"

"Well we unbundled some of the lab tests. That is instead of billing for a liver panel, we bill for each test individually, and then bill for blood collection for each lab tests even though only one blood was drawn. We also have changed the charges for OR time. We now bill for one hour segments. For T and A's we can do three an hour so we get three hours of billing in an actual hour."

"Is that legal?"

"We have cleared it with the insurance companies showing them that although the procedure took 20 minutes we have to have time to set up and take down the room. They approved. We have other tricks; I mean strategies to maximize our billing on the throughput. Re: the MRI. We are glad to have this latest version of MRI. The staff is excited and it will no doubt help us immensely on our quest to be named number one Children's Hospital by US New and World Report. We are looking to add to our radiology staff to get someone skilled in MRI interpretation. John Spirito admits that this new imaging is not his interest or skill so he is happy to add to the staff to work in this area. We have a search firm looking into applicants. We are looking into ways to better serve the community. I have discussed these plans with Bunky the other day. She is excited about this important part of our mission to serve the community of South Creek as well as serve the needs of children throughout the nation and hopefully international patients as well. They are the ones with cash payments.

I will be bringing to the board some exciting ideas about renovating the hospital to provide the right environment for the new advances in medical technology. We are not ready for this but have been working with a committee of the board to explore ideas. We are in the process of hiring Rapsky Associates to help up with dealing with architecture firms. They are architects who now are consultants to hospitals to make sure the project architects do their job and to advise us on planning and scope of the project."

Dixon McIver bends over to Thomas Heatherton "Where did we get this guy? He is terrific. I don't know how much he gets paid but he should get a raise. He is a national treasure."

"He talks a good game but I want to hear more before I give him the bank. He already gets big bucks to run this place."

"In my business that is peanuts, we give that much in bonuses at the end of the year. 1.5 mil is pocket change."

"Any report from the Finance people. Al?"

"Our books look quite good. As you heard, our numbers are up in billing. We have 2.4 in cash, after transferring funds to the endowment fund. We have to keep numbers in that range as the union contract comes up later this year. It is hard to go into negotiations with large cash accounts. We have our big fund raiser coming up, as you heard. Hard to claim poverty with too much cash."

"Thanks Al, I think we can do without the editorial comments, Al. Just stick to the numbers."

"Is he as big a schmuck as he sounds? Doesn't he know that this is a public record? Say,,,, Dixon, how's your boat?"

"Which boat? The one that my captain drives or the one that I run."

"You have two boats?"

Sure, I have the 125 foot honey and the 55 foot fishing boat. My captain does not let me get near the cockpit of the big one. And you?"

"I have a 15 foot sailboat. Enough for me."

"Nice."

Norman Oppenheim asked "What about the new bonus plan that was discussed before?"

"We sensed your concern, Norman at the past meeting so we have hired compensation consultants to look into the conflicts that were mentioned."

"Where do you get such consultants?"

"Dick checked around and found out who was experienced in children's hospitals."

"Is that a conflict? I have a problem with the person who pays the consultant to determine if the payor is getting the right pay. On other boards that I serve on, the compensation committee engages the consultant without the executives participating in the negotiating."

"You have a good point, Norman. But it is done so we will see when they give the report. Anything else? Yes Bunky."

"I went into the emergency area and it was not clean. The toilets were not nice. There were papers all around."

"What day was that? We found that Monday is a bad day after the busy weekend."

"Why is that?"

"The weekend staff is not as large as the week day staff."

"But the census is busier on the weekends, I checked into the figures. Is it because of the overtime pay for weekends? Dick, what do you say?"

"We don't worry about the cost of cleanliness. I will look into it."
"Is I will look into it hospital speak for 'up yours?'"
"You're bad, give him a break, he is trying to make money"
"For his bonus?"

"I would also like to announce that Mrs. Kirby Jackson will head up a new project called South Creek Reads, our approach to building up literacy in the community. Mrs. Jackson has run the South Creek Bakes, when we sold brownies throughout the community to raise money for the home care nursing project. She is a real dynamo, doing a great deal to raise funds for the hospital. I think we should look into getting her on the board."

Gayle Jackson, the energetic wife of Kirby Jackson, stands out as a good example of 'only in America.' Born as Galina Piertrokowski she came from a small town outside of Pittsburgh called Shikalillity where her father and grandfather worked in the steel mills. Her mother took care of the kids and house and attended Mass at St. Andrews every day. She could make kielbasa and pirogues with the best of the community but her forté was baking. She had no good words for her contemporaries who abandoned the old country for Sara Lee or Entenmanns's but fortunately for her family; she wanted to continue the Polish traditions of baking authentic cookies and cakes. Galina worshipped her mother, especially her cooking, so she was a willing assistant, learning as much as she could about the fine art of baking. Like the other graduates of St. Vladimar High school, she only thought about getting married or working in a factory or diner. Gayle did both, she married Thomas Waskotova and went to work at Rosie's Café where the food was like her mom's and the baking done on premises. The customers were mainly office people from the steel plant and, between meal times, the local ladies came in for coffee and pastry. Galina worked the counter initially, but soon told Rosie that she could bake some special items that would boost business. That was all Rosie had to hear. "More pastry, more dough" was her retort to the idea of expanding the menu. "Galina, get into the kitchen and show me your best stuff." Galina was an instant success. Her kolacky and rugelach went over well . Soon the café offered take-outs and was busier at 10:30 and 4 than it was at the usual meal time. The offerings increased to accommodate the season and the many holidays. Galina stuck to tradition, only baking certain goodies for appropriate saints. No canned fruit but thanks to Peruvian grapes and strawberries, some special treats were made in the winter as well as the summer when local produce was available.

One of the men from the marketing department of the mill told her she should go on her own then franchise the bakery. Her pastries would be a hit for non-Poles as well as the fellow countrymen. Galina only knew about McDonald's franchises and how the Steelers would designate a franchise player. She did not reject the idea but talked to Mike, one of her loyal customers who was manager at the McDonalds on Holiday Street. He liked the idea. She could not get much help from her family about franchising, so she decided that she needed to get smarter-she was going to college and study franchising. On her day off, she met with the admissions officer at Allegheny County Community College, telling him she wanted to go to college and study franchising. Her charm exceeded her high school record; fortunately the admissions director took a chance on her gut feeling. She got accepted on a probationary level. If she did well, she could stay and if she was below the middle of the class after one year, she would be back at Rosie's.

"Fine" replied Galina, "now I want to get a work study job at the college, the highest paying one. I don't care what it is but I need to get some money." She was assigned to pot washing in the school cafeteria.

After two years, she was near the top of the class but had not learned much about franchising. So she transferred to the University of Pittsburgh Business School. She learned a great deal about franchising, especially how much money the person with the original idea could make. All she needed was start up funds and a business plan so she learned how to write a business plan as she looked for an investor to help her open up the first bakery. Her Uncle Sam came to the rescue. She applied and got a Small Business loan. Grandma's Cakes and Cookies was born in Sommerville Heights, a suburb of Pittsburgh where young executives had discovered 4 bedroom, 3 baths finished basement houses. These people, fond of desserts but too busy to spend the time in the kitchen, flocked to the bakery which soon started to serve latte and cappuccino, never seeming to mind the mixed culinary metaphor. Another bakery and another opened until there were 5 bakeries spewing out high calorie delicious treats. After 5 years of success, she was approached by another bakery owner about merging their businesses and going big time. The franchise dream was coming true. Things moved quickly. Ten bakeries allowed them to go to the bank and get loans to expand. After they hit 50 they went public, an IPO was organized by a classmate at Pitt. Galina was a millionaire, so was her mother and father. As she got her first check for 8 million dollars, she cried out, "Only in America." Her husband got his in the form of alimony as Galina was on a tear and not going to be held back by Tom who was happy with his Iron City beer, his kielbasa and the Steelers. At first, she was taken in by the glitter of the Wall Street visits and interviews on CNBC, she soon found herself unhappy with corporate life and quit. She loved to bake and this corporate life did not allow much time in the kitchen. She had enough stock and money from secondary offerings to keep her quite comfortable. Now she needed some social polish to go along with her Dunn and Bradstreet rating so she moved to New York, changed her name to Gayle Piel, became an Episcopalian and soaked up what she thought was high class life.

Her blond hair and blue eyes appeared regularly on the social pages but she realized she was not content without a job, so she volunteered at Lenox Hill Hospital. There she met Kirby Jackson, recently divorced also and a rising star in the cardiothoracic surgery world. New York was just about large enough for these two achievers who moved non-stop into all areas of social climbing via charity balls, dinners with Donald Trump and more charity balls and items on Page 6. Sunday Styles in the Times showed their faces about twice a month. At Lennox Hill Hospital, Gayle found a new home, organizing the hospital fund raising events. She married Kirby about a year after they met. Courtship was one party and dance after another. After they honeymooned in Antigua, they returned to a 3 bedroom apartment on Park and 63rd. Life was exciting at first but Gayle's social drive was exceeded only by Kirby's sexual energy. Predictably, Kirby started to wander away with almost anyone whom he met while Gayle took on more and more parties. Kirby gained a reputation for one of the best cardiac and vascular surgeons in New York; Gayle became the social climber's party planner. Neither complained nor felt slighted. Then Kirby got the chance to head up the heart surgery team at CHUC with a million plus salary and a special institute devoted to vascular and cardiac surgery. Happy to leave New York, Gayle relished the new opportunity, immediately took over the fund raising parties at CHUC. Kirby took over all the eager young and not so young nurses, secretaries, volunteers and contributors that he could. A delicate balance.

So it was natural that she was a favorite of the Board, having raised over 7 million dollars since she arrived in South Creek. Happy in this narrow restricted area of operations, she had no interests in other causes or other hospitals.

Their private life was another story. They were not really a couple but more like 2 year olds involved in parallel play. He played the hospital staff and she played the party life. Both seemed content in these roles.

Chapter 16

S ara Wright was busy in the medical clinic seeing the usual colds, ear infections and asthma problems. Somehow she continued to think this was fun, even though it was not the most stimulating work. She took the attitude that even though the concerns were not very challenging, the parents who came to the doctor were worried about their child's problem. She liked helping people and seeing the kids. She felt herself moving away from the idea of going into oncology and becoming instead, a general pediatrician. Then there was always the excitement of finding the one person with a fever who did not have an ear or urine infection but rather was in the early stages of rheumatoid arthritis or had an unusual infection. The first patient she saw when she started her training was a child with a fever who turned out to have acute leukemia. That experience led her to suspect leukemia in everyone for the next 6 months. After failing to find a second case, she eased up on that concern. The most difficult task was to separate out the problems such as pain. Was it appendicitis or someone that did not want to go to school or compete? Was it tension based or a brain tumor? Missing organic diseases still bothered her. She has not moved along in her experiences to be upset if she missed a psychological based problem but that will eventually happen. Her list for today had the usual: two babies in for a check-up, one ear pain, one case of diarrhea and one with fever for 4 weeks.

She breezed through the well babies; they were always fun especially the first babies for the parents. They usually tell the doctor that the baby is not eating enough. Their worry is quickly resolved when she tells the parents that the baby was gaining weight. She loved to use a trick she learned from Dr. Farmer. At the end of the session, on the instructions sheet, she records the weight and put a big "A" on the top, then tells the parents to show the grandmothers this mark of competence. This always works. Her next patient had an ear infection followed by a three year old with and diarrhea. The next child with a fever turned out to be a real challenge.

Irma Snow was a 10 year old who had fevers for 4 weeks. Wearing pink Crocs and a purple shirt that said "Hand over the chocolate and you won't get hurt," she sat quietly in her chair as her mother went into great detail about the fevers.

"We have had a lot of fevers; so many that I could not keep track of them so I charted them in a notebook, then transcribed the temperature values into my Excel program and graphed it out. You can see the color in the background- red for summer months, tan for fall, blue for winter and yellow for spring. At the bottom under the graph are highlights of that time. See the notes on activity, outside temperature, diet, pains, school absences and other symptoms." Mrs. Snow looked up at Dr. Wright awaiting her approval for the mother of the year award.

"That is some work of art; I think you could hang it in the Museum of Modern Art. I have not seen anything like this before. Mrs. Snow, how did you get all this information on this sheet? Amazing job!"

"Well I wanted you to get all the information, get the whole picture of what we are going through."

"Great! Tell me more about when the fevers started?"

"About 4 weeks ago. Yes, it was four weeks as I remember she was starting a new term at school. She gets such good grades. I am so proud of her. She had a cold and it seemed like the others we get. Sniffles and a cough. She took Tylenol and it seemed to run its course. I kept her home from school for a few days and then wanted her to get back to her studies. But the fever did not go away. It was 104 at times and other times it was 99. But we always had a temperature. She ate well and seemed not to be in pain."

"I see from the questionnaire that you filled out that she has had all her immunizations, she had not traveled, been exposed to anyone with an infection."

"Oh no, we stayed away from people who were sick. No malls, no movies."

The history continued with no hints why she should have a fever.

"OK Let's take a look. How are you Irma?"

"Good"

Irma sat on the examination table. She looked like a typical 10 year old, not quite ready to enter puberty. Her cheeks had a hint of rosy color, her face slightly round. She spent time with her hair as it was neatly combed with a flower beret on the side. She did not volunteer much information as Sara tried to engage her in some small talk about school or friends as she went through the physical exam.

"Your physical exam is perfectly normal. Aren't you glad to hear that?"

No response.

"You look too well for any of the bad causes of fever. But strange things happen in strange presentations."

"Which strange things are you thinking about? Mrs. Snow moved to the edge of here seat.

"There was urinary tract infection, inflammatory bowel disease, TB, brucellosis, tularemia, malaria and juvenile rheumatoid arthritis. She just does not fit the pattern of these problems. I mention them not to worry you but to let you know I was considering a long list of possible causes of fever." Because she had seen one young patient who came in for a fever and was eventually diagnosed with leukemia, that diagnosis was in the back of her mind, but she did not share that concern with Mrs. Snow.

"Wow! I used Google but did not come up with many of these diseases. Let me write them down."

"No need to do that. Give me some time and we can do some tests to focus our lists of possible problems."

"Thank you doctor. I am glad you are so thorough; we are so worried."

"Will you tell me what are you worried about?"

"Her fever, of course."

"Sorry, I mean which diseases have you on your list."

"None in particular, but now that you mention it; I wonder if she has leukemia."

"Why did you name leukemia?"

"Well I had a cousin who died of leukemia when she was about 10, just the same age as Irma."

"We can easily check that out for you with a blood test that I am ordering when we finish this visit. It is time to check with Dr. Pitman, who was the attending in charge of residents that day."

Dr. Pittman had a busy practice in South Creek but volunteered to work with residents one afternoon a week. For him, it was a break in the office routine. For the residents, it was a treat to learn his practical pointers. She remembers his first lesson- 'Listen to the patient they are telling you the diagnosis." Dr. Pittman did not like to do a lot of lab tests so Sara wanted to see how he would work through all these diseases that she thought of, all of them required some laboratory work to clinch the diagnosis.

"Dr. Pittman, I have a great case that I need your help with." Sara went over the case with him and her extensive differential diagnosis. Larry Pitman smiled as he could read her mind about the laboratory tests. He was impressed that she had such a good list to work through. He was not of the electronic age so he did not realize that she consulted her iPhone that contained several textbooks before she spoke to Dr. Pittman. A few clicks and the differential diagnosis appeared.

"Let's go in and speak to the Snows."

"Hi Irma and Mrs. Snow, I am Dr. Pittman, working with Dr. Wright today. I understand you have had fevers for 4 weeks. Say, that is a nice ring you are wearing, are you engaged?"

"No," Irma's rosy cheeks got a lot rosier.

"I understand that you have no other symptoms. How do you feel when you have a fever?"

"I feel funny."

"Funny how."

"Hard to say, just funny."

"Do you stay in bed with the fevers?"

"No."

"What do you do?"

"I watch TV or read my books."

"Good. What kinds of books do you like?"

"She loves reading; she devours anything she can get her hands on. Of course Harry Potter tops the list."

"Nice. I like to read too. But I have not read the Harry Potter books."

After going over more questions and striking out for any positive clues as to the cause of the fever, Dr. Pittman looked at Irma and gave her the game plan. "Dr. Wright will order some tests to see where the fever is coming from. I would like you to do a special test for me."

"What is that?" Irma now looked nervous at the mention of special test.

"How do you take her temperature?"

"We use a digital thermometer that she puts under her tongue."

"Great! I want you to get a chart and record her temperature every 8 hours and…."

"Mrs. Snow is a great chart maker. You will be impressed," Sara interjected.

"On the chart you will enter the temperature and at the same time I want you to get a urine sample and I want you to take the temperature of the urine and pair it up with the temperature. You will need two thermometers, one for the urine. I don't want you to mix them up."

"Gross!"

"Then you come back next week and we can go over the tests and the fever charts. Are you clear on this?"

"Yes. Thank you doctor, you are so kind. Both of you. We have not gotten any satisfaction from our doctor so that is why we came here. I am glad that we did. I think we are getting somewhere."

"Any thing else I should know? No? OK, Any questions? No again. OK. See you next week but call if you have questions."

When they got outside, Sara looked puzzled. "What was that all about? Why the temperature of the urine. I know you do not like lab tests but that seems to be a little strange."

"You might be surprised but I am sure we will all learn something. I leave the laboratory tests up to you. But be kind to her pocketbook or the insurance company when you set up your orders."

"You know, Dr. Pittman, if she were seen by some of the other doctors here, we would be knocking off a few thousand dollars in lab tests. OK if I order a CBC, urine culture and sed rate?"

"Fine with me."

The next week.

Mrs. Snow was eager to see what was next; Irma tried to look bored. "Here is the chart. I am not sure what I was supposed to do but it shows her temperature is still high except for her urine. I guess that is because the bladder is insulated from the rest of the body. Is that right?"

"Not exactly but first, tell me how is she doing."

"I am still worried about the fevers."

"I would think so. They range from 104-106."

"That is pretty high! But how is she otherwise?"

"She is still staying home. Watching TV and trying to do her homework. She is so smart that she gets the homework done so quickly. I check it when I have time but she always does it correctly so I don't want to interfere with her work. Give her some space, you know?"

"What do her friends say about her missing so much school?"

"They seem to be tired of the same old story. They don't call as much as before. I wish we could get back to school. I really do."

"I am sure that you do. Kids belong in school and interacting with their friends. Tell me what about her eating, sleeping, activities."

"She eats like a teenager and sleeps like a teenager. Lots of eating and sleeping."

"So what is the signal that makes you take her temperature?"

"Nothing special. I try to take her temperature at least once a day but sometimes when it is really high, I take it several times."

"So if you just looked at her, would you expect her to have a fever?"

"Not really, that is what upsets me. I seem to be able to catch it for most of the time when she looks well, she has a fever. Hard to figure that out."

"How are you doing, Irma?"

"Fine."

"Anything hurts you?"

"Not really, my stomach still feels funny and once in awhile, my leg hurts but it goes away. Oh I also had a mosquito bite on my arm. I put some lotion on it."

"Can you tell when you are getting a fever?"

"No. I feel OK except for the fevers."

"Does anything hurt when you have a fever?"

"Sometimes I get a headache but not always." Irma looks at her mother as she answers.

"What about your friends from school?"

" They called me for the first week I was out, but then they stopped checking in." "Why don't they call you anymore?"

"I guess I am out of the loop. My friends are always on the go and I can't see them because of the fevers."

"Maybe it is time to get back in the loop. Did you call them?"

"No. I guess they are tired of my illness and more interested in school and their friends who are well."

"And you?"

"I wish you could find out what is wrong."

"I will. I promise you. Anything thing else I should know?"

"No."

"OK, let me check her out and see about her ears, lungs and throat.

After an exam which was normal, Dr. Pittman looks puzzled. He turns to the mother and daughter. "Good news again. The exam is normal."

"OK now for plan 2. A new assignment."

"What is that? I am getting tired of all these games."

"Why do you think they are games?"

"We keep coming back here and nothing changes."

"I understand your feeling that way but give me another week. Can you do that?"

"OK but just one week. What do we have to do now?"

"Glad that you are still on board. Mrs. Snow, I want you to get one of those ear thermometers and use it instead of the electronic oral thermometers. You still measure the urine temperature at the same time you take her ear temperature. Use the same kind of chart that you used before and check back next week. Any questions?"

"No but is this the last week? Soon I will look like a medical supply store. Promise."

"Promise."

Next week.

"This is amazing!"

"What do you mean?"

"Her fevers are gone!"

"Gone?"

"Yes she has no fevers this week."

"How could this happen?"

"Maybe something was wrong with the oral thermometer."

"Good thought. Must be the oral thermometer."

"How was the urine temperature?"

"Pretty close to the ear temperature."

"Wow!"

"How do you feel about this, Irma?"

"I don't understand what is going on. But at least this is the last week."

"Are you ready to go back to school?"

"We tried that on Thursday, but that did not work."

"What happened?"

"She had a severe migraine so she went to the nurse and was sent home."

"Good try. I am sorry that you got a headache, Irma. Did you ever get one of these before?"

"Not like this, this was a real migraine."

"What do you mean, real migraine?"

"Just like they describe in the book."

"What book?"

"Health for Dummies. It has all the diseases in it. I read it a lot."

"But you are not a dummy."

"You don't have to be a dummy to read it. That is just a sales trick. I like it because they don't use big words."

"OK. Irma could you step outside and let me talk to your mother."

"I want to stay here."

"I know you would. But there are some things that I need to talk to your mother about. Personal things, you know."

"I still want to stay."

"Please Irma, listen to the doctor." Irma finally leaves the room but does not close the door completely.

Dr. Pitman slides his chair to the door and gently closes it.

"What is going on Doctor Pittman?"

"What do you think?"

"I don't know. This is very strange."

"In some cases that I have seen in the past, some children find ways to make the thermometer warmer than their body temperature."

"How can they do it?"

"They can rub their tongue over the thermometer to cause friction and heat. Here, you try it."

"Look at temperature go up. My temperature is 104 too."

"Now do it without any friction."

"I am 98.6."

"That is quite normal. Congratulations."

"But why would she do that?"

"Do you have any ideas why she wants to be sick?"

"She does well in school so there is no need to stay home to avoid the work."

"People stay out of school because there are problems in school, like academic work or social acceptance by friends."

"She has many friends and gets mostly A's in school."

"The other reason they stay home is to be at home. Some kids stay home because they worry about whom ever is at home."

"Why would she do that?"

"How are you doing? How is your health?"

"I am OK for my age."

"What does that mean?"

"I am always tired and I get headaches and my joints are starting to wear out."

"Does Irma ever ask you about how you are doing? I wonder if Irma is worried about you."

"I never gave it a thought. Maybe she does. I do complain a lot."

"What do you complain about? Give me the top five."

"Oh the usual things for a single mother with a pre teen girl. There are a lot of things to make me tense."

"Like?"

"What do you expect? I work and I come home and I worry. Not much else."

"What about Irma's father? I never hear about him."

"We are divorced. We have been since right after Irma was born. She gets to see him at times but there are no fixed visitations. Hey, this is getting complicated. Is all this my fault?"

"Fault? No body is at fault. What would you like to change in your life?"

"That is pure daydreaming. Nothing will change. I am in this rut and I have to deal with it. I don't see anything good happening or in the future. Oh there I go again, crying like a baby. Sorry."

Dr. Pittman pulls out a tissue from his jacket and offers it to Mrs. Snow. "Sometimes it is good to cry but you don't want to get your silk blouse wet. Here take a tissue."

"Thanks, and I am so sorry that I showed you how I spend a lot of time after Irma goes to bed. Things are so messed up in my life."

"Messed up how?"

"Nothing seems to be working. Do you have any magic pills for me?"

"Fresh out of magic pills? There seems to be a lot of things that need to sorted out, now that we know the fevers are gone and the elevated temperatures readings are a way for Irma to communicate her worry about you."

"See, I know it was my fault!"

"We are not here to assign blame but to get to the motivation for a nice healthy girl like Irma to be at home."

"Maybe we are all crazy, the two of us."

"I don't like to use that word, crazy, but there seems to be some family issues that need to be sorted out."

"How can you do that?"

"That is somewhat out of my range of skills but how do you feel about taking Irma to see a psychiatrist? I know a great one that has a special charm with young ladies."

"Irma is not crazy and I don't think that Irma would have any part of it."

"Dr. Matson is skilled at working through this resistance. Let me give you her phone number so you can set up an appointment. She likes the family to call for an appointment, rather than the referring doctor. If you are OK then we can talk with Irma and tell her the next plan."

"OK you try but I am not sure it will work."

"We need to be positive and find a way to make it happen. I will call Irma to come back in the room so you two can talk it over."

Dr. Pittman leaves the two of them alone while he goes out of the room to make some notes on the chart. In about 10 minutes, the Snows walk out to Dr. Pittman's desk with a more relaxed look.

"Irma was not as resistant as I predicted. She seemed relieved that she would have someone to talk to. Many of her friends had seen Dr. Matson so she was tuned into what would transpire at the visits."

"Good for you Irma. I am sure that Dr. Matson will take good care of you. Please call me in a month to tell me how you are doing. You know that Dr. Wright and I are here if you need us."

When the Snows left the room, Sara Wright gave Dr. Pittman a high five. "You really pulled one off. I was not sure what you were getting at with all those thermometers. You just eased into the refocusing the issues. It was not the fever but the reason for staying home."

"But if it seems like the mother is the source of the dysfunction, why did you send Irma to see the shrink?"

"Dr. Matson is a family therapist so although Irma is the entry point, it will be obvious that the whole family is involved. She will be able to work with Irma to have her return to being a young lady and not her mother's caretaker and she will deal with Mrs. Snow's depression."

"Brilliant. I will never forget this"

"I am glad you learned something. As the old medicine man told his trainees, "I can show you the steps but you have to hear the music." It is pattern recognition. Healthy kids that have signs of illness, in this case, a fever, makes one look at the school, parents and social contacts."

"I think I had my first music lesson, thanks."

WINTER

"Youth is wasted on the young."
George Bernard Shaw

Chapter 17

"I am tired of standing out in the street while my roommie continues in his quest to seduce all the 18 to 40 year old women in South Creek."

"You do look tired. What are you talking about, Lester?"

"Oh Dr. Barstow, I didn't see you sitting there. I was just venting while I got my coffee."

"Come on and sit down and get some caffeine in you. Maybe you won't be so tired. What is going on?"

"Oh I don't want to bother you Dr. Barstow."

"No bother. I heard sex and I am all ears."

Adrienne chimes in. "Lester is always having trouble with Felix, his roommate. They decided to share an apartment and split the rent since they would have so many nights at the hospital, they would not interfere with each other after work."

"But my roommate is always working deals so that he is home more than I am. We have a signal that when there is a blue star showing on the door, the room is occupied. Blue used to be my favorite color, not any more."

"I know the feeling, I had a friend that borrowed my apartment but soon he was the occupant and I was the guard out in the street."

"You too, Dr. Barstow! Just like Jack Lemmon in the Apartment movie."

"Same story. So now you are out in the cold."

"That is the truth, more than you know. I have had it but can't afford to live alone."

"I heard that story before. Loans and debts put a dent into the good life desires."

"I told Lester he could move in with me and my roommate" volunteered Adrienne.

"Do what? Live with two girls. Now that is an option that I did not think of. I lived in an age with single sex dormitories and bathrooms. I even went to an all girl's college."

"Oh, that is not the issue. I would not impose on the girls and who knows, I could face the same problem with them putting out the blue star on their door."

"I only wish that is an issue. Not in our lives. We have an extra room that could serve as a bedroom with a little fixing up. It is painted a strange color but you could live with that or paint it yourself. The landlord would welcome the new décor, I am sure."

"But living with girls, I am not sure that would fly. What if my parents came to visit?"

"They would be thrilled. I think it is a win-win-win deal. Our rent goes down, you get a place to stay rather than on the street and we could continue our coaching. Only Felix gets shafted and from what I hear, he deserves a little of that activity."

"What do you say Lester? I think it would be a good experience for you."

"Oh, Dr. Barstow, you can say that but you will not have to be around these ladies, fight for the bathroom and avoid the drying laundry. I like things my way and have problems with people who do things differently. Take, for example, toilet paper.

"Toilet paper?"

"Yes, toilet paper, people don't know how to put the roll in the holder. If done correctly, the paper will come out on top of the roll. That way, you don't touch the wall and scratch the paint or tile. When you place it so that the paper comes out on the bottom, the paper may droop or you have to go digging to get it. It is just not right."

"I never gave it a second thought. I put the paper in the way I find it."

"You better not invite me to your house or I would be forced to inspect your toilet paper installations. So, you can see, I have doubts about sharing a bathroom with others."

"There must be some positive side to this proposal. From my vantage point, it sounds like an exciting arrangement with a lot of possibilities."

"Name one." Lester snapped back.

"I think you need some more coaching Lester. Try it and you might be surprised."

"Surprised at what?"

"You may learn something about life. And maybe Adrienne will get you to hospital rounds on time. That would be a plus for starters. Think about it, Lester. You will have a good time and who knows what will happen. They will like the security of having a man to protect them."

Freezing when he thought of sharing an apartment with two women, Lester sunk into his familiar shell and did not comment but began to raise and lower his eyebrows, a sign of deep thought. Adrienne was thinking of all the possibilities of a co-ed dorm.

• • •

"Sorry I am late; I got a ticket on the beltway. Speeding ticket, can you believe it after all these years of driving on that straight away at 70-80 per hour? Today I get a ticket."

"Couldn't you talk your way out of it? I thought you were good at that, Mr. Beardsley."

"I tried, believe me, Caroleen."

"What did you do?"

"I was very polite; I stopped and pulled to the side. He told me I was speeding doing 75 on a 55 miles per hour speed limit. I asked him if I could ask him a question. He nodded. So I ask him why do I get a ticket when the whole pack of cars was doing the same speed, about 70? He smiled and said that everyone but me slowed down when they saw me. Then he gave me the ticket."

"So did you learn anything?"

"No, I won't let that jerk change the way I drive. So now to business. How is the plan working out? Are we making a profit? I expect that our plan is pushing us far into the black."

"Not exactly Mr. Beardsley, You know we implemented the new billing and unbundling of the charges so the income has gone up but Caroleen will give you the bad news.

"As Al has reported, the income as far as billing has gone up. We have not yet seen it in reimbursements. You know how the insurance companies are. They reject everything on first billing so we have to protest which delays the payment and sometimes we have to file another request for funds so it will be a time before we will see much more money coming to us from this new billing scheme."

"That is not so bad. Is there anything else?"

"Yes, our expenses are much higher than we anticipated."

"The installation of the MRI has gone way over budget. It seems that the old wiring was not up to code but the inspectors let it pass when we had the old system. But with new equipment, they are insisting on appropriate wiring. The room needs additional cooling, that calls for more wiring. We needed to do some carpentry changes to accommodate the new equipment. With the increased usage, we have to make more space in the waiting room. The bottom line...... expenses are considerably up. We have not started to use the MRI so there is no additional income, only more expenses. Our payer mix has not improved, we have too many low payers and not enough fully insured who pay most of our charges. Seams like those with better reimbursement are still going to Philadelphia or New York, even all the way to Baltimore."

"So what are we going to do? I promised the board that this was a great idea that would be profitable. How can we adjust the books, can we depreciate the electrical jobs? Do we need new PR? Should we blockade the turnpike so that the patients cannot get to the big cities?"

"We need to expand our services. The best pay back is neonatal units."

"But we have too many beds there already. The census is about 60%. No way can we justify new neonatal beds."

"We can if we have new programs."

"The other age group that we do not offer many services is adolescent. We could make a profit on acne and obesity. But there are not many procedures associated with those diseases, maybe a few operations for weight loss, but then we would have to get new scales, new beds etc. Not much room for profit."

"The big draw back is the lack of GYN services. You know the hospital policy that we don not offer birth control pills and perform abortions per Dr. Randolf's edict."

Why can't we get around him? He is ready for retirement soon, I hope. Isn't he near 65?"

"Not really, he is late 50's."

"I guess his young wife has aged him, he looks older. So what can we do? What about depreciating our construction? I have done that before."

Caroleen started to make notes in her notebook.

"That would make some difference but not enough to reduce the expenses or build up our income. Maybe we can cut wages of the executives? How would that fly with the board? I bet they would like it as much as we executives would hate it."

"We do have a large overhead from the executives, legal and consultants. I think we are in the top 5% of all Children's hospitals for salaries. But that is my philosophy, pay them enough and no one will complain. We can follow the U.S. Senate and cut services to the poor and decrease education expenses. Don't we have too many trainees? Can't we get more nurse practitioners?"

"If you replace them with nurse specialists, you will need three to do the work of one intern. They do 8 hour shifts and get premium salary."

"I guess that means we have to cut some executive salaries or drop a few people or programs from the payroll."

"We need to do something before the next board meeting or I am going to get cooked. Caroleen, you do a few run throughs with the various plans we talked about."

"Including the shifting to depreciation?"

"Whatever it takes to get some black ink on the page. Let's meet on Friday and see what plan we can make. Try to make it as legal as you can."

"Right we don't want to go to jail or lose our jobs."

Beardsley noticed that Caroleen seemed to glow more than usual. Her walk had the slightest hint of swagger that seemed new. Either her she gained a few pounds or her clothes shrank but her breasts looked bigger than he remembered. Something was going on in her outside life but he was smart enough to stay away from that. It did make him a little jealous that someone was getting what he thought about whenever he saw her. Lucky bastard, whoever you are. But it did not stop the fantasy.

Beardsley got the information that he wanted but now had to make up some issue so Caroleen would still be at the table instead of leaving for some important kind of work.

"Do you know anything about the bathrooms in the clinic? Are they clean? Is there paper on the floor?"

I don't know Mr. Beardsley. I don't get to the clinic very often. Spending a lot of time in the surgery section, you know."

Right, right. I know how hard you are working. Do you know anything about the new tapas restaurant that opened recently? In addition to keeping Caroleen in his office, he also tried to find out how active her social life was.

"What is a tapas?"

"Some kind of foreigner's food, I guess. I am more into Spanish food, myself. I was in Barcelona last summer, you know."

Al could not hold back, "I think tapas are Spanish, from what I learned on the internet."

"Could be, Could be."

Beardsley saw that this type of conversation was showing them some of his shortcomings and Caroleen was not opening up to him, rather she spent the whole time either looking at her watch or writing in her notebook. "Well I am sorry to cut this short but I have to get back to running the nation's best hospital and I am sure you have things to do too."

• • •

"We have a patient in heart failure in room 8" shouted the Sarge Cranford. This is music to the ears of the emergency docs but strikes fear in the young trainees since by tradition, the new doctors get a chance to look at the patient while the staff doctors look over the shoulders to make sure that the patient gets good care and that the plan of treatment is acceptable. Keith Aaron is first up. Despite his arrogance and negativity, he is a good doctor especially under fire. He pulls his stethoscope from his back pocket as he runs into room 8, trying hard to hide his fear of difficult problems.

"How in the hell do you treat congestive heart failure? Let's see, diuretics, and oxygen and ace inhibitors." he mumbled to himself. "Let me check her and get things started."

"Sabba is about 6, breathing hard, fluid coming out of her nose, chest shows retractions." Keith observes, "Looks like heart failure, smells like heart failure, the Sarge says it is heart failure, so that must be the DX. Let me check her chest. Fast heart rate, no murmurs but hard to hear because of the loud chest sounds. Very wet lungs and quite anxious. He pauses and then continues. OK let's get started. Diuretics. She weighs about 50 pounds – 25 of lasix IV. Oops we need to get an IV started and some oxygen too. Get the rays people here to get a chest film."

Karl Strem the chief resident is supervising Keith and agrees with the initial plan so he stays in the background. The ER nurse gets in the IV line and confirms the order of the diuretic.

"I took blood and sent it off for lytes and metabolic panel. Anything else?"

"No Just save some blood, we may need to come back later to check on the chemistries before treatment. Give it a blast and let's dry this baby out so she can breathe. Fire away! Let's get respiratory therapy down here to watch her airway and notify the ICU that we have a player for them." Karl smiled as he thought of this guy 6 months ago who would be sitting in the corner, figuratively sucking on his thumb and trembling with fear of a sick child. This is one of the bonuses for the chief resident - to see doctors coming out of the medical student cocoon and starting to fly on their own.

"Who has the pulse ox? We need a pulse ox!"

"It is on and 96"

"At least that is good."

Since it takes time for the diuretic to work, Keith gathers himself and opens up his pediatric treatment handbook on his Blackberry to the section on heart failure. He reviews the suggested plan and adds milrinone to the orders.

Sabba calms down a little with the oxygen mask but still is quite anxious. The nurses are connecting all the monitors to measure blood pressure, respirations, pulse and temperature. Keith comments again. "Her skin is dry but there is no fever. That does not make sense."

The x-ray tech arrives to take the chest x-ray. Since the digital x-ray system requires no time in the developer machine, the results appear quickly on the hospital intranet. "Heart size is normal, chest is full of fluid. "Hey wait a minute... the heart is supposed to be large in heart failure and the liver is supposed to be large. Something is amiss. But let's get going with the heart failure treatment. As they say, if the patient gets better with your treatment, keep going. If not better you need to change your plan. But it is too soon to see if things are going to better. The diuretic needs time. We will keep her airway open with suctioning the frothy stuff coming out of her nose. More suction and deeper."

Sabba breathing is slightly better with the suctioning but now she begins to convulse. The seizures lasted about 30 seconds but seemed like hours to this frightened group of trainees. "Hey, this not part of heart failure, she has good oxygen levels, but we need to keep her breathing and her heart beating while we treat the failure. Give her some ativan. That should calm her down. We better get the cards down here and get an echocardiogram. Something is amiss. It just does not fit. Do a search for heart failure with normal sized heart. Maybe this is something odd like fibroelastosis that is it. She has EF! I bet she has EF! I remember reading about it in medical school. Get the cards! Get the cards! They can learn something about a rare case."

Fortunately, the seizures stopped but over the next hours she did not show the expected improvement from the heart failure treatment. Still full of secretions, she was hard to arouse, that could be explained either from the ativan, the late hour or the still undiagnosed problem. Keith wanted to hold the course but was beginning to doubt his diagnosis, although he had did not have an alternative. After all, Cranford, an experienced nurse said it was heart failure and she is never wrong; at least that is what everyone says. The staff doctor from cardiology fueled the doubt about the diagnosis when he looked at Sabba and said it did not look like failure to him.

"I'm calling the ICU for transfer, she is too sick for this unit." He got off the phone, still looking worried. "The intensivist was tied up with a complex trauma case but he said he would be here shortly. Has anyone seen the family?"

"They took off right after the baby came into the ED."

"Strange," Keith thought but he could not dwell on it as the child was going down hill. "Ask the social worker to call the family to get back in. Maybe they could shed some light on the problem."

The therapy continued as the diagnosis remained in limbo while the treatment was keeping him breathing and the blood pressure remained stable. This situation continued as the evening shift was almost over and the nurses were preparing a sign out report for the next shift.

Julie, the nurse who was going to take over the case for the night shift had an opinion, as she usually does. "I wonder if this is the poisoning that I heard on the news. Seems like there have been some cases of that poison insecticide."

Keith, annoyed by this butinski nurse, smiled but he was thinking "Hey lady get out of my way. I am treating heart failure and we need some time for the drugs to work." Karl, raised his eyebrows and nodded, showing that the difference of a few years of training plus his confidence allowed him to listen to others. Although he felt that heart failure was a likely cause of this girl's distress, there were pieces to this puzzle that did not fit. He quietly left the group attending to Sabba, heading for some help from the internet. He slides over to the computer at the doctors' desk and calls up the toxicology reference. After entering the symptoms, the information guru concluded that there was a high probability that this girl was a case of parathion poisoning. The program recommended immediate treatment with atropine, with PAM as a backup drug. He called over the nurse with the key to the emergency treatment cart and asked her to get a syringe with atropine. So armed, he moved back into room 8, cleaned off the stopper on the IV tubing and injected the atropine. Almost immediately, the little girl began to breathe normally, the secretions dried up and she looked around to see what was happening, wondering where she was. Keith was astounded. He saw Karl with the empty syringe and asked him what the magic medicine was. "Just a little pixie dust mixed with atropine for the parathione poisoning." Then he gave Julie a high five for suggesting poisoning.

"Wow, I guess I was too focused in my differential diagnosis."

"And I hope you learned to listen to other people's suggestions and not blow them off without additional thought."

"That too."

Just as the adrenaline in their bodies was wearing off, Sabba began to display the same symptoms. Keith, now fully in command, called out "Another slug of atropine, please. And order up some pralidoxime, we may need it soon." He was following the educational model of see one, do one, teach one. He also had a chance to consult the toxicology section in his Blackberry.

Sabba again responded to the treatment.

Now Karl took over. "She needs to be washed off to get rid of any residual poison. This stuff is absorbed through the skin. Where are the parents? Who brought her in here?"

"He came with the EMTs in the ambulance. The parents are not here. They checked out saying something about kids at home."

"Well call them!"

"They do not have a phone. We sent the police."

"Good idea, we need to know where she got this stuff. This is an agricultural agent, not used very much anymore, according to the book."

"We will get in touch with the police."

Sabba settled down after she was moved to the ICU for monitoring. The group of residents went back to work. Karl moved into the conference room to write the transfer note and to review the toxicology web sites to make sure he was not missing anything. He told the group that they would meet at the end of the shift to go over the case.

In about 30 minutes, the police arrived with the family and took them into the conference room where the team had already assembled there, sitting around the long rectangular a long laminated table. Three lamps, one at each end and one in the middle provided spot like lighting. Karl sat under one spot, the parents sat under the light at the other end. The father, looking nervous, began to sweat as he took his seat. "What is this, the line up? I didn't do anything, I swear. The last time I was in such a room, they were questioning me about a hold up at the 7-11."

"Hello Mr. Ledger, I am Karl, one of your daughter's doctors and these other people are the students and residents. Take it easy, we did not accuse you of doing anything. We just want to ask you a few questions."

"So why the police and why this third degree room. In the movies, this is where they beat up the people that are accused of the crime. Where is the rubber hose? I didn't do any crime."

"What kind of crime? We are not accusing you of any crime. What are you worried about?"

"Nothin, but I get upset when the police come after me. I swear I am innocent."

"Oh," Karl smiled, "I guess this does look like the detective's room but it certainly looks better than the movies. We wanted to ask you some questions about your daughter. She is doing much better but she is still quite ill, we have her in the intensive care unit. You will be able to see her when we finish here. They are doing some tests on her right now. We have everything under control; the team did a great job. We sent the police to get you because we had no phone number to call. You see it is important that we talk to you about Sabba. She came in here with great trouble breathing. We were concerned about heart failure since she was breathing like other people we see who have heart failure she did not respond to the first treatment so we questioned the original thought that something was wrong with her heart. We gave her some other medicine and she got better almost immediately."

"Thank you Jesus. Thank you Jesus."

"We were treating her for poisoning, something she was exposed to, like an insecticide. Do you know of any kind of chemical she was exposed to?"

"We ain't got no insecticides in our house. No way!"

"Well somehow she got in contact with some insecticide chemical. This kind can get into the body through the skin. Does she walk around bare foot?"

"Yes she does. She is our barefoot princess."

"Anyone else sick at home? Any one with breathing problems?"

"No."

"Well tell me about where you live and who lives there?"

"We live out beyond the big mall on route 40. Kind of what you call horse country. I work at the stables on one of the estates. There is me, my wife and two kids. Sabba, the one who is here and Angeena, she is 10."

"Where is Angeena now?"

"She is home with my neighbor. We get along well with our neighbors. Can't I get to see Sabba?"

"In a few minutes. Are you sure that there were no chemical around the house? Living in the horse country, there must be a lot of chemicals. Have they sprayed around your house? Any spray for bugs, for trees, for fertilizer, for weeds. It is important to know since others can get sick and even die if they are not treated. Do you understand?"

"I understand. Let me see. Can I talk to you privately, Doc?"

"Sure, come out in the hall. There is another room out there."

"What's up?" Mr. Ledger?"

"Well, I have a confession. I stole some insecticide from my boss and sprayed it all over the house. We had a lot of bugs and roaches there. I know I should not have taken it but they don't pay me much and I wanted to clean up the house. Is she going to be all right? I don't like to lie but with the police and the room that looked like the detective grilling room, I was afraid I was going to lose my job and go to jail."

"No jail for you. We want to make sure all the people in your family are well and you will clean up the spray from your house before you return."

"No jail?"

"No, not tonight or tomorrow either."

"I will go home and scrub down the place after I see Sabba."

The door to the room opened. "Sorry to interrupt Karl, but we have another young girl who is in heart failure. I got Keith on the case immediately and I thought you should go there."

Karl runs down the hall followed by Mr. Ledger.

"Oh my goodness, it's Angeena. She is having trouble breathing."

"What's up Keith?"

"Oh, just another case of parathione poisoning I suspect. I have ordered the atropine and started the drill of oxygen, suctioning. They are hooking her up to all the monitors. Routine stuff you know."

"You are a pro, Keith."

"Think of it an hour ago I never heard of the disease and now it is my second case. This is getting boring. No variety in this hospital. Where are the colds and lacerations? Boooring. …..but I love it!"

"Where the dickens is the atropine? We have to get this young lady to a party. She needs a good bath to get rid of the chemicals too."

"Speaking of parties, Karl, are we set for the journal club. You know it is just past midnight so today is Friday and the party is on Friday night. The troops are getting thirsty. Thirsty for knowledge, I mean."

"Of course, I am here to make sure you get educated, whatever it takes, and you will get educated."

Both girls recovered and were discharged after Mr. Ledger cleaned up the house. No charges were filed but the case was reported to the county health department.

• • •

LATER FRIDAY

Lester drifted back to the coffee shop and sat in his favorite chair, next to next to Jim and Evil Eva, the secretary who makes the schedules and cares for the residents in more ways then one, especially the male residents who want to get moon lighting jobs.

"Hey Babe, What happening?" Despite a few months of coaching from Adrienne he did not have any other opening lines, just this one from Felix. Social skills is the only course that Lester did not get an A in all his years of schooling. He could recite lectures, word for word without referring to notes He could give you the history of The Balkans or the kings of England, but he was at a loss for anything to say except "Hey Babe. What's happening?" Other than failing opening lines, the coaching deal was going well. Adrienne was helping him be more social. Now he talks about the weather, asks who is going to win the game but he was not sure what game he was asking about. It did not seem to matter for everyone had some game of interest and was eager to comment about the outcome. He moved on to what you are going to do on your vacation. He was now approaching social gadfly status with all his small talk.

"Have a seat Lester, we were talking about Andrew Wyeth and could not remember the name of the woman who he painted, sometimes in the nude. That was the part that interested me."

"Helga. He painted over 240 pictures between 1971 and 1985 in tempera, watercolors and pencil. At the end, she was more of a dried up prune. Why did that interest you?"

"Well if she could get his attention with that body. There must be hope for me."

"Oh come on, Eva, you are young and I bet in better shape than that old lady Helga or whatever her name is."

"Helga is her name. I bet she is a nice lady."

"Want to take a peak, Lester and see if I have a better body?"

"Why would I want to do that, Eva?"

"Just for fun. I like to get compliments. Don't you want to do some moonlighting? They need people to cover the walk-in clinic at night."

"Maybe. When I need some money."

"Well you let me know and I will see what can be worked out. You know these jobs pay well and lots of people want to get them."

"Sounds like I have to qualify. I have my PAL certificate."

"Not that kind of qualification but I would like to see your stuff."

"This is getting embarrassing. Don't you get the picture?"

"Picture of what? Helga is not my taste."

"Tell me Lester what are you going to do about your apartment?"

"Apartment? Oh, I took a room with Adrienne and Sara. It is working out well. I have my own room and they invite me for dinner when they are home and feel like cooking."

"What about privacy?"

"Oh it is private, except for the bathroom. But we work it out. We have a 5 minute limit but I don't need that much time. I think they like having a man in the house, for safety, you know."

"I bet. They have had smiles on their faces for the past few weeks, now I know why there are smiling."

"Why? Just because I am there to protect them from aliens and cockroaches."

"Not exactly. But since you have not changed your facial expressions, I guess everything is platonic."

"Platonic? Right of course."

"What did Felix say about your leaving? "

"Oh he was fine with it. Seems he met some divorcee who pays the rent for him at the old apartment. He did not want to kick me out but we were both irked for about a month before I told him I was moving out. I guess that is what you call triumph-triumph."

"I think the common expression is win-win."

"Right."

"So that is why he seems less on the hunt than before. I guess the old lady has some tricks for him to master. He never liked homework but I guess it was the wrong kind."

Adrienne and Sara joined the group.

"So are you coming to the party tonight? It is the last Friday of the month and we always have a party in the clinic building after hours."

"When did that start, Sara?"

"Since Adam met Eve."

"Adam who?"

"Oh, come on Lester, we are joking."

"Oh yes, I am supposed to laugh when you tell a joke, even if I don't get it. Right, coach?"

"Right." Adrienne replied. "Will you come to the party? I don't want to leave there after dark. You can escort me home. You are my protector."

"Thank you."

"Well that is settled. Now what are we going to do about the news that they are cutting back on the house staff next year?"

"Who said that?"

"Well I heard from Ann Ranier, Beardsley's secretary that he is taking a trip to Africa to make some arrangements with a medical school in Ghana about an educational exchange program. I also heard from Eddie the shoeshine man that there were some Africans who were meeting in Roger Saltzman's office. Eddie knows everything so he filters all the rumors into a coherent story. This is the best scenario we can come up with."

"I think you better go back to Eddie for a new version. That one does not make sense."

"Just think about it, they will work for less money, they don't have loans to pay off."

Karl sits down at the end of the table and butts in when the rumors get out of reasonable fiction. "This is bullshit. Next story."

"Does anyone know where Luda hangs out? She never bothers with the rest of us. She comes to work and she leaves. I don't think she has much of a social life. She always looks so sad."

"Oh, you know those people who came from Ukraine. They seem sad when they are having a good time. They shake their head and frown, even when they are agreeing with you. Luda has been here for at least 4 years, but she has not picked up the New World smile. I guess what she has been through will make one sad. That communist junk, always being cold and hungry in those dark winters, but that is not the story now. She is warm and well fed. We have to make an effort to include her into the group."

"I guess we are so caught up into our own stuff, that we let her slip by, even though we can all agree that she is not a joiner, but we need to make an effort. She is bright and pretty. Those blue eyes and long legs are killers. I could be jealous."

"Has any one ever asked her to join us?"

"Not me. I don't know if anyone else has. Maybe she is waiting for an invitation."

"I am sure someone has hooked up with her and she does not want to share him with us." "But you are right; we need to make an effort to include her."

February is the low point of the year- past the excitement of the first few months, after the confidence level moved out of the scared as hell category but far from the end of the year and the move the next level of training. The days are short, the sky usually overcast, especially bad for those with seasonal affective disorder, the job becomes more work than fun, more demanding and less educational. Moods are low and tempers short especially for those who were working the night shift. The coffee shop is the couch for people to express their feelings and blow off some anger about the system when it was really fatigue that was causing the negative moods. The negativity is so heavy this night that at any moment, any spark from a light switch or a cell phone could cause a bolt of lightening to move through the coffee shop and most likely kill one of the complainants near the metal columns.

Karl Strom, sensing that the group's jeremiads may cause some bad decisions for the patients, jumped into the discussion. "I always believed that you would not trade this experience that you are getting at CHUC, despite some down times. February is a bad time, so don't let it get to you, March will soon be here and things will get better. Tell me, Keith, who would you like to be and where would you like to be?"

"If you really wanted to know, I should have gone into archeology or stayed in Oregon," pouted Keith. "I am only here because my girl friend wanted to come east so I told her I would come but only for a few years of residency. It is hard not to be bitter now that we broke up but I am still here waiting for the year to end. I got a raw deal. But you know, I am also tired of being pissed off. You can only stay mad for so long and then it begins to affect your life. I am sure there could be better times if I could get this anger out of my system. I hate to admit it, but I am learning a great deal and I enjoy being with the kids. I am almost ready to have a good time. I remember feeling this way when I was a teenager. My parents were splitting up, I did not have a lot of friends and I was miserable. I just wanted to be alone. I was about to burst open with my sadness. One night I went out of the house into a field next to the property to look at the stars. There was no moon so the stars were quite bright, I could even see Venus, the evening star, you know. I sat down on the ground and stared at the sky. For some reason, I decided to take off all my clothes and stare at the stars. No one was around to see me and report me to the authorities for public lewdness. Such freedom! So natural! The more I stared, the better I felt. Life was not that bad. I was in a good school, I was getting good grades and despite the divorce proceedings, both parents were extremely kind to my sister and me. I fell asleep with almost a smile on my face. Daylight woke me up and it took a few minutes for me to figure out where I was and that I was nude. I looked around; still no one was around to see me. I grabbed for my clothes and then I saw that I was sleeping in a poison ivy patch. Talk about itching and being miserable, I was King Miserable the First. In a few days, the rash appeared, my eyes were swollen shut and I had to be sedated to keep me from performing total body dermabrasion. Then I had a real problem that seemed to put the rest of the crap out of my mind. So I guess this is better than another case of poison ivy. Same conclusion. I am lucky to be here and have the training that I am getting. I am working with a great bunch of people and in a few months, summer will be here and things will be better. I have no reason to feel sorry for myself all the time. Maybe I am just horny."

Adrienne could not wait to chime in. "I can't help you with that problem but I know what you are going through. I feel the same way.

Usually, I am upbeat but this place is really getting to me. I have no complaints about the work or the hospital. I, too, am lucky to be here. I just did not know that the work would be this hard and I could get this tired. One day after another day; not much feedback or thanks for all this work. I liked school better when you could take a test and get a grade that told you that you were doing well. Part of me would like to be in school where I can study and take tests. That was real fun. Here, everyone seems to be into themselves so no one has the time to say a few kind words. Only my mother tells me that I am doing well and that the patients are better because of what I did."

"What the hell does your mother know about your medical skills?"

"She works in a hospital; she is the one who raised us."

"What was her specialty?

"She was very good at bed making, so-so on bed pans but her best was the wet mop, you know when they put out the yellow sign, "danger-wet floor." You guessed it, she was in house keeping, they called it then. Anyway, she was the one who raised us. She worked the system to get me and my brother into private school. That was the trick that got me out of the rut that I was born into. From there I was able to get a scholarship to Brown and then onto Yale. So I rode the crest of minority admissions projects, call it special treatment but I could do it and got here with little debt and a lot of serious papers for my wall. I am really fortunate, I love being a doctor.

"But get off the cheer leader stuff and answer the question about where you would rather be."

"For real?"

"For real."

"Is any body listening? I would rather be home with a few babies."

"So what are you doing here?"

"I am old fashioned, before babies; I need a ring, not a teething ring but one of those Tiffany things first. None of that heroic single parent crap for my life. It is so hard to find someone, working this schedule. I am not against meeting someone, but to make things easier, I need an educated, tall black man who is not so full of himself and has cut the cord between him and his momma."

"You are too particular."

"Maybe so but I am not ready to settle for second best."

"All the knights, including black nights are dead, except for the Black Knights of West Point."

"For real? That is no fun."

"So what are you going to do?"

"Sit here and bitch about the work and learn as much as I can. As my mom will say, things will get better. I am not going to sing that song; it's tough out there being a smart ass. But I am done complaining for one night. Short term, I could do with a little sex. This place is like a convent!"

Eyes turned to Lester who was tapping his fingers again, deep in thought. "Lester what about you?"

"I am not sure what this is all about. We picked this place and they picked us. Just like Cezanne, he could have worked in a bank like his father but he wanted to be an artist so that was his life. I picked medicine and I am not about to change, what am I going to do? Work in an art gallery or museum? I love art but that is not the intellectual challenge that medicine offers me. Understanding pathophysiology, figuring out which enzyme or what genetic mutation is causing this problem is what medicine is all about. Look, we picked this life, the year is over half done. Next year will be better."

"Better how?"

"More specialty clinics, more intensive care, lots of interesting problems to think about."

"Did you ever think that some poor soul has this interesting problem?"

"What soul are you talking about?"

"The poor kid with the electrolyte problem or leukemia. That's who."

"Oh them, well I did not give them the problem, I am only trying to figure out what is going wrong with them. My father, mean old bastard, was always blaming people for mistakes or bad results. I am not a blamer, just a thinker."

"Did you ever think about how the disease affects the child or the family?"

"Affecting them how? You mean genetic transmission. And guilt for a mutation of an amino acid."

"Not even close. So Lester, what would your alternative career be?

"I'd write books on Croation art in the 16th century."

"What about you, Sevestra?"

"I'd never thought about another career. This was the one that my parents picked for me. They are both physicians so it was natural that I follow them. They are traditional people even though they left India many years ago; they act as if they are still living there. They expect me to follow the family pattern. You know, arranged marriages, traditional wedding, frequent trips back to visit relatives, traditional foods-the whole package of the old ways in the new country."

"How do you feel about that predetermined life style?"

"The more I am with you all, the more questions that I have about who the real me is. My brother is following the family life style. He expects the parents to move in with him and his wife, as is the tradition for oldest sons. I am not sure I can accept the arranged marriage thing. I don't have anybody in mind right now but if I meet someone to my liking, I don't think I could drop him and go through the Indian routine. What makes things more complicated for me is I come from part of India that is Christian so I would need to find, not only an Indian but an Indian Christian. My father has already put in ads in the church newspaper in the U.S. I am described as a "medical school graduate with no school loans." What a testimonial! I am embarrassed to see that ad. But it worked, there were a few responses. Not much to interest me though. I am happy here but not sure my parents are. They did not want a pediatrician but someone to follow them in pathology and research. I like people too much to sit in a lab or look into a microscope all day. They cannot see why I am going into such a specialty that calls for long hours and below average pay. They cannot see why I do not stay home and study rather than go to parties and clubs. Of course they are against my dress, especially the 4 inch heels and the low cut jeans. Unfortunately, I sent them a picture of my party from medical school. They called immediately to voice their concern about seeing my navel exposed and transmit to me their unstated disappointment in my lack of traditional values. So far they have not seen my tattoo."

"So answer the question, what did would you like to be?"

"What would I like to be? I would like the chance to be me."

"Why complain, Keith?" Luda, who just arrived at the table during Sevestra's story, "You seem to have had a good life but enjoy feeling sorry for yourself. What do you have to complain about?"

"Oh, Luda. Welcome to the group. I guess I have a worry and sad gene. In any new situation I have to go through these steps of self pity and anger. I know what you are getting at but I cannot help myself, it is genetic."

"I am so glad to be here, away from my miserable life in Ukraine. I am so happy to have a hospital with equipment and supplies so that I can take care of the patients by giving them what I need. I miss my family in Kiev but you just don't know how good this is. Fresh fruit, unspoiled meat, no fear of Chernobyl radiation in the ground. This is paradise compared to what I have experienced. You just don't know how good it is here."

"You make it sound that you did not like Ukraine."

"Things are different here. I started medical school when you all were going to high school. We had no books, no computers or internet, all we got was lectures and more lectures. The notes from the lectures were pasted on the wall outside of the auditorium. Rounds were impossible. A large group of students would follow the professor on rounds who would spout off to the people near him. The rest of the people just stood in line. There was a lot of favoritism so that people politically connected got the best jobs and those who did not have influence were sent out to the country side to fend for themselves. We lived at home in government housing so the only way to live away from the parents was to get married. I got married when I was nineteen. At first the freedom was exciting but slowly I learned that my husband, like so many other underemployed men, drank a lot. The less he worked, the more he drank. When he was drunk, he would beat me. This became so frequent that I had to make arrangements to get out of that house. I could not get my own apartment as you all can, I had either to move back to my parent's home or continue this arrangement with my husband."

"Couldn't you get a divorce?"

"Oh I got a divorce but I had to stay in the apartment with my ex-husband since the government did not provide housing for single adults. For some reason, he stopped beating me. I guess he was afraid of being sent to jail. It was one thing to beat your wife but not your ex-wife. At that point I made my mind to get out of the country and come to America or Canada or anywhere but Ukraine. I could only see myself getting married to an American or Canadian to get away. I was so desperate to leave, I did not care if the new man would beat me too but at least I would be free to enjoy the freedom that you have here. So I joined the group of women that appeared at the local hotels where tours of lonely Americans would come to find wives. This was quite a scene! Groups of attractive but desperate women would pack into the lobby of Hotel Moscova or Dnipro to meet a bunch of nerdy American men who obviously could not find anyone at home to match up with. The girls prostituted themselves jumping from hotel bedroom to bedroom, hoping to make a connection and get out of the country. Eager as I was to get away, I could not get into that game. I even tried to meet someone on the internet. There were so many sick men that I got scared and quit that. Fortunately, I heard about scholarships that allowed one to come to America. I applied for a grant and got to the interview stage. The first person I talked to was not very nice. He kept asking me about what drugs I used, why my grade in Chemistry was not over 90%. "You must have been on drugs when you took that course" he blurted out, not giving me the chance to tell him that that was the highest grade in the class. I kept my cool and tried to change the subject by asking him about the internet and the access to libraries for doing clinical research. After about 20 minutes of inquiry about drugs, he did answer my questions. I almost cried, thinking how wonderful it would be to have all that information so accessible. The next interview went better. Now I know that I was part of the good cop-bad cop duo. But then I was so upset, I almost ran out of the office and skipped the second interview. The irony of this day was after I got accepted to come to America, the first man wrote me a note to tell me how much he enjoyed meeting me and offered his assistance to me when I come to America. Go figure that one!"

"So how did you get to CHUC?"

"It was a long story. First the group that sponsored me was a Protestant church. They found a spot for me in Oklahoma at the medical school in Tulsa after I took the entrance test and did well enough to demonstrate that I learned something in Kiev. Two of the summers, I spent on missionary work in Texas and Mexico, working with newly arrived people from Mexico and Central America. That experience convinced me that I was happiest working with children. So I applied to pediatric programs and did not get my first choices in Boston and Baltimore but did get into this program. I love it here and treasure the opportunity that I have here."

"Did you get married again?"

"Oh no! No marriage and no beatings. It is a good deal."

"But what did you do for fun in Ukraine?"

"Fun, I am not sure if what we called fun would meet your definition. Before the Communists left, we lived in fear of the KGB. You could walk through a park and hear only kids playing. Adults would not talk because the KGB was listening to what was spoken. At home, we would pull down the window shades, put a coat over the phone and then be able to laugh and sing and dance."

"Why the coat over the phone?"

"Because the phone had a microphone in it so they could listen to what we were saying. The coat would muffle the sound so they could not hear our words. When the communists left, the clubs opened and then we could go into the main part of the city and walk around and see our friends. Most of the clubs were full of ex-KGB and mafia people. So we walked around the streets. The first thing I got for myself was a miniskirt. All my friends did the same. That was the beginning of freedom but not like the U.S. Me, I want to be here and I want to be me, just as I am. No complaints. I am happy as I ever was."

"Wow! That is quite a story, Luda. I hope you can keep your optimism about your position here and I think the others will remember your story when they think about complaining. But it is time to get to work. Maybe we can discuss these ideas more at the party tonight. I hope you will make it, Luda."

• • •

At the other table in the coffee shop, a group of doctors are discussing their pension plans and Sweet sixteen basketball pools as Jackie Lawrence the chief of nursing walks by the table and gives them a warm smile. Roger Saltzman nudged Sam Salivari. Something is up; she rarely comes down here and never smiles at us. "Check your wallets. She is up to something."

"You are right, for a change, I may add. Jackie Lawrence has been quiet for a while but that is a dangerous sign, she must be plotting something. What could it be? A revolution where the nurses will take over the operating room and the surgeons will hand them the instruments and talk to the parents. I don't think so."

"What could it be?"

"We will find out soon enough. You have to watch her to see she thaws out."

"You think the Ice Queen, BS, MS PhD, FAAN can thaw out a little?"

"If she wants something, she can raise the temperature just enough to get what she wants; her version of charm."

"She is talking to Al Sharptee, the CFO. This is getting serious. I bet she wants some more money. That means someone is going to get their budget cut. I hear the hospital is having some financial pressures."

"No way. They have a huge endowment. There is lots of money."

"You never know. The new board members are averse to taking money out of the endowment for new programs that have no return on investment. The Queen would have to be very innovative to have a program that actually makes real money instead of those fuzzy things like good will and patient satisfaction. They are nice but not for return on investment that the MBA people require."

"When Jackie comes to the coffee shop, watch your door, your job, your empire."

Chapter 18

The party started out as usual, but there was extra energy in the air that seemed to indicate this would be more than the usual Friday afternoon forget the week's problems kind of drink fest. The usual people were there, Felix of course acted as the maitre d' even though he was less active chasing the ladies.

"He must be getting older," remarked Claire, a former target.

Lester was hanging out with his new roommates, Adrienne and Sara. Evil Eva, the secretary in the education office came to see what resident will accommodate her to get some extra moon lighting jobs. She scanned the room looking for likely partners for the night. Not much picking. She liked the days when there were more men in the residency group. But she remained optimistic. As she got older and the residents stayed the same age, she took on a motherly role to the boys, providing them with experience and an opportunity to get some extra work covering the nursery or emergency room at $800 a shift. She was smart enough not to neglect the women who wanted the extra work, but there were few takers. Fortunately for Eva, many of the women were mothers and wanted time at home despite the lure of dollars. Other women wanted time to have some social life. After screening the room, she settled on a few prospects. Not Lester, she could not understand him; too many details and facts. Who cares what the history of the whatever? She was afraid he would be sitting on the edge of the bed, explaining how the hormone levels change with sexual activity, the average strokes per encounter and comparison of frequency of sex in each year of residency. He was so full of facts, that Eva feared he would not finish his recitation until the mood passed. Eva was more from the just do it- Nike school. Then there was Keith. Eva thought Keith was so miserable because he did not get enough sex. She had a theory that needed to be tested. Maybe she could help him with his presumed problem. Jeff Cole was another prospect, but he was engaged and Eva, evil as her reputation, was not interested in breaking up a couple. Jeff Marian may be the one tonight. He has no known girlfriend, has interest in moonlighting and has a pretty good body. "Yes," she concluded, "Jeff Marian is the male de jour."

The first year residents were not all together in their usual corner but actually talking to the seniors, feeling more confident that they say something right without fearing that they would make a mistake. Some of them actually combed their hair and dressed in clothes other than the usual scrubs or baggy slacks and sweaters. Joe Schultz, the Pharm rep from the infant formula company was holding court, telling stories and mixing up his Brandy Alexanders where he substituted his company's baby formula for the cream. He was the best rep in the company for getting the message across to the new doctors and future prescribers of infant formula. Of course he supplied the formula for the mixture; somehow the brandy and crème de cacao appeared. No questions asked. For those on a diet, there was the usual vodka and various mixers as well as a group of diet drinks and juices. Today there were not many takers of the latter. You could correlate the intensity of the bar activity with the past week's events. Patient deaths, more work and covering for sick residents all contributed to the drinking and subsequent noise level. Unlike the bar full of spirits, there was no drug distribution area, but from the look of some of the eyes, a few smokers or users were present tonight.

Joe Schultz was in his glory when he had a group of residents listening to his stories. He warns them that he has a lot of Irish in his blood, thus the story telling which sometimes stretched the truth but were very entertaining. Rarely, one of the faculty would come to the parties. Today Donna Barstow and her colleague Don Isaacs were there, telling stories of their days as residents, the days of the Giants, they reminded the group. Back then, they worked every other night, which means two days in a row for either Thursday and Friday or Saturday and Sunday. No such thing as an 80 hour week. They did not mention that in those days there was no ICU or full time laboratory or x-ray services so there was not much to do at night.

As the increased noise level was indicating this was some kind of a celebration, suddenly the room quieted. Heads turned towards the door as Luda, the antisocial one, appeared. She was wearing a light blue angora sweater and the tightest slacks that showed off her long legs and trim figure while still allowing her to avoid intestinal obstruction. Apparently the urging of the people at the coffee hour worked and she decided to make her first appearance. She smiled at the people she knew and walked up to the bar and asked for straight vodka. "I drink wudka, Absolute. In my country, we drink it straight. We have the best vodka. Yours is not bad, but Hettman vodka is my favorite." Felix was transfigured. How could he have missed this young thing, blonde, blue eyes and spectacular legs. He moaned "they should have a law against women wearing scrubs, especially the ones with bodies like she has." Even Lester noticed Luda, tearing himself away from his long discussion on the value of abstract art as a metaphor for world economic conditions. Not that anyone understood what he was talking about, but it seemed intellectual, an area that few had time to think about this year.

"Good to see you. Sara greeted Luda. 'You look great in that outfit. Where did you get it?"

"This thing? I got it at the thrift shop, the one on River Avenue. That is where the rich people drop off their things for those less fortunate but who appreciate fashion. I love to get the real bargains. This one is Donna. Twenty five dollars."

"No way. Is it open tonight? I want to get something that nice."

"Maybe tomorrow, you cannot always get this kind of deal but you have to go often to get lucky. I guess it is not lucky but persistence that pays off."

"Have you been coming to these parties? I don't think I have seen you before."

"No, this is my first time. I usually don't want to go to parties but Janet and Barbara asked me to join them so I wanted to be polite and attend. When they asked me to come, I realized that I have not been too social this year. This is a hard year and I don't adjust well to new situations. I don't see them here, have you? What do you do at these parties?"

"Oh we just talk, mostly about how hard we work and what are we going to do with our lives. The usual. Not much culture. Just time to vent a little and get ready for the weekend. The bar is over there. Stay away from the milky drink. They are awful."

"I ordered Absolute, but this tastes like absolutely not."

"I am not sure you will find Absolute here. Most likely, you will get something like Over the Mountain in a gallon bottle. The cheapest."

Luda goes over to the bar and refills her glass with vodka and returns to the group.

"And who is that cute guy over there?"

"That is Keith."

"Yes, I remember seeing him in the ED. He looks different to-night."

"For a change, he has combed his hair. And the light is different in this room. Look he is coming this way. He must have heard you mention his name."

Keith, who is the usual grump in the group, is smiling, looking like he already has had his attitude adjusted, early in the evening. "Hi, I'm Keith. I know you are Luda but that is all I know. Here let me fill your glass, it is almost empty. What is this? Water?"

"Wudka."

Keith took the glass and made his way to the bar and returned to Luda, almost salivating at her blond hair, athletic figure and the long muscular legs.

"Are you a dancer? I could not help seeing how good a shape you are in. Maybe a jogger."

"What means jogger?"

"Let me explain. Let's go over there where it is not so noisy." They moved over to a sofa on the edge of the room.

"So much for shy Luda. She is more complex and less quiet than we thought about her. It must be that trace of accent."

"Why are you repressing her blond hair, blue eyes and more than average sized boobs? That helps with the intrigue, even if you had a hearing problem."

"I guess we will get lucky when we stop trying so hard. This year is tough on the old hormones, hard to get the level raised to the fun zone."

"OK, did anyone have any action on eHarmony this week?"

"I got 32 hits from my latest version of the questionnaire that I sent in. I decided that the picture was not representative and my comments were too serious. I think that emphasizing the medical training only evoked fears of a huge student loan that comes with the bright future. So my strategy worked. I did not like most of the matches but there was one that seemed encouraging. He is a computer science PhD at Stanford. Best thing was that he did not have the requisite thick lens glasses. I could tell that he did not wear glasses since he did not squint or look like he could not see the camera. Likes sailing, cooking minimalist Italian, I hope that means something above opening Ragu spaghetti sauce. He is from the Midwest, which is a plus for being nice. Did you ever meet someone from the Midwest who was not nice? Oh I take that back, I forgot about those birds in Washington. Some of them were from Missouri and Illinois and the Dakotas. But he looks promising. If he goes to work for Google, it would be better. We could pay off my loans in a few years."

"Hey, you are paying off loans before you meet him. That is a little out of synch."

"But that is what I worry about and if he has all those stock options, then he can help me. That is only fair."

"So when are you going to meet him?"

"He is coming in next week."

"No way, next week? That was fast."

"He has to come to New York to a conference. That is my luck and shows that stars are favorable."

"How come I fill out those questionnaires each month and never got such action, at least so quickly."

"You forgot about the post office worker who had already worn out his welcome at the Asiangirls.com and PacificrimQueens.com and now has returned to the US and hits the internet to see who is available. I guess it taught you to stay away from the free date matching sites."

"Who would think I would be reduced to this? Working in the hospital is not the best way to socialize with the real world."

"Next year will be better."

"But look at Luda; she is warming up to occasion. And Keith, I never thought he could smile."

"It looks more like drooling to me. I think it is going to get embarrassing in a few minutes. There they go for more vodka."

"The party continued for about an hour more. Those who were fortunate find someone, even if it was not leading to romance, were going through the preliminary mating dance of tapping the other person, some physical contact when making a point. The ladies were running their fingers through their hair; the laughter was higher pitched than before. That is why they called this the attitude adjustment hour."

Suddenly there was a loud whistle. It was Joe Schultz. "We are running out of booze. Does anyone have a key to the pharmacy? We can get some ethyl alcohol there."

"But what about the mixer. I can't drink alcohol straight."

"That I can take care of easily but we need to get to the pharmacy."

"Well Jerry, what do you say?"

"Jerry, the pharmacist, turned red. Why me? I just work there."

"That is why we look at you. Can you get us some ETOH?"

Jerry who was having a good time, as always, did not need much encouragement. "OK let's go but be quiet about this. I need the job and the benefits."

"Shortly he returned with a few quarts of ethyl alcohol. Joe came back from the kitchen with grape jelly and a few packages of lemonade mix."

"Voila! A new set of drinks. Purple lady and Lemon pickups. Courtesy of CHUC food services."

Now Eva Masters has toured the room, making sure that the residents were happy and trying not to be too obvious about settling in with Jeff Marian. She had already chatted with him once when she bumped into him at the bar. Not obvious at all, she thought. Now she returned to Jeff, who was talking to a few of his friends at the bar about sports, of course. They were talking about the up coming football draft.

"They are a bunch of overpriced spoiled brats who hardly ever justify the millions of signing bonus. Why don't you guys talk about a real sport? Hockey is the real game. A fight, hits, scars blood on the ice. That is a real sport."

"Eva, I didn't think you cared about hockey. I am an old hockey player from North Dakota, you betcha."

"North Dakota? How did you get in this program? It must be your good looks."

"Me, good looks? I didn't think that my picture did me justice."

"It was a good start but I do admit you are better looking in real life. She grabbed his arm. "Wow, those are real muscles. How much time do you spend in the gym?"

"Not enough. I have an important day job. I don't do much moonlighting so I get to the gym when I am not working at night."

"You don't do any moonlighting; I have not seen your name on the list for moonlighting jobs. Are you interested in getting some more work? I have something to do with the assignments."

"I understand you do. Yes, I would like to get some more experience in night work."

"Not to mention the cash. Maybe we can discuss it later. Do you have a car, I need a ride home."

"Oh sure, Where do you live? It does not matter; I will give you a lift whenever you are ready to leave. I am ready when you are."

"Let me get my coat. I will meet you in the lobby."

No one was paying attention to Lester tonight. But he was busy chatting with Adrienne and Sara, talking more than usual and not noticing that the girls were   attentive to him by refilling his glass. He mentioned to them that he noticed the change in the last drink, the ethanol-grape jelly concoction. Since he was sitting down, no one could judge his ability to stand or walk a straight line. Adrienne did detect a slight slur to his speech, especially with his s's.

Luda, having moved away from Keith who passed out on the couch, was now dancing with Will Miller, the cardiologist. He was one of the few staff members that always attended the resident parties. Luda and Will Miller were so involved in their conversation   that they did not notice that the noise level had dropped as the crowd was thinning out. Who knew Luda had that much to talk about? Adrienne stayed near Lester, getting him a drink when his glass was empty and as usual, was talking almost non-stop with him, slamming her glass down when she was making a major point. She did not appear drunk, maybe a little energized as she continued her animated discussion and drinking too much of the grape jelly special. Her lack of sexual activity was getting the best of her. She was not ready to buy a vibrator as some of her friends had. Adrienne figured that Lester was her only chance, even if he was her roommate, "OK Lester, lets get going. Time to get home."

"Hey what is the rush? This new drink is great. Did they get a new bar tender? I never had a grape drink before. You know grapes vary depending on the soil and ambient temperature. That changes the sugar content especially the short carbon chains, or is it the long carbon chains. Where is my Blackberry? I need to check it on Google."

"Later Lester, Lets get going."

Lester stood up and held on as he regained his balance. "I guess it is time to get home. I think my alcohol level has elevated beyond the safety level. Are you driving home?"

"You bet your life. Let's get going."

He did get into the car without difficulty although the lights seemed brighter and the traffic buzzed by them on the way to the apartment. Fortunately the apartment was on the first floor so there were not many steps to negotiate. When they got into the apartment, Adrienne made some strong coffee for Lester who now was slumped over in the kitchen chair.

"Here take this, I am going to take a shower and get ready for bed. I will be back to check on you. There is more coffee in the pot."

The coffee worked. It should have. He got a triple shot espresso mixed with a small amount of hot water. He drank the first and then took the second one immediately. He felt a little better but he had not really tested his mobility. The room was not spinning; he lost his need to sing Puccini arias or to vomit. When he heard the sound of the water running in the shower, he announced to no one "I have to pee." Although he did not have this opportunity at college where he lived in an all male dorm, living in the apartment for the past months, he got used to sharing bathroom privileges with the girls, but he was usually hesitant to walking into the bathroom when one of his roommates was in there. "That water from the shower is making me crazy, I can't take the pressure on my bladder. I can't wait." So he slowly arose from his chair and hesitantly made his way to relieve himself. Always the efficiency expert who tried to minimize movements and time expended, he pulled down his pant's zipper as he headed for the bathroom. He bumped into the side table and then the door jamb but finally got the bathroom. After a polite knock on the door, he walked in ready to fire away. "Oh no, this is the clothes closet. I almost inundated the girls' finest frocks." Before he let go, he backed up and surveyed the room. "I think this is the bathroom." He knocked and entered. The room was so steamy that only the outline of Adrienne could be seen through the glass shower door. Lester was sober enough to lift the toilet seat and let go. "Oops. I think I missed the bowl," but the reverberation from the bowl reassured him that some of the urine hit the target. "I do detect a great deal of wetness on my feet. But at least, I feel better. My vesical pressure is reduced. Maybe the steam helped too. If only the room would stop rotating."

"Lester, while you are in here, could you wash my back. Oops, this shower has caused a minor flood on the floor. I'll turn down the water so the floor does not get any wetter."

Lester then began to analyze the task. "Should I wash her back, side to side until the level of L2 but not below that to exclude the entirety of the buttocks or should I go head to foot direction with the same limitations of the integrity of the buttocks. This is a complicated choice." Adrienne could not hear him but she knew that he was doing some kind of mental exercise and probably would be paralyzed for the next few minutes chided him. "Come on Lester, I am freezing. Here is the wash cloth."

Seeing the wash cloth interrupted Lester's machinations and his stability. He took the wash cloth and touched her back. Nice paraspinal muscle group, he thought. "Hey, I never noticed that you had a tattoo. Roses, did you know….." As he touched her back with the soapy wash-cloth, he slid forward as he slipped on the wet floor and fell into the shower. Adrienne turned to break his fall. There he was, fully dressed but soaked. His face was buried in Adrienne's well formed breasts which produced a new and wonderful sensation in his pubic area. It was not a full bladder this time but a rather full sized erection. He struggled to his feet, now laughing uncontrollably. Adrienne was torn between being shocked and excited too. As they finally stood up in the shower, she took the opportunity to do something she was thinking about for a long time. "Here, Lester, let me help you take off those wet clothes, you may catch a cold."

"But, but." Lester was worrying about exposing his erection. Adrienne had already noticed the bulge in his pants which led her to the decision to go the disrobing pathway.

"Let me warm up the water. It's getting cold in here. Lester."

"I am worried about my wallet getting wet so I think I concur with your suggestion. Off go the pants."

"Here, let me unbutton your shirt!" Adrienne was in overdrive now. She threw her arms around his neck and closed the gap between their bellies or as Lester would say put their abdominal recti in close apposition.

"Hey." Lester said. "This feels good."

"Here let me soap you up."

Obviously a new situation, Lester felt uncomfortable, not having time to analyze his options or plan his actions so he acted instinctively. He leaned forward and kissed her, his first encounter with such activity, but executed with passion and appropriate force. He liked this but was unprepared for Adrienne opening her mouth and forcing her tongue into his oral cavity, as he would later describe this encounter. This was more than his naiveté could stand. He began to move his hips forward and backward until he felt an electrical feeling as he emptied the contents of his spermatic duct on Adrienne, another first time event done without his own hand being involved.

"My, you are a major league lover. How do you feel? I think it is time to wash off and get out of this passion pool."

Lester, sobering up quickly, could only utter his remark of surprise. "My word! This could make me take up drinking. That was incredible. What else do you have in your trick bag?"

"That was not a trick young man. I have been negligent in my coaching you. We have been all talk and no action. That is what we call a real back scrub. Next we will do the back massage. It is even better and not so wet. Come let's get to bed. We have to get to work in the AM."

"I don't have to go in until noon. Let's try something else. Can't we do the next lesson?"

"I think this is enough for one night. We have to digest this night and see if it needs more practice or can we go onto the next event. I am not on the pill and I assume you have no condoms so let's not get into real sex until we are better prepared."

"Maybe we could examine your estrus cycle. How long has it been since your ovulation into the Fallopian tubes?

"Right now I bet that little egg has gotten a jolt and is ready to pop."

"But that was just an appetizer. I am hungry for more."

"Try a snicker bar. I am tired. Maybe you can keep me company in my bed tonight- we can snuggle, I mean snuggle and nothing else."

"What ever you say, coach."

After the shower escapade, Adrienne could not stop smiling, she was always upbeat and positive but now she had that extra bounce of energy, smiles and swagger. Casual observers did not see any behavioral change in Lester, Those who took the time to look closer could see and extra lift to his gait- he lifted his heel as usual but then added an extra hitch to the heel lift. To Lester watchers, this new twitch meant he was ecstatic.

• • •

"Dick, this is Norm Oppenheim, I need a favor from you."

"Great what can I do for you?" He was excited to get this call since he felt Norman was not on his side and had seen through some of his fancy footwork with the numbers and deals he has presented to the board. Now if he did a favor for Norman, he might move him from being a doubter to an approver.

"Listen, I have a colleague who has a sick kid. I am not sure how old she is but she is little. She has had an infection for several weeks that has not responded to a group of antibiotics. The only doctors we hear about at CHUC are the surgeons but I know they must have pediatricians in a children's hospital but I don't know any names. Can you get someone to see her today? The only doctor I know at CHUC is

Carter Randolf. My friend is worried and we need to get to the bottom of this. The kid does not look well."

"No problem, as you know, we take care of kids at our children's hospital. I will get back to you in a few minutes."

"Thanks Dick, I owe you one."

"No problem. I am glad to help you. You are an important member of our board but we try to give everyone blue ribbon service."

"Sounds like you are running a car agency. By the way what are you driving these days?"

"Beemer, today, the Porsche is in the shop. Waiting for the new ones so I can trade this one in. How about you?"

"I got a little Maserati for short trips. Works like a charm. You should get one."

"I tried one but my garage is not large enough for it, too much junk I've collected takes up space. What do you have for longer trips?"

"For long trips, my driver prefers the Maybach. Enough toy talk, lets get that baby cured."

"Good idea. I will ring you back shortly."

"Ann. Get me Robert Farmer."

Robert Farmer was looking forward to this day. It was his one day a month that he closed his doors and took care of writing letters, trying to put together some observations into a paper to submit to a pediatric journal. This so called free time made up for all the weekends and nights he worked on clinical matters. He was not a golfer so these academic activities were his game. He had, early on, decided that basic research was not his forte or interest, but he always had some case studies to share with other clinicians. His job gave him an exposure to unusual cases and his observation skills allowed him to get a number of cases published. As he opened up his files, the phone rang. This was unusual, since his secretary usually blocked all calls on his academic day. On the caller ID, he saw it was Richardson Beardsley calling. That explained the reason the call got through.

"Yes,"

"Hi Bob, Beardsley here." He got that opening from the World War II movies when the Brits always gave a last name followed by a here when answering phone calls.

"Good morning. What's up?" Beardsley was not a favorite of Farmer or for any of the medical staff as his cost cutting and self aggrandizement annoyed them. Beardsley just did not understand the differences between practices in the hospital and those in a general pediatric office. The people had special problems and required more attention and time to reach a diagnosis, coordinate services between consultants and carry out the treatment. Communication with the family, so important to success, required time. This was not the scenario that the bean counters could understand as it was not billable time. Robert still laughs when he thinks of the call he got from the business office wanting an explanation why the patient visits dropped off one day last January. The patient numbers dropped that day but so did 20 inches of snow, a fact did not show up on their spread sheets.

"Listen Bob, I just got a call from Norman Oppenheim, one of our board members. He was contacted by a friend whose child has what sounds like an eye infection, a strange infection, not responding to antibiotics. He asked for someone to see the kid today. I would like to send him over to you. You are the man for this, I told him. We have to coordinate the throughput of the workup so the output will be typical of our quality CHUC care."

"Sure," he said as he looked at the files on his desk. "I would be glad to see him. I will fit him in at 11. Sounded like a resistant staph infection, MRSA in increasing cause of difficult infections." Farmer did not want to tell him, he was not seeing patients today or there would be a new edict incorporating the terms input, throughput and output, his favorite but slightly outdated terms of choice. At least he would have a few hours before the visit to get some of his work done. "Throughput, output- where did they come from?"

At 11 o'clock, Tobe Hallman and his parents, Mathew and Suzi entered his office. Tobe, age 3, looked small for his age. He was a preppy in training, blue and white striped button down collar shirt and khaki pants. Blue Keds, white laces. Of course the blond and blue eyes completed the picture. Suzi, no longer with her usual cheerful positive façade, showed the strain of these past weeks of worry. Her diamond inset Rolex was the only thing that sparkled. She looked like she slept in her Blu Marine spongy T with embroidered flowers, all $1100 of it. Matt, likewise showed the strain of his child still being sick after treatment with expensive but ineffective antibiotics.

After the usual greetings and demographical information, they got down to the problem. "My golfing friends told me that Tobe needed 6 weeks of intravenous antibiotics. That was why I came to CHUC rather than listen to my buddies who got their WebMD degree.. I have given this history so many times; I will get through the usual points for you. He was always small but generally in good health until this illness. He had not traveled to exotic places or been exposed to travelers who may have brought home some rare infection. This problem started with redness to his eye which they thought was conjunctivitis. Two different antibiotic drops and an oral antibiotic did not work. The area around his eye was swollen and red. He was tired, had lost his appetite and energy. He was not well. The only lab tests ordered were a CBC which showed no anemia or infection and an x-ray that did not show any sinus infection."

"Wow! You sure did a great job of summarizing the case. I can see you had a lot of practice." Bob first thought about a staph infection resistant to the usual antibiotics but was concerned that this was something more. "Come over here, Tobe. Let me look at your eye. Sure is red but it looks like a bruise in the soft tissue around the eye. Your skin looks a little pale." Farmer felt his neck and found a few lymph glands then he rubbed his stethoscope. "I'm warming up this stethoscope for you. Can you say stethoscope?" After listening to Tobe's heart and lungs. "Your heart was normal except for the rapid pulse. That could be from fright.. Let me tickle your belly." Farmer frowned a little as he felt the liver tip and when he tried to feel deeper in the abdomen, Tobe resisted his fingers. Farmer tried the usual tricks he had mastered over time to distract Tobe so his muscles would relax. "OK, let's try this. Just bend your knees and let me see if I can tell what you had for breakfast. I think I feel cheerios, is that what you had?"

"No, I had fruit loops."

"Well, I was close; they feel the same, I'm not good at feeling the colors." Although not the best examination, Farmer could detect a mass in his abdomen. "Amazing," thought Farmer. "You read about this, remember seeing the pictures in the atlas and here was a case of neuroblastoma with spread the area behind the eye. Not good!"

Bob Farmer finished the rest of the examination quickly, called his secretary to come in so she could take Tobe outside the office so he could explain his findings to the parents. Tobe was excited to get a chance to attack the candy bowl that Mrs. Jennings kept on her desk. "Please get me Dr. Spirito on the phone."

When the parents sat down and Bob Farmer moved from behind his desk, he took his notebook and color atlas and sat facing them.

266

"I am afraid this is more than an infection in the eye. We have a serious problem. I have found a mass in his abdomen. The mass plus the swollen area around the eye makes me think that the most likely diagnosis is a tumor of the nervous system"

"Oh no." The parents looked shocked but relieved as they slumped back into their chair. Shock at hearing the word tumor and relieved that the unknown has is now closer to becoming known.

"This is my tentative diagnosis and obviously we need to get more tests and images to confirm my suspicion. But I think this is what we are dealing with."

"How did you get from an eye infection to a tumor?"

"Let him finish telling us what he found, dear."

"Look at this picture in the book; it looks very similar to Tobe's eye."

"Right, it does."

"This is what we call pattern recognition. Certain problems have common appearances. The bruise around a swollen eye is a classic pattern of a tumor called neuroblastoma, a cancer of the nervous system. I could not get a good feel of his abdomen but enough to feel the hard lump there. What we need is an MRI of the abdomen to see if the tumor is there and another MRI of the skull to see what is the swelling around his eye. We will get that as soon as possible and then sit down to discuss the treatment options."

"Is he going to make it?"

"We are going to do our best to help him. I wish I could answer that question but we need to get more information about this tumor. First we need to confirm the diagnosis and then his prognosis will depend on the type of tumor he has and then how he responds to treatment. I expect the radiologist to call back within minutes and then we can move as fast as we can. My role is to organize the evaluation, coordinate the different specialists and communicate with you. I will be in the boat with you and we are going to ride out this storm together. Tobe will be admitted to the hospital. I know that this possible diagnosis is upsetting and difficult to hear."

"I feel awful about this. What can I do?"

"Our goal is to support Tobe and get him the best care we can provide. We need time to regroup so that we don't scare Tobe and upset him with our fears. Kids are great barometers that sense trouble; they get worried when they sense tension. So take a few minutes and then go out and give him a big dose of hugs and kisses. Time for more questions."

"Thank you doctor for being so forthright and so knowledgeable. I knew we were in the right place, the instant we met you. We are tough people who will do our best to be brave. Tobe is our main interest, just as you said. I want to get started with the hugs and kisses. Can we see Tobe now?"

"Of course. That is a good plan." He opened the door. "Mrs. Jennings, did John Spirito answer his page? Wait a second, the phone is ringing now. Hey John, I have a great young man here who has a black eye and what I feel is an abdominal mass."

"Say no more; send him over to MRI now. I will be there to meet him. Name?"

"Tobe Hallman, age 3. They are on their way."

Farmer hung up the phone and turned to the parents who had their arms around Tobe. "John Spirito is a gem, an old fashioned radiologist who can't sit at a computer terminal looking at shadows. He likes to talk to the patients that come for studies. He finally recognized that MRI is a helpful tool, plain x-rays cannot do it all. He is the ultimate company man so you may find him sweeping the floor to save money on housekeeping expenses. Before digital x-rays, he would develop his own films; being one of the last to buy an automatic film processor because he thought they were too expensive. When the employees joined the union, he then saw the value of a processor that did not require benefits or a 40 hour week. Digital technology has stopped that dilemma for him but he is not happy with spending hospital funds, a marked contrast to today's techies who want the most expensive toys. But as you will see, if you have not already appreciated it, these machines are great advances in diagnosis. Let's get going. Mrs. Jennings will you walk Tobe and his parents to radiology?"

Farmer did not like to talk to Beardsley or what usually turned out to mostly listening to him stroke his own needy ego, so he emailed him that he saw the Hallmans and they are in radiology. He went back to his desk to get to his day's project awaiting the call from Spirito.

As predicted, Dr. Spirito was at the reception desk to greet Tobe and his parents.

"Hello big fella, are you going to smile for the picture?" Looking at the eye lid discoloration, he quickly recognizes the pattern of abdominal mass and color changes around the eye.

"Lets go into the room and let the Star War character take some pictures of your belly and if you smile, it will take one of your handsome face. You are one good looking young man. Just how many girl friends do you have?"

"None! Just my mommy."

"Here hop on the table and let's see what the Star War robot will do."

Tobe climbs onto the table, put at ease by the kind doctor. He cooperates with the technician and stays fairly still while the images are captured.

The Hallmans are waiting outside; Spirito is at the console watching the images of the MRI slices through the abdomen appear on the screen. "Thank goodness for the fast MRI, the old ones would take much longer than these new machines." John commented without emotion. "Oh boy, just as I suspected, a big mass above the left kidney. No question that this is a neuroblastoma. Now to see how much it has grown, Oh boy…. It is a fairly big one. Keep coming, keep coming with the slices. Ronny, when you are done with the belly, I need to see some head shots. Yes, I know, only two arms, I will wait." One did not have to be an MRI specialist to read these images. John knew the anatomy of the region quite well so he could see the tumor sitting on top of the kidney and pressing down on the upper pole. Even John had to admit this MRI series was much better than the old fashioned xray study in the old days. He goes to the phone to dial up Farmer.

"Yes?"

"It's John, this is a fairly large neuroblastoma, we are getting the skull now but as you suspected, it probably spread to the skull, hopefully outside the brain but we don't have the shots yet. They are setting up now for those images. Just like the book, amazing. Hopefully the genetic studies will show it to be a good one, if any of them are good."

"Shortly the pictures of the head did show that the tumor had spread to the area around the eye. The brain MRI was clean."

He came out of the MRI suite to meet the parents. "We found the tumor in the belly and have added an MRI of the head where we can see the tumor there too. I see one of these cases every 10 or so years; it is combination that one cannot forget. I always present several cases of this condition in his teaching sessions so the docs in practice will think of this condition when they see someone with a bruise around the eye. I called Dr. Farmer with the report and he wants to see you back in his office. I know that this is a big dose of upsetting news but at least we know what is going on and can get started getting the oncology service involved so they can begin planning the treatment."

Even though they were prepared for the worst, they had hoped that the MRI would give them a different diagnosis. "Thank you Dr. Spirito. Just think, we have been here less than an hour and all these tests are done. We have to hope that the treatment will be effective. We love our little boy so much."

"Yes, I can see that. We have to hope for the best. There are so many treatments these days; they test for receptors and DNA analysis so that the treatment can be customized to the specific type of tumor. In the old days, we just treated all the cases like this the same, but now it is what we call boutique therapy. But we can't forget our pal Tobe. We need to keep him first. Here Tobe, how about a hug for me?"

The Hallmans went back to Dr. Farmer, trying to put on a positive face but scared about the news they were going to receive. They wanted to disagree with the two doctors who so quickly came to the same diagnosis. Suzi's nails were digging into her palms, Matt's face was red; the veins bulging on his forehead.. As Mrs. Jennings led them into the office, Farmer was listening to the last of the dictation of the study.

The mass measures 4 by 5 centimeters along the left sympathetic chain, pressing down on the apex of the kidney. The head study shows metastases into the left orbital area. The brain is free of lesions.

Final diagnosis: left neuroblastoma with impingement on the left renal apex and metastases to the left orbital area. No lesions seen in the brain study.

Adorable young man. As always, keep me posted on the progress of the workup.

Love and kisses

J. Spirito"

"Come in, come in. How are you doing Tobe? Did you like the machine?"

"No, it was not a nice machine. I want to go home."

" Tobe, will you sit here with Ms. While I talk to Ms. Jennings will I talk to your mommy and daddy?"

Tobe heads for the candy jar. Farmer closes his office door.

"I just talked to Dr Spirito who confirmed what I talked to you about. The mass is middle sized, we have seen larger ones. The tumor

270

has spread to the eye area but he did not see any spread into the brain. That is the good news as it could have been larger in size or have entered the brain tissue. I have alerted Drs. Frank Winston, the head of oncology and Melanie Katcher, the oncologic surgeon who have a special interest in this problem. This is a lot and we have moved fairly quickly. I wish that all the workups could be accomplished this efficiently. But we are not done with all the evaluations as this is the start of a long process. Now for questions."

"First thank you so much Dr. Farmer for all your care. It is hard to hear the news but we do appreciate your expertise and kindness. Do you take care of adults too? I wish we had a doctor like you. When we get home, the tears will come but now we are in your hands to guide us. We will do whatever you say. I do have a question about how you figured out what was going on."

"Tobe has a classic problem. It is on the board examinations and study books although it is so rare that most people will not actually see a real case. The diagnosis is one of those conditions that you have stored in your brain waiting for that rare time when a patients presents with the swollen eye. Then you feel the mass and then the brain fires away. I have a few other pearls that I carry with me, silent until I see the pattern."

"I bet you have a long string of pearls in your brain. What is next?"

"We will have to admit Tobe to the hospital so we can finish the testing and talk about the treatment. But let's stop for a second. I love this hospital and feel we have a talented staff. But you will not hurt my feelings if you want to get a second opinion. I would not advise an automatic second opinion but if there is a doubt or a question about what we are doing, you are free to consult another oncologist. Secondly, I treat all my patients as I would treat my family. In certain situations, there are doctors with more experience and hospitals with more technology than we have here. Then I would send you there. In fact, at a recent research meeting, I heard a doctor talk about some advanced testing that she has developed to better define the tumor type- many tumors look alike but the genetic testing will separate the patients into groups that will do better with one kind of treatment or better with another type of treatment. Or those where treatment will only produce side effects and no benefit. I will talk to the oncologist about getting that kind of testing, I don't think we do that study here but maybe they can send the blood or biopsy to that doctor; I think he is in North Carolina. That is far down the line but now we need to get going with the basic workup. Fortunately, all the pediatric oncologists work together by setting up various treatment plans and then the patients in many hospitals are treated by these protocols to see if the treatment is effective. Otherwise, we are operating by impressions from a few cases. That is the way they practiced medicine in the 19th century. We can always do better using treatment protocols so the oncologists can get more experience with a larger group of patients."

"Any questions now?"

"This is going so quickly, I am sure I will have many questions later but right now, I want to hug my baby and see what you all can do for him."

"OK, One final thought. Even though you did not say anything, I bet you are going over the past and trying to blame yourself for causing this problem. Let me be clear and direct. This is not any one's fault. Most parents will go through the blame stage, first themselves and then others. It is not your fault and you did not delay in coming in here. We are getting more information about genes that show that many diseases are genetic, that is the combination of genes produce proteins that will cause cells to grow and eventually be expressed as tumors, or heart disease or diabetes. There are other genes that are supposed to stop cells from growing; in the case of cancer, these brakes do not work. We can do things that will encourage the genes to produce the proteins. But it is not your fault. When you go home and try to take the blame for Tobe's illness, do not take it too far because it is not your fault."

"I understand. It is hard for me not to put myself into all equations but I will try to remember your advice. This is a lot to take, especially for poor Tobe. But we will try to be brave."

"One thing about children's hospitals, when you see the other kids, you will feel that your problem, big as it is, are not as bad as others. Everyone tells me that. We are a team now and so are the others that will be involved in Tobe's care. If you need some time out or even a shot of vodka, drop by and help yourself."

SPRING

Shit happens- how you clean it up defines your character

Burt Sloan

Chapter 19

Connie Eagleston, the youngest member of the faculty was in the clinic trying to finish up the panel of patients for the day. It seemed that everyone worked faster than she did. As a resident, she was even slower. Her advisors always noted that she, in trying to keep a perfect record by not missing a diagnosis, ordered too many tests which in turn caused her to spend more time at the computer monitor retrieving the lab tests, which in turn generated more questions that required answers and probably more tests. Almost all her big discoveries were insignificant but rarely she did turn up a diagnosis that others had missed, justifying, at least to her, all this extra effort. She did not accept the idea of sequencing the testing, do a few studies and see what the results are and allowing nature or time to remove the symptom. In order not to miss diagnosis, her rate of consultations was the highest in the group. Even though the consultant gave a mini-course on the problem in the final report, Connie continued to get a consultation for the next patient who had the same problem, fearing she would make a mistake or something new turned up in the medical journals that she had missed. Many patients thought she was the best doctor - so thorough. They felt reassured when they heard that "all tests came back negative" They did not like those who used intuition rather than tests to confirm clinical impressions. These differences worked well in the free market place where patients could select the doctor on the basis of chemistry and style. But for those who get assigned by the HMO, the mismatch of the comfort zone of the doctor and patient often leads to patient and doctor dissatisfaction.

Connie's next patient was Rosita, an attractive 15 year old, whose scowl on her face and eyes fixed on the floor signaling that she did not want to be in the office. Her mother insisted that she come to the doctor because her sore throats could be strep infections and she remembered from her mother telling her about strep throat causing such complications as rheumatic fever or scarlet fever, relighting memories of people dying from these conditions. Although she has been in this country for over 30 years, she could not shake off the medical lore of her family in South America including trying traditional herbal cures such as an onion around the neck to prevent colds. It may have been the mystical effect of an onion but most likely it was the odor that kept people away, whatever the reason, the spread the cold virus was hampered.

So Rosita was here for about the 20th time to check for a strep throat. Yes, she had pain, No. she did not have a fever, Yes. It hurt to swallow, No. she did not gargle with salt water. Yes. She took Tylenol, but not every 8 hours. It was about the same as yesterday, maybe a little bit better.

With this information, most doctors especially at the end of the day would take a throat culture and run a rapid strep test to see if it were positive. But not Connie. She took this visit as an entry point into the arcane world of adolescent medicine. A long history covered all aspects of life, school, home sexual activity including exposure to HIV, drugs and socialization plus inquiries at depression and suicide. With all these issues so prevalent in adolescent's lives today, it took a long time to go through the list of potential problems.

Rosita was an average student in school; she wanted to go to college to study landscape design as she had many gardeners in her family. She did not want to work that hard in manual labor but she liked plants and gardens so her choice was understandable. Home was the usual complaint. Too many restrictions, too much housework, not enough food that she liked. Sexual activity was a hard area to explore. For the interview, Rosita's mother was excused to wait outside. Until recently, Rosita's mother, following her cultural practices, would inspect her vagina to see if the hymen was still intact. This was so embarrassing, that she vowed if she had a daughter, she would not subject her daughter to such scrutiny. Fortunately for her, her mother abandoned this privacy invasion a few months ago. So although she was not comfortable talking about sex, at least her mother was not in the room and the doctor was a woman.

"When was your last period?"

"Last week."

"Were there any problems?"

"Just a few cramps, but not so bad."

"Have you had sexual activity?"

"What do you mean?"

"Have you had sex with a boy or girl?"

"A girl. Not."

"How about a boy?"

"She looked at the door, as if she could see if her mother was on the other side of the door listening. "Yes, I have sex with my boyfriend."

"What kind of contraception do you use?"

"We don't use contraception. Our church is against that. We are careful. I know about fertility and ovulation."

"What keeps you from using more effective methods than being safe? You know, condoms, the pill, the injection."

"My boy friend does not want to use condoms and I cannot tell my mom about needing birth control. The church, you know."

"You know girls who became pregnant?"

"Yes."

"That would put a crimp into your plans for college."

"I know and it would kill my mom."

"So what do you want to do?"

"I guess I better bite the bullet and take some responsibility or I will be a teen age mom."

"What about stopping sex until you are older?"

"I don't think my boyfriend would go for that."

"So what is plan B?"

"I guess I would go for the shot. My friends take that even though it is a shot. That way I cannot forget to take a pill."

"Do you think you could discuss this with your mom?"

"She would kill me. I am her only daughter. She would just die."

"I think it would be good to talk to your mom. But that is your choice. What you tell me here is for us and not for anyone else. I need to do a vaginal examination and take cultures. I will call the nurse to set up the exam."

Connie took time to explain what she was doing, especially warming the speculum. "Things look normal inside. Here is a prescription for the injection to take to the pharmacy and bring it back here so the nurse can inject it."

"Sounds good. I think this is the right thing to do. I don't want any babies now."

Dr. Eagleston concludes the visit with Rosa and her mother, who head for the pharmacy.

"In a few minutes, there is a call from the pharmacy. "Hey Dr. Eagleston, this is Jerry from the pharmacy. I know you are new here but we don't dispense contraceptives here. It is against the hospital policy."

"What policy? I have been writing for BCP's since I came here."

"And we sent them to the local pharmacy. The board passed a resolution to prohibit contraceptives from being dispensed at the hospital pharmacy."

"You mean we have been invaded by the religious right?"

"More likely it was Dr. Carter Randolf and his group that has a major say with the board. I thought you knew but we don't publicize the policy. We just refer the patients outside. It just dawned on me that you probably did not know so that was why I called."

"Thanks for the information. Please send the young lady back to my office so I can talk to her."

Dr. Eagleston told Rosita about the need to go to the local pharmacy. They agreed that after paying for the injection, she would bring it back to the nurse to inject it and would call her for the culture report of the throat and the cervix.

•••

Two days later, Sergeant Parkerson calls the chief of security and to the COO Eugene James. "Parkerson speaking. There is a disturbance outside the main entrance. Individuals carrying signs about hospital unfair to women shouting "we want contraception and we want it now." Lots of women lots of shouting. I wanted you to know. So far they have not caused any problems with access to the hospital. The Channel 7 truck is pulling up to film the demonstration. Now this was getting serious, real serious."

James went ballistic. "This was going to ruin the hospital's image of providing total state of the art care. I need to find out what is behind this but I do not want to be seen there or be interviewed by the nosey reporter from 7 NBC. Get me Faith Boringer on the phone. We have a problem, we have a problem!" Eugene stands over the phone as if being there will speed up the return call from Faith.

"Faith, we have a PR code Red! As the head of Public Relations I need you to mix in with the crowd, avoiding the TV cameras, of course, and find out what was behind this demonstration."

"Vera, do you have any idea what has prompted this mess?" Vera, his secretary, was well connected with the hospital staff and usually had good sources for finding out who started a rumor or what the employees were complaining about."

"This is new to me. I had no warning that the demonstrators were coming here."

"Well if you don't know what is behind this, go down to the coffee shop and ask Tom, He knows everything. Since we closed down the barber shop, I have lost my contacts for rumors."

"I'll see what I can find out."

Vera goes to the coffee shop which was not very busy at this time of day. "Hey Tom, what is going on?"

"About hockey or what do you mean?"

"Hockey, I know about, I am more interested to know why the people are outside with the picket signs. What is that about?"

"From what I hear from Cedric, the housekeeping guy who sweeps up outside, it is something about birth control pills and women's rights."

"What is the big deal, we don't dispense contraceptives here."

"I think that is the issue. They want to have pills or whatever given to the patients who ask for them."

"Why do they make an issue of this, they can always go to RiteAid or CVS to get them."

"I understand, maybe there is a group that wants to picket and this seems like the best cause they can find today. I understand Riley from transport is out there with the pickets."

"Riley? What is the man doing out there?"

"He loves to relive his 60's days on the protest line. He keeps his picketing hat with the red letters "Power Now" in his locker so he can get on the line as soon as there is a crowd. He loves to protest and I guess he has some feelings about working at his job while the big guys make so much money. At least that is what I hear."

"Thanks, Tom. I have to get back."

"Didn't you come down here for coffee?"

"Oh sure, coffee. Yes I want the usual."

She takes the vanilla flavored coffee with extra whipped cream and a dash of hazelnut, pays $3.25, puts the change into the tip jar, then heads back to the administration floor then goes right into Eugene James's office.

"Seems the pickets do not like the way we do not allow contraceptives to be distributed."

"We don't have a policy, do we?"

"Right. At the request of Dr. Carter Randolph, we don't encourage premarital sex by giving out contraceptive to teens, not a policy, but that is what we do."

"Is this a written policy? I hope not."

"No. it is not written down, he is not so dumb as to put this in writing. He used his influence with the pharmacy committee to put the ban into effect."

"What influence?"

"Well, he has operated on several of the committee members' kids so he had their vote. He is very convincing as you well know,   the committee backs him. So the pharmacists told the patients it was a non-formulary drug. They did not say it was a hospital policy. It seemed to work."

"Work until today."

"Let me check with Dick. I am sure he knows about this problem."

James goes off to the corner office to call Beardsley. The line is busy. Beardsley is already on the phone.

"Yes, Bunky, I know the pickets are outside. We are trying to get a handle on the cause of the demonstration and I have legal here advising me on the correct course of action. Yes, I know that you are president of Planned Parenthood and have strong feelings about birth control and prevention of teen pregnancy. Yes, I know, I know. Bunky, give me a few minutes to get a handle on this and I will get back to you within the hour."

He hangs up and looks at Joyce Banner, the head of legal. "What can do we do without making things worse?"

"I suggest outside council, someone expert in labor relations."

Is that what we pay you for? To get outside counsel? Don't you have any advice other than that? What ever question we ask you, the answer is the same. Get outside counsel. You know we can get a robot to give that answer."

"This is a hot item that is easily messed up so we need some one in labor relations. Maybe we should hire such a person for our staff, then we don't have to outsource."

"Will you pay the benefits and the huge salary or will we take it out of yours. Sorry. But I am upset that this is going on. Someone find out what is going on and do something to stop it. NOW!!"

Vera returns with the news or rather the gossip. She also related that Faith is outside trying to gather some information anonymously. "So the best thing to do is sit tight until we have some facts. This is not an emergency ….yet."

"As always, you have the common sense that we all need, Vera. I need to speak to Carter to find out how this situation got started with the damned pills. Lets turn on the TV to see if there have aired this mess."

"Breaking news… this is Victoria Cheu, Channel 7 NBC reporting live from CHUC where a demonstration has been going on about the lack of contraceptive services for teens. The leader of the demonstration, Charlotte Adams, is here to tell us the issues as she sees them. Tell me Charlotte; what are you demonstrating about and what caused you to start this today."

"We represent the organization, SWRRL - Single Women for Reproductive Rights and Legislation, It has come to our attention that this hospital will not provide contraceptive pills to women, in this case, teen aged women. The hospital policy prohibits this service, an obvious racial issue as most of the people turned down for contraception are minorities, women of color. We are here to focus attention on this issue and force the administration to change the policy. The motto that they serve all people is not true. This is unfair. We want contraception and we want it now."

"Thank you Charlotte, I see Faith Boringer, head of public relations at the hospital. Maybe I can get a word with her. Faith, Oh Faith, can I speak with you?"

Faith almost choked when she was singled out by the TV reporter. She was recognized by Virginia since they worked together to get publicity for the hospital in the past. She removed her sun glasses, took a deep breath, put on her best Southern Belle grin face and moved in on the microphone.

"We have Faith Boringer, head of public relations at CHUC, thanks for agreeing to speak to me. What do you know about this demonstration?"

"First, let me assure you that we serve all the people in the community and in the nation. Our mission statement is to treat all people in the same manner. You are aware that we are the first children's hospital in New Jersey and here we made such discoveries as having the first infectious disease unit in New Jersey to treat children with whooping cough and we had the largest iron lung service during the polio epidemic of 1949. I don't know why the people are here. I came out to speak to the leaders to find out the issues."

"I understand that they are protesting the lack of contraceptive services for teens at CHUC. My sources tell me that this is hospital policy, the pharmacy refused to dispense contraceptives to a teen age patient. What is your comment?"

"I am not aware of any hospital policy regarding contraception for teens. This question is a new issue so I will have to check into it and get back to you. As you know, CHUC is a leading pediatric hospital and we serve all our patients to the best of our ability. As you know, we have been attentive to the community needs with our satellite clinics in South Creek."

"I know about that but we have interviewed a young lady who reported that her prescription and those of her friends were not filled at the hospital pharmacy."

"We are always improving our communications with the public. This must have been a misunderstanding or a communication problem, you know about communication problems, Victoria."

"Yes I do, but from our information, the young lady, who for obvious reasons does not want to appear on television, has told us she understood the pharmacist completely. She had to go to an outside pharmacy."

"Our main concern that she did get the medication she wanted, we are thankful for that. Of course, I am not blaming her for not understanding. Maybe the pharmacist is new and was reflecting policy at a previous institution. I don't want to go through the possible explanations without knowing the facts. I will be glad to come back to you when I have time to check with the hospital policy books and the members of our pharmacy team to discuss facts, not possibilities. Thanks for the chance to speak with you Victoria; I will be back to you. I have your cell number."

"But, in general, for example, if a girl were raped, would the hospital refuse to provide contraception?"

By the time Victoria finished the question, Faith was gone but Clement Walters Jr. had turned on his TV heard the words 'rape and hospital refuse. He screamed. "This is a problem, we have a problem, the hospital has a problem."

Clement Walters Jr., a former employee of the hospital in the dietary department, left the hospital after his plan to unionize the workers was unsuccessful. His charismatic speaking style and anti-establishment passion segued into his next career as a community agitator. If you have a cause, Walters will be there to lead a protest. He was the delight of the TV news department because he was articulate and eager to get his face on camera. No cause was too small for C. Walters, Jr.. When he heard about trouble at CHUC, he grabbed his jacket, was out of the door and in front of the cameras in 5 minutes. When he spotted the TV truck and antennae, he pushed his way through the crowd and in another minute he was on the hood of a car. "Unfair to rape victims, CHUC is unfair to rape victims. Equal care for all, equal care for all. We do not condone racism." He figured that this was enough to get on TV until he could gather information about the real cause by the nature of the questions. Rape he knew was one, but there must be more. He did not like the administration, even if this group of suits was not at the hospital during the union organizing days. Suits are suits, they all look alike."

"Clement, can I have a minute of your time?"

"I am really busy, Rape is a serious charge and I will pressure the DA to file charges and prosecute to the limit of the law. Busy times when sexual discrimination occurs. We have a problem. A real problem. Sure, I'll talk with you."

"I know you are busy with this demonstration but will give me your take on the issues."

"Issues, Issues, there are so many of them, which one do you want to talk about?"

"The lack of contraceptive services for teens. Are there any others?"

"Well they are insensitive to rape victims. I know a young lady who was brutally raped by three men and they hospital refused to provide her with means to prevent a possible pregnancy."

"That is serious. Was it at CHUC? When did this happen?"

"The case is in litigation so I cannot discuss it but believe me, it is not the only time it happened." Clement had found a rich vein and he was going to mine it as long as his imagination would allow. His superficial sincerity and his manner of talking made the fantasy sound factual so he continued. "Of course we need to protect the identity of these unfortunate young women. I pray for their health."

"Do you think the rape cases had anything to do with this demonstration?"

"Do you think rape is not an important issue to resolve? We need to protect our young women and provide all services to them, especially to women of color. All services to all people." He liked the sound of that last phrase. Before he would expose his fictional medical cases, he turned to the group listening to the interview and began a new chant. "All services to all people. All services to all people."

The crowd picked up the new chant and like a wave at a football game, it spread out to become the new mantra of the demonstration.

Walters left this group to look for the newspaper photographer for phase 2 of the demonstration publicity chase.

Richard Beardsley was ready to explode. "Get me Jerry at the pharmacy and find out what is going on, what is the policy? Who started this nonsense? Of course, I believe 'just saying NO is the best contraception, but when that is not enough, we need to stop these teen things from propagating. Where the hell is Jerry?"

"He is waiting on the phone. Line 3."

"Jerry, what policy do we have about contraception?"

"We don't dispense contraceptive pills to teens. That was the way it was when I got here and we are just following the policy that has been present for years."

"I don't see any policy in my policy book."

"Right. It is an unwritten policy. But Dr. Randolf started this, just after he got here. He wanted no contraception, no abortions, and no morning after pills. From my notes, I see he called down here and demanded that we do not engage in promoting promiscuity. He stated it was policy from his department. Gynecology, as you know, comes under surgery department according to the TO."

"TO?"

"Table of organization."

"So this is not the official policy written in the manual?"

"No sir."

"But, when a patient asks for it, do you refuse to dispense contraception."

"We do not dispense BCP, per Dr Randolf."

Beardsley hangs up and yells. "Page Dr. Randolf. Get me the executive staff here immediately we need to do some damage control. This is ruining the hospital reputation. Why is this happening to me? We need to do something. Anything to get this group of hippies out of here. Those bleeding heart liberals or whatever they are. Maybe we should start a fire or discover a cure for cancer. Something! Something! Somebody! Some body do something!"

"Phone call for you, Mr. Beardsley. It's Clayton Pickering."

"Hey Clayton. How's the family?"

"What the hell are you doing down there. I see on the TV that there is a demonstration about contraception, rape, racism, and now I see a group of musicians and Reverend Peter Stokes with save the unborn fetus signs. When did we get into all these hot buttons? Next we will have the

Supreme Court here to debate the issues. I thought you were in control down there. My wife is livid. You know she is on the board of Planned Parenthood. I am doing all I can to keep her out of the demonstration. I am sure that her group is on their way to join the parade. The only thing we missed is the animal rights group but maybe they will sense an opening to press their cause. I tried to call Henry Wilcox at channel 7 to put a lid on this but they are excited about the ratings possibilities, something about sweeps week. What are you going to do? This must stop."

"We have moved rapidly Clayton. Our crowd control group from security is protecting the doors. We have secured the computer rooms and the accounting offices. Believe me, we don't need a riot in the hospital. Our executive staff is meeting now. We have formed a subcommittee to study the problem, the usual moves."

"Good idea to form a subcommittee, but who is hell started this policy to ban contraceptions?"

"We have no policy; it was a communication problem between one of the staff and the pharmacist."

"Do I smell Carter at the base of this? I know about his feeling on pre-marital sexual activity and his membership in the Rose Hill Evangelical Church."

"From our early research into this matter, it seems that your antennae are correct. Carter has expressed his opinion to the pharmacy and they took it as policy."

"Whose head is going to roll with this fiasco?"

"Let me get all the facts before we talk about heads. Right now we are in damage control mode and I need to get results from the teams findings."

"Good idea, Dick. But get the lid on this caldron. We don't need to create a stew, so déclassé. We don't need any bad publicity. Fund raising time, you know."

"I think it is a little late for that wish. I will get back to you shortly.

Beardsley did not see Karl Strem, chief resident wearing his Red Sox cap, joining in the protest, but Carter Randolf did. Looking out the window, Carter, missing the point of the protest, felt betrayed by a member of the hospital staff showing public disloyalty to his cause. "I am going to get that squirt in the Red Sox cap when I have a chance; he has no sense of loyalty to the institution. His career is over. He is a turncoat and a traitor. I wish I knew the young doctors better. What is happening to this new generation?"

The demonstration was in full force. The hot dog vendors set up their yellow and green striped stands next to the balloon sellers. The representatives from the fundamental Bible school were there with bugles and drums to accompany their singing "Oh Lord, save the poor little children." The Reverend Peter Stokes with his bull horn was quoting scripture, using verses that had nothing to do with any of the issues of the demonstration but they usually strike a chord with the audience. In this mayhem no one could understand him but the cadence and tones of his words added a different dimension to the cacophony outside the hospital. The original group calling for "contraception now" no longer produced the loudest chant but acted like the bass fiddle with a constant rhythm and cycle of tones. The screams of the women against rape sang the soprano part, "no rape, no way." The racial card players sounded like the saxophones wailing, " equal rights, justice for all," up and down three octaves of the scale. David Grunberg, chief of pediatrics and an opera buff remarked to his secretary. "If this were not such a serious problem for the hospital, it could turn into an opera. Benjamin Brittan or Phillip Glass, where are you? Listen to the chant."

"Contraception Now, Contraception Now"

"No rape, no way, equal rights, Justice for all, Now"

"Protect unborn children, now, now, - we will over come, -stop- now"

"Now,- protect now.- contraception- stop rape,- justice, justice- stop, now-now- now.

Victoria Cheu, face flushed and voice raised above the din, sensed a chance to get on national TV. She isolated one of the colorful protesters for an interview. "Excuse me sir, could I speak to you for a second?"

He nodded.

"What are your issues with the hospital? Why are you here?"

"Issues, man. I have no issues. I love demonstrations. We have not had such a happening for years. This is a happening man. It's a my generation thing. I am in heaven. "Stop it now, stop it now?" He pushed his fist into the air.

"What is it that you want to stop now?"

"What ever the beep they are doing? I am against the big corporations beating down on the poor people, I am against the banks and their high salaries and bonuses for the executives, I am against the government, the police and women's lib. We are overcoming man, hear me overcome. Wow! Wow!"

"Don't you agree that the hospital is helping people?"

"Hospital, what hospital? I am against big business and corporate greed."

"This is Victoria Cheu reporting from the demonstration at Children's Hospital. As you can see feeling are running high. That is all from here, back to the studio" She stared at the camera, frozen waiting for the camera man to turn off the camera. He was busy watching some of the protesters wearing skimpy denim shorts and white halters.

• • •

Alan Frome, vice president of government and community relations, naïve as usual, suggested that someone from the administration speak to the leaders of the demonstration to clarify the hospital's policy or rather lack of policy against distributing contraceptives. "I am sure this gesture would defuse the group and disburse the crowds."

"Did you make this up or did you copy this stupid idea from someone in your MBA class?" Beardsley was constantly denigrating advanced degrees, especially MBA's, since he had a BA from some non-descript college Eastern Appalachia at Lookout Hills, West Virginia. "Look out there, this is a crowd that is not going to be dispersed by logic. Look! Look! They are selling friggin hula hoops. Hot dogs, hula hoops, every thing but cotton candy!"

"They have a cotton candy stand next to the duck the administrator booth, sir."

"Maybe we should serve them hot chocolate and cookies."

"I can look into that sir. But isn't the weather a little warm for hot chocolate. Maybe we can serve frozen juice. Cooler and much more nutritious."

"Get out of my face, you idiot."

"Get Faith back here and have her send out a press release to clarify our position for the evening news. I am sure the reporters are asking us for comment. Give them the great democracy and ability to express opinion bullshit but stress the communication problem. Isn't everything a communication problem? Now let's get back to our business of providing children with the best health care."

The next day, the crowd, exhausted by the frantic picketing was much smaller without any spirit so it dispersed without further incidents. Their mobile unit trucks returned to the hospital but seeing nothing newsworthy, retreated to the usual fires and car chases.

Beardsley attributed the lack of demonstrators to his damage control approach: facts, communication problem excuse and ignorance of policy.

Beardsley was not finished. He had an appointment with Carter Randolf at 11AM. Carter's association with the religious right board members was very helpful in the early days when the old guard were the main donors to the hospital. But as that group aged, their heirs were more interested in conserving the principle and living on the interest than contributing to the hospital. Those who were still active in charities supported environmental groups and literacy programs. As the new money from the local business people and entrepreneurs replaced the old money on the contributor list, Carter's influence waned but most of the board continued to believe that he was the most important member of the hospital staff supported by a few bit players. He was worried that when the board discovered how he contributed to the riots outside the hospital, he will lose their support. Beardsley was waiting for that time so he could move into the vacuum and appoint his own man to be head of surgery. Carter Randolf was just too strong to come under the administration spell, since he did not need more money so it was hard to pay him off. To hope that he would be involved in personal scandal was not a likely outcome, considering his conservative Christian values. This fiasco of a demonstration may be the hoped for event to take him down or at least neutralize his power.

That is exactly what happened at 11. Carter came in as usual, with his sails fully filled with his hot air, complaining about too many meetings that interrupted his full OR schedule. Beardsley decided today to use his screaming approach. No one could mount a response to a screaming adversary so the one with the highest volume won the argument by default. Even Randolf squirmed a little when the decibel level got too high.

"Who authorized the policy that the pharmacy should not give out birth control pills? Who was the ass hole that started this? Do you have any idea?"

"Policy, what policy? I told the pharmacy people that we are in the business of treating sick kids, not encouraging pre-marital sex in teenagers. Marriage is sacred and sex should be for married couples, married couples with their mates, I mean. Don't you agree?"

"I think that is a personal decision that does not call for hospital intervention. Do you know how much damage occurred by this disruption yesterday? It will take us a long time to overcome the public relation hack marks we suffered." By now the volume was a few decibels lower than a primal scream.

"What hack marks? My donors are thrilled that we are placing a high value on the sanctity of marriage."

"I am sure they value your high morals and ethics but do you think they would like being referred to as your donors?"

"As long as they keep giving, let me call them anything."

"Have you checked with development office to find out the total donations from **your** donors?"

"I am sure it is quite substantial. When I got here, members of my church were instrumental in starting the post op nutrition service."

"How long ago was that, Carter?"

"About 30-40 years ago when I got here. There was no interest in the effect of nutrition on healing and I started the first post surgical nutrition unit in New Jersey."

"Take it easy Carter. You know we follow Aunt Selma's rule. No stories over 25 years old, unless they are funny. I think we have to invoke Aunt Selma's rule in this discussion."

"Who may I ask is Aunt Selma?"

"I have no idea but I like her rule so it is my policy."

"Haven't we gotten in enough trouble with policies here?"

"One for your side. Yes, we have but stay on the subject. If you look at the donor list, YOUR donors have not matched the new breed of hospital supporters, - wealthy business people and patent holders from the big Pharma who live are in the area. They now hold claim to the donor power positions. For your information, these are people that I cultivate and they listen to me. So take your old farts and accept the modern power structure. We no longer have a sherry sipping board. We are in the 21st century man. Things are changing. Just like laparoscopic surgery, if you know what I mean."

That reference about laparoscopy hit Carter right in his surgical ego. He winced, reflexly, showing he got the point that one needs to adapt to the new changes or lose power, the dinosaur effect. "Enough diversion, what are you plans to clarify the issue in the pharmacy before our hospital gets burned down by the next wave of rioters. We have survived the animal rights and the union organizers but I am afraid the women's health movement can do us in. I know it would be hard for you to get into the middle of this so I suggest that I write a clarifying letter about the hospital's stand. We provide contraception. Period. If you would like, I could include your name at the bottom of the letter along with David Grunberg as the chiefs of surgery and pediatrics. I can keep you off the letter, whatever you like. Then, I want PR to get a picture of some teenager, identity masked, receiving her pills at the CHUC pharmacy. Then I want whoever is heading adolescent medicine to get on TV, talking about teen sexuality, the problems teen mothers face and the need to prevent teen pregnancy. Then PR will get the paper to do a day in the life of a teen mom. Then development will get in contact with Bunky Peterson with the idea of starting a program for adolescent gynecology, emphasis on prevention of gonorrhea, chlamydia and of course, pregnancy. We have to make lemonade out of these sour apples."

"Keep me out of it. I will have enough trouble with my supporters, especially the widows. I am not sure if the men care, not that they have their own need for birth control from what I can see."

Beardsley saw an opening and moved in. "I am glad that you are so cooperative. We are going to have a capital campaign to build a new wing in the hospital so we need to keep everyone happy as they send in their bucks."

Carter saw that he lost his battle but that did not stop him. "One more thing. Do you know the name of the resident with the Red Sox cap?"

"What do you care? Are you a Yankee fan?"

"No I am a Cowboy fan. That moron was involved in the protest. I want him fired and I am going to ruin his career."

"Easy, Carter, you know we can't fire someone. We do have something called the First Amendment."

"Well then I will sabotage his career, when I get the opportunity."

Chapter 20

Robert Farmer finally had chance to sit down in his chair. He hated to admit it but he was tired and did not have the stamina that he had 10 years ago. No surprise, for he was nearing his 60th birthday when many people struggle to hold on until they reach the magic 65 before cashing out and starting a new career of golf or woodworking. He did not play golf but he liked to fish and enjoy the metropolitan cultural life, tempting him to move into New York to be closer to the opera and museums. He had always thought that he would never retire but he realized that he was at the top of his game and began to have moments when the facts and details evaded him. He treasured his reputation as a physician which brought with it, a feeling of accomplishment. The memory of the story about his former chief of medicine haunted him. It was old Dr. Kerr who abruptly retired because he wanted to be remembered by his trainees as the chief who possessed a wide range of medical facts, excellent judgment, and skillful dissection of difficult problems. He was worried that if he stayed too long at the post, the young doctors would worry about that old guy who gets confused in discussions and talks about the same few diseases no matter what the patient's problem. Farmer wanted to go out with most of his skills still apparent just like Dr. Kerr.

His medical credentials were platinum level. Excellent college records at Cornell, medical school at Stanford, Residency in Boston and further training at Rockefeller Institute. No bad for a young guy who started in public school in the Bronx. His fascination with difficult problems helped him move into a consultant type of practice with a special interest in infections. The days when he finished his residency, the few available fellowships were mostly for sons of wealthy families or trust fund recipients, living on the distributions from their grandparents' wills. Having no outside funding, he learned on the job, advancing by earning the respect of peers and patients. Things could not be better in his role at the hospital. Even though he did not make it to the big pediatric academic centers, he was content in his present position. He helped train 30 years worth of interns and residents, some of whom are now heading other pediatric programs, some are still at CHUC. He had written chapters in important textbooks, he had given speeches at national meetings and most importantly, he had helped thousands of children live better lives and helped thousands of parents take better care of their children by focusing them on health rather than worry about diseases that their child did not have. Even though he may have made mistakes, he was always honest with his families and helped them with their problems. They in turn, appreciated his efforts. Fortunately, he never had been sued in 30 years, at least up to now. Yes, life was good. It was hard to believe that it would never change but he knew change was in the future, hopefully not the near future, but he felt his life could not get any better than this.

That covered the medical life. Too bad the rest of his life was not as successful. His first real love, died from breast cancer in her 30's. He was devastated, alone and afraid to get attached to anyone else for fear of losing her. After about 5 years, he met Linda who was perfect for him. After fighting off the idea of marriage, he did marry her on a whim. They flew to Las Vegas and were married in one of the all night chapels. Their first child was killed in a car accident;   killed by an air bag that crushed him. He wore a seat belt but he sat in the front seat, which was OK in those times. The stress of his son's death eventually led to a divorce. Linda needed more attention then he could muster as his grief drained him of his usual supportive manner. He started to drink more than his usual occasional social cocktail. At first, he was able to hide his drinking from his peers but he knew he had gone too far. A colleague at a conference noticed him spending a lot of time in the bar and befriended him by chatting at first and then, confronted him with the thought that he was having trouble with alcohol. This conversation was the spark to change him. With some help from an addiction counselor and a great support group, he abruptly stopped drinking and has not had a drink since. He still thinks about it often, especially when he is away at a meeting in a nice resort. Sunsets do him in, prompting him to think about his past and former good times, giving him the urge to sip a little single malt Scotch, but so far, he has resisted the urge. That may explain why he works so much as he does not like to get into the environment when those feeling arise. Better to work than to think and drink. What looks to others as true dedication, is in part, an avoidance mechanism, a trait common in many so-called dedicated doctors.

Except for small health issues, things could not get better. His career was peaking. He had adjusted to his single status, living in a small condo in the center of town. He had friends and he had his reputation. He had more than enough money. He even had a will that he named his nephew and the hospital as the recipients of his estate. Yes, life was good, hard to beat. Then the phone rang to break up his peace. Since his secretary had gone for the day, he picked up the phone.

"Hello, Dr. Farmer speaking."

"Hi, Doc. How are you?"

"Fine. What can I do for you?"

"Doc, I am worried. My grandson does not look well. He has a pain and I think a lump in his belly. Can I bring him in now? I am worried."

"Sure, I am here. But how long will it take for you to get here?

"No more than 20 minutes.

"Good. What is your name?"

"Gillespie. I will be right there."

Farmer leaned back in his leather chair and continued to think about the future and the past. It was good to take a life inventory. He hoped that he could make it through the next five years and then rethink his position.

In about 30 minutes a knock on the door interrupted the thoughts. He jumped up like the proverbial firehouse dog and opened the door. The first thing he noticed was the man was there but no child. He remembered a similar situation when the parent was so upset and worried that he came to the hospital without the patient. That was not the case today. The man asked. "Dr. Farmer?"

"Yes."

"I have a letter from the firm of R.H. Shelby." He threw the letter at him and moved away quickly. Farmer caught the letter in mid air.

"You touched it, its yours!" This was the old trick of notifying the defendant that a suit had been filed, naming him as a defendant. This time it was a case of meningitis; he was accused of being negligent and incompetent in his management of a one year old boy who came to the hospital for high fevers. As Farmer had not been sued before, he was not sure of the next steps but fortunately he had good malpractice insurance but then again he was not sure since most people think they have good insurance until they have an accident of fire, he would soon find out. He would also find out who else was involved in the case since these lawyers never sue just one person. They cast a wide net and hope to find something about someone that will bring in their 1/3 of the award. The expenses come out of the other 2/3 that the patient is supposed to receive. When challenged about this casting of a wide net to snare the evil ones, the lawyers respond that they are only doing this to make sure the guilty ones are identified, not really answering the question.

"Dammit, these are the times I need someone to talk to."

A child with meningitis is a big ticket item for malpractice lawyers. According to the lawyers, all these children were going to go to Harvard and discover a cure for cancer and receive millions in royalties from the drug company; the hired experts will testify that this was true. The forensic accountants produce a long print out to show how much income this Harvard graduate will be make in her lifetime. Then the liars for hire will appear. These are usually well known doctors who have either retired or have major expenses of their own who will testify that any idiot could have made the diagnosis and prevented the problems, no matter what the issue is and how subtle the signs and symptoms were. Therefore, this accused doctor was negligent and incompetent and should pay huge amounts to send a message to somebody. Farmer had heard enough stories and read enough novels to get the broad outline of the future. The scary part was the loss of control of the situation when the trial lawyers move in and work the jury composed of clerks from 7-11, city workers and others who have no medical expertise. In this county, the more qualified the potential jurors are, the more likely they will be excused from the jury panel. Those picked typically harbor a certain occult jealousy against the multimillionaire doctor as evidenced by the huge awards that come from this local court system. But first he had to read the complaint, get the facts, talk to his lawyer and then try to salvage his reputation.

The case was filed by R.H. Shelby on behalf of Cameron Nelson, a one year old boy from Hillcrest, N.J.. Farmer remembered this case and knew he did not commit malpractice. Unfortunately, sick people may have unfortunate outcomes. His real thought was he needed a drink. He had to find a diversion to keep him busy and not be tempted to open a bottle, although he desperately wanted to, at that moment- the price of solo living. No one to talk to, no instant group therapy to ease the tension. When there is an opportunity to discuss the problem with others, the severity of the issue loses some of its force. He could not sit in his office or go to a bar, so he made rounds, hoping to get distracted by some resident or parent. The agenda for the next morning had just changed, get the records and find out who R.H. Shelby was. He had a feeling it was not one of the usual firms that specialized in malpractice.

Making rounds is great therapy. The resident's knew of Farmer's late afternoon walks through the hospital. So when Farmer came on the floor, he would sit down and nibble on the candy from the nurses' station, while he discussed patient problems and answered questions. Even the residents who had evening plans would stay for the opportunity to hear from this special doctor. They were impressed with his generosity of his time and wisdom. They did not suspect he had few alternatives.

The next morning things became clearer. R.H. Shelby was right out of a paper back novel from the airport news stand. A small office on the second floor of a third rate building. He was not what they call a go-to lawyer. One went to him, when no one else would take a case. That was encouraging. Things got better when he got the chart from medical records. Just as he remembered, the young boy had been seen for a cold two weeks before admission. At that time he looked and acted as one would with a cold. He was given Tylenol for fever and advised to drink a lot of fluids. He was given instructions to return if his condition got worse. The parents did not bring him back for a follow up visit until he appeared at the emergency room 2 weeks later, quite ill. The emergency room staff performed a lumbar puncture which showed many white cells and low sugar in the spinal fluid. He was given antibiotics and admitted to the hospital. That is when Farmer got involved. Usually the fever in patients who are treated with antibiotic for meningitis will remain elevated for several days and then slowly return to normal, not in a straight line drop but more like a feather floating downward. Each day there would be fever spikes but the average temperature was lower than the previous day. The patient also slowly became less irritable and took fluids then a liquid diet. As expected, Farmer stayed at the bedside or in the hospital for the first few days, making sure that the treatment plan was followed and that subtle changes were detected and the management adjusted when appropriate. He remembered the case so well because a nurse had come to him and told him that the father of the boy had recognized her as working on the unit and asked a lot of questions about the care and competence of the doctors, looking for any errors or mistakes that she could identify. This smelled like an embryonic malpractice accusation so when he was told about the father's questions, Farmer wrote long and detailed notes on the patient's condition, the plans and the rationale for all decisions. He also noted that the father not spend much time with his sick son. After the baby was admitted, the father took off leaving the mother at the hospital. Farmer had complete notes about a strange phone call. On the second night in the hospital course, about 2AM, the phone rang on the unit. It was the father demanding to talk to the doctor. Fortunately, Farmer was there.

"Hey doc. I just looked up the information about my son on the internet and I wondered if you checked him for polio, he had fever, was irritable and would not move his head, all typical of polio."

"Thanks for the advice. Did your son have his polio immunizations?"

"I don't know."

"Has he been out of the country later, say to China or Africa?"

"Oh, no."

"Well, I looked at his record and he had full polio immunizations. That plus there have been no cases of polio from the US for many years makes the diagnosis of polio next to impossible."

"Oh!"

Farmer, convinced that he would be sued, wrote a long narrative in the chart about this 2 AM phone conversation and for a change, he put the time and date of the note. The note stretched into one and a half pages. Farmer continued playing newspaper reporter by entering details of conversations along with direct quotes from the father's phone call. That would look good for the jury, if the case came to trial. By the end of the first week, this very sick young man turned the corner and began a typical recovery from meningitis. The severity of the case suggested that the infection spread from the lining on the outside of the brain into the outer surface of the white matter. Fortunately, young people reprogram their brain better than adults can so Farmer remained optimistic about the outcome although he told the parents that time and therapy would help clarify his level of function. As he was too young to talk or walk, it was hard to assess all his neurological functions at the time of discharge, but for a one year old, he seemed normal.

Farmer scheduled an appointment with the hospital's legal department to discuss his views of the case. The hospital was also named in the suit since it was "negligent in not supervising such incompetent doctors." Since most doctors had limits on their malpractice insurance, many of them settle for the $200,000 or $500.000 insurance coverage to avoid the trial and additional financial exposure. The hospital with its substantial assets could potentially be forced to pay larger sums so they had to determine if it were better to settle if the record showed anything that would attract the attention of the jury. If that were not the case, they would fight the case in court. The real winners of the case were the lawyers who either settled for a small amount such as $10,000 to end the nuisance case or if they won in court, they would collect 1/3 of the award. The lawyers who defended the doctors or the hospital collected their $300 to $800 per hour as their customary fee. So malpractice cases were a candy store for lawyers on both sides who publicly proclaimed they were looking out for the little guy who was harmed by those money hungry incompetent doctors and poorly managed hospitals, but the large payouts were the main attraction for many lawyers to sue whether or there was evidence of medical negligence.

Farmer knew he will have to endure the depositions, the disruption to his practice and life while the letters go back and forth between lawyers and judges and the expert witnesses. Farmer was betting that this suit would not get to trial as most cases would be dropped after the charts are reviewed by legal and medical consultants. There is public interest in fixing the system but lobbyists step in to protect their trial lawyer clients. The debates about malpractice always discussed the extremes and not the usual situations when bad patient outcomes, not malpractice instigate suits. Since trial lawyers were major contributors to the governor's reelection campaign, there was little chance of meaningful reform from the legislature. So the cases continued, the custom made suits continued to be ordered and private jets scheduled for trips to the islands or the Kentucky Derby.

The phone rings again interrupting his feeling of frustration about the law suit. It's the report on the tumor type of Tobe Hallman - not good news. His tumor has large amount of copies of the MYCN oncogene. Patients with this oncogene, do not have a good 5 year survival. Although the   initial response to treatment of the neuroblastoma was good, the resistance to treatment will soon take over and limit the years left of his life. He picked up the phone to call Frank Winston to see what the oncologist was thinking, then he would talk to the family about the bad news. This has not been a good day.

• • •

The April board meeting began at noon. The usual group attended, expecting to hear the rosy reports that everything was going well and that they, the board, were doing an excellent job of creating the atmosphere and hiring the right people to carry out the mission that the board had developed. Good job boys! There was no indication that this meeting would be any different. Clayton Pickering, chairman was chatting with Dixon McIver and Thomas Heatherson about the recent quail shooting trip to the low country of South Carolina.

Bunky Peterson, silently fuming that there are only two women on the board, was looking out the window, plotting her move to diversify the board. Carter Randolf approached her as she seemed to be the one who would most likely support the plan that he was going to propose. Nothing like a little back room politics to help the vote. Norman Oppenheim was checking his iPhone for email. The rest of the board was most likely to go with the crowd, more interested in what kind of cheese would be served at the end of the meeting. They were awaiting John Spirito who usually was on time but must have been delayed by some emergency procedure.

"Let's get started. We can go over some minor things while waiting for John. Speak of the devil, welcome John, we were going to get started with some committee reports so let's go. First the gardening committee report about the landscaping on the front entrance and then the entertainment committee report on the refreshments after board meeting. Then we can get into the financial report and report from the CEO.

Daisy Farnsworth stood up, checked her 3 by 5 index cards, cleared her throat and began her report. "The landscaper would be putting in new daisies, (a few chuckles) and the tulips were breaking through because of unusual warm days recently. The committee could not decide which type of ivy to plant in the walkways as one member had recently been in London at the ivy show and saw over 200 varieties of ivy. That surprised me as I thought I knew a lot about ivy. I am doing further research on the types of ivy that would thrive in this climate." By this time her hands were shaking and her face was flushed with nervousness. "This ends my report of the gardening committee." She smiled stiffly and sat down.

"Thomas Heatherson, who rarely spoke at the board meetings, looked pre-orgasmic when he heard about the variety of ivies. "Super idea Daisy, I find the present selection of ivies quite bland. My former college roommate has remained at Harvard in at the botany department has a special interest in ivies that do well in New England environment. That is not a pun but an ivy expert in the Ivy League is someone with whom we should connect before making a decision about our selection."

Sam Rubenstein murmured to Norman, "Did you ever meet a person who went to Harvard that did not mention this in the first two minutes of a conversation? When I was in the service stationed in the North Dakota hills, a new finance officer arrived to the unit. The first thing out of his mouth was to ask if there were a Harvard Club in town."

Prentiss Hall reported that the caterer would change the cheese from Edom to Brie for the post board snacks. Richard Beardsley stood up, asked his aide to turn on the projector and began his power point presentation of the financial report. "I am filling in for the CFO who was attending a conference at the Homestead on Deloitte and Touche's new ways for health care industries to finance capital expenditures. It would, no doubt include many new accounting principles that would require new engagements with Deloitte and Touche." The board laughed.

"The financial report looks quite good. We are up 7% in admissions that produces a 10% increase in billing." The board applauded and looked at each other with smiles of accomplishment. "We are in negotiations with Blue Cross to upsize the reimbursements for the new MRI and expand the scope of laboratory tests. Our billing per patient day has increased 7% because of our negotiations last month for unbundling our laboratory packages."

"Good job Beardsley" called out Dixon. Another round of applause and nods of approval.

"We have, now, an 18 million surplus in cash flow. Our expenses are rising somewhat but well within the safety range set out by the finance committee. Of course we are not going to keep that surplus on the books as we do not want to ruin our not for profit status and discourage our contributors from continuing their donations. We transfer the excess to the hospital foundation to secrete the excess funds. The public accounting reports will show us just eking by. But you all know that as we have been doing that for years."

"Bravo," called out Hunter Johnson and the group nodded their heads.

"So we have a good month financially and if I may, go ahead with the CEO's report. Maybe this would be a good time to serve the sherry or everyone take a deep breath as now I am going to propose that we look into building a new children's hospital. Yes, we should think about a hospital for the 21st century that incorporates facilities to match the needs of our patients and the talents of staff. A hospital that provides the space for present and future technology instead of the jerry rigged operation that now stands in this space. This project will take years of planning and fund raising so we need to start now and be proactive rather waiting for the building to become so dysfunctional, compromising our patients welfare. Therefore I propose hiring a consultant to do a feasibility study and come up with a proposal in 18 months."

"I think that calls more than a sip of sherry, is it too early for some Bombay Sapphire martinis for starters?"

"Is the present hospital so broken that we have to get a new one?"

"Forward thinking, old Beardsley."

Clayton Pickering was about to burst a blood vessel as this proposal was new to him. In his early days, Beardsley would always consult him about any new ideas but lately it seemed that CHUC was Beardsley's fiefdom so he did not need consultation from this group of good old boys. Bunky Peterson was worried that she would be expected to chip in 20 or 30 million to the fund. Although her inheritances totaled over 200 million, she was always worried about running out of money or being dependent on her children in her later years.

Pickering made his move. "Do I hear any objections to forming a planning committee? If not, I will get started. Remember this is just planning and feasibility we are not digging holes or tearing down anything.

"I guess a planning committee will not hurt," replied Beardsley who was obviously miffed by the counter-power grab.

Pickering moved that he be the chair of the committee and Beardsley would be ex-officio. The old timers agreed as they did not want the recent additions to the board signifying new money to have too much influence. Oppenheim, the cynic at large, suspected this was going to be Beardsley's Taj Mahal and probably the source of major kickbacks to augment the already excessive retirement package. But he would have to wait until he had more evidence of such evil motives. Beardsley was trying to put on a good front to hide his displeasure of not being allowed to pursue the new building immediately. He loved the game of working with architects, technical consultants and salesmen while trying to keep the medical staff away from ruining his new hospital.

Pickering feeling better that he had retaken the leadership of the board, asked if there were any new business.

Carter Randolf raised his hand. "This is a timely proposal. I met a woman at my church last week who heads a hedge fund that has been doing extremely well. She was there to present a check to the church for an investment that they made with her fund last year. The check represented a profit of 25% for one year's investment. Needless to say, the church board reinvested the profit with her again. She now has assets of over 750 million and is growing at about 20% a year in new investors. She specializes in not for profit institutions, mainly churches and social agencies although she said she has a few universities and health care systems as clients. Since I know her from church, I am sure I can take advantage of that relationship to have her invest our endowment. I wish you all were there to see how she prays. I trust someone who can pray like that. I showed the sheets to Dick. I am interested in his comments."

"On first read of the financial information, I am impressed with the results and the client list. The return on investment for the Randolf's church is impressive and cannot be ignored. However.......... I am troubled by a few things. First I never heard of the auditor, someone in Easton, Pennsylvania. Why go there? I looked up the firm and it is a one man outfit. Scary to me. The audit sheets show no interest or dividends recorded for the investments in the fund. With the magnitude of funds under investment, there should be some interest from money markets or some dividends from the blue chips. This is bothersome. I am also bothered by the high returns. Either they are legal but the success cannot be maintained or they are sort of a Ponzi scheme. You all know about Madoff. Of course, we can use the money but can we afford the risk? I am worried about a scam. It has all the markings: promise the people something that they want and show that this can be achieved. That brings on more people and more money. At one point, the payout cannot be sustained, either because there are no new investors or the personal expenses of the scammer are too high to provide any additional return to the investors. That makes me wary that we are exposed to huge losses. Does any one know where this gal lives, what kind of car does she drive, where does she spend vacations, what homes and cars does her family own? Before I would invest with her, despite her praying style, I would hold off on giving him any money. I am suspicious."

"That is a good observation Dick. Maybe we can meet with her and get an answer to your concerns. But our church has some payouts to prove the point."

"I am afraid she will get me back to church if she is so persuasive." As usual when Beardsley was out of his comfort zone, he quickly scans the faces of the listeners to see if his reference to religion would cause him any problems. To make sure he looked across the group several times giving him the look of a lizard searching for flies.

"Any other new business? I suspect we have done too much already today." Clayton starts to put his paper back into his briefcase without looking around the table.

"I have one item I would like to present at this time so we can go over it in more detail at the next meeting."

"Yes Jackie. What is it?" Clayton could not bring himself to call her Dr. Lawrence so he used the first name.

"As you know the issue of whether to start another health clinic in South Creek to serve our inner city patients has been discussed, tabled and retabled for a number of years. I am distributing a proposal for you to consider that will go a long way in helping us to fulfill our mission to serve the community while not having a negative impact on the financial balance sheet. The clinic will also serve as an input into our hospital services as these patients will require operations and laboratory and radiological studies, major profit centers. To ease the burden of high professional costs, I am proposing that this clinic be managed by nurse practitioners with backup by the medical staff using telemedicine facilities. This is a head's up to the board so that at the next meeting we can go over the plans in detail. Today it is an IO topic."

"The only IO I know is Ins and Outs for fluids. What the hell is IO?"

"Sorry, Information Only."

"Is this going to be a Doc in the Box like they are planning at the mall?'

"Definitely not, these are master's prepared nurse practitioners."

"You did not answer my question. I don't care if they are Olympic Swimming champions, they are not MD's."

"Nurse Practioners will cost less and therefore add to the bottom line."

"Do you really mean that we will lose less money?"

Only Norman Oppenheim was watching Beardsley as this proposal was being discussed. He had a strange smile; one might call it a smirk as he saw expenses going down and more staff ultimately under his control if the nurses were hired.

"I think we are getting ahead of ourselves. Since this was introduced as an IO item, let's stay with that plan and discuss it next meeting. I think we should adjourn now and head for the refreshments. I understand we are being treated to some special Swedish meatballs and I don't want them to get cold."

Feeling relieved that no one spotted his financial game, he wanted to end the meeting to prevent any new surprises from the board. "Great meeting, we have some interesting issues to keep us out of trouble. So expect a call from the committee chairs to get to work on investments, new hospital planning, oh yes, the choice of ivy."

Carrie Randolf stood up. "Before we leave, I want to remind you all that Dick is being honored by the hospital volunteer national committee. I have the honor of introducing him at the meeting next month in Denver. We are proud of Dick for all his good work and bringing prestige to CHUC."

"Here, here. Way to go Richardson."

As he left the meeting room, Norman Oppenheim pulled David Grunstein aside. "David this doesn't sound exactly kosher. As you know I am relatively new to the board to stir up trouble but after hearing these reports, I am concerned. I am especially troubled by the report as there was mention of billing but not of collections. I know from my real estate business that billing is just a number, collections are real money. I was surprised that no one questioned the lack of collections in this report but this was something that I need to follow up when I know more of the background of the board operations."

"You have got this group diagnosed well, responded David. "The search committee members will not speak out against Beardsley since they were the ones that recruited him. Those who profited by his contracts would not disagree with him as their companies business would be vulnerable. Then there were so thrilled to be on the board that they did not want to do anything that would jeopardize this prestigious seat.

That left a few free thinkers who are either tired or not sure of how to proceed so they keep quiet and let Beardsley ride his ponies. I am not sure if you are aware of how this organization is run but Beardsley has engineered the contracts with the medical staff to give him authority to approve all the physician salaries so before the arguments get too heated, self preservation and mortgage payments take precedence over arguing for what is good for the institution. Norman, I am glad you are suspicious and hope that you follow up your concerns when you are ready to make a move. You can count on me for support."

"Right now I am taking good notes." Norman smiled and got on the elevator.

Chapter 21

The house staff was holding their monthly meeting. Their concerns were less global and certainly less financial but still important to the young doctors who were more concerned with present working conditions and near future career issues than the hospital purchases and executive bonuses. Even though attendance was sparse, Ray Strem called the meeting to order. At this time of the year, it was hard to generate any enthusiasm in the group except for end of the year parties and graduation.

"I am sure you will be glad to hear that Grimely has completed his report on the elevator button pushing survey. I am passing out his report that is briefer than usual for old Grimely."

To House staff
From E. Grimely
Re: excessive use of elevator buttons.

Executive Summary
After a careful and thorough survey of the possible problem of excessive elevator usage, we have completed the survey and have come to the final report.

1. The elevator buttons have shown wear and tear, the up buttons (UB) are more worn than the lower ones on the lower floors while on the upper floors (floor 5-9) show more wear on the down button (DB).

2. Repair rates for up and down buttons are similar with a trend to lower floors having a slightly higher repair rate. The differences are not statistically significant.

3. Elevators 9 and 10 are the buttons with the most wear and repair. These are the elevators that serve the on call rooms and intensive care units on their respective floors.

4. From our survey, we find most button pushing occurs in the 4-6 PM time frame and secondly from the 6-7 AM time frame.

Recommendations.

1. We will mount a thorough education program to alert staff about the need to push the up button when going up and the down button when going down.

2. We will place appropriate information signs at the elevator button sites stating: **For those who wish to go up, please depress the button with either the U or the arrow pointing up. For those who want to go down press the button D or one with a down arrow. For those who wish to go up one flight or down two flights, please take the stairs. In case of fire, do not use the elevator, either when going up or down. Thank you.**

3. We will have security check the elevators during these peak times to monitor the excessive button pushing.

4. We will form a sub-committee to monitor the entire program which will now be known as CREEBP, the committee to resist excessive elevator button pushing. Please volunteer if you want to be on the committee.

Thank you for your cooperation in this important matter that will help us achieve our objective of improved patient care (IPC).

_EG/la_

"Now you can see why I chose not to read this report out loud. The laughter would interfere with our mission to provide the best care to the children."

"Now we have to get to some serious business- selecting a faculty member who will win the resident teaching award this year. I am passing around a list of former winners as we want to spread this award to as many people as possible. That does not mean that a former winner cannot win again, but we want to make sure that some great teachers are not overlooked. This award reminds the faculty that we appreciate their teaching and encourages our staff to continue training us instead of concentrating on their clinical work. Any nominations? Let's get the list of the top nominees, and then discuss them and then vote."

"I vote for Will Miller, the cardiologist."

"Second."

"How about Bob Farmer?"

"Good idea, second."

"How about Freda Watkins?"
"Donna Barstow."
"She's my pick too."
"Any more?"
"Nancy Tappeur from GI"
"I know where she works."
"She is OK with me."

"So we have the list of
Miller, Farmer, Watkins, Barstow, and Tappuer. A good list. Any more names, any discussion?"

"I am amazed that Bob Farmer has not won this award. He is always available, he has great way of making diagnoses for difficult patients. He is always here and willing to teach and discuss cases with the residents."

"I don't like the way he asks us questions. He pimps us by his so called Socratic method. I like people who give us lectures like Tappeur."

"Who pays attention to her? She drones on and on. She puts me to sleep."

"Bob Farmer does not pimp; he tries to make us think. Pimping is when the person tries to embarrass you by showing that you do not know as much as he does. He keeps us involved by asking questions."

"But he is always bringing up stories about the old days when they did not have MRI's. Who cares about listening to the chest, we can get an MRI or an echocardiogram and find out what is happening inside? There is no need to listen for rales or murmurs."

"He makes us justify why we order tests. Just draw off the blood and order a MRI and you have the answer. There's no need to limit tests, except for the cost. We don't pay for the tests, the insurance company does. At this time of the year, I am tired of thinking and just want to get the tests ordered."

"In your negative comments about Farmer, you are describing the attributes of a good teacher; a person who makes you think, is available, likes to interact with students and does not give lectures but has interactive discussions. He has my vote."

"I want to support Donna Barstow. I see she won the award many years ago but she continues to spend her time in the ED helping us deal with the tough cases that demand quick decisions and disposition. She is kind, likes residents and she gives good evaluations. I had her write a letter for my fellowship."

"But she won the award before and I think there are others to honor who have been good teachers and have not got the big prize. That's why I like Bob Farmer. He is the champ!"

"Don't over look Will Miller. He has a great way to teach cardiology. Did you ever see him draw a heart using both hands? And the way he can read echocardiograms. Looks like a dust storm to me but he can make sense of it. He comes to our parties and is a mentor to many of us, even the ones who do not go into cardiology."

"But, I have one big objection to him. He is kind and then hits on the women residents. He came on to me when I took cardiology elective. Beware of those dark rooms reading echoes! He has roving hands."

"So what is wrong with that? If you are not getting out socially, he serves a function that I found pleasant. I did not want to marry him but enjoyed the extra-curricular activities, especially when I have no other options, if you know what I mean."

"He never brings his wife to the parties. She would not approve of his dancing style. I don't think she knows about the echo reading room."

"Maybe she sends him to the parties. I think they have 4 kids."
"Any comments for Dr. Watkins?"
"Nice handwriting."
"Come on. Any comments for Dr. Watkins?"
"Nice table manners."

"I want to add my thoughts about Will Miller. I too, fell under his spell. He starts out as the interested teacher, which he certainly is. No one can make sense of those complicated cardiac cases as he does. He is also a good listener so it is easy to discuss personal problems. Then there is the trip to the coffee shop and soon to the echo room. How many of the ladies here have been down that road."

About 10 hands are raised.

"And how many were offended by his hands on teaching?"

About 5 hands shot up.

"So he does serve a social service to those without other options?"

"I would not say that. I have a lot going on but he was a special trip for me. I always wanted to hook up with a teacher. No ties no long range worries."

"I don't think I will vote for him but let's be fair."

Strem tried to get the meeting away from the gossip about the sexual habits of staff members. "OK that is enough for today. Think about these names and let me know if you have additional people to nominate. I will send out a voting list in 2 weeks. We need time to get the plaque engraved with the winner's name."

• • •

Downtown, the DA and his staff was finishing up their investigation of Beardsley's alleged insurance scam. "We are not getting very far with checking the files from CHUC. All we have is some guilty guy in Cincinnati ratting on Beardsley at CHUC. I know what the defense will say- He ratted on his buddy to get his sentence reduced. We have no evidence that CHUC purchased a computer program to alter the records. We have no hidden files on the computer hard drive. In fact the computer that holds the emails was replaced this summer so all the past evidence is gone."

"Was that coincidence or did he know we were coming and deep sixed the incriminating drive?" asked Paul Jameston.

"We can't spend time thinking about what could have happened. We need facts. Facts convict people, not wonderings." Snapped Harlyn. "We need hard evidence or this creep Beardsley will get away with this scam of his. We looked into his bank records, nada for big deposits. I checked with my buddy at the Federal Reserve and they could not find any hidden accounts in Beardsley's name. He lives well but with his huge salary, he can account for these large living expenditures. We are striking out, unfortunately."

• • •

"Dick, this is Norman. Hey, congratulations on your award. Well deserved old man. I do appreciate what you did to get that little girl taken care of at your hospital. I told you I owe you one. And here is a partial payment. I happen to be flying in my plane out to Colorado the same time you are getting your award. Want to check out some property for condominiums in Aspen. I would welcome you and Mrs. Randolf to join me. There is room for 12 so it will not be crowded. I will be in Aspen for about 5 days so if you like you can use the jet to go someplace while I am skiing, oops working in Aspen. I would invite you to Aspen but I am staying at a friend's condo and I don't think he would welcome any strangers, if you know what I mean. Ha ha. But you can have the jet to check out some place like Telluride or even Santa Fe. Flying there in the Gulf Stream sure beats commercial jets and all that delay for security checks and getting baggage. What do you say?"

"Sounds good to me. You will spoil me Norman, but it sounds quite nice. I will check with Mrs. Randolf. I don't see why she would object. Thanks ever so much for the invitation."

"I told you I owed you one." Norman hung up, Without a TV camera on the phone, he could not see the Beardsley's grin or the saliva dripping out of the side of his mouth.

Beardsley dialed Mrs. Randolf. "Carrie, would you believe it, Norman Oppenheim just offered us a ride to Denver and then use of the plane while he is doing business in Aspen. We could hit Santa Fe for a few days and then pick him up on the way home. No, a Gulf stream for 12, plenty of room. We could get back to Bishop's Lodge, like the old times. I hear they remodeled the rooms and have new owners but I bet the fireplace and hot tubs are still there. It is off season so it should be quiet and peaceful, just what I need. I can taste the enchiladas at the Shed and the margaritas at Gabrielle's, when we went there before it was Las Brisas but again, new owners. It would be like old times, what do you say?"

"Good. I will let Norman know. Amazing how convenient, your introducing me at the conference and then Norman owing me a favor."

"Yes I will be good. I know you are a married lady now. In case you forgot, I am married too. So I will be good as I can be."

"Amazing. Great!"

• • •

Carrie hung up the phone and continue her morning email ritual.

Dear Liz,

Sorry for the delay in answering your last email. You know I am not a good letter writer so I guess you are not surprised in my lack of correspondence until now. No believable excuses. Shame on you for suggesting in your last email, an extramarital affair to cheer me up. I think one bad actor in a family is enough! Not that I am self righteous but sorry to inform you that an opportunity has not tempted me to stray from my vows of faithfulness. I don't consider this upcoming trip to Denver a real temptation since I am going with that creep Beardsley, the hospital CEO. The good news is that he just called and we are going on a private jet of one of the hospital board members.

Other than this, not much is new at home. The usual committees, flower show, planning a summer celebration for the theater group in town and hopefully will get to Newport to see some friends this summer. Things at home are the same but maybe a little more civil as we are both quite busy.

Sorry for the brevity but wanted to check in and let you know I am still being good. How about you?

Love always,

Carrie

• • •

Kirby Jackson was planning his trip to Santa Fe to be inducted into the Society of University Pediatric Surgeons, an elite organization that allowed academic pediatric surgeons to meet with colleagues with similar interests. It was the typical good old boy group, even though a few women were of the age that they could become eligible. Women were not excluded, per se, but up till now, there were few women pediatric surgeons. And they had not written enough papers or made significant contributions to the field, or that was the excuse that was offered. The induction dinners were the highlight of the session. Black tie, top of the line liquor and wine from private collections. After dinner there was a roast of one of the senior surgeons by his trainees and a series of foul jokes, typical of a college fraternity instead of an academic society. Carter Randolf had nominated Kirby for membership, a hint that he may be the heir apparent of the chief surgeon at CHUC. The meeting provided a chance for the rest of the pediatric surgeons to know him better.

Of course Kirby was taking his loyal nurse, Mary Ann with him. She was needed for moral support and unobstructed love making, away from the exam tables or office sofas. She deserved a trip away, nice meals, candle lit dinners and maybe a massage at the spa, a reward for good work and extra duty service to the hot shot surgeon. They did not have to worry about Mrs. Jackson. She did not go to meetings with her husband; she could not stand the people and the super saturated egos. She preferred Manhattan and her gardens. Actually their communication had slimmed down to a few grunts and hellos as they passed each other in the house but at least they were not fighting anymore. The last big encounter was about 2 months ago when she insisted in ordering more stationary from Tiffany.

"Why do you have to order such expensive note paper? You can go to Office Max and they will print up your name on some envelopes and paper the same day."

"I like the feel of Tiffany paper and they emboss their name on the inside flap of the envelope. That way everyone knows that I spend a lot of money for my notes."

"But you have to wait so long to get the notes printed and delivered."

"Six weeks is not so long when you want Tiffany. Besides, it is my money so why do you care?"

That was the last exchange that these two people had.

Kirby could not let his secretary know that MaryAnn was going along too so he went through his usual subterfuge, having his secretary make his reservation, business class and then cancel the ticket and get two coach fares and try to upgrade them at the airport. Since he had so many miles on Continental, he usually could get moved up to business class. At this time of year, getting a room at Bishop's Lodge in Santa Fe presented no problem. With the rates they charged, he was assured of a king sized bed, if not, he would make a scene when he got there. The registrars were usually accommodative but with new owners, he had no special clout. His mouth watered as he thought of the papa fritas at Pasquales and margaritas. Great city. Great times. Can't wait. But enough day dreaming, the trip was not until next month and today he had to get to the OR and fix a few hearts. No problem with the acceptance speech. Thank a lot of people, tell a few stories about the lean days when no one could accept his innovations and then thank his mentors and his wife for being so supportive.

The next month flew by. Beardsley was in a good mood because he thought he had made some progress with individual board members about building a new hospital. His financial scheme was working well. The books showed major increases in margins. He met weekly with Al Sharptee, CFO and his asssistant Caroleen Colombe to make sure the financial reports reflected his devious plan that showed a healthy financial state for CHUC. This report would be critical to his negotiations for his new contract, hoping to get 1.5 million a year for 5 years. That would get his pension just about right for his retirement at the end of the contract. Money is important to Beardsley; it always was. When he was 6, he used to con his sister by volunteering to help her count the change in her piggy bank then he would distract her and palm a few quarters, then return her coins to the bank. In his previous jobs, he was adept at padding the expense accounts, 10 dollars here, 20 there. Now he had just one more contract negotiation and he would be fixed for life. Just think what would have happened if he got better grades in college and was accepted to medical school. He would probably be working for some one like himself, a CEO of a hospital who would be getting all the kickbacks and perks of the office while the doctors work their 80 hour weeks for less than half the income.

Like all good CEO's, he met regularly with the staff to make sure that all the players were sticking to the script.

"Vera get me Al and Caroleen and ask them to come to my office."

In a few minutes, both financial people arrived. Al swaggered in and flopped in the chair next to the window and checked his Blackberry while Caroleen quietly took her chair and opened up her notebook. No more time for polite chatter, it was the bottom line that Beardsley wanted.

"What have you to report?"

"Admissions are about average for this time of year. We have fewer collections than last year for this quarter."

"I want to know about charges, we will get to the collections later."

"Oh the charges are fine. We show a 10% increase in monthly charges due to the change in the way we booked OR rentals and radiology procedures. For the lab, we cannot do any more to the lab fees as we unbundled them last year and got a warning from the insurance company about this practice. The same for outpatient surgery charges. They hit us with an audit for the anesthesia charges and for drug charges. Seems they did not like the 30 dollar charge for aspirin that they had OK'd in previous years. So we did not want to be pigs. We did add on public relations costs to the outpatient department so that inpatient costs were down. That always looks good. We still hide the administrative costs by assigning a percentage to each division, inpatient, outpatient, labs and home care. Our way of keeping the administration costs low. The insurance companies let these little things slip through. They make the rules, we just follow them."

"Good, Good, Nice work Al. Any insights on the collections? Off the record, of course."

"Well Dick, not so good. It seems that the rejection of bills has zoomed. Up 20% from last year. Seems that they are getting on to us. Instead of making the final entry, I have been keeping the bills in the pending payment column. This cannot be hidden but it would take a sharp eye to see that this figure is about 25% higher than last year. I think I have it camouflaged well enough so that it will pass the board's scrutiny until we sign our contracts. I see we can increase the figure we made up for uncompensated care to the uninsured. That plus depreciation will balance the changes in the income side. I don't want anything to look like a profit since we are, as you know, non-profit, I mean not for profit."

"Most of the trust fund holders on the board will accept what we tell them but I am worried about Oppenheim; he is the business type that can read a financial report faster than a newly branded calf can run. I think I have him on my side so we may be lucky. He invited me to travel on his plane so I guess he likes me. Lookout bonuses, we are here!!" Beardsley raised his fist in the air as if he had just kicked a field goal with 22 seconds remaining in the game.

"And we also have contributions. They also help our picture. Unless the donors specify, we can put the money in the operations side so it looks like we are generating more patient income. I have a few feelers out to the Debson family. Seems that they sold their business for a big profit and are looking for a suitable place to put their funds. Caroleen, will you get me a file on their company and their charitable giving history. I don't want to look like a boob when I talk to them. I will go to their house and see what we can do. Baby needs a new pair of shoes ….and a new cath lab for cardiology. Great place for generating charges and the insurance nerds pay us a lot for these procedures. We can do well with the administrative fees that go into the operations too. If all goes well, we can expect a bump in our income; a reward for job well done. You two have done a great job! Hopefully we will get the contract before someone gets on our case. It has been good so far. Next… What are we doing about expenses? I see that salaries are up. Maybe we can get some Indian docs to work in the clinic? I know we can cut salaries down there by 40%."

"You mean add Asian doctors to the staff or get rid of the senior doctors."

"Add to the staff, are you crazy Caroleen? We need to get those high paid doctors off our rolls, especially the senior ones who make the most, and fill in with some low cost worker bees."

"Are they trained well enough?"

"Who cares? They have MD degrees. We just need some robots down there to see the colds and cuts. Anyone can do that. You don't need board certified docs to do that kind of medicine. I am even wondering about what we can do to get rid of some surgeons. After all, a hernia is a hernia. When I was in the Navy, the corpsmen could do appendectomies when pushed. Just think what we could do without some of those highly paid surgeons doing routine cases. Not today. But something we can discuss at the next administration meeting. Make a note of it, Caroleen."

"Right. Mr. Beardsley." Caroleen added this to her list of her assignments in her notebook along with notes about the meetings.

Beardsley's head took a mild spastic turn as noted the formality of her reply. He would never get Caroleen in his bed if she called him Mr., but then again, maybe it was a front so that Al would not suspect anything was going on, if by chance, it were going on. He liked these meetings since it was legal to stare at her when she was talking.

"What doctors are you considering replacing? The doctors in the clinic?"

"Some of them, but I am looking at the big salaries. Farmer, Barstow, even Randolf."

"Wow, how will you get to Randolf? He has a lot of clout."

"You remember the golden rule. Those with the gold make the rules, so they say. And I agree. Nothing is sacred when we are cutting costs."

Both Al and Caroleen did not smile as they could see their own jobs in jeopardy either because they were indicted for financial fraud or they were replaced by a college student who took one semester of accounting.

"OK team, I am going out of town to give a talk, the usual. The children are our number one priority speech and drop in a few success stories. I am going by private jet so I have time to do some work during the flight. I am excited about building a new hospital and maybe the altitude in the plane will stimulate my brain. We leave in the morning so it is too early to start with the booze but maybe on the way home, I can celebrate with a few martinis- Bombay sapphire is my new drink. Last night at the Centennial, they did not have Bombay Sapphire; I had to settle for Grey Goose. Caroleen made a note in her book "This guy does not know gin from vodka. If he is going to drop names, at least he can get the facts right."

When Beardsley got back to his office, there was a note to call the DA.

"Shit, what have they found about the billing problem? Ann, please get me the DA."

"Malcolm Harlyn, speaking."

"Hello, Mr. Harlyn, this is Richardson Beardsley returning your call."

"Oh, Mr. Beardsley, I wanted you to give you an update on the case about the medical records and insurance. You remember we were in your office and took your computer and some files."

"Oh yes, I do remember that. What's up?"

Well, we are returning all the material and equipment to you and your staff. We have gone over all the material and right now, we have stopped the investigation."

"You mean this was a false alarm?"

"I mean that we are returning the material and equipment to you. We checked them and there was no evidence in this computer and the records to support what that what the man in Cincinnati said."

"Good. You mean the case is closed?"

"I did not say that but we are returning what we took from you. You can infer what you want from that. Good day Mr. Beardsley."

Beardsley hung up the phone and then the famous grin appeared.

Beardsley thrust his fist in the air and hissed "YESSSS."

"I am glad I dumped my old computer as soon as I heard about the impending investigation. Yessss!"

With that news he was ready for his trip to Colorado without worry about the DA. He showed up at the airport at 8, right on time. He picked up the New York Times at the 7-11 and proudly carried it onto the Gulf Stream. Norman was already there. He noticed the paper and half apologized. "Oh Richardson, I forgot to tell you that the flight attendant always supplied the plane with the Times, the Washington Post and the Journal." Beardsley assumed it was the Wall Street Journal but did not ask which Journal. Since Mrs. Randolf was not there, Beardsley felt it was a good time to score some points with the one board member that he could not figure out.

"The little girl that you called me about seems to be doing fine."

"That is not what I heard from the family. They told me that she had some bad genetic pattern that will shortly cause her body not to respond to the chemotherapy. They went to Farber in Boston for a second opinion and had a few minor changes in the treatment but she seems to be coming along. But even though she got the bad news, thanks so much for taking care of her for me. The family is most appreciative. What is new at the hospital?"

"We are doing fine. I am working hard on looking at the expenses and have come up with some ideas that can improve our bottom line. The new MRI is working well and ahead of projections for usage and income. The food services are costing us a lot so I am working on some alternatives. More money for the kids."

"What is wrong with the food services? My golfing buddy works for the conglomerate that provides institutional food services. He told me they are doing a great job. He did mention that the payments from the hospital are behind schedule. I stay out of these as I don't want to appear as having a conflict of interests. But I will keep an ear and eye open."

"Good idea. Nothing major. But I like to reevaluate our contracts periodically since we can get complacent and miss a good deal that will affect our financials."

"Good. That's all for medical talk now. We have to get ready for the trip and some fun. I see Mrs. Randolf walking up to the plane. She is driving one of the new S class cars. Very sleek."

"Carrie, good to see you." He gave her the European double cheek type greeting kiss. "Looking very chic in your travel outfit. I appreciate people who travel in nice clothes. I recognize your Kriza, understated beauty. The Italians certainly know their design. Looking like this will get you better treatment when you get to the hotel; I try to look good when traveling."

Beardsley, paranoid as usual, was wondering what was wrong with his custom made sport coat and $400 Oxxford trousers. Maybe it was the shoes. He still can't spend $600 or $700 on a pair of shoes when the $60 Bostonian ones seem to be just fine. He tried to hide his shoes and seconded the praise for Carrie's outfit. Maybe it was time for him to get a suit made in Italy.

The pilot and co-pilot made last minute checks of the plane. Check in and security were easy. No search, no metal detectors; just show your ID and get on the plane. The attendant served cappuccino and biscotti. They all settled in their oversized chairs around the conference table as the plane took off. As they passed over Philadelphia, Norman took charge of the conversation. He wanted to know more about Beardsley but did not want to be too obvious so he started on his life story. Beardsley was looking out of the window to see if he could find the Philadelphia Children's Hospital to see if that hospital would still be larger than CHUC when he got his new building. He liked to count the number of the huge cranes that indicated the level of building activity. The clouds blocked the view so he could not make any comparisons.

"These planes are a real benefit when you have to travel as much as I do. I have so many real estate investments all over the country, it seemed going by private jet was more efficient and obviously more restful than fighting lines and sitting in cramped seats on commercial. Since the flight takes 3-4 hours, we have time to get to know each other."

Beardsley did not want to pry but was curious how someone came to this luxury. Carrie was not afraid to ask. "How did you get into real estate?"

"Long story but the short version is I started out collecting rent in Newark. Back then it was safer and one could go through the downtown area, collecting rent money and not getting robbed. Every so often, I saw a property for sale and worked a deal to buy these houses. Most were about $500. I sold some and bought more. As I worked my way up the market, I got into an area where some major developments were being planned for the downtown revitalization. The developers offered me much more money than I invested in the properties. That propelled me into more expensive deals and then I got out of residential into commercial. Same story. Moved up scale slowly. When shopping centers came on the scene, I had some land that worked well for a shopping center so I became a partner in the deal. After a few developments in the suburbs I worked out a plan for other shopping center owners to join forces with me to build bigger centers with several major tenants. That worked well so instead of competing with these developers all the time, we joined our thoughts and assets when appropriate and created mega-shopping centers. That does not mean we did not compete but since we were colleagues, the competition was fair and usually profitable. I had special relationships with some retail outfits while my competitors had other relationships. So when one of us had a development deal, we invited others to bring in their clients. Worked out well, for the most part. I did not bat a thousand but I used timing to get into and out of properties before the big stores went under or when the structures become too old. Location, location, location and timing. Amazing what you can do when you join forces with others. The big variable is home life. Divorces can ruin a business deal as you lose so much of your assets, your D and B gets messed up. I have had two wives so I know about losing assets. I should have been a lawyer, a divorce lawyer that is where the real money is. But I was not too good in the academics. I did all right for a poor boy from Newark. Now I am into charities and doing some giving back. That is almost as good as making a shopping center deal. My new wife is great but I have trouble keeping up with her shopping bills. We have no kids but I have three from our past marriages. One of the boys is in the business with me, one teaches medieval history at Brown and Abby makes jewelry in Colorado Springs. That is one of the reasons that I am going to Denver. A business meeting and then some time with Abby. Sometimes I wish I did not have a trust fund for her but she is so happy doing her jewelry that I cannot complain. Do you want more coffee? It is too early for Bloody Marys."

"What do you think of the idea of a new hospital? I bet you have some properties that you would like to sell to the hospital for the new building, if it gets approved."

"I would not touch that deal. Too much appearance of a conflict and insider business. I never mix my board life with my commercial interests. But I need to know more about the need for a new hospital complex and the financials. I don't mind debt when I can see long term gain eventually but hospitals are not the same kind of business that I know. Maybe someday we can have lunch and you can explain the details to me. I am not sure that bigger is better."

Beardsley thought that the question would get a much longer answer and prevent him from revealing too much personal information. He looked at Carrie as if to tell her it was her turn. She loved to talk so this was not a problem.

"I guess I am next. Not as exciting as you, Norman. But I have no complaints. I came from Ohio. My father worked at the GM plant and my mother was a nurse. I was the oldest of 4 kids. I always wanted to be a nurse since I was 6 or 7. In high school I was a cheer leader and played basketball. That got me a scholarship to Ohio State where I attended nursing school. I loved pediatrics so it was natural for me to seek out a pediatric center to work in an interesting program for kids. The clinical research center at CHUC was my choice and I loved it. I worked on diabetes projects with Dr Altman. We were doing some amazing things, trying to keep sugars normal and complications down. I met Carter while he was exploring the possibility of doing pancreas transplants for children with diabetes. Carter and I hit it off immediately. He was on the tail end of his marriage so it was not like I was stealing him away. Now I am no longer a nurse but a do-gooder trying to improve things in the hospital and in the city. I have my flower garden that keeps me busy and I am active in the horticultural society's spring flower show. I still keep my fingers in diabetes work. We don't have kids as he has children from number one marriage. Sounds familiar doesn't it Norman? There is a big age difference between us so even though I would like kids he feels too old to start that over again. So my kids are my projects such as the Hospital volunteer group that is honoring Dick in Denver. Oops. I see Dick is nodding off. That seems like a good idea to rest up before all the excitement starts."

Beardsley was not sleepy but he was avoiding his turn to reveal his past. He was sticking to his guiding principle of not put anything in writing or reveal details of his past. No one had to know about his blue collar background. He knew he would not be able to conceal all the details of his past but he wanted time to decide what skeletons to let go from his bag of past activities. He nodded to Carrie to show his thanks for her diverting the conversation back to flowers.

"Norman, have you gone to our flower show? I bet you have. What a silly question!"

"No I have not gone to the one here. I have done the one in London, the Chelsea. Spectacular one."

Beardsley made a note to put that on the list of things to do in London after he checks with Google to find out what it is and the date of the show. Back to closed eyes.

"I have been to Chelsea too. What a show! Then there is the Philadelphia Flower Show which is quite a display. They hold that early March. I never miss that one." The chit chat continued until Norman got a phone call from one of his offices. That allowed the other two to pick up the papers and get some more orange juice from the galley.

The plane landed in Denver without incident. A car was waiting for them at the hanger. The pilot and driver transferred the bags into the car and they were off to the Brown Palace. Norman liked that historic hotel since it had an atrium dating back to the early 20th century. The design was copied in many modern hotels. The Brown Palace was the hotel for the copper barrons and their lady friends. Beardsley looked interested. In the limo, Norman reminded them that the plane was theirs for the next 5 days.

"The pilot will take care of all the arrangements when you decide what you want to do after your meeting. Here is his card with his cell phone number. I will be busy with some deals and family visits. Congratulations with your award. It is well deserved and brings honor to the hospital. Good job Carrie, for getting this all done."

• • •

Back in South Creek, Carter Randolf left the hospital earlier than usual so he had time to pack his bag for his trip to Santa Fe. Since he nominated Kirby for membership in the surgical society, he was expected to introduce him at the induction. It was a chance to get to New Mexico again, one of his favorite places. He had made arrangements at the Bishop's Lodge, a nice place about 5 miles out of town. This time of year, not many people would be there so he would get some rest without all the back slapping camaraderie of the surgical group. What a great time to get away, his wife was off to some ladies meetings in Denver with Beardsley so he would be free from the administration's orders to be more productive. The trip would be a change to get involved in some real sex with his new friend. Life with Mrs. Randolf was not like the old days. Two busy people tired of each other and one with a decreased libido did not bode well for excitement in the bed room. Carter was excited, he did not know if he needed Viagra but he took some along with him, just in case. This relationship with his date just started so he had not had any bedroom activities, yet. This trip was the next level or going for a home run as he used to say when he was an innocent teen. Carter smiled as he thought about what would happen in Santa Fe.

He dialed Kirby again to confirm that they would be on different flights to Albuquerque; he did not want Kirby to be on to his new affair. Kirby told him that he had an early morning case so would not be able to leave until 3:30. That was perfect as Carter had an 8AM flight that arrived about noon, Mountain Time. He reconfirmed his reservation desk a the Bishop's Lodge; hoping they still had the rooms with corner fireplaces and hot tubs. A nice place to spend away from home and his wife. Yes, it was going to be a nice quiet time, hopefully not too quiet, he smiled as he corrected his thinking. He had packed his boots, his turquoise belt buckle and the Western shirt with the red heart shaped polka dots. Thank goodness no one from his church would see him wearing that outfit or meet his young blond companion. Since many older men travel with their young blond assistants to this meeting, his young date would not attract too much attention from the surgeons. Carter had not felt this excited since his residency when he won a prize to attend a national meeting of pediatric surgeons and took his lab assistant with him. He had planned to hide her from the other attendees but when he arrived, there were so many assistants there that it was one happy fraternity party. His assistant eventually became his wife number one. So he figured that it was not really a sin. Then he met Carrie and felt that a person of her background would be better for his image than a former lab assistant in the animal surgery lab. Carrie was younger and more energetic; but she could not keep up with oversexed Carter. His increased surgical practice and the complexity of the cases energized him when he finally got home to bed. That old feeling was returning for this trip to Santa Fe.

He did not want to take his blond friend to the airport so he arranged for a car to drive her to Newark Liberty Airport. He made his reservations on Continental and selected his seat. Then she did the same and selected the seat next to his. They took seats at the back of the plane and boarded early to minimize the chance that anyone could see them together. He asked her to get a brown wig over her blond hair and wear sunglasses. She would use her travel name, Christi to add to the camouflage. After they arrived, they would hide away at Bishop's Lodge, Hot tub and fireplace, sounds good.

These secretive plans were disturbed when he got to the airport. He bumped into John Gross, the president of the First Union bank. Luckily, Carter was alone. John told him that he was headed to the islands. Relieved, he picked up the Times and headed for the gate A-28 and seat 32 B.

They changed planes in Houston and got on the Albuquerque flight with about 10 minutes to spare. Now he had to worry for the next hour if the bags would make the change. Nothing he could do about that so he ordered two Bloody Maries and pushed the seat back. He did not talk to his travel partner to avoid any appearance of familiarity. If the bags did not arrive, no problem. He always looked neat when he traveled, although for this trip he did not wear a tie. If the bags did not arrive by the time of the banquet, he was sure that he could find a tie at some store, even if it were a thrift shop store. So he sipped his Bloody Mary and took a nap for the short hop to New Mexico. When he saw the Sandia mountains near the airport, he took a deep breath of relief that the fun was about to start. They arrived at Gate B2, went past the gift shops and restaurants and made their way to the baggage claim #3 on the lower level. The smell of Mexican food at Gardunos did not tempt him, there was time for burritos later.

Unnecessary worry, the bags arrived. Carter let out a whelp and grabbed both of them, forgetting about his sore back. They got on the bus to the car rental area and went right to the Hertz club; he tapped Christi's arm to show her his name Randolf was on the guest board, although he was not happy with the car position of C-34. He rather wanted A level and a lower number, under 10. He thought that an ego boost would impress his guest. They did not have a red car as he requested so he went to the office to complain. They upgraded him to a Continental to make up for the slight inconvenience. After checking the dashboard and light switch, he cautiously made his way out of the maze in the rental area to get back to University and then Gibson. Although the sign showed route 25 – Santa Fe was to the left, he turned right on Gibson and headed East, past the Lovelace medical complex and at the traffic light at the bottom of the hill he turned left and pulled into parking lot behind the liquor store.

"Where are you taking me?"

"This is Cervantes, the best food in town. Don't worry about the outside, the inside hallway is even more scary, it's pretty dark. But then it will be heaven."

"Do you realize that you have the only car in the parking lot? The rest are pickup trucks and vans. Is that a drive by liquor store? I don't think this is for me."

"Trust me, Christi."

She smiled when she heard that name. "I thought Christi was the name of movie starlets and porno stars."

Just as predicted, the hall way was dark but then they entered the restaurant. A fire was burning in the fireplace in the far wall. The décor included the swords on the wall and portraits of Conquistadors staring at the diners. They took a seat in non-smoking area. The home made salsa moved Carter into high gear "You can judge a Mexican restaurant by the quality of the salsa. This is not salsa made in a factory in Brooklyn, this is the real thing. They make their own and will even ship to your house."

They ordered guacamole, which was passable but the enchiladas and fajitas were fantastic. They finished up the meal with delightful sopapillas and honey. Carter skipped the margaritas as he wanted to be alert on the interstate as the drivers were wild and unpredictable; he did not need an accident this trip.

Back on Gibson, he now took 25 North. The ride to Santa Fe was as beautiful as he remembered it. The only thing new was the gaudy gambling casinos that sprouted up from the formerly barren land near Santo Domingo pueblo. They took the St Francis exit and passed through the edge of seedy part of Santa Fe, past the Veteran's cemetery and turned off to the north side of town to pick up Bishop's Lodge Road. At the bottom of the hill, the Bishop Lodge sign invited them to turn right. The well maintained garden welcomed them as they headed for the registration office. The room in Sunset lodge, as requested was not too far from the dining room. But who cares? They were there and none of the guests knew them so they were free to behave or hopefully misbehave. His only obligation was to show up at the surgical dinner tomorrow night. Once he got to the Bishop's Lodge and the bags were in the room, he was so energized that he could not just sit still. He was not here for an afternoon on the rocking chair but he did not want to be too obvious that he was here for special sex.

"Let's go into town and see what they have in the stores." So back into the car, they headed for downtown Santa Fe. They jumped from a number of galleries, full of some strange and some pleasing art to stores full of souvenirs, pottery and turquoise and silver jewelry. In a little store on a side street, a green turquoise pendent on a silver necklace caught his eye. "Do you like this one?"

"It is beautiful; I bet it is expensive."

"That is all relative. There is a saying that I have heard many times in many places, if you see what you like, get it because it may be gone tomorrow or you may not find this store again. Let's go see what it is all about. And don't worry, it is only money." Carter likes to back up his bets. A nice piece of jewelry would look pretty on her and it would cull up a kind of obligation for later that night.

"This is a rare piece of Cerrillos turquoise, a real beauty, comes from this region. They stopped mining there at the end of the 19th century but people still find some pieces out there. Have you taken the turquoise road to Albuquerque? You would see the hippies there, making jewelry and stuff. This piece is a real rare one. You have good taste to pick this one out. Don't you love it?"

"There are a lot of stores with a lot of pieces but this one certainly stands out. Let me tell you one thing, though, I know about the stores and the prices, I don't bargain, I expect a honest price, the one you would finally get to if there were bargaining. But you only get one shot so give me your best price."

"You a lawyer or what? This piece is marked $2050 but I get your message. Final price is $1250. Final, no bull."

"Just what I thought. Let's go."

"What do you mean? I gave you the piece at 1% over my cost. I need to make something on it."

"I don't want to be a fool and overpay for this thing."

"$1125"

"Sold!"

"I thought you did not bargain. But I am sure you will enjoy it."

"I hope so; it was a pleasure doing business with you. Do you want to wear it out of here, that way at least I can save the cost of a box?"

When the left the store, Carter was quite proud of his purchase. "I would like a dollar for every time the word "rare" was used in this town. They have two levels of honesty- regular lies and really big lies. The important thing is you like it."

"I love it. Thank you so much. You are so kind to buy this. I don't know how I can thank you for this."

Carter grinned.

Kirby did not have the problem of hiding his travel partner as he had taken Mary Ann on many of his trips. His only concern was to get the case done so he could get to the airport on time. His scheduled early morning case was cancelled to clear time for a renal transplant case as a kidney just became available. An 18 year old girl from Millville NJ was killed in a car accident on her way to school with her two friends. She was adjusting the car radio to find the right music when she missed a turn and hit a tree. She was still alive when the EMT team arrived but died later in the hospital ED. Her family, present in the ED when she died, made the decision to donate her kidneys, heart and lungs for transplantation into people on the waiting list. Fortunately, she was a very good match with a boy on the waiting list at CHUC. Kirby's team immediately went to work to notify the patient who was getting the kidney while the helicopter left for Millville. The transplant surgery team worked like a NASCAR pit crew taking over #10 OR.

Tommy Morris, a 15 year old with chronic kidney failure was awaken at his home by his mother who told him that this was his lucky day. Since it was his day for dialysis, he was sleepy and bloated with accumulated water. His eyes were swollen and his legs were twice the usual size. He was not that sleepy to realize that this was the day he was dreaming about since he became sick 4 years ago and found out that his kidneys were destroyed from complications of a congenital malformation. After being on dialysis three times a week for the past 4 years, he was relieved that the wait was over. He closed his eyes and visualized his new kidneys spewing out urine. He was sure that would be the reality in a few hours. 40 minutes later, his parents wheeled into the OR suite.

"Do me" he called to the nurse and anesthesiologist as he hopped from his Gurney to the operating table. "I'm yours. Hey, it is cold in here!" The anesthesiologist placed IV lines into his arms, injected a sedative prior to starting placing the mask over his nose and mouth, placed a tube into his trachea and began the anesthesia. The resident and student began to clean his back and side with Betadine.

Kirby was scrubbing outside, looking at the clock, not because he was timing the duration of the soap and brush routine but calculating how he would get the case done before departure time. He had done almost 150 transplants so the routine was well established in his mind. Barring a complication, he would be sewing up the young man about 1-2 PM.

"What is the word from helicopter 1?"

"They have removed the kidneys and are bringing home the bacon."

"Good let's get started with the case." 9:04 AM. This was slightly unusual since they liked to have the kidney in the room before starting the case.

Allison Zimmerman, the circulating nurse and keeper of protocol and sterile conditions asked, "Are you sure we should start? I think hospital policy states we need to eyeball the new kidney before we start. You remember we had a situation when the kidney, once visualized at the harvesting, was full of cysts and unsuitable for transplant. It was only one case but enough to create another rule for transplantation surgery."

"With all due respect, Allison, butt out. This is my decision, not yours. We will be fine. Let's get started." They broke this rule and began the case since the team did not report any gross problems with the donor kidney. With its usual proficiency, the team went to work, cut through the skin and muscle to get the right exposure so Kirby could remove the diseased kidney and prepare his artery, vein and ureter to receive the donor kidney.. At 10:15, they were done with phase 1.

"Where the hell is the helicopter?"

"The bird has some trouble with its mechanics, so they landed at the airport and are coming home in an ambulance."

"So why the delay?"

"Morning traffic and construction."

"Get the damn police and get an escort."

"They can't get through the mess either."

"Why didn't someone tell me this before we started?"

"They kept reassuring us that they were on target. A series of worst case deals. I guess."

"You're guessing and I am stuck here with an open wound and no kidney. I got to get to the airport sometime today."

"We will get you there, boss. Even if I have to drive you there."

"Through the construction and traffic jams. Thanks a lot. Anyone got a deck of cards; maybe I can make some of my expenses from you birds. How is the patient?"

"Signs stable, we are keeping the wounds covered with saline dressings."

"I hope you did. Get me Tim Warren, ask him to get down here and be ready to take over the case, if I have to leave at 1 PM.

The kidney arrived, packed in ice and perfused with preservation solution to maintain its vitality during transport. The kidney comes with stumps of the renal artery, vein and ureter that would be connected to the patient's corresponding artery and vein. Before the connections could be made, the artery and vein from the donor kidney had to be prepared by cutting away the fat and isolating the artery and vein. "Hurry, hurry" urged Kirby to his team. "This is not a beauty pageant; there will be no photographers to takes pictures of the arteries. Let's get moving. It looks good to me." Actually the vessels were not completely clean but the assistants bowed to the boss' direction and began the attachments at 11:45. Despite all the early issues, the anastomoses between the donor and recipient vessels went well. Now to see if the operation did the patient any good. After the clamps on the artery and vein are removed, the blood flowed into the pale kidney. Immediately the tissue turns pink and a small pulsation is seen. That part of the procedure is working well.

"Now let's hope there will be some urine is coming out of the kidney." All eyes reflexly turned to the ureter. The clamp on the end of the ureter is removed while the whole room stops breathing for that instant. Immediately the clear liquid appears at the ureter coming from the kidney, then it turns into a flood. "HOO-HA. GET'EM COWGIRL! This is great! we got the kidney in place just in time. Better than hitting oil in your backyard. We got real yellow gold. Now we can attach the ureter from the kidney to the stump of the ureter going into the bladder."

"Great, I am taking off. Tim, will you make sure all goes well. I will stop by to see the parents."

Kirby left the OR, headed to the locker room to take off the scrub suit with spattered blood and put on a fresh one and then polished his shoes. He entered the men's prep room and found his locker, #4. Someday he would be chief and face the dilemma move to #1 or keep #4. He would probably stick with #4, his favorite number.

Kirby put on his fresh scrub suit over his golf pants and button down shirt so he could play Superman, morph from Dr. Jackson to Kirby Jackson and be off to the airport. He ran his fingers through his hair to look like he thought he should after a long transplant surgery and found the parents in the patient lounge.

"Hello, Mr. and Mrs. Morris, I am Dr. Kirby Jackson. The transplant went well. They are finishing up the closure. Unfortunately, I have to get to the airport to deal with another organ situation. We have to go when the opportunity calls. My team is quite competent and I have full confidence in their ability to continue. I will call in to get progress reports but I don't anticipate any problems. The new kidney turned pink right away and the urine gushed out of it showing that it can remove water from your son. Now we have a few weeks to see how your son's body responds to the new kidney and to find out if it will remove the other chemicals and body wastes. We will watch for any signs of transplant rejection- that occurs in all the patients, despite the matching that we do. We can treat the rejection with special medicines. I hate to cut and run but that is the life of a transplant surgeon. Any questions? Good."

"Thank you so much doctor, you don't know how much we appreciate all you have done for our son. He is in your hands and your teams, too. Thank you so much. Good luck on your next venture. Safe flying."

"He is so humble, I like that about a doctor. Sacrificing his life so others can live. His poor wife probably does not see him. He is so busy saving lives."

Kirby runs down the hall, takes off his green scrub suit and heads for his car that was already pointing towards Newark Liberty Airport and then off to the land of blue skies and pinions burning in the fireplace.

Chapter 22

The coffee shop had its usual customers at lunch time. Lester was holding court on the topic of the latest book on Cezanne, who he felt was slightly over rated when compared to other innovators such as Edvard Munch, one of his favorite artists, even though he was not French. No one in the group could follow his desultory speech. In fact no one even cared about his choices of favorite artists. The rest of the group was more of the Andrew Wyeth followers. They preferred recognizable scenes, accurately painted. Finally, Sevasta Patel and Sara Wright interrupted him at the same time.

"Has anyone seen Felix? Since he has been on a research elective, he is in hiding. We can't find out what he is doing but hopefully he will have something to show for these three months. I hear that he is no longer seeing his mother figure but has taken up with one of her friends. Maybe he should go into analysis to help him explain his penchant for mature women."

"What do you mean, we are not mature?"

"We are not teeny boppers so we are mature compared to them but we are not mature like older women. It all depends on the definition of mature is."

"Speaking of maturity. Did you vote for teacher of the year? I am favoring Dr. Farmer; it is about time he has won that recognition after all the years he has been here."

"I did not vote for him, I thought he has won it many times."

"Wrong again. Can you change your vote?"

"No chance, if you came to the meetings, you would have known that."

"Does anyone know about the fellowships for next year? I am applying for next year in gastroenterology. They do a lot of procedures and therefore make a lot of money." Scope power, power to the gastro scope! That's my mantra."

"But you see a lot of constipated kids from uptight families."

"As long as they have insurance, I will see them. Got a lot of loans to pay off."

"I guess I have not lost my idealism, I still want to do general peds and work in the community. Lots of challenges and lots of good you can do to help kids get a better start. Touch a life, one at a time. The bills will get paid, somehow."

"You better marry a surgeon or a hospital administrator."

"Right now I will settle for a politician or a baseball player with a guaranteed 5 years. The big question is how to get a position here without going through evil Eva. She has so much to say about our files and thus our careers."

"Old Eva, she never gives up. Still trying to use her position of power to gather favors from the house staff men."

"At least she is straight; it could be problems for us ladies, if that were not the case."

"Does anyone have an interest in a softball team? The hospital league is forming and people expect us to participate."

Why don't they just give it to housekeeping? They are full of superb ball players from Mexicans and Central Americans. They did not make the Mets team so they are here but still very good.

"I thought they were going to exclude them as they are professional level players. It is not fair to the rest of us."

Across the coffee shop, Bob Farmer was talking with Erica Gates, a medical student who has selected him as her unofficial mentor. She had to make some decisions about her future too. Where to apply for residency; how far to move from her parents; should she stay close to home or go as far as California.

"What is your leaning now?

"I want to stay here, like many of my classmates."

"Why, here?"

"I love it here, I am familiar with the layout, I like the people like you to be here to teach me. This is my place."'"

"Thanks for the compliment but that is not the issue, too much comfort will lead to complacency and loss of the energy juices that you get in new situations. As a result of familiarity, you might not get a maximum learning experience. You need to get away from here and learn new ways from new people. You have heard all the lectures at least once and probably twice. You know where the bathrooms are, you need new challenges to rev up your brain.

"But this is the best place. You are here. Why don't you leave?"

"This is not about me. I have been here and I have been elsewhere. You can always come back after your training. Get away for a few years. It will do you good. "

"That is not what I want to hear. I would like to be near from my mother and father."

"Where did you go to college?"

"Barnard"

"So you are an Easterner. Time to leave."

"Can't you say anything nice about my staying here?"

"Look, I have a lot to say about which new residents that we accept her. I guarantee that if you put us first on the resident matching plan, you will be here. This is not a case of residency roulette, put in a wild high choice and see if it works. If you select us you will be here. I guarantee it. It is your choice."

"Then where should I go"

"Go to a rigorous place with high academic standards."

"That narrows the choices down to about 20."

Then where did you get a good feeling that the chemistry was right?"

"DC Children's"

"So what is the problem?"

"I think Hopkins is better."

"Hopkins is great but if you did not get a good feeling, listen to your chemistry."

"You are trying to force me to be rational when you talk about chemistry, which is not rational, it is a feeling."

"You are right there."

"Same thoughts though. If you put down Hopkins, you will most likely be matched there. They are bright people who can recognize talent. Remember, be careful what you select, you might end up there."

"I hear you. I will not forget that advice."

"So what else. What do you do besides go to school?"

"I go to church and work on the homeless project that the students support."

"If I am intruding, just stop me. I mean what about social life, like dating and non-medical things with real people?"

"That is not in my game plan right now. I have so much to do and so many people to help. I am happy with my choice."

"Choice or fear?"

"Fear is not a word I know."

"You will next year, when your patient crashes and you are the doctor. So don't deny fear. It is helpful for learning."

"Right you are. But that is enough about me-me. How did you decide on your residency?

"It was much simpler then. No organized system like you have now, I just contacted the hospital to see if they would take me. I had some references and they took me. It was efficient when someone wanted you but hard on some people because they might have gotten an offer from a hospital that was not their first choice. You had little time to decide. Only the real confident would turn down the offer while awaiting one from a better program. That is why they developed the resident matching plan."

"You seem to be here a lot. Is it too brazen of me to ask you what else do you do?"

"After football season, not much. I used to be very busy with social life but now it is work and teaching that take my time. Keeps me out of trouble."

"So why are you pushing me to move away from the life that I like?"

"You have to give living a chance before you decide on your lifestyle. I did all those things when I was younger. Now I see enough angst in my practice that I don't have to pay to see a play on Broadway. I have my iPod full of opera and classical music so I don't need to catch the flu from a cougher sitting next to me in Carnegie Hall."

"I understand. Thanks so much for all your help. I really do listen to you."

"Excuse me for getting too personal."

"It is good to be challenged. Maybe you should have been a dentist. You bore right into the toothache. To be honest, I am not sure I am in the right field. I love school and learning new things. It was easy for me and then people said you are so smart, you should go to medical school. I got accepted, for some reason, or maybe I really earned it. But I got to medical school and more courses and more good grades. But next year will be work. No tests, not many lectures; it is for real doctors, people who wanted to learn so that they could diagnose and treat patients. I am not sure that I want to do that. I want to help people but I don't like the one to one arrangement, if I make a mistake, I could ruin someone's life. That's more pressure then I need. I may not be the best one for a residency. I am not sure."

"Maybe scared is a better word. Join the group. I am not worried about your doing a good job as a resident. I am more worried about the over-confident ones who are ready to take on the world- they are the dangerous ones. You will not be alone; people are there to help you. Just do your best. Keep your eyes and ears open and ask questions. It is not what you are anticipating. The job and responsibility will fall in place. Many people have trouble with the adjustment from transitioning from a student to being a worker without grades. I have confidence in you."

"Thanks, Dr. Farmer, I will keep you posted." Erica picked up the remnants of the Styrofoam cup that she nervously tore into small pieces during this discussion with Dr. Farmer and left the cafeteria.

Robert Farmer tossed his cup into the trash can and returned to his office to see what surprises were in store for him.

• • •

Kirby's plane landed at ABQ airport without incident. He grabbed his jacket, waited his turn to get off the plane and made a pit stop at the men's room across the aisle from the debarkation gate. Mary Ann with only a small carry-on bag, went ahead to await Kirby's bag at baggage claim 2. They headed for some chili stew at Gardunos as Kirby made a call to the hospital to check on the status of the transplant patient. Seemed to being OK. They hopped on the rental car bus to pick up his car at Avis and headed Santa Fe and Bishop's Lodge.

"Nobody will be there this time of year, perfect! I got a room in Sunset lodge. I know you will like it there." All he cared about was the king sized bed that he and Mary Ann tested out as soon as the bell hop left the room. Maybe, it was the pinion smoke from the fireplace, maybe it was the 7000 feet altitude, maybe it was being away from South Creek and Mrs. Jackson that made the difference, but it was going to be a great Santa Fe time with or without the fancy dinner with the surgical society members.

As if it were ESP, as Kirby was thinking about his wife not being there to bother him, Gayle Jackson sat in her office, uncomfortable with a good dose of guilt for not being with her husband when he was being honored by his colleagues in Santa Fe. She checked her calendar on her iPhone and picked up the phone.

"Grace, will you get me a business class seat to Santa Fe. I need to be there by 6 PM tomorrow. And a car at the airport. Call Clara at Bishop's Lodge, she will know about getting a limo. I running out there to see my husband get inducted in some Mickey Mouse group that has so far only admitted three women. Maybe I will understand this group when I see what they do and who is doing it. After all I guess being there to support my husband is the proper thing to do, isn't it?"

Richard Beardsley was in all his glory at the National Hospital Volunteer's Convention. Fortunately, he only had to appear that night to receive the honor, have his picture taken with the president of the group and then make excuses to get back on Norman's jet and head south to Santa Fe. He decided on Sante Fe without consulting Carrie. He was last there about 10 years ago. Since they were in the area, it would be a short jaunt to get there and with a jet at their disposal, it made sense.

Carrie made a wonderful introduction, praising Beardsley for all his community service, his commitment to the underserved and his personal sacrifice for serving in health care rather than in investment banking or in industry. Beardsley was appropriately humble, starting off by remarking that it was so nice to hear those kind words, it was something that he wished he had written, which in fact, he had. But that was another secret between Carrie and him. His speech- Honesty and Integrity: The Essential Components of a First Class Hospital- went over quite well with this family value group of ladies. Carrie scored a lot of points with the current president of the group who asked her if she was interested in being nominated to the board and becoming second vice president.

Because of the late hour and the change of time zone, they were tired so they returned to the Brown Palace and planned to leave mid morning tomorrow. Carrie was relieved that they were staying in Denver as she did not feel secure about flying over the Rockies at night.

So they discreetly left the dinner, first Beardsley and then Carrie. Stopping at the bar off the lobby, they took a booth in the corner and celebrated with a mojito. After two more drinks, Carrie took the lead.

"I am glad we are staying here tonight. Night flying is not for me. They don't have blinking red lights on top of the Rockies. This was quite a night for both of us. You were the star of the dinner and I got to be the next second vice president of this group. I am bushed; I am ready to call it a night. Let me find my key."

"Sounds good to me, I am tired too. The talk drained my energy---most of my energy."

When they made their way to their room on the 19th floor, at the end of the hall, of course, Beardsley got a second wind.

"No sense messing up two rooms. May I come in?"

"You dirty old man. You want to stay in my room? That is pretty brazen, I hardly know you. But it may be interesting." She paused. "Get your things, I will leave the door open."

He returned in about 30 seconds with his carryon bag, ran into the bathroom, brushed his teeth, sprayed on some more deodorant and popped a Viagra before he put on his game pants, Ralph Lauren boxer shorts. He looked at the little horse on the side of the leg and smiled. "I bet the Polo insignia will impress Carrie."

She was a little more reserved, even nervous, for it has been a long time she spent a night with Beardsley. That was an unplanned meeting when she was on a trip to New Mexico with a group visiting art galleries and attending a course on Navajo Rugs at the American Research Institute in Santa Fe. He was attending the board meeting of Children's Hospital Executives. They met by accident at the Pink Adobe where they both had a few extra margaritas and the Pink Adobe steak dinner. Then he invited her to come to the bar at La Fonda. More margaritas and soon they were in his room. No question that the high altitude played a part in this lustful explosion. There was also a little bit of payback in Beardsley's case, as he was still jealous of all the prestige and adulation that surgeons got while administration took all the blame for their attempts to balance the budget and for all their political games that they played to grab more power from the egocentric MD's. Carrie justified her dalliance as she had just weathered another bout of Carter's infidelity. Whatever the motives, that night was memorable both for the passion and for the intensity. Richard and Carrie agreed that this was a one night hook up and for their respective positions and obligations, they should reset to default positions prior to this night.

That system worked for 10 years until this award pulled them together to discuss the plans for the talk and the trip. Beardsley had noticed a change in her conversation and body language. He sensed she was either facing mid life with concern about the effects of age and gravity or she was putting herself back into play as Carter was aging and no doubt, testosterone deficient. Beardsley was no one to pass up an opportunity for another engagement so he decided to send out feelers and see what happened. Carrie took the bait, she immediately sensed the tone of his conversation and decided that one more night with Beardsley would be fun and without victims or remorse. Who would know and what could happen?

Carrie sat in the chair by the window as she checked out the What's Happening in Denver book until Beardsley got in bed, trying to act nonchalant. She went into the bathroom, decided to take a shower, put on perfume, brush her teeth and don her special black negligee that she got at Neimans. She had thought about going to Victoria's Secret but if Carter saw the charge from there, he would get suspicious. Her Neiman's charge was so full each month; he would most likely miss seeing a purchase from the lingerie department. When she entered the bedroom, Beardsley looked up; his agitated movement belied the nonchalant image he was trying to project. He started to lick his lips when he saw her come towards the bed. He was right. She had, no doubt, breast augmentation. He was not sure about some work on her nose. She looked like someone had glued on two plastic milk bottles that extended at least 4-5 inches from the rib cage while the rest of her had a Renoir like softness with gradual curves.

"You are staring."

"I see you have had some additions or did my memory go bad?"

"You noticed?"

"How could I miss? Do I need a flack jacket before I devour you or is it part of S and M. Come here, let me see.

"Keep you hands off my treasure. Maybe you have a silicon allergy."

"Never had any allergies."

Deciding to forgo her planned Salome type dance, she dropped the negligee and hopped onto the bed. She too, was ready for action.

They attacked each other with more intensity than either had displayed at home for many years. Beardsley was always a hands on manager and this was no different. He explored her body, avoiding the silicone zone. Always a little paranoid, he was afraid that they may rupture and he would get silicosis. Better seen than felt. As they faced each other, Beardsley moved into frenzied motion for 20 seconds and then rolled over on his side, breathing heavily.

"Are you done?" Carrie asked?

"For that one but I think there is more coming."

"That was all you got?" "Maybe you could use some Viagra."

"I took a Viagra and a Cialis too."

That broke the spell. The Viagra effect was gone. Seems that words trump pills.

"Give me some time to recharge." He was off to the bathroom to pop another blue pill.

"Don't worry we have more time and more places to see."

"I will be right back and let me see what I can ....."

All this travel, speeches and activity wore Beardsley out, he fell asleep."

Carrie smiled at the bedroom performance. She was laughing to herself, forgetting about his old nickname- Little Dick. It was true about big Porsche, little penis. You would think that guys like Beardsley would not advertise their anatomical deficiency by driving a Mercedes or a 911. I am sure he does not get the symbolism. Maybe things would improve after the tension of trying too hard was over.

The next morning, they were both smiling and happy for a change. After getting a cup of coffee in the lobby, Beardsley went to the manager, complaining about the cleanliness of his room, not telling him that he did not sleep there. The manager, gracefully issued Beardsley a refund. He kept the bill so he could turn it in with his travel expenses. Proud of his own quick thinking, he grabbed Carrie's bag and they took a cab to the airport and left for Santa Fe about 10AM.

"Private jet is the only way to go," said Beardsley as he sat back in the soft leather chair. Carrie poured some coffee in the galley and they became quiet looking at the Rocky Mountain peaks. "That may be Aspen. Looks like a lot of ski lifts off to the left."

"I like Aspen in the summer for the music. Not much into skiing."

"Yes, chamber music is better high in the mountains."

"Have you ever been to the Aspen Institute?"

"What kind of medicine does the Institute specialize?"

" It's an intellectual institute, Richardson. When do we land in Santa Fe?"

"Not too much longer, I suspect. With a private plane we can go directly to Santa Fe; we don't have to use the Albuquerque airport like the commercial planes do."

"What is the agenda?"

"Get to the hotel and resume our exercises."

338

"Is there anything else to do? I want to go gallery hopping. They have a few museums for Indian and folk art. Of course there are many restaurants. What kind of food do you like?"

"All foods that is my weakness. Suggestions?"

"There is a great place for guacamole and a must according to the book is breakfast at Pasquales. Then, outside of Mexican food, you get a lot of average to above average international menus. The book says that they are there when you get tired of Mexican food."

"Sounds good. Let me see the guide book."

Beardsley was more interested if Mexican food would not cause another flame out like last night; he wanted nothing to impede the bed-time activities for the next two nights.

There was a car rental agency at the Santa Fe airport but no cars at the moment. Usually Beardsley would have unleashed his rage at the clerk at the Hertz counter, but today he was trying to show his best behavior in front of Carrie. She was staring at the mountains to the East and the incredible New Mexican blue sky. While they were waiting for the car, Beardsley asked the clerk at the rental desk if she would recommend a hotel.

"Bishop's Lodge. This time of year it is quiet with no noisy kids that are there in the summer. I can call there and make a reservation."

"Quiet, you say. Sounds good to me. Ring them up." Fifteen minutes later they settled into the red Mustang convertible and headed north to Bishop Lodge.

"Let's stop in town and look around. How about lunch at The Shed. Do you remember being there before?"

"Of course, sounds good to me."

The Shed, hidden in a court yard was unchanged. The blue corn enchiladas covered in chili were as delicate as before. Delicate for an enchilada covered with chili, that is. They shared a flaum and finished the meal with an espresso for Carrie and a cappuccino for Beardsley, who caused the waiter to raise his eyebrow who knew that it was too late for a cappuccino according to his Milanese upbringing. After lunch they did some window shopping and looking at galleries. Across the street, they saw looked at the windows of James Reid Ltd. "Those beautiful belt buckles and tips are incredible."

Then across the plaza and upstairs to Packard's to see the Kachina dolls, as the book suggested. Since they did not know what they were looking at, they were awed by the prices. The salesman, a tall man with a grey pigtail and turquoise bolo, was ready for some visitors so he could explain the origins of the types of dolls as well as the history of the carver. He politely corrected Carrie, telling her that the real name was Katsina, not Kachina. Beardsley made a note to get brushed up on Indian crafts.

The artisans sitting under the overhang at the Palace of the Governors were more their speed. So much turquoise and silver to choose from. Beardsley bought an inexpensive bracelet for his secretary. Continuing down the street, they stopped by a few galleries before reaching the LewAllen gallery, where some interesting paintings by Daniel Morper, railroad scenes with beautiful sunsets and cityscapes attracted their attention. Linda, a saleslady, who initially ignored them as she thought they were typical gallery walkers, changed her attitude when she saw Carrie's diamond ring. Must be three carets she thought. So she left her desk, paged the manager and approached them.

"Did you see anything you liked? Our gallery has the best high end art in Santa Fe."

"We like everything."

"Have you seen the jewelry by Gail Bird and Yazzie Johnson? They are our Santa Fe Tiffany quality artists. These are beautiful ear rings with Petersite & Kyamite set in silver. Here is a spectacular belt buckle of pictorial jasper set in gold was a mere $800. It would look so nice on you, sir. How do you like these ear rings?"

"I'll have to work on my husband. Maybe he feels he owes me a gift or feels guilty about missing my birthday. I will work on him."

"He looks like he is ready to buy you something."

"He will in time, after I work on him."

"You have a beautiful Gallery. I like those Morales sculpture. Out of my price range for a rock with cutouts. I will be back to spend some time with a few of the paintings upstairs. And I love that jewelry. Gail Bird did you say? We are new here so do you recommend any other gallery?"

"Have you been to Peters on Peralta? That is a place to see. They have more traditional works than we do but many very good artists are shown there too."

"We are off. May I have your card in case the old man gets happy?"

"He looks pretty happy now."

"That is just the start."

They got back in the car and headed east. The Peter's gallery, a modern adobe building looked very Santa Fe. Inside the large gallery rooms displayed a variety of Southwestern painters of early 20th century and modern times. Without knowing anything about art, Carrie was attracted to realistic landscapes by local artist Woody Gwyn. Most of his paintings were meticulous renditions of New Mexican landscapes and California beach scenes with mist and large rocks. He painted each blade of grass and every tree branch. The colorful composition made the total effect quite pleasing and provided both a memory of the area as well as eye opener to force the viewer to relook at landscapes that are usually taken for granted. The prices in the gallery were reasonable for collectors but a shock to these two Easterners who did not appreciate Santa Fe paintings.

"Enough of art, let's head to the hotel. Maybe a nap before dinner?

On the way out on Bishop's Lodge Road, Carrie looked over at Richardson and congratulated him. "I am glad we are going out of town to Bishop's Lodge. As you know, Carter is in Santa Fe but I am sure he will stay at the El Dorado where the meeting is held. He needs to be with his group to see how his former trainees are doing and soak up their adoration."

In ten minutes, they arrived at the Bishop's Lodge, parked the mustang in the guest checking in spot and entered the office.

"Yes, Mr. Beardsley, we have your room in the Sunset Lodge. They are newly renovated, I am sure the décor will meet with your approval."

"Does it have a fireplace? I hear the nights are chilly here."

"Of course, and we have a new heating system to complement the air conditioning for the summer guests."

"Thanks for the update but I doubt if I would need extra heat. Just like to look at the flames in the fireplace."

The room was better than described, very New Mexican with vigas in the ceiling, a horno-esque fireplace with pinion wood and paper all ready for lighting. The bathroom, minimalist but spacious including a large shower with four heads. Beardsley made another note to include such a shower set up in his office in the new hospital. The bed was like the ones in the Ritz Carlton, firm inside with a soft cover. He fell asleep. Carrie sat by the fire and read about what to do in Santa Fe. She found an interesting restaurant El Nido at Tesuque, at the junction of Bishop Lodge & State Rd. 591. The name of the place Tesuque intrigued her as did the past history of the place that noted it was a bordello in the early 20th century. She would later discover that many restaurants in the area claimed that they were once a bordello. She also liked the furniture style of the Southwest. Maybe she would refurnish her summer home at the Jersey shore with a Santa Fe look. She then opened the book, <u>Death comes to the Archbishop</u> by Willa Cather, a must read for all the guest of the Bishop's Lodge as the Archbishop Lamy the principle in the book had a chapel that still stands on the hotel's grounds. "Oh, I see why they call it the Bishop's Lodge. Makes sense now."

Even though Beardsley had planned to go to Gabrielle's for their famous guacamole, they decided to go to El Nido, closer to the hotel. The road to Tesuque passed by many large and small homes, the old timers mixed with the parvenus who had scooped up the real estate over that past 20 years. Downtown Tesuque consisted of the post office, a small food market that also served meals and El Nido. They entered into the bar filled by the locals who had a motorcycle gang look in black T shirts and tattoos and the wannabe cowboys in designer shirts and jeans, and $800 boots. Dinner of Rocky Mountain Trout with the usual 5 added features including the requisite sun dried tomatoes and organic vegetables topped by some organic spices crowded on the plate. Sauvignon Blanc from the Russian River in Sonoma was perfect. They chatted like a couple on the first date. Beardsley, losing his executive airs turned out to be rather charming, a welcome contrast to his usual conniving way. Carrie seemed relieved to be away from Carter with his domineering "I am a surgeon" attitude which helped her enjoy the dinner and the feng shui effect of the old whorehouse. She was rapidly slipping into the groove of most new arrivals that fell in love with the area. "I would like to check out the real estate office to find what homes were available."

"Take it easy. You know we are at 7000 feet and you are low on oxygen. You need to come here a few times before you think about buying a house here."

"I have not been this relaxed in years; just makes me think about the future."

"Before you get into any more trouble, let's get out of here."

Back at Bishop's Lodge, things worked out better than the night in Denver. Amazing what a relaxing dinner in a nice atmosphere could do for the libido. Beardsley performed better but was a little short of breath. "I guess the elevation was getting to me," was all he could say to cover up his lack of conditioning.

Carter and his friend did make it to Gabrielle's on his cousin's recommendation. "I hear they have the best guacamole in the world and the best margaritas in the Southwest. I have been around and need to taste them and see if the claim was justified. In addition to my rule is you judge a Mexican restaurant by the salsa, you also have to check out the cleanliness of the place. I never ate in a great Mexican restaurant that was really clean."

The beautiful sunset ride to Gabrielle's gave a yellow glow to the opera house on the left and the casino near camel rock on the right. Finally he took the turnoff from route 84, made a sharp turn past another large casino complex and finally saw the sign for Gabrielles. At the top of the driveway they turn right and found a parking space in the first row. "There are a lot of cars here; that is a good sign." This first impression was substantiated by a high Zagat rating at the doorway. The receptionist told them there would be a short wait for a table to open so they hit the bar and ordered margaritas and sampled the salsa. Carter frowned. "The salsa passes muster but the margarita is disappointing." He turned to the bar tender "has the recipe changed? This is not what I expected."

"Yes, when the old owner sold the place, then called Las Brisas, the recipe changed too. It used to be made with fresh limes and pineapple juice but no more. Regular margaritas are what we have."

"I hope I did not make a mistake coming to this place. I did not think of new owners would change the recipe to save a few bucks. But we are here and maybe the famous guacamole will live up to the hype."

The table did open up and the waiter instantly appeared to ask about drinks and if they wanted guacamole.

"Yes and yes."

In an instant the table was changed into an operating room, relaxing Carter a little. Carlos, the ersatz surgeon approached the table with a stainless steel cart with trays of avocados, limes, onions, cilantro, peppers, tomatoes, garlic and a few items that he could not see.

"Here we go." Carlos cut through the avocado, popped out the large central seed and scooped out the meat into a stone bowl. He repeated this with a second avocado.

"Do you want everything?"

"Of course, the works," Carter answered, feeling better that he was back giving orders and hoping this was going to live up to the reputation of being the best. Then Carlos added all the ingredients in the trays into the gray rock bowl, mashed the mixture with a fork and presented the guacamole as an obstetrician would present a newly delivered baby to the parents. Carter was so excited with the culinary exercise that he almost used his fingers to get started with the tasting. He caught himself and picked up the tortilla chips, forgetting to offer one to his companion. Both agreed that this was the best, the really best.

"Penultimate" Carter smacked his lips as he described the appetizer.

"Penultimate, you mean that there is a better one this?"

Realizing he may not know the meaning of penultimate, he moved on. "Who cares about definitions when we are in heaven? I guess that is why I didn't get an A in semantics."

He gulped down the second margarita and ordered another.

"I could stop here and fill up on this, I don't need all the calories and fat in avocado. The rest of the meal was very good. Carnitas and chicken fajitas were so much better than anything that they could get in the East. The conversation was light and non-revealing. Carter dominated the talking, mostly about himself. She was content to be in the Southwest, realizing that this was a fling, a free travel ticket that was paid back with a little sex. She had many encounters with men who took her to Olive Garden or Ruby Tuesday and expected some bed action at the end of the evening. At least this time she had a trip to Santa Fe and a piece of turquoise jewelry as a gift for her companionship. No complaints from this modern liberated miss. Since she did not charge for her companionship she felt there was a difference between what she was doing and what an escort service could provide. This was really a date as she knew Carter before this trip. Made sense to her. Carter was so consumed with his exploits that he did not ask her any questions, personal or general. She wondered what Mrs. Randolf was like. He did not talk about her, but obviously something was amiss in their relationship. She did not pry.

They were both in good moods on the trip back to the hotel. Like any trip, the home bound part seemed shorter than the trip to the restaurant. They got back to their room in the Sunset Lodge, lit a fire and had another glass of wine. Talk about a mood set.

"Ready for bed?" Carter asked.

"Yes, let me get in the bathroom first, if you don't mind."

"Yes, ladies first."

Carter had time to plan the rest of the evening. He would sleep on the side near the bathroom as he usually had to get up several times each night although he denied it was a prostate problem. With all the drinking, he would definitely need to be near the bathroom tonight. He took his Cialis, put out a "do not disturb" sign on the door and locked it three times to make sure no one could come in. While he was fiddling with the locks, she got into bed and pulled up the covers. That was somewhat of a disappointment for part of the excitement was to see her young cellulite free body glide across the room. Well, he missed scene one so the rest of the play would include more important activities. He jumped into the shower, dried off with the soft towels, combed his hair, took a swig of mouth wash and put on the terry cloth robe. He came into the bedroom, turned off the lights and slipped into bed. He jumped when he heard a scream from next door. It was not a danger scream but a cowboy yell. "HOO-HA. GET'EM COWGIRL!"

"That voice sounds familiar but who would I know in this out of the way hotel in New Mexico? I don't know a soul in New Mexico. Must be a loud mouth Texan."

He rolled over on his side and could feel that she did not have a night gown on. She felt his hand and remarked, "Naked in New Mexico, I love to sleep in the nude. Is that OK?"

"OK," he thought. Wow. He could tell the Cialis was working. This was going to be a memorable night. He had not been in bed with her prior to this trip so he was a little tense about making a good first impression. Then he was hit with a pang of guilt. Maybe he should have been more attentive to his wife back home but they lost all their bedroom desires years ago but he now knew he missed the old days. He felt he was a great lover. She did not say a word to him because she was not sure what he was doing, lots of grabbing, the usual moans finished off by a long aahhh. Not bad, she thought, but he did not qualify for the top lovers of Santa Fe, even though he was the only contestant so far. She did not hear another sound from him except for the heavy breathing of deep sleep, a waste of a long acting Cialis pill.

When they awoke in the morning, he was all smiles but a little edgy.

"I am hungry. Let's hit Pasquale's for breakfast. I read about this place in the book which claimed it was the best breakfast in the Southwest. I don't question the authority, assuming it would be good, if not the best, but to be honest I do worry about book recommendations in hotel rooms. You know they pay for the ads in the book."

"Let's go before it gets crowded."

Down the hall, Beardsley also woke up in with a smile on his face. Carrie had already gotten out of bed, dressed and was sitting near the fireplace, reading more about Archbishop Lamy. She had already walked up to his chapel, a small building near the registration office. She had definitely unwound from the hectic life at home, the tensions at home with Carter and the committees. It felt good not to be pressurized by so called important tasks.

"Give me a minute to get dressed and we can go Pedro's, Pasquale's, one of those names. How are you? Did you sleep well? As you know, I got knocked out early. Hope I did not disappoint you."

"No disappointment, I feel good, so good that maybe I will never go home. But first, I could use some coffee. Hope this place has some good brew." About 30 minutes later they were off to breakfast in town.

No disappointment for Carter. They got to Pasquale's early so there was no waiting line. Luckily they got the last available booth. The waiter immediately poured coffee and announced that they were out of the organic celery but did have watermelon radishes. "Let me check the menu, Hey this coffee is great. Do you roast your own beans?"

"Not yet. We get the best organic beans from Julio's in El Dorado."

The menu was, as expected, fully organic - every item had descriptions denoting its whole grain, hormone free, home made, free range status. Carter selected Papas fritas, a chopped potato dish with cheese, chilies and various diced up herbs, estimated calorie count above 2600. "Give me a Pasquale omelet, coffee and toast"

In a few minutes the plate arrived, a most cholesterol filled delight. "Well, I hope the exercise from last night will burn up some of these calories. It is a tasty mixture somewhat like the guacamole last night. How is your omelet?"

Exotic! Cheese, tomatoes, peppers and a side of chilies. Fresh squeezed orange juice, incredible home made multigrain toast. Just great. And the coffee, the best! Good choice Carter."

Carter beamed at the compliment; his stomach was full but not his ego which always had more room for words of praise. This was the first time she called him Carter, instead of Dr. Randolf.

• • •

By the time Beardsley and Carrie got to Pasquale's there was a line of about 15 people waiting to get in for breakfast. One tall man with

University of Tulsa on his sweatshirt announced that he was told there would be a 30 minute waiting time.

"I would not wait 30 minutes for breakfast, if Guy Savoy cooked it." Beardsley liked to drop names of famous chefs, even if he had never been to Guy Savoy's Paris restaurant. Bunky Churchill told him that Guy Savoy was her favorite restaurant even before it received another star from Michelin. Typical Beardsley mispronounced Guy Savoy by using the American way. Carrie turned her head, impressed with his culinary knowledge but not his French. She had been to Guy Savoy several times with Carter. She also questioned his lack of judgment on how long to wait for a good meal. Beardsley moved past Pasquale's and headed up Don Gaspar towards San Francisco Street. He scanned the area and saw Tia Sophia restaurant.

"Look there are people leaving that restaurant so there will be no waiting. I'm for that."

Tia Sophia was old Santa Fe, dark, a long line of booths and tables. Best of all the cooking odors predicted good food ahead.

"This place is for me- no waiting, lots of local looking people and a friendly host. Let's sit down."

They ordered huevas rancheros with home fries and coffee. They did not say much except comments on the various people in the room, a collection of Santa Fe residents wearing long skirts, colorful blouses, a bunch of obese cute kids and a few old grannies. When the food arrived, Beardsley attacked the omelet as if he had not eaten in days.

"That hits the spot. This place is better than that other dump, and we did not have to wait either."

"I wonder why the books do not mention this restaurant."

"Time to hit Canyon road."

Carrie agreed since she had read about all the galleries on Canyon road. They decided to walk up hill, forgetting again about the altitude. By the time they got half way up the road, they were slowing down, waiting to catch their breath. ---So many artists, so many artifacts.

About the same time, the two at Tia Sophia had finished their breakfast; Carter paid the bill at Pasquale's, and then asked the cashier where to find the best Santa Fe Galleries. She told them about Canyon Road and it was a long walk up a steep hill. Carter thanked her and headed for the car.

"I am not here to set any endurance records, as far as walking up hills, that is. This time of year, I am sure we can get a parking place. I hear it is murder here in the summer season." They rode up Canyon Road and found a parking place across from the Bodega. "Perfect" he proudly proclaimed. "Let's go into this place and see what they have. The Bodega was just what old Santa Fe looked like before the invasion of Benetton, Gap and Starbucks. Many long skirts and peasant blouses, long beaded necklaces and antique concha belts. Being in a good relaxed mood, Carter said "pick out an outfit that makes you look real Santa Fe. I want to give you something that will help you remember this trip."

"Thanks but you already bought me this turquoise piece. The blue sky and the fresh air are enough memories."

At the bottom of the hill, Beardsley ran in and out of the shops and galleries.

"I wonder how many of these bowls are really old. I never saw such prices for clay with a little color as he looked at a variety of Santo Domingo dough bowls. Next some interesting black pots and plates. "Who is this Maria? Her plates are 8000 dollars! For one plate! I do admit they are nice but at those prices, I need to know more about these. I suspect a racket of some sort. I can usually smell one a mile away."

Carrie was surprised for this was the first time that he admitted that he did know all there was about a topic. He made a note to buy a book on Maria and see what her deal was. She must be something special to command such prices. The Morning Star Gallery was another shocker. "$4000 for a kids drawing of Indians done on lined paper!"

The sales lady smiled. "These were from a ledger book, done in the 19th century by Indians who were trying to preserve images of their culture by drawing primitive figures on the lined paper."

"I bet I could get the kids at the hospital to draw me a few of these pictures for nothing. No one would know the difference."

The saleslady smiled while Carrie raised her eye brows.

Before he made a total ass of himself, she led him past the antique baskets. He did notice the price tags of $2000 and kept his mouth shut about the prices but wondered if they could upgrade the hospital gift shop to have items like this.

At the next gallery across the street, he stopped at a well worn basket and scowled. "This basket is only $4500; there must be something wrong with it. Why so cheap?"

The climb up the road got steeper. "I guess this is what racers mean when they say they hit the wall. I have seen enough, maybe we could head back and I could get to the spa. I have an appointment for a massage at 2PM."

"Fine with me. My feet are telling me to quit. This is a fascinating place, I love it here! But starting out in small dose seems prudent."

"You go to the spa and I will ride around some more after I drop you off."

Carter, coming down Canyon Road, expressed similar fatigue as they approached the Alexandra Stevens gallery not knowing that Beardsley and Carrie were inside finishing up their gallery hopping. "I have had it. I can't do one more gallery today. All the things start to look alike. It's time to end the hike here, after all, the way back to the car is straight up hill, I have no interest in going into that gallery to see one more sunset painting or cowboy sitting next to the camp fire. It is time to head back to the hotel." The long day and the long walk made Carter a little testy. "Maybe I will take a hike around the grounds; I see they have a map of trails. What do you want to do?"

"Maybe hit the massage table at the spa," she replied.

"Be my guest, I am not a big one for massages but by all means, you should get one. Let's head back. I have to rest up a little for the big dinner tonight."

Back at the hotel, Kirby Jackson, was on the phone to the hospital to check once more on the condition of Tommy Morris, the transplant patient. "He did what? How the hell did that happen? Did you go back in to re-attach the ureter? Sorry, of course you did. I was shocked that this happened. Did he have a coughing spell? Did he fall out of bed? The sutures loosened up! That's impossible, my stitches are the best in the East. So how is he doing now? Good, good. What did the parents say? Of course, I will talk with them. They know I am out of town and I signed out to you. But I want to talk with them. Call me on the cell when you see them. I will wait for your call here. Thanks old man, for all your help I owe you more than one."

"What happened?"

"A suture line broke and his ureter started to leak. His urine leaked into his abdomen. Fortunately, he was in the ICU and on antibiotics." I never had this happen before. Maybe I hurried too much. I guess I should have taken more time to prepare the ureter, but I was in a hurry. Now, I am waiting to talk to the parents."

The phone rings, Kirby did not answer immediately, trying not to appear anxious.

"Dr. Jackson speaking. Hello, Mr. Morris, I am so sorry to hear about the complication. I take full responsibility for the surgery and likewise for the complications. I have never had leakage at the suture lines of the kidney tube. But it does happen. I am glad that they detected it and tell me, how is Tommy doing now? .....Good, I am glad to hear that. I feel badly that I was out of town when it happened but Dr. Warren filled me in with the details. Yes, he is an excellent surgeon, I agree. That is why I feel secure when I signed out to him. I expect to be back tomorrow night and will go straight to the hospital. You can get my cell phone from the doctor there so you can call me whenever you need to contact me. And let me have yours. Right, right, 984 good, I got it."

MaryAnn was glad to have a break from the bedroom. The king sized bed was much better than the exam table in Kirby's office. But as her grandmother said, "enough was sufficient." "I need a dip in the hot tub to take down some of the swelling from last night." She was walking like she had been horse back riding but she was afraid of horses so that was only a description, not the source of her gait.

Kirby liked horses so he decided to go to the stables and ride around the trails. He was not a horseman but was sure he could find an old horse that would not throw him.

MaryAnn did go into the hot tub. It was delicious. She stayed there for about 20 minutes and then headed back for a nap, not upset to be alone for awhile.

Carrie stopped by the front office to mail a letter and headed for the spa.

"Am I late?"

"No ma'am" We are not busy this time of year. Oddly, today we have another lady from New Jersey before you. Are you on a convention?"

"No, I am here for a few days to get away but I think I have caught the Santa Fe virus and will have to stay here until I get over it, if that is possible."

"Just stay away from the realtors. They love people like you. Buy this year, sell next year."

"OK, what do you suggest for me now?"

"From the look on your face, I think you would like our Adobe massage."

"What ever you say."

The massage had the classic Santa Fe fluff, herb wraps, ground pearls in avocado paste and a variety of eclectic aromas rubbed in the skin." After an hour on the massage table, Rosa, the masseuse lit a pinion candle and bought a fresh terry cloth robe to Carrie.

"I am so relaxed; it's hard for me to get off the table."

"You have a lot of things going on in your life; I can feel it in your muscles."

"Yes, but you seem to be getting them out of me with those strong hands. I should see you every week. This is heaven."

"You can stay in the room as long as you like. Maybe you will find the vibrating chair will continue your relaxation experience."

Carrie, a little wobbly, made her way past the fireplace to the black leather chair covered with pale green towels.

"That is perfect. Let me close my eyes."

Even the wail of background music seemed perfect for the experience. Memories came back of good and bad times, friends not seen for many years, choices she had made and opportunities rejected. She was almost in tears as she thought how much tension there was in her life. About 20 minutes later, but it seemed like a month, she woke up, feeling much better and certainly more relaxed so she slid into the warm pool in the next room and picked a spot near the jets that continued her back massage. She liked the Mexican wall tiles and the vigas on the ceiling. At the far end of the room she noticed plastic flaps separated the indoor pool from the heated outside pool. She ducked under the partition and settled on the bench facing the Sangre de Cristo Mountains to the west. The afternoon sun highlighted the rocky surface areas in shades of blue, purple and pink. Her skin was tingling; she had not been this relaxed for years. After finishing her thoughts about her past wins and losses, she began to plan her future. She made a resolve to start the next phase of her life with new vigor and less pressure--- she would start right now.

The background music switched to Liza Minnelli singing New York, New York. Carrie was so immobile she could not even tap out the rhythm as she usually did when Liza sang that song. This song was followed by Somewhere Over the Rainbow, an apt choice for as she was staring at the mountains, the shadows, the clouds- "How could one top this experience?" she asked herself. When she looked to the right of the mountain peak and got her answer. While she was asleep, the afternoon rain shower came and left with a rainbow- she felt paralyzed by this sensory overload, wishing she could paint the scene and preserve this feeling and the aroma of the air. She now realized how far she and Carter had drifted apart over the years as they delved into their work and ambitions, missing the companionship that they had in the early years. Maybe that is why she was here with Richardson. He was a good travel companion and OK lover but his ego tended to dampen the emotional experience. She wished she had children but she accepted that emptiness. It was clear that Carter seemed too egocentric to share with another generation moreover he was addicted to the glory of the OR and the praise from grateful parents. The unlimited need for stroking of his ego and few other interests kept him close to the hospital and away from her. Now it was too late to think of children since he had the vasectomy this year. She was trying to figure out how to redo her remaining life, not that she wanted to dump Carter but that was also a last resort option. Hopefully, she could try to rekindle the feelings she originally had for him. She was definitely through with the creep Beardsley. After last night, it was time for the sorry dear I have a migraine routine. She also considered the plus and minus of going back to school or taking up some new craft when the plastic flaps parted and a young blonde's head arose from the steamy water.

"Spectacular, isn't it. Oops did I wake you up? Sorry."

"No, I was far away in a new life, I mean new world. This place really gets to you, doesn't it?"

"I have never been in such a relaxed mood, this air, the mountains, this hotel; not the way I usually spend my days. I think I work too hard, I have too many pressures."

'Don't we all? I think it takes something like this to put life into focus or maybe to unfocus it, if you know what I mean."

"Right, right, right. Maybe it refocuses things rather than unfocuses them. I may just never go home."

"Have you been here before?"

"No this is my first time but I am converted to the Southwestern life. All I need is a rich husband and I will be here every day. I love the air, the sky, the colors, the smells. I had a great dinner at a place called Gabrielle's last night. Amazing guacamole! Today had breakfast at Pasquales and then hit the Canyon Road scene. I came here with a friend who knows how to show me a good time, day and night. He is so much fun, so caring about me and making sure I see everything. He even bought me this turquoise."

"Very pretty. I was on Canyon Road too. We did not make it to Pasquales, the line was too long. Your friend must like you a lot. He sounds great, you should marry him?"

"No, I am not here to get married. Wow! I see you are, How many carats is that ring?"

"Just three."

"Beautiful, what a wonderful engagement ring!"

"This is not an engagement ring; I got it after a slight indiscretion on my husband's part. Not the seven year itch, but a 5 year fling with someone at work. I was very understanding and this was the payback. You must have heard that joke about the lady that looked at her big ring and said "My ring is lonesome; it is time for him to have another affair."

"No, I never heard that one. But I get the point. How long have you been married?"

"20 years. I was a child bride and he was an old bachelor that worked too hard or maybe had too much fun being single. I doubt the latter as he is deeply religious and does not seem to be the kind that chases around. I am not sure why he had the three carat affair. But we got back together again. He loves his work and provides well for me. Not just for the diamonds but he is a decent person and was a good companion."

"Was?"

"What are you a psychiatrist? I was just thinking before you came in the hot tub, how things have changed in my life and was pondering the changes I could make. I guess though, when I get back home, I will fall back into the trap of daily living, keeping the traditions going and worrying too much about what others think. It is a shame that we cannot bottle up this Santa Fe feeling and take it with us back home.

"I saw in one of those tourist stores, that they sell a can of Santa Fe air. It was on the plaza, right near Starbucks."

"Well, let me inspect you. Young, good looking, great body but no ring. Let me see that turquoise you have around your neck. Green, very interesting."

"Yes apparently, it comes from the Cerrillos mines. People who know turquoise can tell which mine it come from by the color and pattern of yellow, brown or black. My traveling friend got it for me."

"He has good taste. It is a knockout. My husband would never have the taste to pick something so delicate like that stone."

"But you have the big diamond. I have a green stone."

"Oh you will have your chance, don't rush into things. You have plenty of time. Seems like you don't need that advice from me. You look like you are capable of making good decisions."

"Not all the time. I should not be here; I am with someone from my job. One of those working too close and too late at night things. Little by little we started to get too intimate and now, I know it is wrong, but in a funny way, I enjoy being with him. He is so different at work and here. He actually wore cowboy boots today. He says they are comfortable, I can't believe that but everyone says that. How did you and your husband find this place?"

"I am not sure how my friend found it."

"Your friend, not your husband?"

"Oops, I guess the truth serum in this water got to me. My husband would never come to a place like this, although he would like the chapel on the grounds, even though it is not a Protestant church. He works and he goes to church. That about does his spectrum of activities. Our life is what you call civil. No issues, but no spark. Maybe my ovaries fell asleep. Maybe he has a girlfriend, but I doubt that as he is more than religious. You know the anti-abortion type, for low taxes, voted Republican, had a vasectomy to show the world that that is a way to limit the population. I guess I had a weak moment and came here with a man that was attending a meeting with me in Denver. I should not have not done this but I have to admit that I am having a good time. The sex is not that great; seems he does a better job talking then performing. This experience has my juices flowing like the old days, twenty years ago. I even feel sexy at times, a strange feeling from the past. I wish my husband and I could share these moments, sights and romantic times. He loves to operate and politic in the hospital with all the big shots but he doesn't know what he is missing. Tomorrow I will be gone and be back in the real world. You know about the Santa Fe virus?"

"Santa Fe virus?"

"Yes, it is a strange disease. It does not make you sick; you just want to be in Santa Fe. You cannot cure it so you have to keep coming back, like an immunization shot. Keep returning and you won't get other symptoms of the disease. I forgot. You also have to buy a lot of turquoise to keep the virus from spreading. I have never seen it written up in a medical book, but believe me, it is real. I have a big dose of it."

"Maybe it is altitude sickness. I hear that is a problem at 7000 feet."

"No, that is a real illness; I got a mild case of altitude sickness in Telluride, you know it is 9000 feet at the base and 11000 at the top of the ski run. Headache, vomiting and breathing difficulty. Believe me, I know the difference between altitude sickness and Santa Fe virus."

"I understand, now. I think I have been bitten too."

"Do you think your friend is the one for you? I mean to make it more permanent?"

"Oh, no, he is married. But to tell the truth, I enjoy the experience; I have never been involved with a married man. Some advantages as more free time since there is no way we would live together. I was married once but for a short time. I made the mistake of not living with him before we married. I did not know what a slob he was. Just dropped his clothes wherever. I tried to make it work but it was too much work and he was not really worth it. So we split before we had kids. Better that way. I like being single but not too single, if you know what I mean. "

"You must have a lot of beaus."

"I have my share but could do better. I love work and spend a lot of late hours trying to catch up with all I have to do. You know the routine. Work hard and you get more work to do. I always think I am not doing enough so I take on every assignment that is offered. I don't know how to say no."

"Sounds like you need a coach that will help you say no. Sometimes saying yes gets you to nice places, like this hotel. But it saying no is difficult."

"Are you available? You hit it right on the button. I cannot say no. Maybe that explains how I got into a bad situation at work and this trip. No complaints but I know it is not right and so does he. I think this trip has cleared up a lot of questions that I have been unable to think about. Are you sure you don't want to be my coach?"

"No, I think I need one for myself. Maybe I will coach myself. But I know what the right thing to do, I don't want to upset my husband, he has been so kind to me. I know this affair will end tomorrow when I go home. Believe me, I have had enough of my friend and got the fling urge out of my system. Our situations are too complicated for us to continue, even if we wanted to. Right now, I don't want to, I think my behavior was more of a reaction than an attraction."

"I like that. Probably applies to me. I was tired of the bar scene, on line dating and young hustlers who were more interested in the bed room than my brain. I have more trouble than this trip. I think I am on to some financial hanky-panky at my job. I suspect that my boss is doing some things that are illegal. But I am here for this fling, and it is a fling. I intend to end when I get home, even if he wants to continue, which I doubt. I let this nice talking man get me here but I am stronger than that. This trip was special; the things that attracted you to the area also affected me the same way. I enjoyed the art, the food and culture. I can't believe I am telling you all this. But obviously, I have been bothered and needed to talk. Do you take Blue Cross insurance for this hour?"

"I was just going to ask you the same question. I feel better just talking to you."

"What was the name of the restaurant that you went to last night? Maybe you would join us? If it was so good, you might like to return for more."

"I would love to but my friend has dinner plans tonight. I am so full, I think I will eat some cheese and crackers and call it a day or night. The place is Gabriele's. They will give you directions at the desk. It is right out 84 north."

"Nice to talk to you, I hope to meet you again to get a progress report. My name is Caroline, but they call me Carrie."

"Caroline. I am Caroleen. I guess it has the French patina as I come from Lyon. Caroline, Caroleen."

"I thought I detected some French in your words."

"Have fun tonight."

Chapter 23

Kirby was finally tired of sex. It took a long time, but he was now ready to return to the serious world of medicine. He had to think about his short speech after Carter's introduction. He had not seen Carter in Santa Fe, figuring he was in town hoping to find old trainees to pay tribute to their old chief. Kirby was not fond of Carter but he did not want to get on Carter's wrong side now for he had a lot to say about who would be appointed the next chief of surgery when he finally retired. But it was nice of him to come to Santa Fe to make the introductions. Carter was one to stand close to the candle, when someone he knew was being honored, he would stand near him to share the spotlight or the flash from the camera. Kirby had to remind himself that he should not utter any sarcastic comment or anything that could be interpreted as less than praise of his chief. He would keep the talk light and impersonal.

MaryAnn was in the bathroom, washing out her stockings and panties. Traveling with a carry-on bag did not allow for a full supply of clothes so she had to do a little laundry, not a bad price to pay for not checking a bag and running the risk of losing it in the transfer of planes. The rest of her things were already packed in her carry-on as they were heading out early in the AM. Be prepared was her motto. She made one last check of her hair in the mirror and they headed off to town to the El Dorado Hotel to be on time for the pre-banquet photo session for the new members of the society.

Carter was aglow. After he left Caroleen at the spa, he had a great hike along the horse trails. At the top of the hill, he could see Los Alamos to the West and what looked like Colorado to the North. So peaceful. The contrast of this serenity to the life back home made him question why he was pushing so hard. What would he do if he retired? He better get some interests to fill the day. Would Carrie put up with him if he were home all the time? Maybe he could head a foundation or do some fund raising for the hospital. He would miss the chatter of the locker room, if he retired. How could he replace that? He would not answer these questions now as he did not want to break the New Mexico spell that overwhelmed him today. Caroleen looked different when she returned from the hot tub. Still beautiful but she lost her soft look. Her teeth clenched, he could see the masseter muscles contracting.

"Are you OK?"

"Oh I am fine. I was thinking about what I would do when I got home and that made me grind my teeth a little." I think this place is getting to me. Not a complaint. It is so beautiful here; I think I got over relaxed in the hot tub. Looking out on the mountains and sky overwhelmed me. Thank you so much for inviting me here. I am having such a pleasant time."

"Thank you for coming with me. I did not realize how nice it is to travel with such a lovely and appreciative companion. It will be hard to get back to the real world. But enough of this touchy feely stuff, I have to get to town for the banquet and catch up with Kirby at the hotel. He missed a lot by not staying at this hotel."

Caroleen turned her head away to avoid his eyes. She tried to cover the move by saying she was looking for her shoe. "Oh don't worry about me at dinner; I am so full of this great Mexican food, that I can skip eating for a few weeks. I may go the bar and have one last Margarita. What time do we leave in the morning?"

"We have an 11 o'clock flight so we should leave here about 8:30. I like to get to the airport 6 weeks before the flight, if you know what I mean. How about you?"

"Oh I like to get there as the plane is taking off and make a scene about yelling at the pilot and demand that they open the door for me. Not really, but I see no value in sitting around those dingy waiting rooms."

"OK, now that I know your style, I will try to entertain you while we are waiting at the airport. I have to rush. I will cut out before dessert, try to stay awake, miss relaxation."

Caroleen was happy to see him go. After the confession in the hot tub, she realized that Carter would no longer be in her personal life. She went into the bath room, took off her clothes and put her locket on the shelf next to her tooth brush as she was not sure how the hot water, bath oil and perfumed soap would affect the turquoise. She admired herself in the mirror. She did have a nice body, especially after seeing the others in the hot tub and pool. She was young, bright and attractive, she was going to find the right man, right age, and settle down, even if it meant working less and enjoying life more. The mellow feeling continued as she soaked in the tub. This must have been the honeymoon suite as the bathtub was double sized with two sets of controls for the water and the Jacuzzis. Her muscles responded to the water massage but she worried that her poor skin will be de-oiled. The body oil would fix up that minor problem. She turned on the radio, spilled some more bath oil into the water and slid back into the tub. Real peace. About half an hour later, she got out of the tub and applied the body lotion to her legs, arms abdomen and part of the back she could reach. She touched her lower back.

"Oh no!" she screamed. "No birth control patch! It must have come off in the hot tub."

The patch that was supposed to be replaced the day she before she left on this trip. All the excitement and the rush to get her work done, she forgot to change the patch! It has now been three days overdue and missing! She remembered the directions that if the patch is more than 2 days late in the second week of the cycle, back up contraception must be used.

"Wait, don't panic! Sit down and get a hold of yourself."

Then she took a deep breath and remembered the news articles and TV spots showing Carter getting his vasectomy and the follow up check. She felt a little relieved but angry that she was so careless.

"I do not need to become pregnant now and not by a married man."

In her social life, she had other encounters with men other than with Carter but if she were pregnant, he would be the father since up to now, she had been compliant with the use of the patch.

"Stupid girl. I should have been grown up enough to take the hormone shot. Time to sit down and think."

She had to decide if she should she take Plan B morning after pill? What was the policy in New Mexico about pharmacists dispensing the pills without a prescription? If she had her laptop with her, she could look it up on Google. She rushed to get dressed and ran up the hill to the main office to see if they had an internet connection. The night clerk was the only person there.

"Do you have internet connections? I need to look something up."

"The reservation clerk uses the internet; I don't have authority to use the computer. What is the problem?"

"I need to check some information about pharmacy services in New Mexico. I am from the East and not sure of what goes on out here."

"So would the internet tell you?"

"That is what I wanted to find out."

"Seems like most people would use the phone and call the drug store."

"Phone, oh my goodness, of course the phone. May I see your yellow pages, please?"

At that point she realized that she was in total panic, an unusual feeling for her as she was always in control of her emotions and problem solving skills.

"Thanks for your advice, sorry to bother you. Have a nice evening."

"You too. Good night and good luck."

Carrie told Richardson about the guacamole place that a young girl described to her when she was in the hot tub. He interrupted her by claiming to know all about it and was ready to get going. In a few minutes they took off for Gabrielle's. Richardson regaled her with the description of Santa Fe outside of the plaza area. He had checked on the hospital on St Francis and the large number of doctor's offices around it. He had seen the capitol buildings, St. John's College and the Wheelwright museum, the Folk art museum and the antropology museum. "This is an exciting place." What he did not tell her was how poor he felt. This place had real money people. The rich are poor compared to the really rich that lived in the hills of Santa Fe. The houses were mostly vacation homes worth several million dollars. Just what could be the primary residence? The BMW's, Escalades and Lexus SC made his mouth water. He could imagine the furnishings and wine cellars. His money making schemes were peanuts; he could never achieve the Santa Fe standard of living that he saw on his trip. When he got home, he would have to rethink his position and his financial maneuverings. He should have gone into real estate development or done some insider trading; he had a lot of contacts.

The dinner went well. The guacamole was a new experience for them. They decided to order a second round and skip the main meal. Finally, Richard asked Carrie how the spa worked out.

"Just the best." The massage was so relaxing. I soaked in the hot tub. There was a cute young girl with a French accent. I think her name was Kathleen. She and I exchanged stories and some confessions. Seems like she was here with a married man, not her husband. So we had some shared experiences."

Richard was not sure where this was heading so he decided to butt in and change the subject.

"What kind of massage did you get? The usual or one of those where they walk over your back."

"You mean Shiatsu?"

"Yes, is that the one where they press their fingers into your back?"

"Sort of like that but they did not have shiatsu massages. I got the Swedish regular type. Just perfect for me. Of course, they had their usual Santa Fe modifications with aromas, music and herbs, everything but granola."

Beardsley was intrigued with the story about the blond girl with the French accent. It sounded like Caroleen, but what would she be doing in Santa Fe. Of course, she was not the only woman in the US with a French accent and blonde hair. He turned his attention back to Carrie.

"You look so relaxed. I hope this trip was a good idea for you."

"Yes, thanks to you and to Norman for his plane. I feel ready to go home and redo my life. Thank you so much. It was a great trip. What time do we leave tomorrow?

"Any time, the nice thing about a private plane is the freedom from schedules. We have to pick up Norman about 4 PM in Denver. I will call the pilot when we get home."

• • •

Gayle Jackson's plane arrived one hour late in Albuquerque. Fortunately she travelled in her banquet outfit and carried a small bag so she avoided the wait at the baggage claim area. As ordered, the car was waiting for her to take her to Santa Fe. The driver went about 10 miles over the 75 mph speed limit and got to Santa Fe by 6:15. She went directly to the El Dorado and found the banquet room where she stood at the back of the room. The speeches had already begun. Unfortunately, the first speaker was more than long winded. So the next speakers, even the ones who had planned a few words, bloviated in like manner. Finally it was Kirby's time to address the group. He stood up, slowly walked to the podium, and established eye contact with the audience, just as he was told in public speaking class at Choate. He then looked at the tables at the back of the room so he would project his voice. He choked as he saw his wife Gayle standing against the wall. He cleared his throat and began.

"Gentlemen and Ladies, members of the Society of Academic Pediatric Surgeons and guests. I am honored and humbled by the honor you

361

bestowed upon me with membership in this most prestigious organization. I hope I will continue to serve children and their families in the tradition of this august group, many of whom, I was honored to work with at various stages in my career. There is a long list of people I want to thank but I do not want this to turn into an Academy Awards type that speeds through so many names that it becomes meaningless to the audience. I do want to acknowledge four people: Carter Randolf, my chief, Mrs. Roland, my 6th grade science teacher who inspired me to ask questions and think creatively and most importantly, to work with facts. Thanks to my medical school pharmacology professor, Carl Schmidt who said 'the essence of science is measurement.' I checked this in Bartlett's quotation and it does not come up so I guess Shakespeare did not write it before Carl. And finally, to my wife Gayle who surprised me by leaving her busy schedule and attending the dinner tonight. She is my biggest fan and my personal critic, kind of keeps me in place when I act too much like a surgeon. Please wave to the group, Gayle." When the group turned to look for Gayle, Kirby looked over at MaryAnn who was already getting her handbag and moving her chair back to make a hopefully unnoticed exit when the people were busy applauding Gayle.

Mary Ann did get away from the banquet hall through the side door and got the doorman to call a cab. In Santa Fe, cabs are a rarity but tonight she was in luck. The timing was as perfect as the movie scenes when the cab pulls up almost immediately as the actor hits the curbside. She jumped into the back seat and told he she wanted to go to Bishop's Lodge and then to the Holiday Inn on Cerrillos. She assumed that there would be at least one Holiday Inn on that busy and heavily franchised thoroughfare. The cabbie was happy with this kind of fare; he was polite as well as talkative. When they got to Bishop's Lodge, Mary Ann jumped out and reminded the driver to wait, as if he needed a reminder. She hopped up the steps to the room, grabbed the bag at the front door and threw it into the cab. "Let's hit it."

"You must be running from the devil. That was the fastest exit from a hotel I have seen. You are definitely not from Santa Fe, people here don't move that fast. Are you skipping the check out, bill paying thing?"

"Oh, no I did that this afternoon. I have to meet a friend at the Holiday Inn in about 10 minutes. The dinner at the hotel ran longer than I expected. I did not want to be late."

"Oh in Santa Fe everyone is late. You must not be from around here."

"No, I am not, I am from the coast."

"Frisco, I think I detected California in your voice."

"Right Frisco, great city, cable cars, fog and Irish Coffee. Great city. I love it."

"Where are you from?"

"I am from California, too."

"What brought you to Santa Fe?"

"My grandchildren. After I got divorced, I stayed in California, taking care of my mother. She died two years ago so I packed up and moved here so I could be near my grandchildren. Rentals are very expensive so I ended up moving in with my ex-wife and her husband."

"Interesting. How does that work out? Husband and ex-husband."

"Not too good, at first, but now we have our places and tolerate each other. He is more the biker type and as you can see, I am a business man." In a few minutes he continued, "Here is the Holiday Inn. I enjoyed talking with you. I hope you catch up with your friend."

Maryann paid him, grabbed her bag and walked into the registration area.

• • •

At the end of the dinner, Kirby walked through the crowd waving at old friends finally getting to Gayle at the back of the room. She gave him a cheek and a quick hug like a basketball player gives an opponent at the end of a game. "I am so proud of you. Thanks for the mention. I thought I would just sneak in and surprise you when you were finished with this meeting. It was nice to hear those kind words about you and from you" Where are you staying? I have a car waiting for me so I can follow you to the hotel."

Kirby kept his surgical cool, feeling that MaryAnn would use her nursing skills at problem solving and get out of the hotel before they got there. But to insure that they would not bump into MaryAnn, he suggested a drink at the bar at the El Dorado before going to their hotel.

This seemed to work out. Kirby was on a high from the dinner and seeing old friends so he talked on and on. They got to the room at the Bishop's Lodge. No MaryAnn, no MaryAnn's carry on case. He had lucked out.

"Not a bad room. Nice fire place and in the daylight the view of the mountains is spectacular. Maybe we should come back here in the summer. This is not the place for just one person to enjoy."

"Good idea. I am bushed. My clock is two hours different so it is really 1AM in my body. I will brush my teeth and meet you in bed."

Gayle went into the bathroom and noticed the panties and stocking left drying on the clothes line in the bathtub. "Old Kirby, up to his old tricks again. I wonder where she went, who ever she is. Should I pick them up or let him find them and worry himself sick wondering if I saw them or what will I do to him for fooling around on this trip? He will never change his ways. OK with me. I don't have to deal with him so often when he has other play toys." So Gayle dropped the evidence in a plastic bag and put it in her carry-on. She would hold them for future interactions.

She returned to the bedroom and slid under the covers.

"Great night for you Kirby. I'll see you in the morning."

When Carter got back to the room he realized that something was wrong the minute he saw Caroleen. "What is the matter? You look upset."

Caroleen went over the last hour when she discovered the problem of the missing birth control patch. Carter tried to be a patient listener and not jump in with a solution to the problem. She got to the part of about getting the morning after pill from a pharmacy. This complicated his potential fix for her concerns. He had adamantly spoken out against pharmacists dispensing the morning after pill doctors performing abortion since it would encourage promiscuous sexual activity. This was an abstract argument but now, this was real life, not pandering to his religious right contributors. Since birth control patches were new to him, he could not offer a professional opinion but it did not stop him from interrupting her.

"What you want to do, I mean tonight."

"I am not sure. I definitely don't want to become pregnant. The brochure said it is too early to get a pregnancy test and that if the patch was not changed in 48 hours, other forms of contraception should be used. Going forward, contraception is not an issue."

"Not an issue?"

"No, you must agree- abstinence is the best birth control. We are in plan A. On one hand, I know you had a vasectomy, I saw you on TV when you went for a post op visit. On the other hand, there may be a few critters still hanging around down there. That is why I want to go to a pharmacy tonight and get the morning after pill. I would like to borrow the car and go to one of those all night drug stores. I found a few of them in the Yellow Pages. I think there should be one on Cerrillos Road, with all the college students in this town. I am glad that you had a vasectomy. Maybe I am just panicked at my stupidity. But the consequence is not one that I want to face at this stage of my single professional life. Especially, since you are not ready for a shot gun marriage, neither am I. I could always get an abortion. I have always been pro-choice and still am. But I know where you stand. I remember the pickets outside of the hospital about reproductive rights and your opposition to them. How good is a vasectomy?"

"Let's calm down and think this thing through. I agree with you that I am not one to claim fatherhood although if you were pregnant and if I was the father, be assured that I would support you and the baby. I would face my responsibility. But there is one point that needs further discussion."

"What is that?"

"I never had a vasectomy!"

"You never had what?" she screamed loudly enough for the whole hotel could hear her.

Carter yelled back so she could hear him. "I never had a vasectomy!"

In the room next door, Carrie, still in her newly found happiness, was jolted by the roar. "I swear that sounds like my husband Carter. But what would he be doing here?" In her blissful state, she either forgot that he was in Santa Fe for his surgical group or more likely, she was thinking about him so intently that every voice sounded like his.

"A vasectomy. I did not want anyone cutting on me. You never know what complications that could arise. I did it as the poster boy for the anti-abortion groups. I wanted to appeal to some major donors to our program that are right of right wing conservatives and thought that this would be the way to give the movement some publicity and get some camera time for myself. Those smart ass young surgeons are getting all the press now. I am getting too old for this game but cannot give it up. . I am what you call a praise addict. I need the glory."

"If you don't mind me saying so. You are a real son of a bitch.......
a deceiving shit head..........and a bigger than life ass hole. You mean I could be pregnant."

"That is a possibility." Carter had not been called such names since he was a first year resident at Hopkins.

"Then I am off to the drug store."

"I am going with you. I don't want you to drive in an unfamiliar city at this hour of night. Especially with your being so upset."

"You mean I should not be upset? Mr. calm-forked-tongue-fake."

"You are right calling me names. I apologize. When we discussed contraceptives, you said you were wearing a patch, so I did not have to disclose my sham operation. I agree that you should get the pills. I insist on driving you."

"Isn't that against your beliefs?"

"My beliefs are academic; the rules change when it becomes personal. As other things on this trip, this is privileged information and not for public knowledge. Right?"

"Right. No one will know about this."

They got in the car. Caroleen was sobbing; Carter was mulling over the possible solutions to the multiple problems.

"Maybe the Yellow Pages stated that drug stores were open all night but the pharmacies may be closed. Maybe, the pharmacist would not be allowed to give the pills without a prescription. Maybe if I wrote a script and maybe they would honor it even though it was from out of state. Or maybe the pharmacist would not dispense the pill because of religious beliefs.... That narrow minded son of a bitch! Maybe he was like one of the right wingers that I kowtow to back home. I know that this was my punishment for adultery. I am going to change my ways when I get home starting with cutting out the bullshit and beginning to be honest with others and especially myself. I am ready to admit that I am too old for all these activities. Surgery, adultery, pride, egotism."

He stopped this flagellation as he reconsidered his future behavior. "Maybe I was going too far with considering giving up egotism. I will just have to find another place or way to keep my ego pumped up."

They did find a RiteAid pharmacy that advertised being opened all night. "Great, stop here and we can settle this dilemma." Always the surgeon, he sought solutions to problems and rapid closures. They went past the Rite Aid specials, the hair colorings and shampoos and laxatives, finally reaching the pharmacy. Open all night for the hair supplies but not for pills, the pharmacy closed at 10 PM.

"Now what?"

"We will hit CVS, they may be better."

"I hope they have a cooperative pharmacist that does not pry too much."

"Boy, have you changed your tune, mister religious right."

"And if we don't get the pills, we can head off to St. Vincent and get a D and E." He was so upset that he said this, knowing no one can walk into a hospital at night and ask for a D and E, especially at a hospital called St. Vincent. First they needed a positive pregnancy test to be considered for any procedure.

Caroleen did not know rules and that D and E was the same as an abortion so she innocently asked "what kind of pills were D and E. I guess the E is Estrogen."

"Not exactly, but we are getting ahead of the game. Off to CVS."

They did get the pills and a smile from the pharmacist. She saw the man and the young blonde and made up her scenario. "Here is your medicine and instructions. Tell your daughter to be careful so she will not get into trouble again."

Carter cringed. Even though he felt young, he was not ready for that age separation comment, but it was true. "I have to stop acting like a young stud and accept the fact that this acting out will not restore my testosterone levels." As they left the counter, he mumbled to himself. "I am going to change my ways and the policy on women's health at the hospital. I have I now had a better fix on the teens that came to CHUC for help with their reproductive activities. I am fortunate to get out of this one, maybe. But the poor people who do not have all the tickets of admission that I possess to face problems of life and personal issues like pregnancy. I never had to think about people before. I vow that I was going to stop seeing the chief nurse. Well, maybe one more fling before I stop seeing her. Then I will try to make some peace with my wife." Carter ignored the fact that she seems willing to have him stay away from her. But sex is not everything. Or he was going to find out if that last statement were true. He was now more audible. "I guess that this is what they mean by a sea change."

"What did you say? asked Caroleen.

"Just thinking out loud. I am sure this will work out in a positive way. It has just made me start to rethink my life. I am going to make a change."

"I am too. No more trips without a box of patches for one thing."

"I see you still have a little humor left."

"I don't feel pregnant, but not having been pregnant, I don't know what I mean. I think this will be OK. I am glad I got the pills here. Maybe I will calm down and get some sleep. I will be glad to get home tomorrow."

The three couples showed a variety of emotions on their flight home. Kirby picked up MaryAnn at the Holiday Inn at 5:30 AM and caught the 7AM flight home. Fortunately, there were no business class seats available on that flight so Gayle took the 1 PM plane. Kirby was anxious to see his transplant patient, wondering what, if any law suits may ensue from the surgical mishap. MaryAnn was happy to be with him for a few more interrupted hours. On the 10AM flight through Chicago, Caroleen held the barf bag as she was nauseated from the hormone pills; Carter was pondering his future outside of surgery, wondering if he had enough money to survive.

At Bishop's Lodge, when Beardsley woke up in the morning, Carrie was in her chair reading Luxury Estates of New Mexico. In addition to the beautiful adobe houses, she was intrigued with the article on the primitive church in Chimayo that had miraculous healing powers. Now she wanted to experience some Native healing. Going there would be the start of her transformation to her new life and outlook. When she saw Richardson looking up from the bed, she smiled and said "Can I borrow the car? I would like to visit one more site before leaving New Mexico. Do we have time? I will be back before 12."

"What is left to be seen? We have done the town."

"This is an old mission church outside of town, on the way to Taos. I would love to see it. You don't have to go. I will be able to find it."

Beardsley was afraid that she would get lost, get into car trouble, or somehow cause them to be late in meeting Norman in Denver. His principle was all people in the group stay together on the last day. "Don't be silly, if you have to see it, I will go with you but I can't promise that I will go into the church. I am afraid the walls would collapse. Let me call the pilot and give him a head's up."

In about 30 minutes, they were out of the hotel and heading north towards Espanola where they hit route 76 and took the curved road through hills and mesquite trees under the New Mexico sky's characteristic blue behind fluffy clouds. After a sharp left turn at the top of a hill, the road dropped into a valley where there were the usual rural beaten down houses and a few car repair shops. Finally the sign Welcome to Chimayo, altitude 6220, Population 2800 announced their arrival. Another sign, Santuario Chimayo, had an arrow pointing to the right. First they passed the gift shop, a few fast food stores and parking lot for handicapped visitors. Since no one was there, Richardson pulled into one of the spots; he was not going to turn around and find the public parking spaces. At the far end of the courtyard stood the church, built in 1836. Carrie jumped out as Richardson said he would stay with the car while she went to the church. Inside the rough woodwork and primitive art silently added authenticity to the special powers of the church. At the altar was the crucifix that was the origin of the healing powers of this church. Carrie stood there in awe. It was far from presumptuous, but powerful in its effect. No wonder people came here for healing physical ailments; Carrie was sure that mental ones were cured just as well. After 5 minutes of what she felt was meditation, she turned to the left into a smaller room whose walls were lined with crutches, letters of testimony and pictures of Chimayo miracles. There was a small room with a large hole in the dirt floor. People ahead of her were filling plastic baggies with small amounts of dirt from the sacred pit where legend has it that the crucifix was first found. Carrie did the same thing, experiencing even more serenity than she did in the hot tub. This was worth the trip.

Beardsley was walking around the court yard, looking at the small business that catered to the tourists. Good idea, he thought. While people got healed, make a few bucks on the side. This was his kind of place. Maybe he could add a healing site to the new hospital he was planning. The ride back to the airport was appropriately silent as the landscape plus the healing ceremony at the church required peaceful quiet reflection.

Norman warmly greeted Beardsley and Carrie. Carrie, in a pink cashmere sweater, glowed in the darkened cabin. Her body language revealed that all was not pure and pristine in Santa Fe. She was happy and animated in her description of the Santa Fe experience. Beardsley, uncommonly silent, appeared depressed and in another world. Not only he was poor by Santa Fe standards, he had called his office that morning and found that Al Sharptee, his CFO, had resigned. He was not sure why Al suddenly left. Did he get a better job, did he get cold feet about their financial maneuvers, and was he contacted by the auditors? He could not talk on the phone since, paranoid as he is; he feared that his phone was tapped. Thank goodness, he thought, nothing was written down so there was no paper trail, if he were investigated. He was still worried.

Chapter 24

Life continued at CHUC with a full census, crowded emergency rooms, day surgery oversubscribed and the new MRI cranking out studies, 24 hours a day. As usual, the ED, the place with the most unpredictable excitement provided its dramatic actions. Today, there were 2 patients brought there for gunshot wounds from a gang battle, a number of febrile patients, a 2 year old with newly diagnosed diabetes, a variety of kids with lacerations and a 16 month old with asthma. As he gained knowledge and experience Keith Aaron lost his hostility from last summer. He picked up the next chart. He hated to admit it, but he was enjoying his second rotation in the ED.

"Another asthma case." the triage nurse forewarned him.

"Cool, I know how to treat asthma, a piece of pizza." As he read the history, he started to question the diagnosis. "Asthma does occur in young infants but this case of so called asthma sounded different. No cold symptoms, no family history of asthma and never wheezed before made this a different kind of problem... No doubt, this was wheezing, but maybe not asthma. Just like Donna says, all that wheezes is not asthma."

Keith was showing that he was ready to be a second year resident when the thinking pattern changed from 'what is it? to 'what else could it be?' "I am suspicious that this might not be as straight forward at it seemed at first but I am up for the challenge." He gave a high five to the triage nurse and looked for room 4.

The mother was holding George Mesa, a 16month old. She was worried.

"Hi, I am Dr. Aaron. How are you doing?"

"A little tired."

"Hello George. Can you wave hello to me?" "OK, not now, but maybe later. Tell me something about George."

In response to Keith's questions, she provided the following information.

George did not feel warm, had not eaten much solid food but was drinking. He had been around several cousins who had colds but did not get near them. No GI symptoms. There were several members of the extended family who had allergies but George had not shown any allergic reactions. There was nothing in the environment that was unusual, but the air quality in the neighborhood was not good as there was an electric power plant near the house which poured out all kinds of toxins into the air. No new rugs in the house and no exterminator sprays but the hot air heating system was still used, especially in the chilly mornings. They had not changed the air filters in more than 6 months.

The physical examination showed a anxious. slightly obese boy with a necklace of metallic beads draped around his neck. His breathing showed more than usual effort to take in oxygen. The ears, throat and neck were normal, no signs of infection. His pulse was rapid and wheezing, as anticipated, was heard on the left side. But not on the right !! Keith's suspicion that this may not be straight forward asthma was correct. An infection was not high on the list as far as the history goes.

"Has he eaten any peanuts?"

"We have no peanuts in the house."

"What else could he have put in this mouth and then breathed it into his lungs? Toys, carrots, beads?"

"He is always putting something in his mouth. Wait a minute, He was playing with his sister's beads, but I was not watching him that close."

"Bingo. We will find out. Off to x-ray and we will see. Not all objects will show up on x-ray but we need to take a look."

The x-ray room had only one patient ahead of George. After his x-ray was taken, Keith went to the reading room. "There it is. The left lung is overinflated with air and pressing on the right side, a mediastinal shift. Keith's initial reading was confirmed by Dr. Spirito but you know he would look for something else like a bone tumor in the arm or a rare metabolic bone disease. His eagle eyes scanned everything on the x-ray starting with the label to see if this x-ray matched the name of the patient, then the bones, the heart and finally the area of interest, the lungs." first the edges, then the middle" was his motto.

"OK, big boy, what do you see?"

Keith was rapidly losing his confidence for he knew by the question that he had missed something. "I see the left lung full of extra air in the lungs near the center of the chest and not much air at the periphery. The bead is blocking the airway and causing the wheezing."

"Good, but anyone can see that, what else does a CHUC pediatrician see?

"OOPS, I see his name is George Mesa and he is 16 months old."

"Good, and what else."

"He has American Health Care insurance?"

"Look boy, at this oval object in the airway."

"Of course, I thought you could see that, John."

"9 months and 2 weeks. What is your name?'

"Keith."

"You are one of the early birds; I keep a record of how long it takes the residents to call me John. I don't like the doctor business but I don't make an issue of it. I like it when you call me John. Now that we have that out of the way, is there anything about that foreign body that interests you?"

Keith knew that he was getting closer to the point and that John was dragging it out to make a point. A point that he would never forget.

"See that little guy. It is solidly opaque. Makes one think it may have metal in it. Maybe it contains lead. Then a kid will put it in his mouth. Does that ring any bells?"

"Not my bell, John."

"Well, I bet his mom bought some Mexican candy that is full of lead, or won a prize in the gum ball machine. The trinkets from China also have a lot of lead. They are small and easily swallowed."

"Did you get a lead test?"

"Not yet, but the blood will be in the lab in minutes or even seconds. You can count on that." Keith stops at the computer on John's desk, enters his password and orders the blood lead.

"Once again, John Spirito scores a grand slam. Besides that you have saved a lot of brain cells. We may have found the foreign body but not have picked the lead exposure up for a long time, much to the distress of the young man with the growing brain. You are the man, John. The real man."

Keith left the radiology room, so excited about the scoop he was about to declare at the clinical conference that he almost forgot about the need to get the patient over to ENT so they could pass a bronchoscope and retrieve the lead bead. He ran into Karl Strem, the chief resident, and breathlessly told him about the case.

Karl became energized. "We have to do something about the jewelry and toys that contain lead. I was just reading about a case of a 2 year old that swallowed one of those lead bombs and messed up his brain. We have to do something about the lead candy! It is the end of the year and I need something to occupy my time until June. You guys are so competent that I am not needed as much as I was in June. That is why we are here; to train the next group, I guess the first thing we need to do after ENT sees him is to get the lead level results. When that is done, we can then start a campaign to educate the parents about the danger of this kind of candy, shut down the imports, find the people who are bringing in this cheap crap and most important, save a few brains. Are you ready for some action?"

"I am ready and I have some others who will join us. There is Sarah and Jeff. They are the do-gooders on our team."

Fortunately, the piece of candy was easily extracted and the breathing returned to normal. George was treated with antibiotics, a laxative to get rid of the candy from the intestines. Karl sat down with George's mother and explained that they tested the candy and it had lead. He explained how the lead harms the brain so she should never buy that candy again. Karl told her how he was going to publicize the danger of this candy and hopefully, reduce the exposure to lead and the brain damage."

Mrs. Mesa thanked him and invited him to come to her house for tacos, special tacos from her village, made with goat meat. Karl thanked her but demurred, claiming to be a vegetarian. He called public relations to help set up a publicity campaign.

• • •

Kirby was the first in the group to arrive home from New Mexico. He went to the hospital to see Tommy Morris on the transplant unit. The second surgery to stop the leak was holding; the urine was draining normally. Fortunately, there was no sign of rejection of the new kidney. The family, thinking that the leak was part of the procedure, thanked Kirby for all his good work.

"Thanks again, Dr. Kirby. We appreciate your interest and the phone calls when you were out of town. You are a good man and would always be in our prayers."

Kirby left the family, convinced, once again, that good communication skills could prevent anger and malpractice cases. He had a good feeling that this family would not sue him. Even if his charm saved him from a suit, he vowed never again to get caught in such a time squeeze as he did on this case. He knew that, in time, he would forget the vow and have his testosterone level take precedence over good decision making.

Although Carrie left New Mexico after Carter, her non-stop on the Gulf Stream allowed her to arrive home first. Still smiling and singing show tunes while she unpacked her bags, she started to cook some fajitas, like the ones at Gabrielle's. She did not like the taste, something was missing from her recipe maybe it needed some New Mexico air. She had to remind herself, not to let it slip that she was in Santa Fe. She was sure that they had Mexican food in Denver, where Carter thought she was while he was in Santa Fe. For 10 minutes, she looked into the mirror and saw happiness on her face for the first time in a long time. In addition to her smile, she felt a twinge in her lower abdomen. She vowed that she was finished with Beardsley, and would not entertain another affair just because she was lonely or bored. She was going to make a new start with Carter, at least try to make a new start. She realized that she was on the first team of the COT, Complainer's Olympic Team. All she did was to react negatively to her life. The maid was late, the gardener missed some weeds, the food market was too expensive, and Phillipe never did her hair right. Her chronic unhappiness was expressed as displeasure over situations which her affluence provided. That had to change.

She did not know what to expect from Carter when he returned home from a trip. If his trainees made a fuss over him, he was elated; if he did not get the expected amount of adulation, he was more difficult than usual. She tried to see it from his viewpoint. A fragile ego that like a dog needed unlimited amount of stroking. She got out the candles, put on some 70's music on the satellite radio. "Channel seven for the 70's. This is his kind of music and no commercials. That would keep the mood going."

Now into reading faces, she was shocked to see Carter. His smile and loose body movements showed he, too, had changed. Relieved at the first impression, Carrie did not question why. She would enjoy the moment.

"Hi, babe, how are you? How was Denver? How was the meeting? My time in Santa Fe was great, just great."

"Good, good, good. I wish you were there, my dear. Many people asked about you. Of course, Beardsley was Beardsley, egocentric to the nines. He did give a good speech and was a little humble and gracious when he got the award. I love the Gulf Stream that Norman owns. It is the only way to travel. Maybe some day? But that is not important. I made some fajitas for you. I had them in Denver and loved the spices and vegetables. I don't think I will qualify as a chef at Taco Bell, but I wanted to help you to a soft landing before you get into the pressure cooker at CHUC tomorrow."

"Great! I am sure that the fajitas will be fine. Here I bought you a turquoise butterfly. The green turquoise is from Colorado mines; the silversmith was someone famous. It will look good on your pink sweater. Here, let me put it on you. As he placed the butterfly on her sweater, she clasped his hands on the pin and pushed her breast toward him. "Too bad you didn't have another, the right side is lonely but I will give you a chance later on to take care of Mrs. Right."

Carter was in such a good mood that he did not immediately pick up on the change in Carrie's demeanor. She was actually flirting with him, like it was 20 years ago. This was unusual, but nice. He was not going to delve into the reasons why she had changed. Maybe she had altitude sickness and her brain trapped some air bubbles. This was going to be fun for as long as it lasts.

After he finished the dinner, he jumped into the shower and then bed. Carrie finished combing her hair and walked towards the bed, wearing the black negligee that she had worn for only a few seconds in the Denver hotel with Beardsley. After seeing her dressed that way, he yelled "HOO-HA. GET'EM COWGIRL!" Carrie's head turned sharply. Those were the words that she heard at Bishop's Lodge but it was not Carter's voice; she hoped that the voices were different. Carter saw she was stunned but being egotistical as he is, felt she was surprised by his energized outburst, not the words. He pulled back the covers, inviting her to come to bed. This time the black negligee stayed on for about a minute until Carter got the drift that she was not going to push him away or plead for a delay until the morning. This was like the old days, before they got married. It was more like gymnastics than sex but neither person complained. When they were lying on their backs, looking at the ceiling, Carter asked "What were you doing in Denver? That was like the old days. Not that I am complaining but you surprised me. I would say that was an A plus work; I am known as a hard grader as you know."

Carrie did not respond to his question about what she was doing in Denver but asked him "What were you doing in Santa Fe? It must have been the sunsets. Right?"

"Oh sunset, I was so busy I did not see the sun go down. Lots of meetings and socializing with my old trainees. I even had some time to work out. I was really out of shape. I think it was good to get away, puts things in perspective."

"I feel the same way. Getting away is good for many things. I think the altitude must have something to do with it. I feel younger and rejuvenated. I think my ovaries woke up in Denver. The poor old things don't have much more mileage in them. I hope this is not the last gasp.

"I hope not too. This was fun. I need a little time to recharge and maybe we can try that again."

"Anything you say boss." She looked over at Carter and saw that he was already asleep. "See you in the morning."

When Beardsley reached home, he found out that his house had been broken into but after he looked around, he realized that the robbers took nothing, not even his old 32" TV set. He rationalized that they must have been looking for a flat panel TV, not the old box one he had. He thought he had nice things but the robbers disagreed. Obviously he needed some help with the quality of his home furnishing. Beardsley made a note to have a new decorator who would furnish his house in a way that it would be more attractive to future robbers.

He got back in the hospital routine quickly. First on his list was to talk to Al Sharptee to find out his reason for bailing out, making sure to keep the conversation open ended so as not to focus on their financial tweeks. He had played with the accounting methods so much that he did not really know how much the hospital was making or possibly losing; hopefully, Al could fill him in with the real numbers. Richard was relieved to learn that Al was leaving was because he wanted to move back to California, where his family and his wife's family lived. The job was at a smaller but less stressful hospital. He wanted to make the last phase of his working life easier on his coronaries and lining of the intestines. After quietly looking for several months, this offer in Riverside came through. He planned to leave in 4 weeks but wanted to take some vacation time before his departure. Al recommended Jeanene Cartright to be the interim CFO. Beardsley said he would think about it. She was as good as anyone in finance and she did not know about the plan to work the numbers. Since Beardsley's contract was up for renewal, this would work out. Once he got his raise and new severance package signed, he could take time to find a new CFO, Jeanene was too passive to take this as a permanent job. Thinking about his contract prompted a call to Clayton Pickering to check in and find out if any new board decisions happened while he was away.

After he checked the patients in the hospital, Kirby finally arrived home from the hospital, he was shocked to find that most of the furniture was gone; Gayle's closet was empty except for a few pairs of Jimmy Choo shoes. On the kitchen counter were a note and a package. He opened up the package and found MaryAnn's panties with a note in Gayle's hand writing. "Congratulations on your award. Did not know you were into cross dressing." He next opened the envelope. On the edge of the inside of the envelope was a Tiffany imprint. The formal note paper had an address engraved on the top Gayle Jackson, Apt P2, Bainbridge Towers, New York NY, 10012. "Dear Kirby, time to move on. You can contact me at the above address of my new condo in the Bainbridge Towers, if you want to talk." The words were not unexpected but the timing got him. Kirby remembered that it takes at least 6 weeks to get engraved stationary from Tiffany. Old Gayle really plans ahead.

In the legal affairs office, the risk management people were going over the month's reports of atypical occurrences and possible law suits. Margie Kelly, the person responsible for looking at systemic errors in the hospital, gathered information to help determine if the problem in medical care was because of communication difficulties, scheduling problems, laboratory procedure conflicts or was the mess up because of human error or bad decision making. The list was similar to last month: lab report not posted promptly, delay in admissions/discharges and the usual group of unhappy people who liked to sue doctors and hospitals, no doubt prompted by eager ambulance chasing lawyers. The breakdown in suture lines after a transplant caught her attention. That was an unusual occurrence, especially when she saw that Kirby Jackson was involved as he was known for his steady hands and perfect stitches. She looked on the next page which indicated that the parents have not indicated that they were unhappy or had threatened a law suit. In fact, there was a letter of thanks commending the hospital on its great care. She got out the file and saw that although Kirby Jackson was the surgeon, he was not the one to repair the leaking ureter. Tim Warren did that. Strange, she thought. Probably Kirby was outside talking to the reporters or the parents. But they would have called him back, if he were around the hospital. The anesthesia record did not look unusual but it documents what happened on the operating table, not the discussions around the table or movements in and out of the OR. She flagged this case to discuss it with the OR staff to get a first hand report. The system was working. The management office sniffs out the problems before they become lawsuits or big payoffs. She put this chart in the red box for full review by the legal committee.

A few floors above legal, Beardsley met with the compensation committee in the Board Room. He had colored bar graphs that showed the increasing income flow and decreasing expenses. Cash on hand increased. His homework paid off as he sensed they were in his back pocket. It was a great performance, thought Beardsley, if it was only true!

"Great job Dick!"

"You are a miracle worker!"

"I think you are underpaid, you need a raise."

"Beardsley tried to look modest but that exceeded his thespian skills."

"How can we keep you here forever?"

"I guess by extending the term of my contract to 6 years."

"Done, as far as I am concerned."

"Me too. You are one swell fellow, Richardson."

It worked, Beardsley said to himself as he left the room. "1.5 mill with 10% raises each year for 6 year. He would not have to worry about bonuses tied to financial performances, this was hard cash. It will take more than 6 years to find out that the numbers I showed them are slightly off. This is my day, this is my hospital and this is my board. I hope it is my board. They still have to approve the committee's recommendation. Just call me A-Rod of hospital administrators."

He continued to himself. "I have taken it as far as I can without looking manipulative. I have to remain modest, even when I go to the Porsche dealer. I could not be feeling better as no one saw through the number juggling. I provided a strong bottom line for the P and L statement. No one questioned how the numbers were so good; they only worry when there is bad news. No one caught the false entries for the depreciation and the inflated numbers in the accounts receivable. No financial problems for this lucky man. You have to admit, a plain envelope, full of 100 bills slipped to the auditor, had to do something for my cause."

As he walked down the hallway, he heard a familiar commotion outside the hospital. "Oh no, not another bunch of hoodlums, picketing the hospital about women's health, or hopefully, not union organizers trying to entice the nurses to join 1099." He went to the window to check out the crowd. He saw the people but could not make out the focus of the protest as the signs were written in Spanish. He thought he could see the word for candy and of course Mexico. Then he spotted Karl Strem wearing his Red Sox hat with a group of medical student led by Erica Gates on the steps of the hospital, yelling at the crowd. Something about Stop Mexico! "Oh no! Not an anti-immigration rally by the locals." But the crowd was not disorderly, like the last one. Beardsley got on the phone to security and Community relations to find out what was behind this demonstration.

"Faith Boringer, please, this is Richardson Beardsley. I'll wait."

"Yes, Mr. Beardsley, I was expecting your call. It seems that Karl Strem, the chief resident and a medical student got a hold of the TV stations and the local paper to point out the tragic effects of lead containing candy from Mexico. The city's Hispanic population was creating a generation kids with lead poisoning."

"That explains why the young doctor is wearing a T shirt that has the familiar "Get the lead out! This is making the hospital look good. We are not to blame, right?"

"Right you are, Mr. Beardsley."

"Good job, Faith, let's run with the publicity. Call CNN. Call eBay. Thanks for the information."

Beardsley saw this opportunity to strengthen his community interest face. He adjusted his tie, looked into the mirror behind the trophy shelf in the hall way to make sure his hair was combed and went outside to face the TV cameras. How good was this day? he was thinking, A new contract, a chance to be on television to act interested in a group that he really did not care about. It would be hard to top this run of success. He went to Karl Streem, took his Red Sox hat and put it on backwards. Putting one arm around Karl and the other around a protestor, he headed for the Channel 7 TV cameras.

As Beardsley was going out the front door, three people got out of a car in the visitor's parking lot, armed with black leather lap top cases back. They headed for the administrative wing, took the elevator to the 12 floor where they presented their ID's to Ann Ranier.

Patrick Gallagher, Donna Brittan and Roosevelt Howard Jr. were auditors from United Bonding Company who insured the hospital's board of Trustees, Officers and Volunteers. They were concerned about the surpluses that were accruing in the past 6 months. The financials, better than other hospitals in the area and other major children's hospitals, alerted them to a potential problem. Although exceptional management could explain the success, Al Sharptee's resignation triggered an alarm to these chronically paranoid auditors. As forensic auditors, they knew most of the tricks of financial games. Were these numbers from financial cooks or crooks? These investigators were pros; they all had experience with other hospital financial doings and knew where to look for possible fraud. Of course, they had to suspect embezzlement but usually the people in these frauds were not that dumb. Since all possibilities had to be considered, they needed to talk with the finance people, look at their spread sheets and reimbursement transactions with the major health insurers. If the hospital officials were not cooperative, they would seek a warrant and examine all the records and the email files. They had already done a tour of the suburbs to check out the size of the houses of the administrator and finance people and talked to neighbors about life styles changes of their targets. Always pleasant, they assured Ann that they would not be there too long. Ann, likewise pleasant, did not like them snooping around, even though she knew that nothing illegal could be carried out at CHUC. Nonetheless, she paged Beardsley.

"Mr. Beardsley, Ann here. There are three people from the hospital bonding company who want to check on some financial reports. I have them in the waiting room as I know you would like to meet them."

"It must be a routine visit, thanks for the heads up. I will be right up."

"Dammit. Why me? Stay calm Beardsley. Don't blow it now. I was on a roll today but this was not good." In his scheme to build up the financial surplus, he had not thought about insurance auditors. "Slow down, I don't want to look too nervous and reinforce their suspicions. I'll have to use my charm to diffuse their search. I was on such a roll, I felt nothing bad could come of this. I'll just stop for a minute to get myself together; if I ran there too quickly, they may suspect something. Stay calm. I know I can get to them." He stopped in the men's room, checked his iPhone and then headed for his office.

As usual, the three people were polite when they saw Beardsley but their faces had as much emotion as a skate boarder preparing for a run down a flight of steps. All business.

"Richardson Beardsley, welcome to our hospital. Sorry to keep you waiting; I should never walk in the halls, everybody wants a piece of me. What can I do for you?"

The three shook hands with Beardsley. Roosevelt took the lead. "This is a routine visit, part of our regular hospital inspection of our policy holders". They did not mention that they were also looking for signs of guilt.

"We will do anything to make you visit productive and pleasant. Please come into my office. Can I get you something to drink?"

The news of the auditor's visit buzzed though the administrative suite. When Caroleen was in a panic state as she had yet to recover from the Santa Fe and now she was afraid that she would be included in the financial charades that were going on in the hospital. She had nothing to do with the billing or padding the accounts receivable as her responsibility was the ambulatory care units. They did not make a profit and there were no obvious ways to fudge the figures, at least as far as she knew. None the less, she worried that she would be included in any financial ruses. She should have said no when she heard about the plan since she knew it was not totally legal but she was new to the job, had a lot of debt that she needed to cover and did not feel she could go against her boss. If she had said no, she also would not have been sent to snoop around the surgery department as Beardsley wanted her to do. Then she would not have gotten involved with Carter Randolf, not gone to Santa Fe and not had the pregnancy scare. Her period was due soon; then at least she could erase the Santa Fe from her mind. The pregnancy test was negative in Santa Fe and again four times since she came home. She decided not to take another pregnancy test and seek positive thoughts. Automatically, she felt for the patch on her side. It was still there but it was redundant as she had no more exposure to sperm since that time in Bishop's Lodge but she was still worried. Hopefully, the auditors would not involve her but she was still worried.

Beardsley panicked. He could tell that these auditors were talented and experienced.. He knew he had to come up with an explanation for the low reserves and high receivables. Buying off these three as he did with the hospital auditors was not an option. He had to cut more expenses as he had outlined in what he called project Gray Hair. Fire the gray hairs. He could bring in young doctors to work for less money; he just heard about a group of Cuban doctors who defected to the U.S. This was not the time to think about quality. He always avoided all discussions about quality measurements. When the staff worried about quality of care, he challenged his critics to define quality and assess it. That ended the discussion for quality was too subjective a concept except when one or a family member was ill. He knew most measurements of quality came from patient satisfaction surveys. But what did the patients know about quality. In patient surveys, they voted with their emotions. "She was kind, explained my problem clearly etc." but they do not mention if the diagnosis was correct, the studies necessary or the treatment current with the latest evidence based treatment. The least capable doctors on the staff seemed to come out in the upper 50% on the patient ratings.

With plan Gray Hair, he could lop off about $500,000 easily and maybe more, depending how wide a group he targeted for dismissal. Of course there would be severance to pay but most of it would be covered by a decrease in salaries. It was time to move on cutting staff. He sat down at his desk and picked up the phone.

Carrie was on her phone talking with a decorator to discuss changing the color of the walls to brown and turquoise. She asked the gardener to put more blue colors in the cutting garden. She felt great but had an uneasy feeling about the future, optimistic that good times were permanent, as usual, she worried that the mood would turn sour. As she was looking at the garden, she saw a UPS truck was pulling up to the front of her house. "Who could be sending us a package? I have ordered nothing from the catalogue books or the internet. Someone is surprising me with something. I hope it is a diamond."

When the bell rang, she danced to the door, humming Somewhere Over the Rainbow. Valerie from UPS, greeted her, gave her a pen to sign for the package and presented a small box to her. "A present from New Mexico. I hope it is a gift from a friend." Carrie smiled without comment. The return address indicated that the package was from the Bishop's Lodge. She went inside, ripped open the wrapping paper to find an envelope and a small box.

The Bishop's Lodge
Santa Fe NM

Dear Mrs. Randolf,

Thank you for staying at the Bishop Lodge. I hope you enjoyed your stay with us and look forward to your return. After you left, our house keeper found your necklace in the bathroom. Enclosed in the box you will find this lovely piece of turquoise.

Our best wishes to you and Dr. Randolph.

Amanda Olivero
Vice President, Housekeeping services

"Turquoise? I don't have any turquoise necklace. I should just wrap it up and send right back with Valerie," muttered Carrie. "But then, turquoise is a good way to stir up memories of the Southwest, I am ready to go back. But first I will take a peak."

She opened the box and saw the green turquoise stone on the silver necklace. "That looks familiar. Where did I see this? In the store on the Plaza? Not in a museum. No. that French girl that was in the hot tub with me. Obviously, they mixed up my name with hers. We were both staying at the hotel. The maid must have confused us so she got the stone from her room and when she got to the office, she gave the wrong room number. I will just send it back and tell them of the mix up. It is a beautiful stone. I wonder why the young lady, did not call them to tell them of her loss. Young kids, they are so irresponsible. I think I will show it to Carter, just a hint. These days, he would buy me anything. Wait a minute, how did they know my name and address? I don't think Beardsley would have given them my name. Strange!"

That night, she showed the letter and stone to Carter. His blank face showed that he did not appreciate the beauty of the Cerrillos Turquoise. When Carrie told him she was going to mail it back so it could be delivered to the right person. Carter looked almost as green as the stone. He followed his instinct when faced with a crisis. Say nothing, look straight ahead and don't confess to anything. He learned that reponse from his old dog who would not move when he found poop on the rug and asked "Who did this?" He stood there, frozen. "Fine, wrap it up and I will drop it off to the Mailbox store and send it back to the hotel, what was the name of the hotel?"

"Oh I can call Valerie, the driver and she will pick it up."

"No, I will feel better getting it right to the pickup site. The truck may break down or be robbed. You never know. I can stop by first thing in the morning."

"You sure?"

"Sure. Safety first."

The next day, he took the package to the hospital, paged Caroleen to ask her if she had the gift he bought her in Santa Fe.

"I think so, why do you ask?"

"Well I have one in my hand that looks just like the one that you were wearing."

"Oh, no! I must have panicked when I realized that I had not changed my patch. I do remember taking it off when I soaked in the bath tub. Oh no! What a stupid mistake!"

"I tell you what. Come by my office in 10 minutes, I won't be here but when you get it back, don't wear it in the hospital or in town so that my wife will not see it by accident. She does not know you or that you were there with me, so she will never connect all the dots. I would like to keep it that way, you know what I mean? Any more urine tests I should know about?"

"Nada."

"Good."

The other phone Carter's office rang so Jan picked it up on the second ring. "Surgery Department, Jan speaking"

"Good morning Jan, Mrs. Carter here. How are you doing?"

"Just fine, Mrs. Carter. Are you enjoying the spring weather?"

"It is perfect for gardening and fishing."

"What can I do for you?"

"I want to talk with Caroleen, but I don't remember her last name. She has a French accent."

"Columbe. Extension 4474. Do you want me to transfer you to her office?"

"That is not necessary. Thanks, I don't know what is happening to my memory."

"I think it took a walk with mine. Isn't it awful, the way we forget names?"

"It is a major handicap but we should stick together, maybe we forgot different names."

"Thanks for your help"

Carrie collapsed in her sofa in the den. "So that's it. Dear Carter was in Santa Fe with that French parfait. At least he has better taste than I did with that twerp Beardsley. I must have been desperate to sleep with him. But he did get me to Santa Fe, the trip that started my new life. So it was not all lost. Maybe dear Caroleen got him charged up much to my benefit. I am actually having a good time now. Carter is a new person, a better, more humane person. Now if he could only become more honest. But who am I to talk about honesty. At least I did not leave anything in the hotel room at Sunset Lodge,.....as far as I know. I will just file this little episode away in a safe place. I may need some juicy ammunition in the future."

David Grunberg, opened the meeting of the legal committee, the group formed to examine occurrences in the hospital that may lead to legal actions and determine if there were errors in the hospital operations that caused the problem. They also reviewed cases where suits were already filed. In that case they made recommendations about fighting the suit or settling out of court. The panel consisted of David Gruenberg, Jackie Lawrence chief nurse, Carter Randolf, John Spirito, Karl Strem, chief resident, and Faith Borringer PR. Invited guests were: Allison Zimmerman, OR supervisor, Kitty Brown, OR nurse, Tim Warren and Kirby Jackson. "Today we are looking at case RM #53904. You all have the case summary in front of you. This is the case of a patient whose underwent renal transplant by Dr. Jackson last month. After what looked like successful surgery, the suture lines at the ureter connection broke down so the patient had to return to the OR. Fortunately, he recovered and was discharged within the usual time frame."

"Fortunate for the patient and the hospital?"

"Right, Dr. Spirito, we knew you would worry about both parties."

"So why are we going over this?"

"Good question. The second operation was performed by Tim Warren, not Kirby Jackson. We had an unusual complication and a change in surgeons. Further study of the time sequences showed that case started before the donor kidney arrived in the hospital. The helicopter had mechanical difficulties which delayed the delivery of the kidney, and Dr. Jackson did the transplant but left just after the ureters were attached. He did not close the case but he signed out to Dr. Warren who took care of the closing and the post-operative care. Dr. Jackson was in Santa Fe, New Mexico, being inducted into a surgical honor society. Subsequently, there was a leak at the suture line that required a second trip to the OR for repair. There is no law suit followed but we want to be ahead of the problem to see if there was anything that we could do or should do, system wise, that is. I have asked a few of the people who were in the OR and ICU to come in and answer any questions that we have about this case.

There was an incident report filed about the case by Allison Zimmerman, senior nurse in the OR who reported that protocol was broken when the surgery was started on the recipient before the kidney had arrived in the OR. Further study showed that surgery was started before the kidney was in town. As you heard, the helicopter had trouble of some kind."

"Why did you file an incident report, Allison? Do you make reports often?"

"I do. When there is a problem with sponge counts or with blood transfusion reactions, my understanding of incident reports is not tattle telling but rather communication to alert legal that an occurrence occurred, I mean that an incident occurred that may cause legal problems. I did not do this as a personal vendetta against Dr. Jackson. I respect his talents." The other nurses in the room smirked when they heard this denial as they knew about Dr. Jackson and Allison had a romance in the past. He dropped her suddenly when he found a younger lady from radiology. "I know the hospital rules about starting renal transplant cases; this was a violation of that policy."

"What did Dr. Jackson say when you bought this rule to his attention."

"Something to the effect of "Butt Out." I must add that this was the start of the case, so tensions were not increased as they might be when connecting the arteries and ureters. This was mild to the comments made under stress. We are used to those tension relieving utterances. I understand how stress can make you say things that could hurt other people's feelings. It is part of the OR and does not faze me. I have been in the OR for almost 20 years and have heard a lot worse than butt out."

"Do you file incident reports whenever the rules are broken?"

"Not exactly, there are rules that are bruised, broken, or splintered."

"Which one was this?"

"Badly broken, I guess. We either have rules to be obeyed or we should throw out the rules and procedures books"

"Kitty Brown, do you have anything to add. You were the scrub nurse on this case."

"Right. I was the scrub nurse. What would you like to know?"

"Did you see anything unusual about this operation?"

"No, it went amazingly well. The kidney pumped out urine immediately after the hook up."

"Do you think Dr. Kirby was operating his usual way or was there any differences that day?"

"He was fast and efficient."

"Any indication that he was preoccupied or rushed?"

"No."

"How about when the ureters were attached. Anything different?"

"He was on a roll by the time he got to that stage."

"On a roll?"

"Yes. I could not keep up with him, he was moving right along."

"Did you notice anything about the sutures he was putting in?"

"He did that real well. I am amazed how uniformly that he can put those little sutures in that slippery tissue. He is like a Singer sewing machine. Oops, does Singer still make sewing machines? I am showing my age."

"Yes, they do but I am not sure where they are made, probably in China.

"I have a question for Tim Warren. Tim, did Kirby Jackson, sign out the case to you?"

"Yes sir. He gave me the story and I took responsibility for the care of Tommy Morris."

"It is unusual that someone would do a transplant of the kidney and then leave town."

"It has happened. We work as a team. Transplantation surgery is by nature not scheduled, you have to do them immediately when a kidney becomes available. The case gets superimposed on the regular OR schedule or office hours or as in this case, trips out of town."

"Did you have any problem taking over since you were not in on the case?"

"No, I have done many transplants, we work as a team."

"When did you find out there was a problem with the connections of the transplanted kidney to the patient."

"The urine output slowed down slightly, the weight was going up and then I was able to detect fluid in the abdomen."

"How so?"

"The old fashioned way, I examined his belly for bowel sounds and I found that he was slightly more tender than usual and when I moved him on his side I could detect fluid by finding dullness. An ultrasound confirmed the fluid. We went right to the OR."

"What did you find then?"

"I could see urine leaking at the site of the ureter anastomosis. The sutures had broken down in the area about 3 o'clock. It was easy to suture the area and stop the leak."

"Did the sutures look like they were put in by a sewing machine?"

"A what?"

"Were the sutures uniformly spaced?"

"Not really."

"How did the patient do after the second operation?"

"He did great! Just a tinge of rejection that we fixed immediately."

"OK Kirby, your turn."

"You had to leave the OR because you were going to Santa Fe?"

"Right."

"What time was your plane?"

"It was about 4 PM."

"Was there a later plane you could take and still get there?"

"I don't know but I assume so."

"Could you have left the next day and still made your dinner."

"I think so. I knew about how planes get stranded because of weather out west or even here. You know how Newark airport gets hit by bad weather, especially this time of year."

"What do you think we should do to change our systems to minimize this problem?"

"I have been thinking about this a lot. It is hard to make a foolproof system since we never know when a kidney will become available. So we have to go with whoever is around."

"How would you feel if you needed surgery and your surgeon left the case while you were in the OR?"

"I am not sure that is a fair question, John. You know, as dedicated as we are here, we do have times when we need to be elsewhere. Meetings, lectures or testifying in court. Check that, I guess I should not have mentioned court, in this setting."

"As you heard, someone thought you should not have started the case before the kidney was present. The usual sequence."

"I wanted to get the kidney in the patient as soon as I could; I feel they do better when the time without blood flow is as short as it could be."

"So you were starting early to protect the donor kidney."

"Right."

"Have you started the case before you had the kidney before?"

"Sure."

"Why do you think that some of the OR staff were against starting the case before the kidney arrived?"

"I guess you would have to ask them."

"Do you think it was because you wanted to catch a plane?"

"Not really, as I said, there were other planes I could have caught."

"Right."

"So have you changed the protocol for transplanting kidney by following the sequence that you did in the Morris case."

"I really don't have a written sequence or protocol."

"Did you enter a note in the chart that you were signing out to Dr Warren?"

"No. I am bad at writing notes. Now that we have the computerized record, it is even worse for I can't get the hang of the new system."

"Anything else, any body?"

David Grunfeld looked at his watch and moved to conclude this session. "Thank you for coming to discuss this case. As you know, this is confidential so no one should discuss the case outside this room. We are not here to affix blame but to look at our systems to see if we can do something to the structure of the hospital so that we can prevent problems with patient care rather. We have to be on alert to do the best job, not being complacent. Complacency is our enemy. We must constantly retune the engines or violin strings, you know what I mean. Now I would like the panel to remain so we can discuss what we heard today. Thank you, women and men for coming down here today."

The guests left the room.

"Any first impressions about our system?"

I think the unscheduled aspect of the case brings on a multitude of logistical problems. Most of us have our week fairly tightly scheduled so that we have to deal with ad libbing the time."

"What do you mean, Carter?"

"Our scheduled obligations have to be modified when we have emergencies that may take precedent over the scheduled tasks."

"How about not writing in the chart, Carter?"

"A federal offense. I just cannot get the attending surgeon to write notes. I know it is the rule but they were not raised that way so it is hard for them to follow the rules."

"Should we put in writing that the case should not start until the kidney is in the building? This time we were lucky but next time, if there is a next time, we may be unlucky."

"I am surprised the parents are not more aggressive about the complication."

"A good question, John. I think they are nice people who are so grateful that their son is peeing real urine, that is all that matters, writing in the chart is not important to them."

"Again, should we put in writing that the case should not start until the kidney is in the building. Just think what would happen if the next transplant case will be a plaintiff lawyer's child. We could be in for big bucks."

"The problem with making a protocol to prevent a problem means that if someone goes off protocol for a good reason and there is a problem, we have shot ourselves in the foot. Maybe it is better to be faulted for not having a protocol. Then we will be ordered to make one up. Let's close the case then, with a slap on the wrist. But violating a protocol that we made up will be worth millions to some doctor chaser."

"So this was a sham meeting?"

"Not really Karl, we can always ding Kirby for not making notes. Then it looks like we have done something," replied Carter, obviously biased as one could be when one of his team was being subjected to this review.

In the old days, Jackie Lawrence would have defended Carter because of their long history at CHUC. Today she was trying to be an independent voice while supporting the concerns of her OR staff. John Spirito, always worried about the institution, especially when there was a chance for losing money to pay out malpractice claims, wanted something positive to come out of this discussion. He learned that he had to hold back and wait for the comments to wind down and then seek how to come up with a compromise that will please most of the people and appease the extremes. He could see that the surgeon was protective, the OR nurse, used to procedure books and protocols, was pushing for another document to detail who, what and when. The PR person was thinking about what the press would do if they got wind of this or found the document, wondering why we had to write down what was to happen and when, obviously a cover up to a big problem that needs an investigative reporter.

Karl Strem entered the discussion. "It seems to me that he was rushed; think about what we know. The operation started earlier than usual, the next to worst things happened, the kidney transport had trouble. It could have been worse; the kidney never arrived so there would be a big hole in the young man that had to be sewn up and then put back on dialysis, just as he would have been if the donor had not been found. Then we have the broken suture line, sure, it could happen in any case, but Dr. Jackson never had this complication before. Seems he was preoccupied and rushed. We are charged with looking at systems, this issue will occur again so we better come up with some recommendations.

Next patient may not be as fortunate as this patient was. We need to take a stand for the patients and the institution and not support our various disciplines. Especially, we should use protocols to improve patient care and not worry if a lawyer will find the violation of protocol."

After the discussion lasted about 30 minutes, John could not stand any more talk, he piped in "Could we couch the document to say something like "there will always be circumstances that will alter this protocol, but effort should be made to follow as closely as possible. And on and on and on. But I would make a big point that our protocol that requires a note to state that the doc is signing out to a person who understands the case and is alert to the possible complications. They do not have to be enumerated."

"Good idea John, I knew we could get some wisdom from you."

"I would make a special note to Kirby reminding him of the note problem."

"Do you think anything will change after this meeting?" Karl asked no one special.

"Not really, but we tried."

Chapter 25

Once again, the group assembled in the conference room for the house staff meeting. At the end of the year, it was hard to get the residents to do anything but get their patients admitted and discharged. They did not come to lectures or ask questions on patient rounds. The only interest they had was making plans for the break after the end of the academic year in June. A group of singles were going to the North Carolina outer banks renting a house in Duck. No one had ever been to Duck, but the name made people curious about seeing a place called Duck. Since it was off season, they got a good rental price. Others were taking the break to fix up their houses or move to new apartments. A few would be attending weddings. The thought of a week off served as fuel to keep them going through the last weeks of the year.

Karl Strem made the usual announcements about undicted charts and the need to dictate discharge letters to the referring doctors. He then turned to the results of the voting for the teacher of the year award.

"As you recall, we had a few favorites... Robert Farmer, Will Miller from Cardiology, Freda Watkins, Donna Barstow from the ED and Nancy Tappeur from GI."

It was a close race but it came down to Robert Farmer and Will Miller. This year the winner is Will Miller."

"I demand a recount."

"What was the actual vote?"

"Trust me, the election was straight forward. Miller won by 3 votes. Those who do not like the result should check with their non-voting comrades. Only 45% of the house staff voted."

"Poor Farmer, he has never won the award after all these years and all the teaching he does."

"Maybe he should start sleeping with the house staff like someone else does."

"What is wrong with that? I think Shakespeare said. 'It is better to be loved by a married cardiologist than not to be loved at all.' He is a good teacher; it is just the extra qualities that made me vote for him."

"You too?"

"I wish. My vote for him was an anticipatory one. I am looking forward to the end of the year dinner to collect my reward after he gets his award."

"Remember this is confidential. We want Will to be surprised."

"But what about poor Farmer?"

"Sorry, but we live in a democracy. The staff voted."

It was obvious to Karl that those who supported Farmer had strong feelings about letting him know his teaching was appreciated. His manor of asking residents to answer his questions turned many people away from him. They did not like to be embarrassed in front of the group, when they did not know the answer. They were so used to getting all A's on their report card from knowing all the answers. That was not Farmer's intent; he just wanted them to learn what they had not known and to think on their feet, the Socratic Method. Karl had a warm feeling towards Farmer.

"How about presenting a second plaque to Dr. Farmer indicating appreciation for his many years of teaching house officers and providing a role model for clinical care?"

"Good idea! Like a lifetime achievement award. Do it! That will let him know we appreciate his teaching."

"Good, meeting adjourned."

When the meeting broke up, Felix grabbed Lester and pulled him aside.

"I am in deep trouble, my friend."

"Trouble, what kind of trouble?"

"I may get killed."

"What have you done? Not dictated your charts? What ?"

"You remember when I met the volunteer and she began to come to our apartment?"

"Right, that was a major event in my life that made me move into Adrienne's."

"This is not about you, Lester."

"Right, right. What happened?"

Well that went quite well for several months. Then she decided to divorce her husband but was worried that he would, no doubt, hire investigators to follow her to the apartment. So she stopped coming to the apartment. We met a few times at the hospital in the resident's on call rooms but that was too rushed. She moved out of my life."

"So why are you going to get killed?"

"Well, she confided her dilemma to her friend who was also very unhappy at home, her husband was either working or had a mistress or two that took up his time. So she called me and asked to come over."

"What did she want you to do? Talk to her husband?"

"Not really, she wanted to take over from her friend. I got good ratings, obviously."

"Anyhow, she came over and we hit it off. Things were going great. Then one night we were resting up from our love exercises, drinking some wine, and watching the news. She blurted out, "that's my husband.""

"Where? I was grabbing my pants to get ready for an escape out the back window."

She says, "on TV, that's him, being interviewed by the DA"

The caption on the screen said. DA talking to Dominic Mentarento, reputed mob leader.

I almost fainted. "Your husband is in the mob?"

She looked puzzled. "Not really, he works for his cousin in the family business. They sell recycled metals."

I was really panicked now. "What is his cousin's name?"

"Enzo Romanesco."

Lester could remember names and details that no one else cared about until they needed to retrieve some minutia from the past. "I remember that name. Lester, you were with me in the ED when that kid came in with appendicitis; they got Dr Randolf out of bed, even though he was sick as a dog, to do the surgery. Mr. Romanesco than wrote a check to the hospital. It was in the papers."

"I guess that is the hazard of not reading the local papers. So your girlfriend number 2 is connected to a mob member?"

"You could say it that way. I always thought that these women relished the role of the wife for the perks and diamonds, not having a problem with their husband's mistresses since it eased the demand for bedroom service. Who would think that she wanted to play too? Now I am in a fix. If I escape from her, the old man will not find out. But if I escape from her, she may turn me in, just for spite. Either way, I will either end up in the Raritan River with concrete boots or have my balls shot off and then end up in the Pine Barrens like the guy in the Sopranos."

"That is all the choices you have?"

"Can you think of another?"

"Why don't you tell her you were stuck with a needle from an AIDS patient? That so far you test negative but it will take 18 months to get the final test. To be fair to her, you should stop meeting her. That way she will be sure not to become infected with HIV. The only safe way is to abstain. Tell her that condoms are just not safe."

"Do you think she would buy that?"

"I do if you use logic and frame it in terms of safest for her. She will be out of your life in a heartbeat."

"Not the way my heart is racing. No one moves that fast."

"OK in a string of heart beats."

"Maybe you can get a rash on your face. That would scare the libido out of her."

"Do you know where any poison ivy leaves are? That will give you a rash in a few days."

"Brilliant! Thanks a lot. I am so into myself, I did not ask you how you are doing. How is Adrienne? What is up with you two?"

"Thanks for asking. That was a result of Adrienne's coaching. She taught him to say 'thanks for asking.' Things were going great."

"Were?"

"Yes, in the past tense." Lester related the episode in the shower where she pulled him into the shower and then to bed. As Lester began the story, he paused as he thought about how exciting those early bedroom scenes were. Then he realized that he stopped the story in mid-idea. "So things went well until about a month ago. We had a nice night watching PBS and then went to bed. It was getting serious; I mean we were talking about the future."

"You are getting married?"

"Well. We kind of talked about it. First I was going to meet her parents in a few weeks, when we both had a free weekend without call. We discussed that a lot, how to act when I got there, what to say. What not to say. You know ....protocol things, I guess you would call it. The talk stopped when the sex began. Pretty good, I must say. I usually take a shower when we are done and then go to sleep. So I am in the shower and I heard this wild scream."

"You were robbed?"

"No, nothing that simple. I ran into the bedroom to find her sitting up in bed and screaming at me. "You're Jewish. I can't take you home to my parents. It's bad enough that you are white, a doctor but a white Jewish doctor. That is more than my parents could take."

"Wait a minute. I did not convert to Judaism today. I was Jewish when you met me, I do not consider that scene in the shower was a conversion baptism, far from it. So why is it an issue now?"

"We were not going to my home back then. Now that it is in the plans. Now it is an issue."

"Let me get this correct. Your mother is half Irish and half Black. Your father is Spanish. That sounds to me that they could make a commercial for Campbell's Soup. Did you ever notice how a house where Campbell's soup is served looks like a sub committee for Youth United Nations?"

"Lester, you can't keep on track in a serious conversation; you always have to digress with comments about your observations.

That is right about who they are. It does not mean they would welcome a white Jewish doctor into their house. That is not how they were raised. They are entitled to be bigoted like the rest of us. Maybe they would like me but I doubt it. They would be intimidated by my vast knowledge, especially about art. They think art is for rich smart people, not their kind."

"You mean her father married someone erroneously labeled as Black, raised her as a black girl and they have prejudicial thoughts about religion?"

"Yes, it is the only area that they can focus on for their negative feelings."

"I can understand their feelings about being Jewish and maybe white but what is wrong with being a doctor."

"A doctor symbolizes meritocracy. They are against anyone rising about his natural state."

"So what about Adrienne?"

"She was considered the rebel and a failure in the family. They feel they failed when she decided to go to medical school. The family black sheep."

"What did they want? The family white sheep? I doubt that. So she is the total rebel. Getting an education. A medical degree and now in bed with a white Jew. How low can you sink?"

"She says to me, that is what I love about you. You can take an issue and shave all the emotion away and see the core of the issue. How about a hug and I give you a blow job and we can figure out the next step when we wake up in the AM."

Felix sat erect in his chair, his face flushed. "Lester, how lucky you are. You kept her and had a blow job too."

"It's not that kind of blow job I thought it would be or the one you are thinking of. She wanted to dry my hair with that electric machine because she did not want to get the pillows wet."

"Little sweet Adrienne, has a bigger wild streak in her, more than I realized."

"Wild is the word, despite the goodie girl appearance in the hospital Ever since we got premium cable TV. She watches the late night programs that teach about wild sex. I though we got the premium package so we could watch reruns of the History and Discovery channels. But she went right for the mature audience programming. That was a close call."

"Did you ever meet her parents?"

"No we decided to wait for the graduation time and invite them to come to the closing ceremony."

• • •

It was about 2 weeks since they got back from Santa Fe, Carrie and Carter were like two oversexed teenagers. Instead of "later, honey," it was "no time like the present." People remarked to Carrie that she looked radiant, her skin was beautiful, and her friends were looking for signs of a face lift or Botox. Maybe she gained a few pounds too. She noticed that she had to tug on the buttons to close her blouses. "The dry cleaners must have shrunk this blouse. I will go and complain to them."

Carter knew differently. "I think your breasts are enlarging. Must be all this sex stimulating your estrogen production, honey."

Carter had renewed interest in his training program, he decided to let the residents do more of the cases, and he had changed his concept of ego enhancement from doing the cases to training the next generation, sharing the limelight with his trainees. He admitted that it felt good and was less taxing on him. He woke up in the morning with new energy. Carrie woke up this morning and threw up. "It must have been the eggplant parmigiano" she reasoned.

"Maybe you should see your doctor and get a pregnancy test." Carter was always one to get to the point, surgeon's linear thinking.

"A what test? I am too old to get pregnant, more over I have lived a long time without children and am not interested in assuming the responsibility for a newborn. I have not been very careful about birth control since lately my periods were quite irregular so I figured that I was early menopause. Besides, even though you had confessed that you did not have the vasectomy, we had never conceived a child in 20 years of marriage, when they were trying to start a family."

She was now beginning to panic. She knew about Carter's pro-life stand. This was going to be a major barrier to any plans she had. Now she broke out in a sweat. Was that a hot flash or was it her nerves? Take a deep breath, she told herself and get a pregnancy test kit from the RiteAid store when it opens at 9am. She used to joke that instead of showing a blue plus sign, they should sell two types of kits, one where positive pregnancy test displays 'congratulations' and another one should display 'bad news.' Right now she was not sure which form the results should display. Carrie lost her sense of humor as she waited out-side the drug store for 15 minutes. She was slightly embarrassed when she failed to find the pregnancy tests and had to ask the clerk who had you are too old for that kind of stuff lady look on her face.

She bought 2 kits in case she messed up one test and raced home.

A blue plus sign! "I'm going to be a mother." She screamed and reached for her cell phone to call Carter. She had wanted to see his face when he heard the news but could not wait to tell him; she needed to talk to someone. Having already checked the internet for information on mifepristone to end the pregnancy, she was prepared to take the treatment.

"Sit down, big daddy, I have news for you."

"Wow! Great news. I am glad the urologist was able to hook me up again. One never knows about the success of undoing a vasec-tomy…..Wow! You're pregnant! …..Amazing…… What happened? A baby at my age. I can't believe I did it! I don't think I can change dia-pers. Let me sit down. Oh, I am sitting down! What does all mean? I never thought I could get you pregnant. Do fathers still hand out cigars or has the anti-smoking lobby ruined that tradition too? Imagine, me being a father, at my age. Imagine."

Then Carrie took a deep breath again. Maybe you are not the father, she said to herself, maybe it was good old Beardsley. That we will never know since this is my secret to keep. I am through with Beardsley and he does not seem to want to change that. We said good bye at the airport when we got off the Gulf Stream and that is how it is going to stay. It would be easier on all of us if I just kept quiet and went to my GYN doc-tor and get the pills. Maybe I should have kept this news from Carter but I was so excited that finally all my systems worked that I had to tell him.

When he came home that night, Carter was pacing around like a proud rooster. He looked like he was ready to crow. Maybe that will happen when the sun comes up in the morning.

"How is this going to play out?"

"What do you mean?"

"With your face all over TV with your vasectomy, how are you going to explain that to your public?"

"That will be easy. I will say that I had the vasectomy reversed. That happens all the time. No big problem."

"About an hour later, Carter came back into the bedroom. " Maybe you don't want to go through with this pregnancy?"

"What are you saying?"

"Maybe you want to see your GYN doctor and get RU 486."

"Boy, you really have changed. You are the poster boy for the pro-life people."

"This is different. My public face is what I thought my public wanted from me. My private face changes depending on the situation. I could not make you go through a pregnancy against your will. You don't have to answer this now, just opening the discussion so that we can continue our lives as we have been in the last weeks. This is real fun. We can talk about it in the AM."

The next morning started with another bout of nausea, just like college drinking binges that ended up at the toilet bowl. "I think it is a girl, I can feel it."

"Feel what?" Carter asked. I did not think morning sickness started so early in pregnancy."

"I was never one who did things by the book."

"I have been thinking."

"About what? May I ask?"

"About me, of course. I have decided that I am going to quit this place.

"This place?"

"CHUC place. I am going to step down as chief of surgery. I am going to change careers …… and locations."

"You are quitting and leaving me?"

"No, No not leaving you. You are coming with me. Where would you go if you left South Creek?"

"Any place?"

"Name it."

"To New Mexico."

"Why New Mexico?

"It sounds like a place that would be about as opposite as this mess but still livable. Where would you go?"

"Strange, I picked New Mexico too. I saw just a little of it but I know that it is the place for me.

"Would you have to get a medical license to practice there?"

"Not where I am thinking about."

"What do you mean?"

"I am going to work for the Indian Health Service in some small rural unit. You are in the Public Health service so you don't need a New Mexico license. I am too old to take any more tests."

"You are going to some rural clinic and give up all this glamour and technology?

"Right. I see the handwriting that says I am getting old and not keeping up with the modern things like laparoscopic surgery and all those sporin antibiotics. I am too old to learn which cephalosporin goes with which bacteria. It is true that surgery is a young man's game and I am getting old. I don't want to mess up any patient because I hung on too long. It is time to give the young ones a chance. My pension is huge, my investments are more than adequate so we can live quite comfortably. I know that the Indian Health Service doctors get nice salaries, not what I make but enough that we can go out to MacDonald's, if they have one out there. How does that sound to you?"

"Sounds like heaven to me. I can see the sunsets and smell the fresh air already. I wonder how long it takes before you don't see the sunsets or get sick of Mexican food. With those words, she grabbed her abdomen as a wave of nausea hit her."

We could find out. He hugged Carrie and pinched her rear, his usual sign of affection."

"I think I will go see Beardsley today and submit my resignation."

"There he goes again," thought Carrie. "Thinking of himself while I am the one who is pregnant and not sure of the next step. But that is why I picked him out. When he is thinking about himself, he does not bother me. I guess I treasure that non-interference more than being the center of attention. I realize that there is no way he could stop being a surgeon. That is why it is hard to be a wife of a surgeon if one needs to feel like a special individual. He needs all the stage, the applause, the forced reverence from the OR staff. He is really a needy person who needs his ego stroked every day or every hour. I guess that is why he is stepping aside but not down. Needy, lovable son of a bitch."

$$\bullet \; \bullet \; \bullet$$

Beardsley was in his office earlier than usual this day, phone on his ear as usual. "Thanks for the heads up about the auditors." He slammed the phone down. "I knew those guys would find the amount of reserve funds was far lower than the average for the amount of hospital charges submitted to the insurance companies. I was a fool for thinking I could get away with that dumb move but it did get me a new contract - 1.5 mil is not a bad deal for me. I did not figure out that Sharptee would resign so quickly which in turn invited a deeper level of audit. Only a dunce could miss the cover up of the reserve funds. I know my lawyer will handle it. I have been in hot water before and he helped me survive."

He pulled his backup plan from his secret file, hand written of course.

Memo to self
Re: Plan B: damage control to cut expenses to minimize the losses that were about to be discovered.
Plan to save 3 million dollars.
Cut out the gray hair.
- **Get rid of Randolf, Barstow and Spirito and senior staff. Sharptee was already gone.**
- **Replace the primary care doctors with just graduated or the foreign graduates from Pacific Rim and Cuba who would work for 50% less than he was paying the US docs now. (After all, they were just seeing colds.)**
- **Hire radiologists from Mysore University in India to read x-rays over the internet.**
- **Bring in Nurse practitioners who would work for even less.**
- **Reduce by 10 the number of house staff.**
- **Get rid of most of the PR and human resource people**
- **Outsource the housekeeping duties to a company (disregard fact that they may employ illegal immigrants).**
- **Cut in salary for executives 25%**
  - **The recent raises for them would still net them their 350,000 salaries.**
  - **Fire the vice president for legal affairs (not worth a dime let alone 350k)**
  - **Same for the human resources VP. (Note: we are going to be diverse at less cost.)**

- - No one would quit since even with the cut in pay, they still were getting paid at the 90 percentile for people around the country for that position.
- Close down one of the community clinics.

Immediate savings 3 million before going after the real redundancies in the organization.

• • •

He dialed his secretary. "Please arrange individual meetings today with Sprito, Randolf, Farmer and Barstow. No particular order."

Beardsley knew he should check with the board before he did it but he wanted to move quickly so he planned to call a few of the usually agreeable board members and stay away from the real thinkers. He was not sure who would get the first axe but that did not really matter.

His phone interrupted his scheming.

"Mr. Beardsley, I have Dr. Randolf's secretary on the phone, he would like to see you today."

"He can come right now if he likes."

"Dr. Randolf said he could be there in 30 minutes."

"Fine Vera. Show him in when he gets here and no interruptions when we are in the office." The smirk appeared on his face. "See all good things have their place. Carter will be the first one to go."

"Hello Richard, You are looking good. Things going well with you?"

Beardsley was taken back by such a friendly opening. He wanted to jump right in and get this awkward discussion over as quickly as possible.

"Yes I am doing fine. I hear you wanted to speak with me."

"What a coincidence, I wanted to meet with you, too."

"So go ahead Carter, you start."

"No you start. What I have to talk about can wait." For a change, Carter did not have to be the first speaker in a discussion.

"Are you sure?"

"Sure. Go ahead."

"Well Carter, I have some bad news. I know when one is discussing bad news; one should come right out and give the bottom line."

"I heard that is the current thinking. But sometimes I move slowly to build up the case before dropping the axe."

"Or the guillotine as sometimes happens."

"The Guillotine. That sounds drastic. Go ahead Dick. You're first. My reason for being here has nothing to do with axes or guillotines."

"Carter, O man, I am asking for your resignation. Nothing about your work or you. We have a financial problem and I have to let a group of people go, I decided to start with people near retirement age. Your pension is good and I assume you have adequate funds."

"You are getting rid of me after all these years of dedication and service?" Carter decided to play it out like bad theater. Look shocked, he told himself. Don't ham it up. Don't be too agreeable and for good- ness sake, don't let him know that you were going to resign today. "I can't believe that you are going to drop me like you would if you bit into a jalapeño pepper. My life, my career, my patients." Hey, don't over emote he reminded himself. Beardsley may just feel sorry for you and change his mind. "There are 37 in your heaps of veeps. Why not can them instead of dropping me?"

"Correction! There are only 36 vice presidents. I am not dropping you. Of course you will get a nice severance package, medical coverage for life and a nice cash settlement. I hate to do this to you but for your information I am taking a 33% pay cut and so is the executive staff of vice-presidents. I may even cut one of them out. Now what did you want to see me about?" Beardsley conveniently omitted the fact that he had just given the VP's a 33% pay raise before this blow up.

"It does not matter. This is hard to accept and process. I need some time to sort out this conversation. Of course you know you are open for legal issues such as age discrimination. I guess if is easier to drop me than canning women or minorities, if we had any. Avoiding my law suit should be worth something in the severance package."

"I will keep this in mind. Thanks for not getting hysterical."

"Not my nature. I await your severance offer, in the mean time, I have a few lives to save in the OR." Carter almost danced down the hall but was worried that Beardsley had TV cameras checking the hallway activity.

That day Beardsley met with John Spirito, Robert Farmer and Don- na Barstow as well as others from general pediatrics, administration and human resources. He called the union chief who accepted the news of outsourcing as well as an envelope of cash with a promise of only a token fight and demonstration.

Carter could not hide his joy. He called Carrie with the news about the firing and the severance pay. "This could not have worked out better. I was so excited that I forgot to say my prayers. I guess the prayer from yesterday was still working."

John Spirito was not as accepting; He had always thought he would die in the reading room, scanning x-rays for hints of rare diseases. His loyalty to the institution did not include passively taking dismissal from the place he loved. Having no outside interests to take up the void in the day frightened him. His first thought was to fight this, so he called his lawyer to find out who could take on his case of age discrimination and firing without cause. Too bad he never had a contract with the hospital.

Robert Farmer's reaction was similar to Carter Randolf. He knew his time to stop medicine had arrived. He was ready to quit but could not make the move. He was tired and running out of gas but he never wanted to die with his boots on as many of his friends did. Getting fired from his job at CHUC would be good for him; now this decision was made for him. Donna Barstow was devastated as her whole life was the ED, the students and residents and of course, the patients. She knew she could find things to do or even a new hospital but CHUC was the home she never thought of leaving.

When Caroleen heard the news, she realized that the auditors were on to something and Beardsley was using this staff massacre to divert the attention away from his financial culinary tricks. It was time to get out of this messy place and start a new life. Losing her job at CHUC was not the worst scenario as she could go elsewhere with a fresh start.

John Spirito's anger increased when   he heard that the hospital was contracting with a group in India to read the x-rays over the internet. He felt he had to move quickly; not for himself as he was sure he could find another position   but now his mission was to protect his kids who needed someone on site who could talk to them, to make sure the right study was done and oversee the radiology technicians. Too often the outside radiologists read the studies after the patient left the radiology suite so there would be no chance to pursue the diagnosis with additional studies at that visit. Who could vouch for the quality of the readings? He got on the phone and called Norman Oppenheim, the one board member that seemed to have both the interest of the hospital and the balls to speak up and challenge the leadership to explain their decisions and to shake out all the spin from the discussion.

"Norman, this is John Spirito. Have you heard about the shakeup at the hospital? You have not? Let me give you the highlights, or the low lights as they may be." John went over the last 24 hours of decimation.

"No, I have not heard about this. From our board meetings, everything seemed to be going well in the hospital, especially the finances."

"So that little bastard did this without the board's approval?"

"Sounds that way. But I will get busy and round up the team. Don't pack your bags yet. John, we have some work to do. I have been suspicious of some shenanigans and have had forensic accountants in my company go over the financials presented to the board. I will expect a report from them momentarily so I will ask them to show me what they have."

The buzz in the hospital was stronger than usual when the firing news leaked out. Soon everyone knew that the best doctors and mid level administrators were on the firing list. No one figured out why this was going on but they knew the consequences, patient care would suffer and the reputation of the institution was at risk. Those who were not fired were frightened fearing they would be next. Twittering served as an emergency support system. Norman Oppenheim held two phones, calling fellow board members to alert them and to organize a meeting to assess damage and make plans. Since Clayton Pickering was out of town, Norman took charge of getting the board members together. He had called Beardsley who made excuses about being tied up in budget meetings but told Norman that he was alerted to a problem and had already instituted some major cost cutting in the staff when the auditors alerted him about a deficit.

"Can I see the auditors' reports?"

"That would be nice but I can't do it as there was no written report just a phone conversation."

"You mean that you whacked all these people without an official report? Do you think that is fair? Fair to the mainstays at the hospital. Dr. Farmer? Dr. Barstow? Dr Spirito? To name a few. Who else did you can?"

Beardsley did not realize that Norman knew the names of the released doctors, even though he did not mention any names when he called Norman. "Carter did not seem to have a problem with stepping down. I could not wait for reports to stop the hemorrhages. I owe it to the institution. People are important but I did not want to interfere with the welfare of our patients or harm our hospital."

"I think you owe something to the people who make the institution, like respect and consideration. Who are these auditors? I need to speak to them."

"They work for the bonding company and have been told not to talk to hospital people."

"So how did you get the information?"

"I begged them to give me some inside information."

"Well give me their names and I will beg too."

"I am afraid I cannot do that."

"Why?"

"Security."

"This is crazy. I suspect there is more to the story and I am exercising my duty as a board member. I don't want to sound accusatory but this sounds like stonewalling. What are you covering up?"

"I don't like the tone and content of your comments." Beardsley was using tricks he learned in the negotiation tapes he brought from QVC. Trick #5- get aggressive.

"That does not bother me what you don't like. My responsibility to the hospital comes before your feelings. If you have nothing to hide then you will cooperate. I want you to know that I am calling a meeting of the board as Clayton is out of town."

"Did you call him?"

"I have put in a call but he is fishing in Canada and does not have a cell phone."

"Is this meeting legal? I doubt it. I will check the constitution and let you know what it says."

"I thought you were tied up in budget meetings."

"I will multi-task it."

"I will call you when we are done."

The next phone call was to James Chao, the partner of Baum, Andrews and Chao, the auditing firm for one of Norman's real estate investment funds.

"Hey, James, have you heard anything about the hospital finances? The CEO fired all the big guns on the staff, claiming that the auditors gave him an oral report about falling income and high costs, mainly the salaries of these doctors."

"He said what? I know the auditors who have been at the hospital doing the routine procedure when a CFO leaves. I guess it did not take long for them to find some funny business. I bet it was the reserve funds. That is hospital administration 101. You need to keep the reserve funds at a certain percentage of the charges. It is also auditing 101. Look first at the reserves when going over income statements. Only a rookie would try to pull such a trick. I thought Beardsley was smarter than that but I guess he was so proud that he discovered this trick that he did not check his lecture notes from college that usually has many case histories to show that this is a fool's strategy."

" I wonder if Beardsley actually went to college. But why was this not picked up before? Seems that such a fundamental accounting procedure should have been detected?"

"You are right in the long run. But the scheme will work for a short time by increasing the reserve fund just before the yearly audit and then dropped it back to low levels after the inspection. They could not keep this up forever but for a year they could pull it off. Because the auditors came in unannounced, they got caught. Have you talked to Sharptee, the old CFO?"

"He would not talk on the phone or without a lawyer."

"So it looks like Sharptee is the culprit. How about Beardsley?"

"I don't think he would be that dumb to pull a stunt like this. I plan to talk to him as soon as I can."

"He must have known that this was being done."

"Not necessarily. He has a lot of responsibilities so maybe this was pulled off without his knowledge. This will be a bombshell that we don't need right now, when we are trying to build a new hospital and need the community support. They are not going to donate to a stained institution."

"You are right about that. But how do you keep it quiet?"

"As best as one can. I am just a board member, not the communications director." Thanks for reminding me, I need to talk to Faith Borringer in PR. We need to do some major damage control. It is bound to leak out soon as the public hears about the layoffs, I mean resignations."

"That will be a tough job, Norman."

"And James, will you look into all the consulting contracts from CHUC because when I first joined the board, I was suspicious of these arrangements, especially the ones from the compensation experts.

"We can do that; I will have one of our compensation people get on it."

"Hey, thanks for speaking with me James. I have to go to the board meeting and make some plans."

Chapter 26

"Thanks for coming in on such short notice. As you know, Clayton is out of town so I took the responsibility to call the meeting of the executive committee today. You have heard Richard Beardsley notified the senior staff that they were dismissed. So far, Carter Randolf agreed to a buy out. The rest of the group has not agreed to a severance and a few have indicated that they are going to court to fight the dismissal. There are financial problems that are being uncovered as we speak. The auditors have recently been here and find that the income stream has increased slightly but the reserve fund to cover the gap between what is charged and what is collected is lower than standard practice calls for. Apparently these reserves were being juggled to make the financial statement appear better than it really was. Up to now, they were able to hide these deficits from the auditors. We, now have to come up with a plan to cope with bad publicity that will, no doubt come soon. I have Faith Borringer coming from PR to help us. We may have to go outside to get some damage control experts if this is as bad as I think it will be."

"Do you have any ideas how this could happen? What does Beardsley say?"

"I had a brief conversation with him. He was in budget meetings all day."

"I think Beardsley should be in on this meeting. After all he has done to build up the hospital. He is our leader and we should hear from him."

"We will hear from him when he is available and when we get more facts. Just let me see, how many people heard of a reserve fund?"

No hands were raised.

"Just what I expected. We are all negligent in not knowing about how the hospital works. We are here to be involved in the institution and oversee the administration of the hospital. I am afraid we were being led by the administration, being fed information that may or may not be true but what we wanted to hear. We all drank the Bombay Sapphire martinis. Does anyone think we should have been notified of the staff firings?"

Those present remained paralyzed.

"You mean that by not raising your hand, you agree that the firings are none of our business?"

"OK, that is better. We should have been informed of the upheaval. We should have known the findings of the auditors, too. Agreed?"

"Why weren't we?"

"That is a good question, Tom. Either someone thought it would blow over and did not want to bother us. Or maybe someone was trying to do some maneuvering to soften the news. To defuse it."

"That was stupid, if you don't mind me saying so. Right?"

"Sam White, what do you have to say?"

"I am not sure who will be snooping around here to uncover the problem. But it is my feeling that we have our own investigation with some outside legal counsel to keep us in line. I would hate for this investigation to be muddied up with some well meaning but stupid moves."

"Sam, Bunky and Tom. Will you help me look into this mess? Anyone else who wants to join us? Please let me know. I realize that this in not what you would use as a model for following the sunshine law. But I wanted to get started before the whole state of New Jersey knows about this and impedes our work."

After 20 more minutes of discussion, the group broke up.

• • •

Henrietta Rowland, a features columnist for the South Creek Express had been camping out in the hospital for the past three weeks, searching for human interest stories. Her article about the public demonstration against lead poisoning from Mexican candy was published last week. Relatively new in town, having come from the Lebanon Daily News in central Pennsylvania, she had not known about CHUC before she saw the live coverage in Channel 7 news. So far she had followed a patient admitted for leukemia and another one for William Syndrome as he visited the variety of specialists who cared for his multiple problems. She was now doing a story on the evening shift, the time in the hospital day where emergencies and changes in patients' condition garnered the staff's attention rather than scheduled admissions, tests and surgeries. Tonight she was shadowing the security department to see what kinds of issues call for their attention. Henrietta had just left the cafeteria with Lt. Parkerson who had stopped for a few minutes to grab a coke and apple pie, both items he did not need as evidenced by his 44 inch waist. As they strolled down the main corridor towards security central, they heard a roar "go man go, go man go" One officer, obviously from Texas, shouted "hook 'em Horns" as he made the Texas sign of index and little finger extended like horns. As they got closer to the office they could see at least 6 security officers plus Percy from housekeeping crowded around the panel of monitors. They were all holding cards with numbers on them, like the ice skating judges in the Olympics. Most were 5 and 6 with one 3.

"Excuse me, gentlemen, what is going on and keep it down. This is not Memorial stadium, it is a hospital."

"Not the stadium but more like Cheryl's, the gentlemen's club." commented Nate, the sergeant in charge. "Look at this, lieutenant."

Lt. Parkerson could now see what all the excitement was about. On the monitor was a couple in the missionary position on the new MRI table in radiology.

"Is this being taped? Whoever the jerk is, he will be fired and we need the evidence. Can anyone identify the perpetrators?"

"Never saw the dude before but I can tell you one thing. He could use some pointers from me. I never saw such wimpy sex. They don't call me beauty in motion for nothing. I am the champ."

"He needs some lessons on how to salsa with the senorita. He is like Tommy Two Step, Shake it man."

"This guy is a disgrace to the dude gender. She looks like a blow up toy from Jake's sex shop. But it is more fun than watching people on the monitor entering the main door. I give this daddy a 3 or 4 with points off for creative style and bad position."

"Have you ever done it on an x-ray table? Not the best place for a power sex award. Because of adverse conditions, I give him a good 6."

"Poor approach, average entry and not much splash at the end, a 5."

"How did you guys get this on tape?" asked Lt. Parkerson.

"How did we get this on tape, Percy was doing the floors and saw someone enter the radiology MRI suite. He called to security and we beamed up that new security TV camera in MRI."

"Good pick up Percy, now that we had the porno show for the night shift, who is going up there to scare them away?"

"I don't think that is necessary, they are getting up now. Hey I know that cat, he be the boss from administration. He gave me a candy cane at the Christmas party last year. Tape off, no one saw this right? I don't want to lose my job over a little hanky panky in radiology."

While they were dispersing, Henrietta peeked at the sign in book and saw that at 8:33, Mary Conrad from Pediatric Imaging Diagnostics signed in the guest book. Henrietta jotted the name and the company in her note pad to follow up in the morning.

Someone else at the newspaper had done some snooping too. The next morning the front page showed a picture of Beardsley over an article written by investigative reporter George Fox.

Cream of Children's Hospital skimmed off by CEO.

Financial Problems prompted move

According to unnamed hospital sources, most of the senior staff was informed yesterday that their contract was terminated immediately. The hospital person, who asked not to be directly quoted, said that a problem with the hospital finances required the removal of the heads of surgery, radiology, ENT, anesthesiology and several pediatricians. The source went on to remind this reporter, that the CEO makes 1.5 million annually plus benefits and retirement contributions. The chief of legal affairs makes 400,000 a year as does the vice president for human resources. None of these people was removed from their position but took a pay cut of 25%. The physicians who were fired earned from $125,000 to $250,000, depending on their specialty. There were rumors in the hospital that international doctors from the Cuba and India have being recruited to replace the doctors and others on the staff who are still employed seeing the bulk of the patients in the ambulatory section. These rumors, unconfirmed, were generated by the recent visit to the hospital of Ahmet Gupta, well known head hunter that places graduates of his for profit medical school in India to work in US hospitals, mainly in rural areas that are short of U.S. trained physicians. Gupta also has a company that places Filipino doctors in the U.S. Richard Beardsley, CEO, did not return calls. Al Sharptee, the CFO, recently resigned from the hospital for a job in California in a smaller hospital. We did confirm that Mr. Sharptee was in California in the Palm Tree Hospital, a 95 bed general hospital in Riverside. He was not aware of any financial problems at CHUC. Calls to the doctors fired yesterday were referred to their lawyers.

Our sources also told us that an audit of the hospital finances was just conducted when Mr. Sharptee left. No one would comment on the results of the audit. We contacted several board members of the hospital who were surprised that the doctors were leaving CHUC. The board had not discussed these moves with Mr. Beardsley but was planning a meeting this noon at the hospital. There was no record of a board meeting yesterday as would be required by the state sunshine law.

Thomas Crouseman, age 15, a long time patient at CHUC was almost in tears when he heard that his doctors were no longer going to take care of him. He had been a patient since he was 7 months old when a tumor was found in his abdomen. After the initial surgery, he has been seen in oncology, radiology, dermatology, nephrology and gastroenterology to care for his cancer and complications that arose from radiation and chemotherapy. "These men saved my life, without them I would be a goner. We need them to return. Why don't they fire the boss? That would be a good way to save money."

Nick Genel, state attorney general, read the article on the internet and emailed it to Newark office fraud team who investigates non-profits.

After Norman Oppenheim saw the article, he knew he had to make a public move. The so called private meeting yesterday, trying to keep the problem secret, was not working. He called Vera Cunningham.

"Vera, this is Norman Oppenheim. Will you set up an emergency meeting of the board and try to get word to Clayton on his fishing trip?"

Vera told Norman, "The insurance company that bonded the employees had just appeared at the office. They had called in the hospital lawyers who were making arrangements to take all the computers in the finance office to check emails, memos and letters that may relate to the shortfall. I felt like telling them not to bother to take Beardsley's since he avoided using computers, it would be empty."

"Do your best to get the group together, Vera. I think the hospital is in trouble."

At the same time, John Spirito was meeting with the fired doctors to plan their strategy. Carter Randolf begged out of the meeting as he was happy with his buy out. He had already bought an SUV for his trip to New Mexico and had contacted a realtor to sell his house. Only Robert Farmer could not make it that day but sent an email that he was interested in being part of any action the group decided to do. John scratched his head, then banged the coffee cup on the table. "Let's get started. We have a lot to do today. We are all disappointed in Beardsley's action. I feel that the quality of care would be harmful to our patients if the administration outsourced to inexperienced doctors to do the main clinical work. Secondly, I have the name of a labor lawyer who specialized in professionals who felt they were unjustifiably dismissed. You know that the newspaper had already written an article about the firings."

After much venting and discussion, the group agreed to begin legal action against Richard Beardsley and the hospital with the plan to drop charges against the hospital once they hopefully would begin negotiations to return to their jobs. They were firm in not letting Beardsley off the hot seat.

Beardsley was in deep thought in his office while the doctor's meeting was occurring. After reading the article in the paper, he began his counter campaign. Not one to shy away from confrontation, he was sure that he would prevail in any dispute.

"Vera, get me George Fox at the Mid Jersey Express.." Beardsley did not want to be interviewed by the author of the article, but rather saw this as an opportunity to provide what would be a leak of information to defuse his position in this about to be discovered scandal. He hoped these things would pass over if he could weather the initial public reaction.

"Hello George, Beardsley here. I saw your article about the hospital in this morning's paper and wanted to know if you had questions for me. I am sorry that you could not reach me yesterday. Budget time you know. I noticed that you mentioned the recent resignation of Al Sharptee. This is off the record but we were concerned about some of his accounting procedures and were beginning an investigation of our finances to see if everything was on the up and up. Of course, we have not gotten the report, but, off the record, I was wondering if this was a coincidence that he left so suddenly. Makes you wonder, doesn't it? I am also concerned that the assistant CFO is in on this. She is a young lady that was involved in billing and collections. I can't say that she did anything but many fingers are pointing at her. You may want to pay attention to her when you are doing your background checks. I am concerned about her. I hear that she has a lot of personal debt. That is all I can say now since as you know, there is an investigation going on and we don't, as you know, discuss on going investigations. But when we get solid news, I will call you George. We want to get to the bottom of this and get back to our job of caring for sick kids and their parents. Nice to talk with you George." Beardsley hung up before George Fox could ask him any questions.

He looked at himself in the mirror on the wall next to his desk to check to see if his smile was still confident, feeling quite good about the launch of his damage control campaign.

"Who the hell are you guys? Didn't you see that I was on the phone?"

"We are from the DA's office and want to download your computer. We have a warrant here if you would like to read it."

"Who got the warrant? I need to talk to our legal office."

"They are the ones that asked for the warrant after the Board requested some action to see if there was a felony perpetrated on the hospital."

"A felony? That means time in the brig. You will find me most cooperative, I like my freedom."

Beardsley still had the phone in his hand so he pushed the intercom button and called to Vera to come in to see him.

"What the hell is going on?"

"The best I can tell is that Norman Oppenheim called a meeting of the board, they called in legal and then got a warrant for all the computers and financial files about budget."

"Why was this done without my approval?"

"You best talk to Mr. Oppenheim about that. He has retained an outside firm for legal advice. They are on their way up here to talk to you. I just heard from Mary Powtol that the doctors have hired a lawyer too to fight for their jobs."

"Who am I? The janitor, I am in charge here. No one makes a move without me. You understand?"

Norman Oppenheim, John Spirito and several dark suits appeared at the door.

"Norman, are you aware of all the nonsense that is going on here, behind my back? The place is out of control. It is good to see you, Norman, old man. How is your plane? But who is that with you?"

"Richard, I want you to meet Mitchell Schwalm, from the law firm that I employ for my companies. Richard is the head of the white collar crime section at the firm. For the past 5 months when I noticed some irregularities in the financial reports in the hospital. we engaged him to look into the hospital finances As we suspected, there is some problem with the reserve funds; they are lower than average for hospitals, especially for children's hospitals. We were not finished with the audits but when the uproar started with the staff firings, we had to move to step 2. As you know Clayton is away so I took over. As of this moment, you are relieved of duties as CEO until we can sort everything out."

"This sounds like a bad TV program. You are looking at the CEO; you should be going after the financial people. Sharptee and that blonde one who worked with him. I suspect that Al Sharptee's sudden resignation had something to do with this. The young girl. What is her name? Cindi or Crystal, Carol….. Caroleen, that is her name. I am sure she was the one who messed up the books. Billing and collections is her bailiwick. She must be the one and so is Sharptee. I reacted to the information, the lies that they fed us. I am surprised as you all are. Why pick on me? You know I can sue you for defamation of my name, unlawful seizure and false accusations for a start. I have a contract and I intend to see it enforced. I want you all to know that I was unaware that this was going on. It was not discussed with me at any time. I had no choice than to make some moves to restore our financial status while continuing our world class reputation.My job is to set the standards, to make sure that we do things right as well as do the right thing. I am the sugar that attracts the big donors. Yes, the majority of my time is building up the endowment and building buildings, at least getting the donors to underwrite the construction. I think you will agree that I have been quite successful in that arena. The quicker we get this sad situation finished, the quicker we can get on with our business of taking care of sick children. Are you going to talk with Sharptee that is where the money is? That is where you will find the cause of this problem. Do you agree with me?"

"Not so fast Dick. We have a charge to look into the reasons for our present situation and find out the reasons that we are in this financial trouble and the reasons for the miserable staff morale."

"Have you checked out that girl, what is her name Carolyn?"

"Do you mean Caroleen, Caroleen Columbe, the woman from finance?"

"Right. I have been suspecting her of playing with the books. I don't trust those finance people with MBA's. Over trained with theory and no practical sense. Don't you agree?"

"We will see about Caroleen later. What do you understand about the reserve funds?"

"What do you mean? Of course I know about them. Standard accounting stuff.

"Who determines what number is assigned to the reserve funds?"

"That is my point. It is that girl who does it. She is the one that got us in all this trouble. I don't get involved with that low level activity. I am at the top of the ladder, which does not involve reserve funds."

"How about setting contracts for major capital purchases?"

"Contracts, no I don't get involved in negotiating contracts for equipment."

"How about for million dollar purchases of a MRI?"

"MRI? Why did you use MRI as an example? Our capital budget is 20-30 million a year. I usually get requests for major equipment from department heads, who in turn, put out a call for equipment needs to their staffs. Then the capital equipment committee will meet and set priorities. When the budget is created, we approve a figure for equipment and then send a note to vendors to submit a proposal. So, for example, the radiology staff will request the MRI, the chief of radiology will both approve it and send it on to the committee or keep it on the list but not with the highest rating."

"Do you know who initiated the request for the latest MRI?"

"No, I do not. You can ask John about that. If it gets to me, then John approved it and put a high rating on it. Right John?" After he said that, his eyes did the rapid scanning movements, searching the faces of the audience to see if they were buying his excuses, false as they were."

"Come on Dick, you know that John did not approve it. In fact, he spoke quite clearly against the purchase of another MRI, emphatically stating that the hospital did not need it. I remember his saying that we should not give up the space for it, and we did would have to install new wiring and that security camera- that camera caught the porno scenes that were recorded entertained the night staff the other night."

"What porno the other night?"

"I guess you did not hear the tales from the security guard. Well some guy was having his way with a young woman in the MRI suite. It was caught on videotape in security."

Beardsley stared straight ahead like a Cotton Mather in front of a bunch of Pilgrims. Despite his controlled behavior, his clinched teeth and perspiration on his forehead displayed evidence of his emotional state.

"Ease up, Richardson, I don't want you to get sick. Enough of this diversion, we need to hear more about the decision to purchase the MRI. I have a difference of details. The usual procedure is a bottom up one, but in this case it seems like a top level decision. How did you determine the price of the equipment?"

"The usual, list price minus a discount for non-profit institutions.

"Did we get three bids and then compare the price with other hospitals to see if we were in the same ballpark."

"I did not."

"Would it surprise you to know that our price was 10% higher than the other MRI that the vendor sold to Pacific Children's about the same time?"

"10% seems high. It must have been the extras."

"We have our contract and information from the other purchasers. Yes, 10% exactly. Then the extras for wiring and extra cooling made it more than 10%."

"Someone must have erred on the comparative expenditures from our sister institutions. Yes, I remember now, it was the same girl, Caroleen that was supposed to do the comparisons. She failed me again."

"I think I heard enough for now.

"I have a contract that guarantees me my salary for 3 years. I expect the hospital to live up to their financial obligation that is in my contract."

"Does the contract stipulate your continuing pay while you are in jail? We have been collecting information since we were alerted to this deception, including extensive files on the real financial condition and the ones you approved as true, even though you were aware of how the were altered to make our financial condition look so positive. No one would notice a 5 percent variance between this hospital and other similar children's hospitals. But 15% was hard to explain if the numbers were true........and legal."

"I suggest that you forget the contract and leave. The other option is a long trial and huge expenses and most likely a jail term."

"I expect a severance to match my contract. Right?"

"Are you out of your mind?"

"Yes, you cannot stand the bad publicity either. Seems like the board will be exposed as a bunch of good old boys."

"We'll see about that. I hope you have a good legal team."

"The best! You won't get me."

Beardsley stomps away from his desk and walks towards the outside door.

"Believe me, all this is legal and has been approved by our counsel. Right now, you should leave the hospital and avoid a scene with security carrying you out. The papers and TV station are in the lobby looking for some action. You can take the service elevator down to the garage level and skip out without a scene. I think that is the best plan."

"You do? Do you know who you are taking to? I am the CEO. I am in charge!"

"I think I am aware of your title but you are not making a good decision, if you plan to fight this. Why don't you call your lawyer or the hospital lawyer?"

"Those bunch of weenies. All they know is to get outside counsel. They are not worth one tenth of what I pay them. Useless bastards, all of them. I don't need a lawyer. Come on and get me. I am innocent. I don't know your game but it will be costly when I get through with you. You can take your lawyer and your warrants and shove them far up your ass."

Beardsley s face was purplish red, his hands were shaking. Oppenheim was concerned that he may suffer a stroke.

"Now calm down Richard and try to cooperate. We have a lot of information about you and your role in this problem. I think you better cooperate and go to the garage quietly. If you are innocent as you say you are, my apologies."

"Save your apologies for after the trial when you and the hospital will pay me big bucks. Leave quietly; not on your life. Bring 'em on!"

"OK. Lt. Parkerson, escort Mr. Beardsley out of the hospital."

Parkerson led a team of oversized guards that looked like some over the hill linebackers for the National Football League. They lifted Beardsley up and carried him out to the elevator. The car descended as swiftly as hospital elevators moved, eventually the doors opened on the first floor.

"Ladies and gentlemen, we have a celebrity here, please step aside." As the entourage headed for the main door, they passed the security office. One of the guards who saw him on the TV monitor in radiology last night yelled out. "Hey boss, don't ever videotape yourself having sex. You are never as good as you think you look. I am available for coaching." The guards' loud laughter drew more attention from those in the lobby to this perp ride.

"Have a nice rest of the day," Officer Higgins said as Beardsley was deposited on the sidewalk outside of the hospital.

Beardsley, as usual, did not show any emotion other than defiantly jutting his jaw as far as it would go, in the best Mussolini pose he could muster.

When he got to his car, Beardsley called Caroleen on his cell phone. "Caroleen, did you see what they did to me? They kicked me out of my hospital. You better watch out, as they may come to get you too."

"They were already here and took my computer again. But hang up, this phone may be tapped."

Beardsley liked the idea of a tapped phone. "Be careful and get a lawyer because I know that you were in the center of this mess. I have already put the finger on you. Be prepared. My name is good and I will be cleared, once they get to you."

• • •

Norman Oppenheim, real estate developer and philanthropist, looked pretty comfortable sitting in Beardsley's chair in his new hospital CEO role, called in Vera to tell her that he was acting CEO. She smiled but said nothing except "anything you need me to do?"

"Yes, get John Spirito on the phone, please."

"Hello John, This is Norman Oppenheim speaking… Norman Oppenheim, new acting CEO. We have had a little coup in the administration. Richard Beardsley was just removed by the guards and is on leave from the hospital. He did not want to go peacefully so the security had to remove him. As acting CEO of the hospital, the first move I am making is to reinstate all the doctors that were recently let go by Beardsley. You get back to work and read your x-rays. We need the income. Sure. No problem. We have to do what is best for the hospital. You are the best and we need you."

Norman could hear a cheer in the background.

"Thanks a lot Norman. We are glad to get back to work. I don't think anyone will turn down your offer except Carter, He is hell bent to go to work at an Indian Health Service hospital in New Mexico. Strange place for such a prissy guy but that is what he wants to do. I wish I could have seen Richard's grand exit. Do you think it will be permanent?"

"I doubt that he can do much from prison. We have a lot of evidence about his cooking the books." Then Norman hung up the phone.

Chapter 27

When Donna Barstow got back to the ED, she heard Code Blue, ED. Code Blue ED on the overhead speakers. The EMT from the fire department was wheeling in a small boy who looked dead or close to death. An IV was running, there was a cardiac monitor that showed an irregular heart beat. The tech was squeezing a bag that delivered oxygen. When Donna went over to see the patient, she recognized that it was Samir, the young boy that was seen many times for child abuse. "Looks like someone was still after this unfortunate young man." Donna noticed that his one pupil was dilated "This poor guy has major brain problems. His lack of movements may be from the acute brain swelling or it may indicate more extensive damage."

"Call Neurosurgery stat and send out a Code Blue alert," the triage nurse shouted at the ED clerk. Within minutes, Ray Bartlett appeared at the ED. He did a quick but satisfactory physical exam and saw that he needed to get to the OR quickly to stop the bleeding in the brain. "Alert the child abuse team. We have one of their frequent fliers here again. This time it is serious. I knew they should not have him return to his home with that troubled man there. I wonder if he is back at his old tricks of beating up little kids. See you all later. Got to go save a life."

Vivian Nusbaum was called to see what she could find out about the person who abused Samir. She remembered Samir, as she did many of the children who were in the child abuse program at the hospital. She was not convinced that the boy friend of Samir's mother did it, but he was the prime suspect. Samir's mother seemed so protective of him and so involved with his care, that she was not likely to have harmed her son. But all options were open, so Vivian and her team reopened the file on Samir. She spoke to the mother Shana. Her assistant called home to speak to Allen. No one answered the phone. Maybe Allen finally got a job? She reported back to Vivian that no one was home.

"Shana, where is Allen? Did he get a job?"

"No Allen, he be in jail."

"Jail?"

"Yes, he got caught in a drug raid. Sold some junk to a policeman. That was not very cool."

"So who was home?"

"Just me and the kids."

"You were home alone with all the kids. Do you want to tell me anything about how Samir got hurt?"

"I don't know. "

"Who else could have injured him?"

"Maybe the neighbor."

"What is the neighbor's name?"

"I don't know, Mary or something like that."

"Mary? Not many people named Mary these days."

"Maybe it is something else."

"I want to repeat what I said many times before. We are here to help you. Otherwise Samir will continue to get injured if he pulls through this time. You know he is very sick and maybe he will not live. He is very sick."

"You don't think he will live, my little Samir?"

"Yes, that is why we have to get to the bottom of these injuries. Do you want to tell me anything?"

"You mean he may not live?"

"That is a possibility."

Shana began to cry. Vivian put her arms around her and offered her a tissue. "I just lost control. I did not mean to do it. I really didn't. He is so active and he got to me and I lost it. I didn't mean to do it. I didn't mean to do it. I got overwhelmed by 3 kids and no one to help me. Can you help me, please?"

"I know you did not. We are here to help you."

In the OR, Ray Bartlett had things under control. He did not have the time or interest in calling Sam Salivari until he started the operation. He removed the bone flap in record time. It was obvious that Samir had another epidural hemorrhage. Ray cleared away the blood clot to expose the leaking artery which he repaired. "Good that stopped the bleeding. Let's pause to make sure there were no leaks. Someone call Sam and tell him what we are doing."

The group stood by, waiting for an assessment from Ray.

"So far so good, we will worry about he extent of permanent damage that the brain sustained later; right now it was so swollen from the injury and decreased blood supply from the pressure of the hematoma. Less is best is my motto, so we don't want to do much more. Time will tell us more. Kid's brains are amazing in their ability to adapt to damage and to reroute of circuits to restore function. Hopefully Samir would finally have some good luck."

Ray closed the scalp after putting in drains to remove the fluid that would form from the initial injury and the surgery. He said his own prayer as he wrapped the white bandage around Samir's head.

The team in the neuro-intensive care unit would attend to decrease the swelling with steroids and cooling of the body to slow down metabolism. Since Samir was not responsive, he offered no resistance to being placed on a cooling blanket. Fortunately for Samir, Katie was going to be his nurse. As usual, she took over with her expertise and confidence.

When Samir was stable, Ray finally had time to talk with Katie. "Last week, Sam Salivari saw Anthony, your pal who fell on his head last year. He was walking, talking and finishing school with a tutor. He has a mild limp and still a little slow with higher mental functions but does well as long as you do not change subjects too quickly."

Katie thought back of all that poor Anthony went through and said, "I call that recovery a full success. I wish he would stop by so I could give him a kiss."

"Now I am jealous!"

The newspaper did report that Beardsley stepped aside as CEO of the hospital but no details except that the hospital discovered some problems with the hospital's financial statements. No finger pointing, no accusations, no quotes of excuses. But on page 1 of the second section, there was an another article by Henrietta Rowlands

Night life at CHUC

There is no down time at a hospital but activity is different after the sun sets. Offices are closed and most of the administrative staff leaves for the day, but few supervisors are there to solve problems and deal with new issues like massive accidents, unruly visitors or unusual events. Reduced laboratory and radiology staff await emergency cases or patients whose condition changed dramatically, but routine studies waited until the next day. The emergency room stays busy, feeding work to the other services in the hospital as sick patients are admitted for further care.

Last week, I shadowed the security force under Lt. Lance Parkerson. He has been at the hospital for 20 years, starting as a guard in the emergency room and progressing over the years to sergeant and recently exchanging his uniform for a suit as he was promoted to lieutenant. His shift started at 4 PM when he got the sign out from Nelson Rivera, the daytime lieutenant. "Not much happening today. I had to go to adolescent unit to calm down some teens that were too noisy for the nurses and other parents. A guard was already dispatched and took care of the problem by turning off the radio. There was an emergency case being flown in by helicopter so they would have to provide escort service to the elevators and clear out the cab while the patient got to the ICU. Sanitation trucks were expected at 11 PM to clear out the day's pile of garbage and waste. Nothing else."

So for that reason, at 8 pm he was able to sit down in the cafeteria and hit the machines to get some unneeded calories. Twinkies and diet coke. "Diet drinks make me feel like I am doing something about my belly. I try to get the Twinkies that have the calories removed before they are packed" he smiled with a twinkle in his eyes. "See, it is gone. No calories visible." Everyone seemed to know him as they passed his table; they made comments about his nice suit, his family and the NFL draft. He was a rabid Washington Redskin fan. "Time to get back to the office and check on the guards. They are a good group but sometimes when things are quiet they get rowdy." So we left the cafeteria and headed for security central.

The guards were out of control with their shouts and cheers. I could make out a few words between the laughs and shouts. "Go man Go." Parkerson jumped into the disturbance. "Gentlemen, Gentlemen, you are in a hospital. Your job is to keep the building secure but also to act like adult security officers." When he moved to the wall with the security monitors, he saw what was causing all the excitement. Either someone had slipped a porno tape into the system or there was some hanky panky in the radiology unit. Initially Parkerson kept a straight face but shortly, he was smiling. When the officers were making comments about the style or lack of style, according to the group, Parkerson lost his lieutenant face. "That is enough, men. Stop this!" The group broke up, but not before they flashed their scores. By my quick unofficial count, the final score was about 4.5. That includes taking away the top score 5 and the low score 2 as the judges do in the Olympic skating. One of the guards put it into perspective summing up the episode as you are never as good as the videotape shows. The calm was short lived as the couple got off the MRI table. "It's the boss!" I was not sure which level boss they meant. Security boss, personnel boss of even higher up. I assume it was not the latter since rarely the hospital top administrator would be in the hospital at night unless there was a fund raiser or similar event. I can assure you that it was not Bruce Springsteen either.

I asked Lt. Parkerson if he had ever seen this type of porno in the hospital. "I have not seen any action on the monitor. We do not have cameras in the on call rooms but I suspect when you have young people in scrub suits, you may get a pajama party; working close together as these young people do, things will happen. I cannot prove it but the word is that the young dudes would actually pay to work in house keeping as they then have full run of the hospital, especially on the night shift. As I say, things happen. We caught one guy dealing drugs in the locker room before we could nab him, one man from dietary was found dead in the toilet with a needle in his arm. That was a few years ago, nothing like that recently."

So the hospital never sleeps. In addition to doing the great work that it does, it is a miniature city with all the issues and problems that we face in South Creek. Now that news about the financial problems at the hospital has become public, are they planning to peddle porno tapes of "Hospital Gone Wild" one solution to the deficit? Or should we wait until they put cameras in the on call rooms?

The buzz in the coffee shop centered on the identity of "the boss." For a brief time the financial problems, the firing of senior staff and the forced removal of Beardsley dropped from the discussions. The medical staff were trying to figure out who was still working, who would fight the dismissal and suggestions for returning most of the doctors to work. Wayne Sampson from the lab stated that he saw some Indian doctors looking around the emergency department. He was sure that they were the replacements that Beardsley had talked about during one of his frequent tirades on saving money. As usual none of the comments had any facts to back up the statement.

In the neuro-surgery intensive care unit, Katie Berg was checking all the lines connected to Samir. After his surgery, he showed some small signs of recovery by opening his eyes and responded to painful stimulation, a small change from his condition when he came to the ICU. His vital signs were stable and he was being fed by IV which provided fluids and vitamins but not much more. The nutrition staff was coming today to meet with Ray Bartlett about increasing calories. Ray came by at 7:15 on his usual rounds. This was the best way to start the day shift for Katie. After a slow but cautious start, their relationship has blossomed into an exclusive but still chaste arrangement, much to the disappointment of the clerical staff in the ICU who were looking for signs of more physical contact. They were experts in interpreting body language especially for those couples who having sex. Nothing for these two.

During daytime, the interaction was purely professional. When they were away from the hospital, they were a beautiful couple, enjoying being together. Although not an agenda item, they talked more and more about the future. Places to practice, type of house, number of children but not about sex. They were playing that area right out of their upbringing. Neither one would deny that they were not tempted or found each other sexually attractive, but they had their principles. Ray was being courted by the hospital to stay on as a staff neurosurgeon, working under Sam Salivari. But after he presented some of his research on head injury at the last meeting of the University Neurosurgery Society, Yale, Stanford and Michigan have given him invitations to visit their centers. All three offered junior positions. The major medical center patient variety and the chance to continue his research work were attractive but after so many years of training, he would like to be better compensated and more independent of the administrative and hospital politics. Not that he could escape some politics but some places had less than the big centers, their major concern was keeping the beds filled. Katie was not in any hurry to pin him down; pregnancy was not an issue that could push Ray into marriage so she figured that after he got a contract for next year, wherever it may be, they would have to decide about their future. Right now it was Samir that was their concern.

"What do you think?"

"Some progress but very slow. He must have been banged around quite a bit. They try to say this is shaken baby syndrome, but shaking does not do this. He was banged against something hard like a wall or floor. Poor soul"

"He will make it. Right?"

"Sure he will make it but who is going to care for him? He is certainly not going home."

425

"You can never tell. Some soft hearted and soft brained judge may be taken in by the poor repenting mother. I have heard about many cases where the judge gets swayed by promises rather than past performances and return the kid to the home where the battering occurred. You know the song and dance. 'Children should be with their mothers."

"It will be hard to return Samir to his mother if she is in jail."

'Do you think she is going to jail?"

"With this track record of multiple occurrences, that is a good bet; depends too on whether or not the judge has a bad breakfast on the trial day. Then no one knows what will happen. Please don't burn the toast, I pray."

"So he will be in foster homes?"

"That is the usual story. Many homes which is definitely not what he needs."

"We have to make sure he pulls through before we get ahead of ourselves in worrying about placement. Are we OK with the meds, calories, lungs, tubing, joints, and skin."

"Yes sir, we are weaning the steroids, he is on hyper-al, sugars OK, liver enzymes normal, chest clear, pulmonary percussion every 2 hours, tubes changed yesterday. PT working on keeping joints mobile, he has splints on wrists and ankles to prevent wrist and ankle drop. We have him covered."

"Good, when is your break, I can meet you in the coffee shop. Today is a slow OR day and clinic is not until 1."

"I can meet you there about 10:15.

"Sounds good."

Ten o'clock is the usual meeting time for the group in the coffee shop. As the year was coming to a close, the talk was mostly about summer vacations, present social life or lack thereof and any new dating services. So far, no one has come up with lonelydocs.com but Felix was thinking about starting one. He has rejoined the social group after finding out his paramour was a mafia wife. He was now focusing on getting a fellowship. The applications are due in June for the positions one year after the match is made. He first thought about dermatology since that involves the least amount of work and high return as long as acne cannot be cured and viruses still cause rashes. But he needed more challenges than looking at skin. The other high paying specialties such as cardiology and critical care are too work- intensive with too much night call. That leads him to gastroenterology, lots of procedures with good reimbursement and unlimited kids with constipation to clog up the office schedule. So he was leaning towards GI. He would apply to the usual Boston, New York, Philadelphia, Los Angeles but have a few places less traveled such as Seattle, Cincinnati and St. Louis. They need some Eastern hubris to balance their extra nice local guys. Lester, being on an arthritis elective, would show up eventually. Linda from the nursery sat with them today and of course Evil Eva, who was constantly trolling the group for after hour's entertainment.

"Any news about internet dating service replies?"

"None for me today. I just may start my own romance hook up page. I think we need more important information In addition to the usual, age, favorite foods and football teams, I could have categories such as outstanding loans category: over $100,000, $50-100,000, under $50 and none. Why not put that up front so you would not fall for a greater than 100k especially if you were a 100 thousand or rarely, no loans. This has to be the greatest impediment to finding a suitable partner. Just think, if you had leprosy, you could get a cure, but if you have big loans, it will take years to get out from under that, especially if you intend to stay in pediatrics. Then the match up could look at things like interests, social climbing skills and type of clothes. Anyone want to invest in my website? No? I thought so."

"What is wrong with the usual ones? They cover the same topics."

"But not as direct. Think of the flow chart. Are you interested in a doc? If yes go to lonelydocs.com. If not interested go to the others. Why not be up front? The site can attract daughters of investment bankers, no problem with debt there. Or slackers on trust funds who need some prestige in their lives. I am psyched. Need some capital."

"Speaking of lonely docs. Does anyone have pictures of the new residents coming here in June?

"What is it worth to you, Felix? asked Eva Masters. "I have the pictures and more. Who wants to come to my office after work and take a look at my pictures?"

"I will if I can bring security services with me."

"Why don't you put the pictures on the intranet?"

"Do you want to help me?"

"How about the weather? Does anyone think it will rain on June 11?"

"Trauma alert, 2 minutes, ED trauma alert 2 minutes"

"Sorry gang, we have to go."

Just as the table cleared, Katie Berg arrived at the coffee shop. "What happened? I arrive and the place clears out." She spied Carla Adams, her friend who worked in the cardiac unit. "Hey Carla, how are you? Why so sad?"

"I just got my period. Again....but I wanted to be pregnant, not potentially pregnant. This is my third shot at in- vitro. Another 10K going down the drain. "

"Sorry to hear about that and sorry for being so unfeeling. I did not know."

"That's OK. It was not something I would put on my Face Book page. I guess I'll have to adjust to a childless home. That is OK. Many people live good lives without kids. I would not like to join them but now that is the way it is."

"Why don't you adopt some baby? Those Chinese girls are so cute. My neighbor adopted a girl from China last year. They are doing fine."

"That sounds good. But we used up a lot of money for the IVF. My mother would not be happy with an Asian grand daughter. She is old fashioned and a little prejudiced.

"Maybe she would change her mind if you explained what you have gone through."

"Maybe she would but not right now. She is taking care of my father who is not well."

"Sounds like you need a social worker."

"That is probably what I need, you are right. Enough of me, how are you doing."

Ok. I am at an earlier stage than you. Still not married ....yet."

"Anything pending?"

"Not yet, but I am working on it."

"Really? Are you and Ray talking about marriage?"

"Not in so many words but you know Ray, a man of few words. I am not the modern miss who would be more aggressive about our relationship. I prefer the old fashioned way- wait for him to propose. He is talking about our future so I guess there are some assumptions built into that type of talk. I am ready and optimistic. It will be easier when he decides what kind of job he will take at the end of his residency. He has many offers but I think he is leaning towards staying here."

"Time is running out, July is not too far away. But knowing Ray, I would not worry about him. But you looked a little stressed out. What is happening?"

"Oh the usual, a sick kid got readmitted with another bout of child abuse. Epidural hemorrhage this time. So sad. His mother seems to be the one. An overwhelmed 23 year old with three kids and a boy friend in jail. Talk about needing a social worker. Ray was supposed to be here but maybe he was called to the ED with the trauma alert."

"Maybe you will be my social worker on the side. I feel better just talking to someone about my own little issues when we work around people who have much bigger ones. I just need to change my attitude and reset my life plans."

"It is just when you give up that something good happens. I hear so many stories about people who get pregnant after they adopt a child or when the give up trying. I haven't even started to try so I don't know what I am talking about."

"That qualifies you as some kind of expert but I hope you are right about things happening once you give up. That is where I am right now. Good to see you and I hope that little boy with the epidural makes it. What is his name?

"Samir"

'Not a very Waspy name."

"Far from it. But he is so cute."

• • •

Norman called the meeting of the executive committee of the board of trustees and the medical executive committee.

" I thought it best that we meet here as a group. The room is clean; I checked for hidden tape recorders or cameras." At the mention of cameras, all eyes reflexly turned to the TV monitor. "As you know, we have a problem; yes, a crisis at the hospital discovered by the routine audit of the hospital after the CFO resigned. Let me backtrack briefly, Even before Al Sharptee left the hospital, I thought it best to have someone come in to review all the consultants' contracts. I wanted to make sure that we were not running into conflicts as I am aware that many consultant firms have several divisions that are set up to cover the usual client's needs- accounting, organization restructuring and compensation. This offering of comprehensive services is also a setup for non-objective advice."

"Excuse me Norman, what do you mean by non-objective advice?"

"There are many variations to the process but for example, if a firm is called in to advise on executive compensation, they will recommend a generous package that puts them in good light with the CEO. When the hospital needs help in reorganizing their structure or settling turf battles between specialties, the same firm gets that contract to help with the organization revision. Kind of indirect blackmail: recommend high salaries for us or we will send our other business elsewhere."

"You mean like the Wall Street firms that recommended the stock of a company and then got other financial business like loans or new offerings."

"Same kind of conflict."

"And greed."

"So what did you men find out, Norman?"

"The report is not complete but they did find out that the auditors have a subsidiary called Executive Strategies for Health Care, the firm that the hospital hired to review the administration pay packages."

"So we have odor most foul in our castle."

"Not ready for conclusions but your shot at Shakespeare is noted, Bunky. There is more. About 6 months ago, Caroleen Columbe came to me in confidence. She showed me notes from meetings with Mr. Beardsley and Al Sharptee where Beardsley concocted the plan to doctor the books by altering the reserve funds. She also showed me minutes of meetings where the MRI contract was forced through the system over the objections of the staff. There are no notes about the 10% premium, but I have an idea who profited by this extra money. I confronted Richardson with this information about the MRI purchase and, if course, he denied everything.

This consultant morass plus the bonding agency's auditors finding that the recent monthly reports were inaccurate regarding the reserve funds were underestimation starts to build a case. We have asked outside auditors to look at the next phase to see if there bogus patient bills with no record that the people registered or the doctors saw the patients. Additionally, during the audits, computers were checked for emails and documents to try to find out how we got into this muddle."

"So what is next?"

" For starts, as you know, when the news of shortfalls emerged, Dick initiated a program to remove senior faculty in an attempt to reduce expenses. That move was not justified. With all the financial subterfuge, the bad publicity in the paper, the chaos in the medical staff, I have asked Beardsley to step down He refused to leave so he was removed by security from the hospital. As temporary CEO, I have decided to countermand the firings and restore the doctors to their positions. Before this goes any further, I thought we ought to sit down and discuss the problems and hopefully come to some reasonable solution. This is not a court, this is not an inquisition. It is the start of discussions that hopefully will bring this problem to a positive conclusion."

"How did we get into this mess?" asked Dixon McIver. "Who was on watch? The ship has left the harbor and no one was on guard."

"Nice metaphor Dixon. Really nautical," chimed in Tom Heatherson.

Norman was getting impatient with his fellow board members. "We should get some advice from outside counsel and get this guy punished. The bottom line is the hospital is in deep financial trouble and we, as board members are responsible for this financial disaster."

"We have insurance to cover our liabilities, right?"

"That is right Dixon but the news sullies our reputation and is a big embarrassment. We will be the laughing stock at our clubs plus the development office would go crazy if the word got out. Our fund raising would drop to below zero. We would be drummed out of the leadership of NACRI. We should let him go quietly."

"Tom, what the hell is NACRI?"

"NACHRI, the National Association of Children's Hospitals and Related Institution."

"But this guy is a crook," Norman protested.

"We have lots of crooks but only one reputation."

"I think we have him on his knees. He has no claim to anything but a jail cell. We have to finalize our disposition of this crook Beardsley."

"So what are we going to do with him, Bunkie? After all he has been so good to the hospital and building up the endowment, all the new construction and equipment; we owe him a lot so I am against any legal action. We should come up with a severance pay and begin the search for a new CEO."

"Wait a minute, Tom. I think we have criminal actions here and as a board member, I want to execute my fiduciary duties and make sure that we get some of the money back from Mr. Beardsley."

"Not so fast, Bunkie, We need to put on our public face too and not let the community know what really happened here. The newspapers will forget about this in a few days and we can all return to our supervision of the hospital affairs. Just think what they would say at the club; you know there are a lot of members who would just about kill to get our places on this board. I remember, my father told me about the time when the administrator of the hospital was caught taking his wife on a trip and charging it to the hospital, at least I think it was his wife. That was in 74, before I was on the board. They kept it quiet and no one made an issue of it. We should follow what worked in the past."

"Not today with newspapers and the internet; they are always looking for scandals to fill up the air time. I bet the MRI porno tape is already on YouTube."

Norman interjected. "Wait a minute, ladies and gentlemen. We have to look at the bigger picture. We are insured for any financial chicanery. We have the public to consider as they are our biggest supporters. This is not a good situation so do we open it all to the public or let it pass as Tom suggested? Do we let him go with some payment or do we subject ourselves to huge legal fees and public ridicule?"

"I am against feeding those lawyers any more money than they already get from us." John Spirito chimed in. "Even though getting fired by this bastard was not a pleasant feeling, I am back at work and I have my health so no harm, no penalty."

I appreciate your feeling John, as you say, you doctors were the only ones directly hurt by Mr. Beardsley's actions. Your reaction to this is a good lesson for all of us. Isn't that what they say in church- to turn the other cheek."

"Not if it is your cheek, I am afraid to admit."

"Maybe we could hire a PR firm to do some damage control."

"More money spent. They do not always work out well. Look at what happened to the pollution case that the Banner Pharmaceutical had to face. They got one of those Madison Avenue types to help them with PR and the whole thing exploded as the lawyers found more damage than originally suspected. I remember my father telling me to cut your losses. He did not do that in 29 and the family lost a bundle. But then we got into real estate and made it up after the war. Thank the Lord for shopping centers."

"Interesting family vignettes but enough history, Tom. Can I make a motion to negotiate a severance package with Beardsley and give him a one way coach ticket out of town."

" I make a motion that we form a subcommittee to work with our lawyers to create an equitable severance for Mr. Beardsley with the caveat that the details are not released to the public."

There is a motion on the floor. Any further discussion? All in favor, raise your hands. Opposed?" The motion is carried 7-3.

• • •

The auditorium was packed with residents, family and guests for the graduation ceremonies and awarding of prizes. Since the word was out that Dr. Farmer was being honored, his secretary invited some of the patients that she remembered. There was Jackie, the young girl with Turner Syndrome, and Rusty, all fixed up after his heart surgery. They looked good and were excited to hear their doctor being honored. Dr. Esposito walked on to the stage at graduation, looked at the audience and waited for them to settle down. "Good morning. It is with great sadness, that I have the unpleasant duty to inform this group that last night, our colleague and friend, Bob Farmer died in his sleep........ You were probably not aware of his condition but in the last few months, he was complaining of being tired. Then last night he had a massive heart attack. Typical of Bob, he did not complain or burden us with his problems or let his problem interfere with his love of patient care and teaching. He stood out in his ability to diagnose common and rare diseases; his sensitivity in taking care of families was without equal. Bob was able to practice medicine in a way that many aspire to but never match. He was naturally competent without trying. He did the right thing because that is the only way he knew how to proceed. As you know, he was asked by the chief resident to be the speaker at this graduation. He had hoped to make it here today to share with you his thoughts. A few weeks ago, he stopped by my office with his speech to ask me if I would read it. Typical of Bob Farmer, he was prepared with a plan A and a plan B, just in case. Today you will hear his words which are not only a graduation talk but now, a farewell speech. So let us rise in honor of his memory and have a minute of silence for one of CHUC's real giants....." There was not really a need to ask for silence as the audience was stunned at the news of Robert Farmer's death.

"Thank you." John Esposito fighting back tears, opened the folder containing the talk, cleared his throat and began.

"Congratulations to you on your completion of your training at CHUC. I want to spend a few minutes with you to talk about your life outside of medicine, your conduct and relationships. Rather than continue with a group of truisms about your responsibilities and moral guidelines, I will continue my interactions with you, as I always did, by asking questions.

The first one is "what will it take?" In my medical school times, there was a dean of a prestigious school in Philadelphia, who opened the convocation of the first year students with the command. "Look right and left, one of this trio will not be here next year because of academic failure." Fortunately we don't play that game any more, as you already know, most everyone accepted to medical school will graduate. But I have changed the conditions. Look to your left and, if the conditions don't change, one of you will be divorced. So I ask you "what will it take to change those numbers? Now repeat after me, the career is not as important as the family. One more time..... Whether you are going into practice, a fellowship, research lab or a career in the pharmaceutical industry, you will be tempted to work, just a little bit harder, see one more patient, write one more paper or run one more experiment. If you are tempted to take on more, your family will have less time with you at home. When you get divorced and it is your night to spend with your children, you will not take on that extra task. Then your family will have priority over the temptation of working more. Family time is sacred in the post divorce era. Maybe if your family were a high priority for you initially you would not have to go through the anguish of divorce.

For the 50% of you who do not get divorced, you are not off the hook. Make your family come first. Before you take on more in your professional life, ask yourself are you spending enough time with your kids? If not now, you will, when your child has a problem in school, with drugs or risky sexual activities. Look at the numbers of how many teens are in some kind of trouble, do the math, you are testing the odds if you let them on their own while you are busy supporting them. Did I say support? You know what I mean.

Now, for the second main question. Why are you going to be tempted to do more professionally? Maybe seeing one more patient will be more money? Making more money will allow you to get more material things for you home, car or vacation. Accumulating material things makes no sense if you are not home to use or enjoy them. Write one more paper? When you look back at many of the papers that took you away from your family, you will smile, even laugh at how unimportant that paper is even though it took many hours to write, even a bad paper. Serve on another committee? Believe me, the person who asked you to be on the committee was probably looking for a warm body to represent the department or division rather than selecting you for your skills. Senior people, tired of committee chatter, are happy to find people who will say yes to committee assignments. Watch what happens to the person who says no. Nothing happens to you. If you say no, the person who asked you will nod, even smile and then pick up the phone and call the next person on the list. A friend of mine gave me this advice about saying no. He told me it took him many hours of psychotherapy to learn to say no. You are so honored by the request that you say yes before you think about what present activity will be replaced by this new obligation. "Gee, they picked me. I am special and respected by my boss." Not so fast. I am giving you this advice for no charge- professional courtesy. Try to separate out the honor you perceive that you. and not others, was asked from the task you are being asked to do. Do you really want to do that task?

At the end of your career, you will look back and, if you are honest with yourself, you will question the value of many of the papers you wrote, talks that you gave, extra patients that you saw but who failed to follow your advice. Lots of wheel spinning, for what? Pay more attention to your family.

Enough questions. Now for some directions to have a better life. You know me. I speak in direct statements. But now I am changing that. The following are rules with mixed messages. First piece of advice is --Grow and don't grow. Continue to learn, to get more experiences and improve your skills. That is why they call this practice. Real pros practice every day. So grow in your knowledge and skills but don't grow in weight. Take care of yourself. If you are stressed, you will eat and you will expand. Don't grow around your waist.

Next, --- change and don't change. As you age, you should be open to new ways of thinking; do not become so rigid that you will not adapt to your environment. Look for new experiences to enrich your life. But do not change your spirit, your idealism, your quest for new knowledge. You are a unique group of people.

Those of you who know me will expect a few rules. I will not disappoint you. This is directed to your family life; hopefully you will be blessed with a nice family.

First rule, Get involved in sailing. You don't have to buy a boat, unless you want to. But take a few rides. You will find that even with the best plans, you have to adapt to changes in the wind direction and tides. Sometimes to get from point A to point B, you can go in a straight line but when the wind changes, you cannot get where you want to without zigzagging, not a straight line. In a word, you must plan, then evaluate how the plan is being executed and then adapt, be able to change your plans.

Two. Next get a dog. With a dog, you will learn the effect of unrestrained love. Even though you make demands of the dog to sit or stay, the dog will love you and forgive you for being tough. Additionally, you will see how many rules you have for dealing with life will not work when applied to your family. When you expect your pet to follow your rules, you may find that some work and some do not. The dog will find a workable plan that may differ from yours. Dogs eat when they want to eat, not when you tell them to eat. It is not a case of your dog winning and you losing, but more that the dog has another workable plan that will show you there is more than one way to success. Then when you deal with your family or patients, you will, hopefully, be more flexible. You are not infallible and your rules or plans are not always perfect. Get some feedback from the people around you. Be open to new ideas. You may eventually reject them but listen and learn something. My former teacher opined, "You should entertain new ideas but you do not have to invite them to stay for dinner."

Finally read the sports page. Look at the best players. The best baseball player may get a hit only one time in three at bats; the best basketball player will usually score only half of the shots at the basket. The best quarterback will complete half of the passes. No one, not even the all stars are perfect. Ease up on your expectations. Do your best but live with your mistakes and learn from them.

So slow down, make your family come first, be ready to adapt your plans when necessary as you learn from experience.

It has given me great pleasure to work with you, to teach you and to learn from you. You are a treasure to me. Thank you for allowing me to share these years with you."

Dr Spirito put down the paper, wiped his face with his palm and looked up at the audience. Silence with a few sniffles and sobs could be heard from the audience.

Finally John Spirito looked at the audience. "The last of the giants. We will all remember Bob Farmer. Following his lessons in medicine and life will honor his memory."

After the graduation, the residents had a few more days before the first year ended; there were still patients to see. These were the lucky patients that came in while the experienced team was still working. If they came next week, they would face the new house staff who worried about missing some rare disease rather than thinking of common problems before the unusual ones. Bob Gardner was back in the ED. He was working in the trauma unit taking care of possible fractures and lacerations. He had just sent a 6 year old boy to x-ray to rule out a fracture. Peggy Gallagher, the triage nurse today asked him to check out a minor hand cut. With his confidence, came smiles. He was actually having fun.

"Hi, I am Dr. Gardner; I understand your hand is cut. May I take a look at it? No I won't touch it. I just want to look. First can you feel this pin on your thumb- How about over here? I see. Well I will wash out the wound and get the hand surgeon here to see what he thinks about the nerve."

Sarah Wright was doing her last well child clinic of the year. Just as she started the year, she was again seeing a child with a large head. This time she was primed. After the first fiasco of trying to make a diagnosis of hydrocephalus in a normal child with a family history of large head, she first asked this mother about family head sizes. Sure enough! She asked about head sizes in the family and bingo. Another case of familial macrocephaly. No need for a MRI.

The hospital continued to provide excellent care. Despite all the turmoil, the staff continued to serve the patients well. The loss of a few people could not change the level of care. The rough around the edges group of residents last July was now a NASCAR pit team, confident, experienced doctors who take care of patients in an efficient manner, fixing the problem and sending the children to resume their activities. The waiting time in the walk in clinic and emergency room shortened. People with colds did not have to have leukemia ruled out. People with coughs had allergies rather than cystic fibrosis. The laboratory and radiology services had fewer tests to deal with as the residents honed down their testing to prove the diagnosis rather than ordering a group of fishing tests to see what they could catch. Although they felt good about their skills, it would take some interaction with the new doctors next week to appreciate how much they have learned in the past 12 months. When one is busy worrying about her medical decisions, tired from the long hours and lack of sleep plus trying to have some personal life other than eating and sleeping when not in the hospital, she does not appreciate the massive amount of material and skills that have been amassed in one year. The comparison with the next years new doctors would validate her progress.

The only constant was Felix who was ready for the next group of new residents. He had, against his poor judgment, courted Evil Eva so he could get a peak of the pictures of the arriving residents. There were at least 3 good candidates who were not married, 3 more who were.

It was at the end of the year when the hospital staff would no longer be a united team. Many of the residents will stay for more training while others will move on to other hospitals to start their next career, practice, fellowship or research. The medical staff will continue their routine, happy to see the young doctors mature and move on while they braced for the next group of rookies. As usual, the staff continues to meet at the 10 o'clock coffee hour to discuss cases and hospital gossip. The new house staff quickly found out that the coffee break was the time to socialize and develop their support group. You could tell who the new people were by the tenseness of their jaw muscles or vacant stares at the clock. At the corner table, the physician staff took their usual places, leaving one chair, Bob Farmer's seat, empty. John Esposito sat down, stirred the coffee cup, scratched his head, looked at the young shining new faces of house staff and grumbled. "It is good that July comes only once a year."

EPILOGUE

"You are where you want to be."
Mesha Zev

Life continued after June 30th. Richard Beardsley's supporters on the board voted to give him half of the money promised in his new contract over the next two years. The official explanation, released to the press, was that he was going to spend more time with his family and take up wood working. He was all smiles as thought of the next two years as a well paid sabbatical leave. Then he received the bill from the lawyers who claimed about 25% of this settlement. Taxes took about 30%. His wife, having enough of his dalliances and worried about his ability to support her, divorced him and got half of the total severance package. The rest he invested in a hedge fun that went bankrupt. Once the word got out about his financial dealings, he could not get a job in hospital work so he became a consultant, which means he was out of work. He took an apartment in what was known in South Creek as Divorce Towers, a high rise that leased apartments for short terms.

Beardsley felt relieved that he was broke but not in prison. He did beat the system but it was a short lived victory for about a week later, he got a call from the DA's office informing him that they now had enough evidence to make an indictment regarding the kickbacks. Beardsley was confident that he could beat this one too. At the discovery phase of the trial, the evidence was quite strong because the computer files were found. When the investigators checked Beardsley's computer, they found it was relatively new. Suspicious that he may have junked the old one with incriminating files, they found out that the original server was discarded, not destroyed. Further field work found the server in Anthony Herman's office. He had retrieved it from the discard pile of used equipment and replaced his old computer with this new one. These files contained everything. Beardsley pleaded guilty eventually and spent 2 years in prison where he met his counterpart from Cincinnati. They formed a hospital administration consulting company when they got out of prison.

Nick Genel, the New Jersey Attorney General, had formed a task force to investigate not for profit organization. His findings provided another problem for Beardsley. He did not pay taxes on his kickbacks from contractors as well as account for the construction work on his house done by builders seeking work from CHUC. Another trial is pending.

Lester and Adrienne got married in a civil ceremony. He took a fellowship in endocrinology with a special interest in intersex problems. Adrienne started an emergency medicine fellowship but left after one year to enter law school. She was then planning to get an MBA and raise her three children.

Samir, the boy who was abused several times, was adopted by Carla Adams, the nurse who could not get pregnant. As often happens, she conceived about 2 months after the adoption. Hunter Evans, a blond blue eyed boy, and Samir became known as the chocolate and vanilla siblings.

Karl Strem initially worked with WHO fighting AIDS in Africa. After 20 years, he became health commissioner of San Francisco. He is now organizing his campaign to run for Senate from California. Keith, the curmudgeon, finally came to terms with his wrong decision to be a doctor. He joined a series of pharmaceutical firms, slowly rising to be a medical director of a start up company that developed a new treatment for glaucoma. His company was bought out by DuPont. He took his payout and opened a book store in a newly redeveloped part of Newark. He now smiles most of the time, except when there are too many customers.

Ray and Katie were married in June at Katie's home. Ray took a job in Palo Alto, starting a head injury service at the Packard Children's Hospital. Katie started as an ICU nurse where her talents were recognized so she was recruited to head up humanism in nursing for the nursing service.

Erica Gates, the medical student who got involved with the lead poisoning rally, worked at the NIH studying the effects of toxins on brain development, then got a Masters in Public Health degree at Hopkins. She worked with the Doctor without Borders, and then she spent time at the Rand Group, trying to develop a national health plan. Many years later, she will become president of the Kaiser Family Foundation.

Carter Randolf did make it to the Indian Health Service at Fort Defiance AZ. with Carrie and their daughter, Rainbow. Carrie became a jeweler specializing in turquoise necklaces.

Will Miller, who won the teaching award, then stopped teaching as it got in the way of his productivity. He did make an arrangement with

Luda the resident from Ukraine, who took a fellowship in cardiology to be closer to him. So far, Will has not divorced his wife. He will shortly leave medicine to work for a drug company, doing clinical studies on cardiac drugs.

Caroleen decided that health care was not a good field for her. She took a job as auditor for an insurance company plus volunteering to be treasurer of the local volunteer fire company where she discovered the president and vice president were embezzling funds. Now she is testifying against them in a criminal case. She decided that working in finance was not good for her life so she quit her job and opened up a cookie franchise from Gayle Piel's company.

Kirby Jackson never settled down. His paramour, Mary Ann, married a used car salesman in Prescott Arizona, where she opened up a diet clinic and held sales parties for sex toys for women.

Donna Barstow is still in the ED. John Esposito was diagnosed with colon cancer but seems to being well after surgery and chemotherapy. Felix? Well Felix did complete his residency, took a Robert W. Johnson fellowship in political affairs, and became part of the government relations section of Dacis Pharmaceutical. He married one of the daughters of the founders and now heads a family foundation where he is supporting such right wing causes as encouraging teens to practice abstinence.

Author's Note:

This work of fiction deals with an imaginary hospital and personnel. There is no Children's Hospital of Union County. In my experiences as a pediatrician, I have worked in and visited numerous hospitals ranging from general county hospitals serving the indigent, military hospital and numerous children's and university hospitals where similar, but not identical, situations occurred as described in this novel. Many of the characters are composites of a number of individuals. For example, the problem of the elevator buttons incorrectly being pushed occurred in Florida, the person who loved memos was in California and the effort to turn this into a research project happened in Pennsylvania. Likewise the administrator Richardson Beardsley was created from stories that colleagues shared with me about executives they knew. I guess every teaching hospital has their own version of Felix the predator; the name came from someone observed on the beaches of St. Thomas. Likewise, the surgical ego is present in every hospital so it was easy to caricature

Having spent my medical career at the Children's Hospital of Philadelphia, I made sure not to include any of the characters from there, even though many people were hopeful they would be mentioned in this book and requested Brad Pitt or George Clooney to play their role, if a movie is made from this story.